THE

PREACHER'S WEB

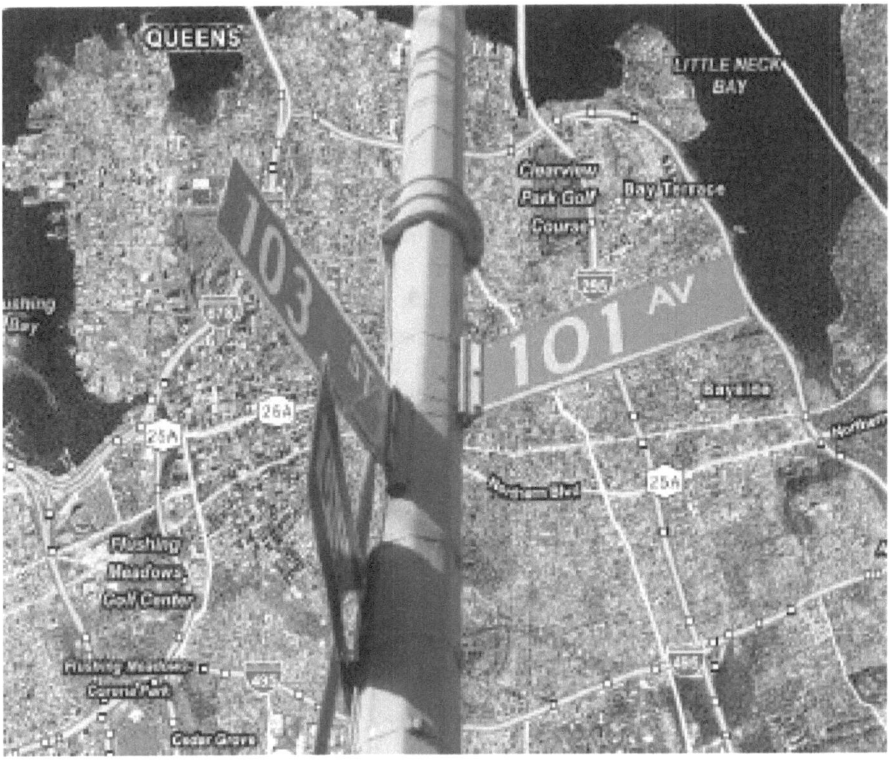

Marc A. Beausejour

S.H.E. PUBLISHING, LLC

THE PREACHER'S WEB

Copyright © 2016 by Marc A. Beausejour

For information contact : www.shepublishingllc.com | info@shepublishingllc.com | Tel: 219.515.8032

Library of Congress Control Number: 2024932581

ISBN : 978-1-953163-91-2

Edited by: Leslie E. Stern

Second Edition : February 2024

10 9 8 7 6 5 4 3 2 1

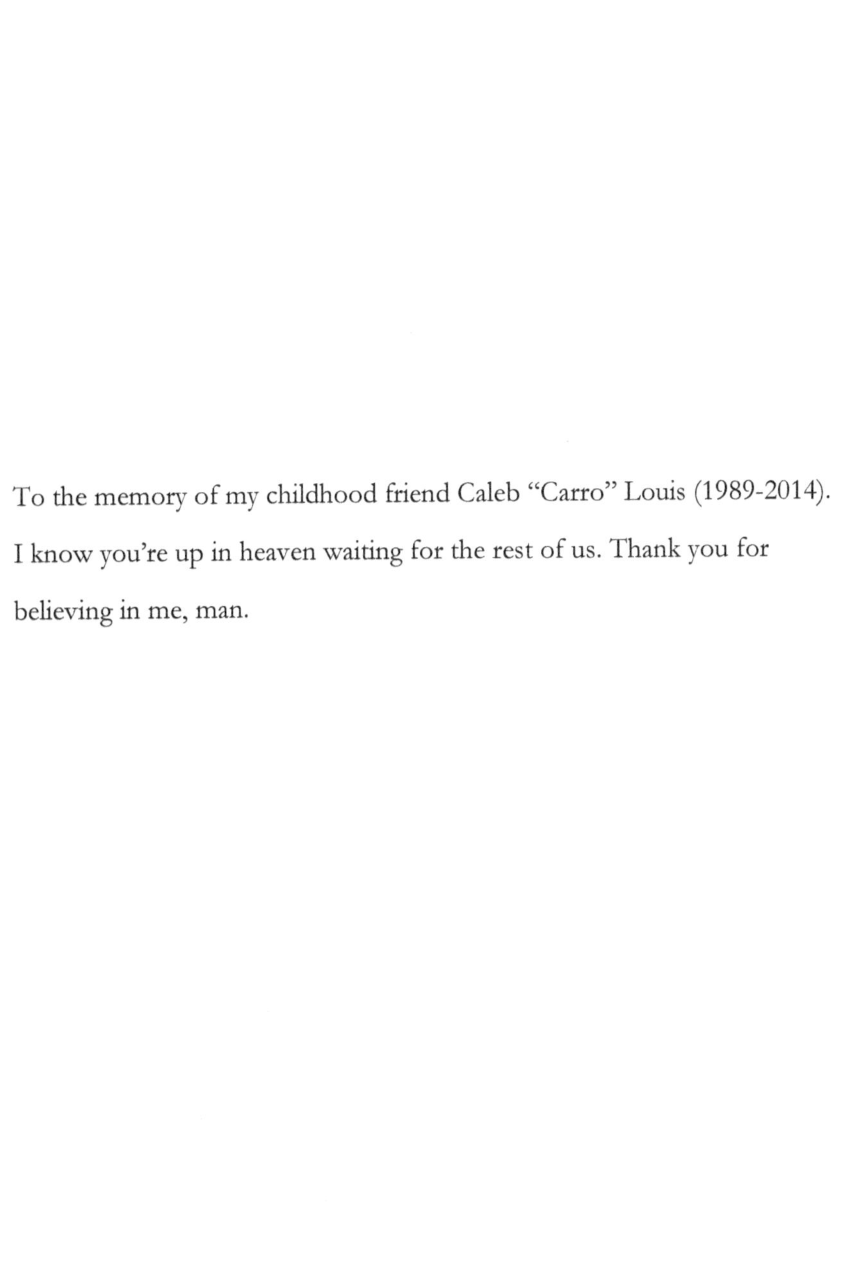

To the memory of my childhood friend Caleb "Carro" Louis (1989-2014). I know you're up in heaven waiting for the rest of us. Thank you for believing in me, man.

INTRODUCTION

Just how far can forgiveness go? How long can it be measured? Do we forgive people because we are obligated to do so, or do we forgive because it is the duty of mankind? We love to draw lines and put rationality on deep topics such as this, but where do we draw the line? What if the people that we have to forgive are the very people that consistently disappointed us; that we took as our trusted friends, allies and family betray us to the point where we can never reach the point to forgive them? The story that lies before you is a gritty morality tale wherein the characters are faced with the choices to forgive those that have wronged them, betrayed them, isolated them, forsaken them; even physically abused them. This story, set in the very pulse of Queens, New York is not based on real or actual events or characters. To all my readers and listeners, I give you fair warning. There is constant use of negative verbal language, profanity, racial slurs, and insensitivities that some of you may find uncomfortable if you choose to continue to read this story. Please do not think this is my disposition or my mentality. I understand that this book may be offensive for some people to read. But the best way to tell the story is to tell it in its entirety, without concealment, borders, or fences. As the story begins, reflect on yourself, and find the peace that lies within you.

M.A.B.

CHAPTER ONE

A game, that's all it was. The first man who got the business took care of it. In this life, second chances were rarely a possibility and even if there could be second chances given out, there was no way that those chances were going to come in these parts. A man is born, grows up and goes to school, where he would hear the same song that everyone could be somebody, if they put their minds to it. There was a life beyond those streets, a way out of the 'hood. All it took was finishing an education and receiving what the government called a diploma and then going to college where a degree could be attained after four to eight more years. That's what everyone thought life was like in this neighborhood. Maybe that's the way it was in California or one of the southern states, but not in south Queens. Not in Richmond Hill, New York, where the school message was taught the same, but it was more perceived as "A life you COULD have but it wasn't going to happen." You wanted to be a doctor who treated patients and prescribed pills and other forms of medicinal drugs. That was a fantasy. That would never happen in the real world.

Never had this been more painfully true for anyone as it was to Nate Plummer. Born in nearby Jamaica Hospital off Van Wyck Expressway, Nate attended elementary, intermediate, and high school in the New York school system. Attending Richmond Hill High School, Nate was a student who excelled in many different sports, including track and basketball. Standing at six-foot-two with long arms, Nate was one of the most explosive young point guards the school has ever seen. With the ability to control the tempo of the game and the ball-handling skills that only hours of practice at the courts in the park can give a person, Nate was on his way to success. Unfortunately, the one problem that derailed Nate was his poor grades. Although he was dynamic on the court, he was unable to translate that success into the classroom. Nate never wanted to admit that he was never intentionally lazy, but Nate never saw the significance of homework, long assignments, or quizzes day after day, week after week. Nate was averaging a low C average in his classes and that was good enough for him. That's when the game changed.

At age seventeen, Nate was introduced to the world of drug dealing in the streets of Queens. His favorite dealing corner was the corner of Lefferts Boulevard and 101 Avenue. When he began dealing drugs with his friends, Nate was still attempting to go to school during the day, so he would not draw suspicion from his coach, his teammates, or his parents. It went pretty well for a while. Nate's parents did not permit him to get a job until he graduated high school, which infuriated Nate, because everyone he knew was working at least part time and making a little bit of money. Besides it was hard enough getting home. Nate lived near Francis Lewis Street, which was a little more that forty-five minutes away from Richmond Hill High School. So he had to take two city buses just to get to his street where his small apartment building was located. That was a dollar a day, at least for cab fare, plus Nate wanted to buy his own food once in the while. He just couldn't get with the school food, and he would normally just skip out on eating during lunch or borrow money from his friends to go eat at a McDonald's down the block. Nate was very popular in school, so he rarely had any problems borrowing money. His longtime friends Gary and Mike would spot him a couple dollars every now and then. But Nate started to get tired of asking his friends for money. He wanted to make his own money and considered finding part time work in a grocery store. He continued trying until one day on his way back from school, as he walked to his bus stop, Nate was confronted by Tony Payne and Deshawn Curry, both of whom were in Nate's graduating class of 1981. The only problem was that neither of them would be eligible to graduate, having dropped out of school to continue their drug dealing business. They proceeded to teach Nate all the tricks of the trade and Nate found out that every week they would rake in more than thirty thousand dollars. Unfortunately, most of that money went to the supplier of those drugs, Earl Canter, also known as "Big Earl."

Earl had connections to most of the drug imports and he did not hesitate to show the rewards of his booming business. A massive three hundred twenty-eight-pound man, nobody messed with Big Earl. Earl was known to be a highly short-tempered man and if a deal didn't go his way or if his fellow dealers who worked with him did not make enough money to meet street value, he would let anyone know immediately. As soon as he was taught the ways of the street game, Nate was fully inducted into the drug trade. Nate's grades soon began to slip lower and his career as a rising basketball player was rapidly fading as the allure of the streets began to entice him more and more. Worried about his plummeting grades, Nate's homeroom teacher soon contacted Nate's parents and informed them about Nate's academic failures. On more than one occasion, there were shouting bouts between Nate and his parents. His father who was a telephone pole repairman was very upset that his son did not want to apply himself. His mother worked in a nursing home and shed more than a few tears whenever Nate would explode with anger and rage at them.

One warm night in April, Nate's life came to a crossroad. Nate, who had not attended school in two weeks, and he began receiving letters from the school stating quite clearly that he was in danger of not graduating. While the letters didn't sway Nate one bit, they became the last straw for his parents. They forced Nate to pack his belongings and promptly threw him out of their apartment. Nate called one of his friends Gary McKey, who lived in an apartment building on the first floor, so he had basement access and stowed Nate discreetly away in the basement, without his parents knowing. The basement was a little adjoining room with old boxes, dusty couches, and roaches scurrying around him. Nate cleaned the place up and slept on one of the couches in the basement. Gary's parents never went to the basement, so Nate was well concealed, and it was there that Nate spent the next two years until he found a place of his own. Gary would graduate from Richmond Hill and so would Mike Hillman, who was an All-Star quarterback for the Richmond Hill football team. Both Mike and Gary took turns trying to convince Nate to stop dealing drugs and stop abusing drugs as well. During these years, Nate became a user himself and was on everything including crack-cocaine, weed, and heroine. The changes that took place in his features were all too telling. His skin sagged, his eyes were bloodshot, and he would sweat profusely whenever he stopped using. One night Nate was nearly a block away from the trap house where Big Earl was sitting watching TV when he saw a typical business deal going on between Tony and a young man who appeared to be a gangbanger. The two men were standing next to a closed corner store. It was about eleven o'clock that night.

"Wassup, my man!" Tony greeted the young man as he slapped him a five, before looking around for witnesses. Seeing only Nate watching, Tony continued the deal. "Iight, so I got three bags of powder and a tube, man," Tony said as he took three bags of cocaine out of his pockets and under his cap. The gangbanger took a look at the bag, staring at it intently with a look that showed that he didn't believe Tony.

"Sho dis shit's real? I need that real shit, you know what I'm sayin'?" he asked as he looked at the bags.

"Hell yeah it's real, nigga. What you think I am?" Tony replied as he placed the three bags in his hands.

The gangbanger thought it over, then put his hands in his pocket to take out a stack of $50 bills. "All right then, how much?" he asked.

"I got you at $350 dollas kid," Tony replied as the gang member paid him the money then took the bags before walking off into the clear night. Tony crossed the street to walk over to Nate and said "What's up man? How much you made?" he asked.

"Not much, man. Block's been empty as hell," Nate responded. It was true. Nate only had a few fifty-dollar bills in his pocket but knew most likely that it was all going into the pockets of Big Earl.

"Damn man. You betta make that money before Big Earl stabs yo' ass," Tony replied as he walked back into the building to give his earnings to Big Earl.

As Nate turned back to the street, he saw someone walk towards him. Although there were streetlights in the area, Nate still couldn't make out the figure walking towards him until she got nearly a block close. At first, Nate couldn't believe his eyes. It had been two years since he had seen her, maybe longer.

"Nina, is that you?" Nate called out to the figure. He wasn't so sure, but it had to be her. As her image came to light a few feet away it was confirmed that it was Nina Martin.

Born to black and Hispanic parents, Nina Martin was once the object of every boy's desire during her days at Richmond Hill High School, where she attended as well. As a matter of fact, Nina and Nate had known each other since their sophomore year at the school. At that time Nina was petite, slender, and beautiful. She had a light skin complexion with brown copper eyes and thin lips. She was on the cheerleading squad and was on the beta club at their school. Even Nate wouldn't have minded dating Nina back in those days. But Nate didn't do that for many reasons. One of the reasons was the fact that Nina was already dating Mr. Big Man on Campus himself, Mike Hillman. Mike was something of a lady's man and he had the girls dangling from every doorway as he walked through those halls, hoping to catch word that Mike was single. But Mike loved Nina and they went steady for a while. But then the drugs kicked in. Although Nate had been using and dealing before anyone else did at school, Nina was one of the few girls who was also involved in doing crack cocaine and heroin, the latter being her drug of choice. That was the other reason why Nate hadn't dated Nina. In Nina's instance, if she didn't shoot herself up the arm every once in a while, she would completely lose it. She would hallucinate, suffer terrible emotional swings, and just make the mood around her unbearable. There were times when Nate would walk the hallways and when he would pass the girl's bathroom, he would hear ranting and raving to the walls. He would wait a couple of minutes, then go inside where he knew Nina was alone there and verbally snapped her back to reality. Nobody else knew this. Nate was like a big brother to Nina and the last thing that Nate ever wanted was for Nina to suffer as he did with drug dependency.

While Nina and Nate's friendship grew, Mike and Nina's relationship began falling apart. Mike didn't like the drug use of either his girlfriend or his friends, so by the time the second semester of their senior year came around Mike had rid himself of any communication with Nate or Nina. Although Nina's drug use may not have been the sole reason for their split, rumors swirled that Nina had hooked up with Gary, who was tall and athletic and also played on the basketball team as well. Whether the rumors proved to be true or not, all Nate knew was that by the time he dropped out of high school and his friends graduated, none of them never really spoke to each other, although Gary lent Nate a room after his parents kicked him out.

After high school, Nina got sucked deeper and deeper in the drug world, working as an informant for Big Earl and often transporting drugs for him as well. Nina did this for about three years. Then one day she disappeared without warning. Nobody knew where she was hiding. Fear and paranoia washed over the group of the dealers. She might have gone to the police and sold them all out. Nate feared that possibility as well, but when no police asked about their mysterious activities, they soon took that notion out their minds and began to relax again. As Big Earl often said, "I knew there was no way that bitch was gonna open her mouth, anyway," After that everyone moved on about their business. No one was going to mourn the loss of one little girl. When one girl left, there were always three or four more girls willing to take her place. So Nina was never seen and never heard from again – until that night.

"Nate, is that you?" Nina asked as she came closer.

"Yeah, what's up girl? Long time no see," Nate responded as he came forward to hug her. As Nina's visage came within view, Nate suddenly saw that she had been using. She was twitching; not terribly but the sudden movements were undeniable, like she had a tick on her shoulder. She started to look a little frail and gaunt in her figure. She still had her pretty brown eyes and fair skin but the drugs were taking a toll even to her skin as well. Nevertheless, Nate still embraced her. "Where you been all this time?" he asked.

"Well, I moved out to my aunt's house in Hollis and started working at a pharmacy store there," she replied. "I'm so sorry I didn't tell you anything. I just didn't want to leave any tracks of anyone possibly following me out there. I just had to get away Nate. My parents had walked in on me shooting up once and I got in huge trouble for it," Nina added as Nate held her shoulders to keep her warm as the night got chilly again. Nate was happy that she got out of 101 Avenue, because anyone who got out of those streets always had a chance at a better life. But one thing bothered him.

"If you liked it over there so much, then why'd you come back?" he asked her. At this, Nina sighed.

"Actually, I came here to look for you, Nate. During the time that I left, I was still dating Gary on and off. Eventually I got pregnant with his son. Then I realized that Gary was not the man I thought he was. I gave birth about a month and a half ago, Nate, and I came home. Then I got a letter from Gary telling me that he moved to Jersey, and he was not ready to be a father," she continued. She went on to explain that her parents refused to help take responsibility for the baby, Nina had been forced to have sitters watch him while she worked before and during the pregnancy and she had gone into rehab to get clean. But the mounting responsibilities and pressure of being a single mother with no one to turn to had driven her back to shooting up heroin again. Nate, taken aback by what happened from Gary leaving his girlfriend and child behind, to the fact that Nina was back to her old habit, and it was destroying her already frail relationship with her parents. "Nate, all I need is a few hundred dollars to get some things for him. Please," she begged him.

A few hundred dollars? Nate thought. I barely got that now and most of it has to get to Big Earl by tonight. Nate knew that if he didn't meet the numbers or didn't get Earl his money, he would be in for at least a beating, if not death. But Nina was his friend. Nina was like a sister to him. Nina, who was once a free spirit, now had a burden that she could not carry on her own. Nate had to do something. He looked at the small wad of cash in his pocket and he looked at Nina, who seemed so small and helpless, wrapped in her brown sweater. Nate was forced to make a decision. He may not have been the best guy in the world but he wasn't careless. There was no way he was going to run out on Nina the same way all the other boys in Nina's life had done. "I'll tell you what. You can chill at my spot with the little guy for the next couple weeks, cuz I ain't got that much but I'm gonna figure something out," Nate said.

"But what about what you're doing now? How you gonna get by?" Nina asked. Nate hadn't even given that a thought. But he decided that he needed to quit this game and get himself an actual job. He had always thought about getting his GED since he never got his diploma and go pursue a career; a life that kept him away from these streets where the possibility of prison or death awaited him.

"I'll be ok. Let me go to the motel where you stayin' at right now and help you get your stuff, ok?" he asked. Nina nodded. They walked by some single-story old buildings that had either regular wire metal fences or broken wood fences. As they approached a house where the gate in front of it was broken at the top and only a few sharp wooden spikes remained of the fence, they heard a booming voice.

"HEY YOU, WHERE YOU THINK YOU GOIN'? WHERE MY MONEY AT, NIGGA?" it thundered. Nate's heart suddenly sank like a stone. He had been hoping to slip away in the dead of night without being noticed but apparently the plan had failed. All the dealers must have turned in their money and left and Earl noticed that Nate was the only one not accounted for. Now there he stood, just a few feet away from Nate and Nina, his hands starting to ball into fists. Nate knew he couldn't take Big Earl on by himself, but he wasn't a punk. He was not going to back down. That just wasn't how things were done in the 'hood. Besides, with Nina now next to him and needing help, he felt an obligation to protect her.

"I'm done with this, Earl. I could give you a little bit of this money, but I'm taking the rest of it, cuz my homegirl needs it," he responded gesturing to Nina. It only took a few seconds for the realization to kick in on Big Earl's face.

"Little Ni-Ni. So I see you finally came back home. Why don't you give big daddy a hug, huh?" he leered as he approached Nina. "Ni-Ni" was the name that Big Earl called Nina during the earlier days when she was still working for him. He may have seen it as a term of endearment, but Nina hated that name and took it as an insult, like he was addressing a child.

"Get the hell away from me, you damn psycho!" Nina replied as she backed away from Earl into Nate's arms.

"Damn psycho. You weren't saying that to my man Slim earlier today when you brought a couple needles from him huh?" Earl asked, smirking with satisfaction when the look of shock registers upon Nina's face.

How did he know what I bought earlier? she thought.

"You think I didn't know why yo' bitch ass ran out on yo' own crew a couple years back?" Earl continued "You really thought you could get away from me? Did you really think that I wasn't gonna find you? You ain't got nowhere to go baby. You mine and you always gonna be mine till you die. The mouse is always gonna run back to tha' trap if it falls for the bait," he sneered as he grabbed the back of Nina's hair and jerked it back, painfully. Nina yelled and tried to fight back but Earl was too strong her and continued to drag her by the hair.

"Get off her, man!" Nate yelled as he jumped on Earl's back. Nothing but Nate's instinct forced him to commit such a stupid act because he couldn't have been using his common sense. Nobody messed with Big Earl.

Earl flung Nina to the ground then grabbed Nate by his shirt collar and knocked him to the ground with a huge forehand. Nate saw stars and little lights popping in his head but realized that Earl was headed toward Nina again. Nina began calling for help and before long, her voices must have been heard because one of the neighbors, awakened by the commotion outside called the police. As Earl grabbed Nina again, Nate decided to attack Earl head-first. He rushed at Earl and managed to plow into his wide frame, but Earl barely moved an inch and with both hands, delivered a bone-crushing blow in the middle of Nate's back that made him double over in pain. Nate got up and rubbed his back. Suddenly he heard a yell of pain from Earl. When Nate looked up, he saw a couple of scratch marks on the left side of Earl's face, below his chin. Nina had scratched him. When Nate stood up again to rush toward Earl again, what happened next was so quick, yet it played over as if it was slow motion. Big Earl lifted Nina up by both of her arms and flung her, almost effortlessly to the side of the yard where the broken wooden fence splinters were. Unable to break her fall in time, Nate watched Nina fall backwards into the sharp spiked area. Nate could only look on in horror as the sharp edges of the fence entered Nina's body. She gasped in pain that only a mortally wounded person could make. Nate quickly rushed over to Nina's side. Tears began streaming down the side of her face and she began breathing in short gasps.

"Nate... Nate," she murmured as the life began draining out of her. This was an out of body experience for Nate. This couldn't be happening. This wasn't real. His friend of over 7 years cannot be laying there, bleeding to death, with a hemorrhage in her abdomen area.

"Come on, Nina. Please don't die on me, girl. Please don't leave me like this," Nate sobbed, tears running down his eyes as he took off his shirt to stop the bleeding. As Earl looked down on what he did, Nate's eyes met his. "This was between me and you, man. You didn't have to do this shit. She was never involved. I'm the one that took your money," Nate said with anger and primal rage coursing through him. The police sirens blared, indicating the police were nearby.

Big Earl pointed at Nate and said "It ain't over between us, nigga. Don't ever forget that your blood is here. You ain't goin no damn place. You ain't gonna be no damn body. Remember that!" he said as he ran.

As the police came to the scene, they discovered the horrific scene. Nate explained everything that happened and as the paramedics came to the scene, Nina took Nate's arm and pulled him close to her so she could whisper in his ear.

"Please take care of him. I left him with a sitter by the name of Tiffany. Please look after him. Please," she said. Nate nodded; tears still wet in his eyes.

"You know, you never told me his name," he said smiling a bit. Nina started to say something but at that same moment, she slipped into a coma.

The police came to gather information and get a statement from Nate, but he wanted nothing more than to accompany Nina over to the closest hospital. The doctors worked fervently to save her life but with too many major organs punctured and the massive loss of blood that transpired, Nina Martin was pronounced dead at two-thirty AM the following morning.

Nina's parents arrived at the hospital and were devastated upon hearing the news. Nate knew he was going to have to answer to the police and face charges of involvement in the murder but throughout every facet of police investigation, Nate made it perfectly clear that he did not kill Nina and knew that if more evidence was released, he would not face extensive jail time. Unfortunately, Nate would serve some time for dealing illegal drugs. Before he was arrested at his apartment, Nate asked that Nina's son remained with Nina's parents but the old couple, who both had frail health in their age, handed him over to an adoption agency. A family soon adopted the little boy, and he was safely raised in Jamaica Estates. After Nate was cleared of all charges, he left Richmond Hill, and went to live upstate. As for Big Earl, he disappeared from 101 Avenue and Lefferts and was never seen again.

CHAPTER TWO

Eighteen years passed and the streets that had once echoed the tales of nightly activities and was void of any bystander or citizen was now filled with pedestrians bustling as some waited for the city buses under square-shaped bus stops and others walked to reach their destinations. Some even chose to take the grime-filled stairway that led to the subway system. It was a warm, sunny day, although the color of the impending fall season began to display on the leaves as the tips began to turn a shade of yellow. The air smelled of a toxic yet addictive smell of the pungent combination of Chinese food, bus exhaust, and pizza. The crowd of people walking did not resemble the zenith that was Manhattan. Nobody was relaxing. People in Richmond Hill, New York were involved in a huge rush to prepare for the opening of the educational institutions that awaited young upcoming students. This bustling scene was a stark contrast to the dark, grisly scene that was seen nearly two decades earlier. Many of the dark alleys that were once clearly visible from the streets were either filled in by land development to create new block stores, hair salons or were now small side apartment buildings for tenants.

After the disappearance of Big Earl and Nate's departure, the crew that Earl had assembled were scattered and spread across Queens. Many of the drug dealers were either currently imprisoned or had given up the drug game to begin a new life outside of the streets as law-abiding citizens. They became average everyday workers who worked to support a family by clean living and community awareness programs. Of course, when the older drug dealers would wise up and leave that lifestyle, there would always be new kids on the block attempting to continue the game.

Law enforcement has increased surveillance over time so that if there was even a hint of suspected drug activity, the police would show zero-tolerance. Perpetrators were arrested on site and either held until bail was posted. The younger kids – those still under legal age – who were still attending school were either sent home to their parents or were sent to a juvenile delinquent hall.

With school on the horizon and drug laws cracking down everywhere, there was only one safe haven for many young black men, and that was the basketball courts within the many public parks that were scattered all over the tri-state area. Lefferts Blvd Public Park was the place for most of those boys. The courts may not have been the most desirable looking recreational facilities built – there were no nets on the eight basketball backboards and rims and most of them were bent from its normal circular shape due to past on – court battles and constant dunking by taller, more experienced players, but the courts were like a second home to these boys. Pick-up games, trash talk and showcasing skills were the norm in the city and if one couldn't play the game very well, they would let the weak link know about it. Public humiliation would be the least of their worries. The most committed and dedicated ball player would be out on all days; even cold winter days, as long as there was no snow on the ground. If a player showed improvement and got better, he can then shut the mouths of all his doubters. If not, he was humiliated even worse than before. This wasn't a novelty; it was the rule of the street. It was ostracize or be ostracized.

On this warm September day only two full courts were occupied as players aged fifteen and above engaged in full-court pickup games. These games were competitive and very rarely did any of the younger kids see any action. The games were rough and physical and played on asphalt terrain, so it wasn't a playground or any place for small children. One kid that knew about the hard knocks of the blacktop was Jamal Samuels. A skinny, black fourteen-year-old, Jamal was not entirely new to the courts, having played there for about three years. He was not the best player during those times when he would play on the courts. He knew that for sure. Most of the older players would just pick him because they needed an extra person so the game would even out. More times than not, guys had frozen Jamal out in most of those games, refusing to pass him the ball. Jamal would never let his emotion show outwardly but he was embarrassed when they would do that to him because in his heart, he knew he wasn't that bad, and he could contribute. He guessed that maybe it was because of his age, but he refused to use that as an excuse at all times. He was not going to let his stature, or his age affect his game. If anyone knew how to survive through these trials, it was Jamal.

Jamal was the only child of Isis and Robert Samuels, who had been divorced since Jamal was five years old. The breakup was so bad that Robert ended up packing and moving down to his native state of Florida, where he currently resided. From time to time, he would talk with Jamal but as far as Jamal was concerned, his father was like a dead leaf to him; blowing in the wind and landing wherever it settles. It was a cruel thing to think, but it was the truth.

Since the divorce, Isis has been searching for some comfort, any comfort that men couldn't seem to give her. She would find it in attending different churches in the area. She must have visited five churches in Jamaica Avenue before settling at the Rock of Jacob Church on Liberty Avenue. Jamal had been attending church with her and he had enjoyed their services, their functions, and the caring environment. They had opened their hearts to welcome Jamal and his mother three years ago. It was the church that had finally offered the support that Isis needed, and she felt that the Lord was the one who could give her that much needed strength. Jamal also believed in that power but at this current time he wanted to test his physical strength on the courts. However, Isis demanded that before Jamal even thought about going to the park, he had better get a haircut. Jamal protested.

"Mom, who cares how my hair looks? It's not a big deal. It's only the first day of school on Monday," he said. But Isis always made sure she stayed on top of her son when it came to taking care of business.

"That's all the more reason that you need to get your haircut, honey," she said. "This is your first day of high school. You want to look your very best on Monday. If you don't do it, you can't go to the park. Ok?" she asked, only she really wasn't asking, it was more rhetorical than factual.

Sighing, Jamal put on a T-shirt and his athletic shorts while grabbing his basketball from his closet. Then he rushed out of the door to head downstairs to the first-floor lobby area of the five-story apartment building on 106 Street where he lived with his mother. Checking his wallet to make sure his Metro card was in there, Jamal stood at the closest bus stop, basketball in hand. Looking around nervously, he hoped the bus would come sooner than later because he really wasn't comfortable standing there, basketball in hand, waiting for a bus to come by. Anyone could leap out, jump him, and take his basketball away from him. As a green-lined bus came to the stop, Jamal swiped his card and sat in the middle section of the bus. His mother told him about a barbershop in Lefferts Boulevard. As the bus approached the intersection where the barbershop was, he began to pull the cord inside the bus to get off at the stop. Jamal got off the bus and proceeded to walk inside Ozone Park Barbershop. The moment he walked in the barbershop, he heard talking right away.

"You mean to tell me that dude ain't gonna get drafted in the first round?" one of them said.

"Nah man, that brotha ain't good to me at all. At least not first round good; I can think of three other guys that coulda went above him," another barber said as he was finishing one of his customer's haircuts. Jamal sat in one of the waiting seats.

One of the barbers, a thin, balding man saw him and asked, "Who you waiting on, young man?"

Jamal looked around to make sure nobody was ahead of him before replying, "Anybody. It don't matter," he replied mildly.

The barber cleaned his station and wiped the hair from his last customer off the side of the chair, then beckoned Jamal to sit down. He showed him the hair chart of different hairstyles. "Which one you want, youngblood?" he asked. Jamal looked at the chart, thinking for a moment. Then he made his decision.

"Ok let me get the bald fade with a lineup," Jamal responded to the barber. The barber then put the chart away then started brushing Jamal's short, disheveled hair. While he prepared Jamal's hair for the cut, he heard the barber's bell on the door sound, indicating someone had entered the barbershop. Two older boys had just walked into the barbershop.

"Them workouts gotta be brutal as hell," one of the boys, a dark-skinned wiry boy, said to the other boy who walked in with him. The other boy was light skinned, with eyes that seem to pierce at anyone that he stared at. Both boys were tall; about six feet six or even taller.

They must be ballers Jamal thought. The light-skinned boy wore a t-shirt that read RICHMOND HILL ATHLETICS and blue basketball shorts with Nike sneakers while the other boy wore a Nike brand shirt with black basketball shorts.

"Yeah man, it ain't no joke. Season ain't even started yet and coach got us running like crazy," the light skinned boy responded as he and his friend sat on the waiting chairs to wait for the next available barber.

"Well, well if ain't Mr. All City himself. I hope you over there doing work for the Red Storm this season," the balding barber said as he continued to cut Jamal's hair.

At first Jamal didn't know which one of the boys the barber had addressed, until the light skinned boy responded, "Oh you already know, Clark. I'm definitely going after mine this year."

The light skinned boy seemed to have a lot of confidence in himself, as far as Jamal was concerned. But living in the Mecca blacktops, overconfidence was nothing new. If a person could play ball well, he had to flaunt it as much as possible, as long as he had the skills to back it up. Far too many times, when Jamal goes to the courts to work on his game, he had seen a poor sap being ostracized because earlier in the day he had been talking up a storm, only to be silenced forcefully by his opposition. All basketball towns were the same and Richmond Hill, New York was no different. If a person couldn't play ball very well, they would let him know it in a heartbeat. Then it would be advisable to take up another sport that was best suited for someone as inept as that person was, like billiards or playing Chinese checkers with the old people at park benches.

As Jamal adjusted his head for the barber to reach the back corner of his head for a lineup, the light skinned boy glanced at him. It was a quick, fleeting moment but the boy nodded his head upward slightly which was a silent greeting for what's up. Unfortunately, Jamal couldn't nod back because the barber was focused on lining his hair up sharp, so he was careful not to move.

Another barber, a few feet behind Jamal indicated that he was ready to take another client. At this, the light-skinned boy got up and said, "Well I'm gonna roll onto Duke this time, man, since you still cutting homeboy here."

Duke was the name of one of the other barbers in the shop. He got his nickname for two reasons: He was a fan of the Duke Blue Devils, and he loved listening to Duke Ellington. The barber gave him a look of mock disappointment.

"Oh, so I see what's up. Now since you a superstar and all, I guess you don't need lil ole me cutting you anymore. Choosing the Duke over me, huh?" the barber laughed.

"Naw, it ain't like that, man. You still ma dude. I'm just gonna change it up a bit cuz I got somewhere to go after this, you know what I'm sayin?" the boy replied, laughing as he made his way over to Duke, who cleaned his chair in preparation for him.

Throughout the day, the barbers cracked jokes and talked about their favorite sports teams. It took the barber seven more minutes to finish cutting Jamal's hair. While Jamal paid the barber eight dollars for his haircut he asked about the name of the light-skinned boy who was now getting his hair cut.

"You mean to tell me you don't know who that is?" the barber asked Jamal incredulously. Jamal nodded his head, indicating that he didn't know who the boy was. Even though Jamal has lived in the Richmond Hill area for three years, he still considered himself relatively new to the area meaning that he didn't know any of the local high school athletes just yet. "That young man right there is Trevor McClain, son. Fresh off his senior year at Richmond Hill High School, where he averaged about 20 points and eight rebounds a game. All City and first team All-Defense. I mean there's got to be a reason St John's recruited him, boy," the barber responded shaking his head as if he still couldn't believe that Jamal didn't know him.

Jamal looked over at Trevor. Man I wish I was as tall as he is. I may not be the best baller out here but having the height wouldn't hurt at all Jamal thought as he left the barbershop to walk the four block route to the nearest public and recreational park, but not before he stopped by a corner store to buy a sports drink. Requesting a plastic bag so he could conceal the drink and keep it cool, Jamal finally reached the courts. He surveyed the eight-goal/four court asphalt spread that lay before him. Most of the rims didn't have nets on them, except for the main center court, which also happened to be the court that everyone liked to play on because they still had nets hanging from them. It was at those courts where the young men were playing their full court five-on-five game, so Jamal chose a corner hoop on the far back end of the courts to practice and work on his game.

As he walked by the baseline and passed the older players, he took notice of some of their skills from the fluid motion with which they shot the ball to the way they broke their opponent down with the dribble. He saw the way they flicked their wrist when they put their shot up. He made his way over to the court and began working on his game. Jamal wasn't the best player. He had a suspect handle, and his shot was not yet defined. He started out by making right-handed lay-ups which were his specialty and then switched over to shoot left-handed layups. As he practiced, he looked toward the busy Liberty Avenue. His friend Omar Keaton was supposed to meet him on the court about twenty minutes ago. He began working on his perimeter game, shooting from the top of the key and mid-range elbow shots and baseline shots, which was the hardest shot, since you had to shoot from an angle. He was practicing so intensely that he didn't notice the older guys had finished playing their game and some of them were heading toward their cars in the parking lot or walked out of the park into the sidewalk. He also didn't notice there were two other individuals who had been shooting hoops at the other end of the court and at the last couple minutes, they had stopped to watch Jamal warm up. At the last moment Jamal dribbled back toward the three-point line and released a shot, knowing that it was off because he didn't put enough arc on it. The shot fell a few feet short of the rim. He heard a short sound of laughter from behind him and a low whistling sound as the ball missed the rim. Trevor and the friend who had been in the barbershop with him were laughing and shaking their heads at his direction.

Great Jamal thought. Just what I needed; two older, more experienced ballers clowning me and school ain't even started yet.

"Ayo son, appreciate the breeze you just gave us," Trevor said, laughing.

Breeze? Jamal thought. It was eighty-two degrees this day and there was barely any wind felt. "What breeze?" he asked Trevor.

"The breeze from that air ball you just shot. Felt real nice too," Trevor answered, laughing. Jamal tried to laugh off this situation, but he couldn't believe they saw that failed attempt.

"Yeah, I'm a little rusty right now, but I'll get it," Jamal responded as he went over to get his sports drink that he kept in the plastic bag underneath the rim.

As he took a swig out of the drink, Trevor asked "Aye man, can I get a waterfall?" Jamal looked at Trevor. It did look like he was fatigued as well, due to the sweat starting to form in the front of his shirt.

"Yeah man. Here." Jamal offered as he handed the drink over to Trevor. Trevor let the liquid stream in his mouth without putting his lips on the bottle. He then handed the bottle back to Jamal and introduced himself.

"Trevor McClain and this is my boy, John Strickland. What's yo' name, dog?" he asked.

"Jamal Samuels. What's up?" Jamal replied as he dapped Trevor and John. Dapping was an expression that meant the same as giving handshakes, but in a certain way; a certain style. They walked under a tree shade to stay cool.

"So what grade you in, man?" Trevor asked.

"I'm about to go to ninth grade right now at Richmond Hill High," Jamal responded. At this Trevor perked up a bit.

"Oh ok, that's cool. My old stomping grounds. Now, I'm gonna keep it 100% with you. It ain't all fun and games there. People are gonna try you a lot over there, even the teachers. But that's why I kept to the court. Kept my game up, ya know?" Trevor said, while spinning the ball in his finger.

"Yeah, I heard you were recruited by St. Johns," Jamal replied.

"Recruited?" John retorted. "Boy, they practically begged this man to come play for them. My boy was unconscious last year droppin' 30 point games on dudes, they was on their knees beggin' dis fool to come play for them," he boasted.

"Shut yo ass up, nigga!" Trevor exclaimed, laughing. Then he turned to Jamal. "Nah, but they gave me a full ride to play for them. So right now I'm conditioning until season starts," he said.

"That's what's up," Jamal replied. Looking at them made Jamal a little envious and insignificant. If these are the types of players that play for Richmond Hill, I got a long way to go he thought.

Trevor seemed to have read his thoughts because he asked, "So you tryin' out for the squad this year?" Jamal made sure that he gave his upcoming response some thought. He didn't want to appear too cocky to act like he can make the team with no sweat, but he didn't want to go out like a punk either.

"Yeah, I'm tryin' out for ball. But I'm trying out for the freshman squad though. I already know the varsity squad got their team locked," he replied.

"Well I wouldn't say all that now. Some freshmen have been good enough to make varsity," Trevor said.

"Did you make the varsity squad as a freshman?" Jamal asked Trevor.

"No. He never even played ball until he became a senior. He was tired of ballers like me doing him up on the hardwood," John joked. Trevor fake-punched his friend and they laughed.

"Ayo, son, don't listen to my dude over here. He be talking cuz he hatin' on players that be crossin' his clumsy ass over three times a day," Trevor replied.

"You going to St. John's too?" Jamal asked John.

"Well I been getting letters from Iona College, Boston College and Seton Hall but I'm weighing my options right now," John replied. At this, Trevor gave John a look that said Boy please!

"Look, don't be lying to homeboy. You working at the mall right now, going to York College," Trevor retorted, seeing through the facade that John was putting in front of Jamal.

"Well, right now I'm between jobs, so my peoples are talking to their peoples," John laughed.

Jamal was relieved at how calm and collected these guys were. It wasn't like Jamal was bullied on a regular basis, because he could hold his own and defend himself when he had to, but sometimes taller guys would give him a hard time because of his height and skinny frame. Picking up the basketball after their short break, Jamal resumed dribbling the ball and shooting. Trevor got up and joined him in shooting around. But the moment he did so, Jamal instantly regretted letting Trevor use his basketball because it seemed every shot that Trevor took went in. He had exceptional form, and his movements were fluid. Normally if a person was shooting around in the park and made a shot, they had a chance to keep shooting until they missed. But Trevor was automatic. It didn't matter where he shot from; the ball swished gracefully through the hoop. Jamal, in one ten-minute session completely understood why St. John's wanted him to play for them.

John had just begun to join them in shooting around, when he suddenly stopped and stared out into the street at the corner intersection was and said, "Shorties, three o'clock."

Jamal and Trevor turned toward the intersection, following John's gaze. "Shorties" was a loose term for hot, sexy petite girls who knew they were beautiful, and they flaunted it in every way they could. In this case, there were two of them. Both girls were wearing tight jean caprls and blouse-like shirts. The only difference in clothing was that one girl was wearing sneakers and the other girl was wearing designer sandals. One of the girls looked about nineteen, brown-skinned and her hair fell to her shoulders in a bundle of curls. The other girl looked younger and her skin was a shade of light brown-olive and she had straight brunette hair. Jamal couldn't help but look as the girls were talking and laughing at a joke that he was sure made them oblivious to the boys now watching them. One thing that Jamal as well as the other guys noticed was that these girls were packin. A term that meant they were voluptuous; well-endowed in the chest and backside. Jamal must have been drooling or something because the next thing he knew, Trevor and John exposed him.

"Look at this boy, staring all hard. You like that, right?" John asked Jamal with a sly smile. Jamal did like it but he knew it was wrong for him to like it. Since he moved to 101 Avenue, Jamal has been attending church with his mother and has heard teaching that it was a sin to look at a woman and lust after her, so he was no stranger to it. However, Jamal couldn't seem to take his eyes away from the beautiful, female bodies that walked into his view. Trevor then turned to him, giving him the same sly smile that John gave him earlier.

"You want me to hook you up? Miss Brownskin might be a little out of your league but lemme get the other one for you," he said. Jamal looked at him in horror.

"Wait, wait no, no, don't do it..." he stammered but it was too late. Trevor began calling out to the two young women.

"Ayo wassup? My boy Jamal, was tryin to holla at ya for a minute. Is that cool?" Trevor asked. Jamal did his best, but couldn't hide the blush and the grin of embarrassment that began to display on his face. The young women began to laugh.

"We would, but we actually going to the store right now. Maybe lata'," the younger olive-skinned girl answered as they walked past the park still laughing and glancing at Jamal. All Jamal did was shake his head and had his hand up to his forehead.

That could have gone a whole lot better Jamal thought. Turning to Trevor he wondered what led Trevor to put him on the spot. "Why you gotta play like that, man?" he asked. Trevor only laughed.

"Yo relax, G. She was feelin' you too. I can tell these things. I bet you gonna see her again. She look like she still in high school anyway," he replied.

I hope I don't see her again. She probably thought I was a pathetic loser Jamal thought. "Yeah, I guess," he replied.

"Yeah man, don't even sweat that. The one thing that turns a female off is a dude that's too thirsty or too nervous," Trevor said as they began shooting more hoops. Jamal nodded his head, readily agreeing to what Trevor said. He hoped Trevor wouldn't ask the next question that would come out of his mouth. "You a virgin, man?" Trevor asked with a sly smile.

Jamal didn't want to answer that question because he didn't want people knowing about his personal life. He didn't want people to know that he was still a virgin. Sure he was young, but Jamal had a lot of stories from older friends and influences that they took the choice to have pre-marital sex, even before they reached the age of eighteen. Jamal decided to flip the question back to Trevor.

"Are you one?" he asked. Trevor laughed and said with full confidence that he was not a virgin and during high school, he did everything in the book and then some.

"Watch bro, the same way that girls were all up on me in high school, I can give you the appeal," Trevor reassured.

"Gee, thanks," Jamal said sarcastically. It was almost five in the afternoon. Jamal was sure Omar was not going to make it to the court, so he had no choice but to start getting ready to go home. He informed Trevor and John that he was going back home. As he took his basketball and went to wait at the bus stop, he was very pleased that he made a couple of friends that did all his talking for him. They did joke about a lot of issues and you couldn't take them seriously but Jamal felt as though these guys came along just in time. They gave him great basketball pointers and tips because he would need that for this year if he tried out for the Richmond Hill squad. He had to prepare. School was around the corner – just two days away – and Jamal want to make sure he had everything prepared for his return to school. As he came back home and laid down on his bed, he thought about what a good day it had been and he couldn't wait to see what his future would hold. He was also going to try to be more open towards other people because he knew that one day he would need them. Isis Samuels, his mother, would return home with an armful of food so he could help prepare dinner with her.

CHAPTER THREE

One Sunday morning, as the rays of the sun penetrated in brightly patterned lines upon the trees and sidewalk, a man awoke from his bed and slid his feet into his brown slippers. He yawned and stretched his arms as he shook off his fatigue with one single motion. Next to him, under the sheets, his wife was still asleep. He took a loving look at her and smiled as he ran his coarse, rough hands across her shoulder and her head. She stirred slightly but didn't fully awaken. After a minute, the man walked across the tiled floor of his two-story duplex side home to the bathroom. As he turned on the bathroom faucet, he gazed at himself in the mirror and studied his visage. A well-built, broad shouldered man of forty years stared back at him. He looked closer and he could see the developments of the fine age lines creased across his forehead and his hands. He splashed some water on his face and began to brush his teeth. After he did so, he walked across the narrow staircase to the small kitchen that he and his wife had inhabited for many years.

The room across from the bathroom belonged to his eighteen-year-old daughter. Along the wall of the staircase, there were many photos and portraits. There were pictures of his family throughout the years; memories of him and his wife when they had first met many years ago. The one lingering memory that stood out among this mini museum of sorts was his high school sports memorabilia. His All-City football picture when he was still a star quarterback at Richmond Hill High School did nothing but gather dust like the rest of his photos. The man used to glance at the photo whenever he would travel up and down the stairs on his way out of the home because he would enjoy reflecting on how different his life turned out. When he was young and he had all the ability and talent in the world in his particular sport, it seemed success was what was expected for his future. The world could have two choices for someone whose future didn't pan out the way they expected. It can be an excuse to mope around and lament on what could have been, or it could be an opportunity to get up off the ground, let go of whatever doubt, hate, denial or anger has instilled within, and keep moving forward. Pastor Michael Clark Hillman decided to go with the latter.

Not a day passed, when he wouldn't think of those high school days and reflect on how reckless he used to be and how he would be influenced by his friends to do what he couldn't even fathom doing now. He liked to consider himself the most level-headed of the people with whom he had associated himself. He had been no better than they were. He had his demons, and he was sure his friends at that time had their demons as well – some more challenging to overcome than others – to the point that he had to cut them out of his life.

A young, naïve wayward man he was when he was in high school. He had a specific group of friends that he considered more than merely friends. They were almost like his brothers. The irony was that Michael actually a younger brother who was five years younger than him, but they lived as if they were total strangers. They never met eye to eye on anything. As a result, when they each graduated high school, they went in totally different directions. Michael had dealt with depression after his close friends and high school girlfriend did what he took as an act of betrayal. He withdrew himself from the world, comforting himself with the bottle. Even though he was underage, and he wasn't old enough to drink at that time, he would somehow find his way to a bottle. His family, who had supported him and who, ironically, were church-going folks too, could never identify or relate with his struggles. He gave up playing football, although many schools had offered him a full scholarship. He never saw the point of playing anymore. Contrary to people who wanted to play a sport only for the promise of a financial benefit in the future, Michael loved football because it was a connection with his friends. It was also a connection with his girlfriend at the time. It was even a connection to the life that he wanted to share with them; a life that he coveted and ultimately the life he would never live.

Throughout the entire summer after his high school graduation, Michael wandered aimlessly through life, wondering what it was and what it meant to live, when Trayback Collins came into his life. Collins was a minister at Liberty Covenant Church when Michael stumbled his way through its doors one night.

"You ok, son? I don't think so because it looks like you fittin' to do something wrong," he said.

Actually Michael wasn't going to do anything that particular day, but thoughts of suicide had been swirling in his mind.

"No sir, I'm not fittin' to do nothin'. I just wish I knew what to do. I just don't know anymore. Everyone that I trusted don't give a damn about me," Michael responded in frustration.

"Well someone does care about you," Collins said and at that point he began telling Michael about Jesus Christ and His sacrifice for mankind. Michael listened to him as he explained the Gospel and it was amazing how he fit the basics in a one-hour session. Michael thanked Mr. Collins and walked home, thinking about what the minister had said.

That night he had a dream in which he was visited by the Lord and He spoke with him and urged him to rebuke the spirit of depression in the name of Christ. It was as if Michael was nauseated the whole evening until the Lord visited him that night and spoke those powerful words to him. He awoke in a cold sweat. He ran to the bathroom toilet and retched violently. He vomited, not food but an evil black liquid that came bubbling up from his system. He didn't know if it was the bottle of spirits he had drunk earlier or something else. But one thing was for sure, Michael was no longer depressed. Inexplicably, he felt rejuvenated and reinvigorated about transforming his life. He attended Nyack College and studied the Bible and theology in depth. He also took a physical career path to become a marble specialist, which had become a great pastime for him because he appreciated colors, patterns, and creative designs. He had always been good at math, so the measurement portion came to him easily. Eventually, he worked his way up the job ladder and finally opened his own small non-profit contracting company, Hillman Marble Co. Michael quickly earned a reputation as a very fair and polite person with whom to do business. People began to refer to him affectionately as Pastor Mike Hillman because he had ministered at Rock of Jacob Baptist Church for over 10 years. He met his wife, Robyn, when he was still at Nyack and after they married, they had one daughter, Shania, who attended Michael's old school, Richmond Hill High School.

In the meantime, Mike's brother, Blake, has moved to Texas where he started a successful medical career. Even though he was getting his career together, Michael knew that he had to continue praying for his brother because he knew that his brother had not developed a personal relationship with Christ. He called him numerous times, attempting to encourage him to visit his church one day and share the Gospel with him, but Blake was either too busy or just never gave the Gospel much weight.

This Sunday morning in 2003 as he reflected on his past and how it brought him to where he was today, he realized that it was nothing but divine grace; grace that he didn't deserve and a sense of peace that eluded him for much of his younger life. As he brewed his morning coffee, he walked over to his desk study, which was built on the side of the kitchen and took his Bible and sermon notes and read over it for about five minutes. He bowed his head in prayer.

"God, of Abraham, God of Isaac and God of Jacob, today I come before you in spirit of humbleness and reverence. For ten years, you have bestowed upon me the great responsibility of leading your people to you. You have been indescribable in you traveling mercies and your wonderful grace and cheer. I lift my congregation in prayer this morning as they will hear not just me, but you as well. Speak to your people today Lord Father and let the Holy Spirit fill this place today. I pray for my family, Lord, that they speak life in their thoughts and their actions. I also pray that you would forgive my sins and the sins of my family and our shortcomings. I pray, not because I am worthy but in the name of your son Jesus Christ, my Lord and Savior. Amen," he entreated with his whole heart. He then turned the volume up on the small kitchen radio that his wife had plugged in the kitchen to listen to while she cooked. The old song, "Every Time I Feel the Spirit" sung by a choir came wafting through the radio, bringing a smile instantly to his face. Mike took a sip of his coffee and began humming the song. Looking at the clock, he saw that it was a quarter past eight. Placing the cup down, he began to shout.

"Rise and shine, beloved. In the words of James Brown, get on up!" Michael said emphatically as he walked to the small hallway corridor towards the rooms, stopping at Shania's room. "Shania are you up yet?" he yelled as he placed his ear next to the door. A small, muffled groan gave him confirmation that his daughter was awake. "Couldn't you stay awake and watch with me even one hour? Keep alert and pray," he said, reciting a Bible verse.

"Matthew twenty-six verses forty and forty-one," the groggy voice recited back to him.

Michael smiled and walked toward his bedroom. This had been a ritual they did every Sunday morning since Shania was little. From the moment his daughter was born, Michael vowed to teach his daughter all the ways of the Lord and train her in the church. It was very encouraging to watch her grow up fascinated with the Bible and she would draw Biblical stories Sunday school classes. As a result, Shania and her father made up a little game whenever they woke up on Sunday in which they would recite a Bible verse to one another, and they had to identify the book, chapter, and verse. This was an excellent tactic to ensure they were both doing daily Bible readings and devotionals. Sure it would become tough with their schedules of school and work, but Michael always said that people always had at least ten minutes a day to read the Bible.

Walking into his room, he kissed his wife on the forehead and Robyn opened her eyes. Robyn Hillman had straight black hair which she recently cut and fell just above shoulder length. With hazel-brown eyes and full lips, and a full figure, sometimes Michael couldn't believe how blessed he was when he married her. There were times that he would look at her and even though she had age lines, Michael still saw the same beautiful young woman he met at Nyack when he was trying to find himself. She had also been in a Christian family in Yonkers, and she had excelled academically in high school. Robyn had even become her school valedictorian. Her twin brother, Arthur Blaylock, was a successful lawyer in New York City and was just as strong and self-driven as his sister but that was where the comparisons stopped. While Robyn had a spiritual relationship with the Lord, Arthur couldn't be more far removed from the church. He did not find going to church particularly interesting and he was more concerned about his business, just as Mike's brother. So Mike prayed for his brother-in-law to be reconciled to the Lord as well. As Mike kissed his wife, he recoiled playfully to the side.

"Oh baby, you know I love you, but morning breath don't mix well with me!" he joked.

"Whatever, Michael!" Robyn exclaimed, laughing as she got up, her long silver nightgown draped over her body.

As she headed to the bathroom, Mike couldn't help but wonder if his wife had been distracted as of late. Although their relationship was as strong as it had always been, he couldn't help but feel that at times the fire in their relationship had dimmed slightly. When Mike and Robyn first got married, they made love almost all the time and neither could breathe without the other. Yet lately it seemed that work and family life had superseded their love life and as a man, Mike had to admit, it was discouraging. However, he didn't want to dwell on it because Robyn worked as a New York City school system social worker and her hours were long and when she returned home, she was often very tired, and it would require a great deal of effort just to prepare dinner for the family. So Mike took that into consideration and just prayed to the Lord for strength because his family needs far outweighed his personal needs. There were two bathrooms in the apartment but only the hall bathroom had a shower. Mike entered the bathroom to enjoy a long hot shower. One shower and one nice solid-black suit later, he walked into the kitchen. Robyn was in a sky blue cotton night robe and was drinking the coffee that her husband prepared earlier.

"So did you sleep well, honey?" he asked.

"Yeah, I did," Robyn replied, smiling at Mike. Even though it didn't appear that she was as in love with him as she once was, she still loved this great man of God. He had come from the first time they met. She appreciated all he did for his family, and she knew she was blessed. That's what made her even more fiercely protective of him; she knew her husband was in the public eye at times and there were more than a few women waiting to shatter their harmony.

"Sometimes I think about the kids that I work with, and I'm surprised how many of them have broken homes and fathers that don't seem to care about them. When I talk to them, I'm more thankful that I have you and Shania," she added.

"Did you invite them to our family?" Mike asked. He always referred to the church as family because that was how they were as described in the Bible.

"I always pass out the business cards that I have and hope to see them one day but I never do. That's when I get really worried," Robyn confessed.

"I know. Sometimes I fear for these young men and women out there. We live in a system and a social structure that's built to keep us at a disadvantage, but it's always important that we keep showing God's love to them because that's what He would do," Mike said. "Where is Shania? She needs to hurry up because we got to go in another ten minutes," he added, looking at his watch. Robyn looked back into the hallway corridor.

"I think I saw her coming out of the bathroom a short while ago," she responded. Mike got up from his chair and started to walk to the room. "Go easy on her, honey," she called after him. Mike lightly knocked on her room door.

"Shania! We are not going to be late to church this Sunday, I need you to put some pedal to the metal. I don't understand how you can be a track runner at school on weekdays and on Sunday; you act like you running on quicksand!" Mike said, half exasperated, half amused.

Shania ran track and field at Richmond Hill High School, and she was starting to get the athletic recognition her father had once gotten in his heyday. She had local city newspapers boasting her name after winning her races. The apple didn't fall far from the tree. Shania was long and slender with the same brown eyes as her mother. After a minute or two, the door opened, and Shania stepped out.

"Ok Daddy, I'm ready now. Are you happy?" she said rolling her eyes but smiling slightly.

Mike wasn't happy though. He looked at the outfit that Shania had planned to wear to church. She was wearing a black dress that fell barely below her thighs, so it certainly didn't cover much of her legs. The front of the dress was low-cut; not extremely, but enough to attract male attention. That did not sit well with Mike at all.

"No you are not ready, young lady. Where do you think you're going? Church or the street corner?" the pastor asked.

"What? Come on, Daddy, there's nothing wrong with this dress. It's cute and it's not too revealing at all," she countered.

"I beg to differ. No daughter of mine is going anywhere dressed like this. Robyn, do you see what your daughter was about to wear going to church? Come out, Shania and show her what's left of that dress," Mike stated and Shania stepped out. She walked down the hall, model-runway style, even pretending to wink at people who weren't there just to show off in front of her father. Robyn didn't seem too concerned.

"Oooooh, kill em' girl!" Robyn said as they both raved on the beauty of the dress. Michael just shook his head. He wasn't amused one bit.

"Robyn, Shania is not going to church this way. This is not up for discussion. I'm sorry. With the young brothers that we have coming to church now, this would be too much of a distraction," he said.

"Mom, why does Daddy have to be such a stick in the mud?" Shania asked. Robyn ran her hand through Shania's wavy black hair.

"It's only because he loves you so much, sweetie. He's seen so much in his past where young women as beautiful as you were taken advantage of by young men. He's just protecting you," she answered. Shania rolled her eyes again; then returned to her room to change. After ten minutes, Shania reemerged in a nice floral, summer dress that complimented her figure but was far less revealing than the previous dress.

"That's more like it! Now when we get back home, we are going to discuss where you bought that dress and how you can kindly return it to its original owner," Mike replied. Shania just took her Bible and walked outside to their Nissan Maxima and sat in the backseat, staring out the window while they drove to church, avoiding her father's eyes as they stared in the mirror back at her on occasion.

"Jamal, come on wake up. We have to get ready for church!" his mother, Isis Samuels called through his room door while knocking the door.

Jamal was awakened from his groggy stupor and stared at his alarm clock. It was eight thirty-five. How did I sleep through the alarm? I could've sworn I set it last night at eight o'clock Jamal thought with a shrug. He got up out of bed and prepared for church. His mother had gone to the dry cleaners that week and had prepared his favorite white pastel and navy-blue slacks. He laid them out on his bed and searched for his blue and black striped tie. Sunday was his favorite day. Whatever problems he had encountered during a regular school week or work week and however he felt about somebody personally, Sunday morning church services always seemed to alleviate them. Jamal loved Rock of Jacob Baptist Church. He and his mother started attending that church three years ago when they were still searching for a church family. After his parent's messy divorce, Jamal noticed a change in his mother. All the joy was gone from her life and the lighthearted fun she used to enjoy with Jamal, she no longer did. They had stopped going to the park or occasional bowling trips. They didn't even take their yearly trip to Coney Island like they had before the divorce.

Then, through a reference from one of her clients at the beauty shop where she worked on Jamaica Avenue, she found out about Rock of Jacob Baptist Church. From the time she started attending the church, she fell in love with the church community. Jamal participated in the Sunday school classes and activities of the growing youth group in the church and she especially enjoyed hearing the messages preached by Pastor Mike Hillman. What she found most intriguing was the effect Pastor Mike had on Jamal. He had a way of preaching so that the youth of the modern-day era related to him. It was as if he had walked in their shoes and faced decisions that they faced. Pastor Mike encouraged them to change their lives through obvious understanding. The way he stood on the church podium and spoke was so influential and even fiery at times; so much so that Jamal had told his mother that he had aspirations of being a pastor one day as well. Isis was thankful for Pastor Mike and since they'd become members of the church, she has noticed a change in her home. She became much more forgiving and throughout the problems that she faced with her ex-husband and Jamal's father, Robert, she was much happier again. As they entered a new chapter of life where Jamal was about to enter high school, she knew how important and much more instrumental Pastor Mike would be to her son's growth than Robert had ever been.

At nearly midday, it was almost a packed house inside the Rock of Jacob Baptist Church, which was located at the corner of 95th Avenue and 111th Street. A two-story building which had been built about twenty years ago had seen its share of changes and development over the years. When Pastor Mike was ordained as the pastor of the church, it only had forty-five or fifty members and only three deacons. There had been only one main Sunday school room where all the kids would be squeezed into one room. Since that time, the number of members in the church had more than doubled, reaching about ninety-eight members with six deacons, two ushers and one pastor. They had also expanded the number of Sunday school rooms, building two more rooms on the lower level of the building that was easily accessible down a thin flight of stairs.

The classes were separated by a series of revolving walls. One class was known as the primary class of children who were preschool through seven years old. The next classroom was reserved for the intermediate ages which seated the eight-year-olds to the preteen level kids. Then the third class was used for the teenage and young adult ministry. It was a unique setup and was taught by some of the most caring and charismatic teachers. A woman by the name of Betty Wilson taught the children with great enthusiasm; teaching with song, videos and games with different activities. The preteens would also watch videos of the topics but they started doing devotionals and keeping journals of their daily Bible readings which they would present to the teacher before class started. This class was taught by the pastor's daughter, Shania.

When Jamal started attending the church, his first Sunday school teacher was Shania, and he would be the first to admit that he did have a little bit of a crush on Shania. He knew Shania was way out of his league and she perceived Jamal more as a little brother than as a romantic possibility. When Jamal was finally elevated to the young adult class, he kept the journal that Shania gave him when he was still in the intermediate class and he continued to write entries daily. The young adult class was taught by Wesley Richards, and he was more practical at his teaching approach; more Bible readings, more real-time applications, and at times there would be movie presentations as well. Only by God's grace was the church able to flourish the way it did, and Pastor Mike did not take its success for granted. He was happy to provide a home for people who needed shelter and happy to provide hope when the people needed optimism. He was most grateful that his congregation was telling others about it and through word of mouth, his ministry was expanding. That was Pastor Mike's mission; to help the church grow so it could be a positive influence in the community.

The adult choir sang a selection for the church, choir conductor Raymond Cline led the congregation to the rendition of the hymnal 'How Great Thou Art.' At the conclusion of the song the organ player, Julie Macland, played a chorus while the ushers passed the offering plate for tithes. During the service, the adults sat on the right side of the church and the youth classes occupied the left side of the church. The deacons were appointed ministers and church officials, whose jobs were to oversee the service and make sure the sanctuary rules were adhered to and were anointed, baptized, and inducted into the ministry. Kevin Garrett, Ronald Plank, Clay Hudson, Charles Lee, Max Nelson, and Marie Joseph were the six individuals that were chosen to be deacons for the church. They were responsible for greeting the churchgoers after the ushers greeted them and would often be chosen to pray over the communion ceremony when it was being conducted. They were also a vital part of developing different ministries in the church. Ronald Plank headed the newly formed singles ministry and Charles Lee headed the mission trips and organized picnic events yearly. Each member was a body and each member had a purpose to serve in the church. Besides Julie Macland, they also had guitar player Tremaine Guy and drum player Louis Canty. They were an integral part of the service and the family and Pastor Mike were very thankful for their contributions to the church services.

As the offering was finished being passed around, Pastor Mike was called to the pulpit to begin preaching. As he approached the dark wooden pulpit, his eyes fell on Isis Samuels and the rest of the congregations on the left side and to Jamal and his friend Omar Keaton on his right. He also saw Shania with her best friend, Loree McAfee. He began his sermon.

"Beloved, let us turn our Bibles to the Book of Acts chapter twelve verses six to eight. When you have found that passage, let us stand so we can read it together," he said. He paused for a moment, allowing everyone to turn their Bibles to the highlighted book and chapter. When he had confirmed that every-one has turned to their Bibles accordingly he proceeded to read.

"The night before Peter was to be placed on trial, he was asleep, chained between two soldiers, with others standing guard at the prison gate. Suddenly, there was a bright light in the cell, and an angel of the Lord stood before Peter. The angel tapped him on the side to awaken him and said, 'Quick! Get up!' And the chains fell off his wrists. Then the angel told him, 'Get dressed and put on your sandals.' And he did. 'Now put on your coat and follow me,' the angel ordered. Brothers and sisters, this morning I want to meditate on what happened to Peter in that prison cell. The brother was trapped and chained between two guards, with no way out. But was Peter distressed, beloved? No, he was not distressed because he was asleep. He did not know when the miracle of his freedom would arrive, but he knew that it would come. Peter was in a position where he could have panicked, and he could have given up hope beloved but he believed in the power of the man named Jesus!"

The crowd shouted "AMEN!" in unison. The pastor continued.

"Many of us find ourselves trapped, imprisoned, and contained in our sin, in our struggles and in our situation and we have fallen so far from the faith we forget to look upon the author and finisher of faith, Jesus Christ. We have people who are bound by drugs, people who are bound by the spirit of hate, anger, lust, sloth, and alcohol. And as I stand before you all this morning, I can also attest that I, too was bound by the spirit of depression which caused me to depend on alcohol rather than to depend on the Lord God who created the heavens and the earth. I wanted to use alcohol as my relief; as my way out, as a way of getting past my anger, my ignorance and my selfish vanity and pride. But instead, it held me even deeper. This morning we have folks present who are depending on these outlets and have forgotten the meaning of prayer and forgotten that the battle is not yours, but it's the Lord's!" he said emphatically while the church shouted "AMEN!" again.

A woman shouted "PREACH!" The pastor continued.

"In the verses leading up to verse six, it said that the church prayed earnestly for him while Peter was in prison. Brothers and sisters; let us not underestimate the power of prayer. Even the Word instructs us to pray without ceasing. When we see a brother struggle in the streets, don't discourage him or put him down. Help a brother out and if he refuses your help, just pray, and allow the Spirit of the Lord to go to work! The world is already on a mission to destroy our young people already and we don't need to give them a hand. Instead, we need to give them the nail-scarred hands of Christ and allow Him to break the chains as he did for Peter in prison. When you listen to the words that the angel instructed Peter after the chains fell off his hands, he says, 'Quick, get up' and instructed him to put on his coat and follow him. The Lord is telling you this morning that whatever your situation is this morning, get up from it. The Lord is breaking your chains this very morning. Get up and take your stuff and follow Him! Don't delay and don't wait for the enemy to realize what has happened. Get them chains off and shout that you are a free person in the name of Jesus Christ. I want you to turn to your neighbor and say 'Neighbor, this morning I am free. Sin no longer has a hold on me.'"

Jamal turned to Omar and stated those words and Omar repeated them back to Jamal. Shania turned to Loree and repeated the words.

Robyn turned to the person sitting next to her and repeated those words. The pastor continued.

"Sin does not have a hold of you. The Lord wants you to let go your spirit of doubt and fear and anxiety. Let go of sexual frustration, immorality, riotous living, and jealousy. In the name of Jesus, you will not be bound by your imperfections. You will not be bound by drugs. You will not be bound by your haters. Tell your hater I'll see you later!" he said to a loud AMEN and bits of laughter on the clever line. "Today is the day you will no longer wait for a person to rescue you. You won't wait for a politician to rescue you. You won't wait for the police to arrest your sons, because the Lord has taken care of you, and He will continue to do so!" the pastor continued among shouts of cheers and "AMENS" echoing through the church walls.

When the service ended, the people began to file out of the church but not before shaking Pastor Mike's hand and thanking him for the message that he preached. As the people began to fellowship with one another, shaking hands and greeting others, Isis came up to Pastor Mike.

"Pastor, thank you for that wonderful message today," she said. "I felt like at times I was trapped just like Peter have been discouraged but it is always good when the Lord uses his servant and speaks through him."

The pastor shook her hand firmly. "Thank you very much, sister, I appreciate you coming today as always. So where's the little guy?" he asked, referring to Jamal. Isis looked around and saw Jamal talking to Omar and another kid the same age.

"He's right here, pastor. Jamal! Come over here and greet the pastor," Isis said and Jamal did as he was told.

When the pastor shook Jamal's hand he asked, "So are you ready to start school this week, young man?"

"Yes, sir I'm ready," Jamal answered.

"That's what I like to hear, Jamal. My daughter has told me that when you were in her Sunday school class you were one of her smartest students. I hope you keep up that good work when you enter high school.

It's not easy and there will be challenges, but keep your head up, pray and persevere. Got it?" the pastor asked.

"Yes sir, I'll work my hardest this year," Jamal said.

CHAPTER FOUR

Sleeping in a misty blue room, window bars frigid with the cool September night, Trevor woke up and made his way outside the room to the dark hallway. He had no idea why, but he knew that he had walked this hallway before. He could hear the voices of people talking outside about sports. Unfortunately he couldn't tell which sport they were talking about. It could be baseball or basketball but who knew? He looked outside the small window at the end of the hallway where the full moon was shining at its full strength. A chill went through Trevor, and it was as if his bones were frozen raw and the more, he breathed, the more he saw the air mist coming out of his mouth. Then, out of nowhere, he heard a baby's cry. The cry started as small, heartfelt gasps but soon progressed into all-out bawling. It was not the cry of a baby that was hungry, or cranky or tired. It was a different cry. It was a cry of abandonment; a heartfelt cry by a child whose mother was nowhere to be found. The screams grew louder and louder and more piercing. Trevor looked for the source of the sound. He jogged back to the room where he had been sleeping but he couldn't see anything. He then realized the baby's cry was downstairs on the first level floor of the building. Trevor walked downstairs, hoping he wasn't going to find an abandoned baby in the garbage. Too many times, he had heard stories about how far a drug-addict, or an alcoholic would go to satisfy their desires at the risk of an innocent baby; left alone in the streets to starve, shiver, and ultimately freeze to death in the cold.

As he turned to his left upon descending the staircase, he saw the baby, wrapped in several layers of blankets. He stepped closer, expecting to see the baby sleeping on a crib or a small bed, but instead, the baby was lying down on what looked like an electric heater. Trevor ran quickly to save the baby before it started to overheat, but then realized the heater was not hot at all. As a matter of fact, he wasn't even sure if the heater was turned on. Then, in the small corner of the room, adjacent to where he was standing, he saw a woman hunched over; her back turned to him as she was busy. Trevor didn't know what she was doing, nor did she seem to acknowledge that he was even there; he only that she was very much entranced and occupied by what she was doing. Trevor couldn't understand it at all. A helpless baby was lying on top of an electric heater all alone and this woman heard it crying; yet she wasn't doing anything about it? It didn't make any sense.

Filled with anger and indignation, he asked, "Lady, is this your baby? You don't hear it crying?"

The lady still had her back to him, as if she hadn't even heard what he said. Trevor started to get more annoyed. The one reaction he hated more than being insulted was being ignored when he addressed somebody.

"Lady, you can't hear me? Are you deaf or something?" he asked angrily.

It took her another two minutes, but she finally turned her head slightly over to him and stared into his eyes, Trevor gasped. In the woman's hands were 2 needle syringes and a number of cotton swab balls. The woman had black hair and a thin body, but her eyes appeared bloodshot and sunken. Her skin was a pale yellow, in comparison to the complexion that she must have had before she began using drugs. Two huge rubber bands were tied to her arms and when he looked closer, he saw the syringes were empty. Trevor could see right away that she was a heroin addict. Trevor started to speak to her again.

"Hey lady! Listen! Your kid probably wants something to eat, and I think..." his words began to trail off and stop in mid-sentence, because what he witnessed next was not of this world. It couldn't be.

The lady's face started to sag, and it began sagging more and more. Trevor felt sick. It was similar to watching an age progression chart only instead of taking fifty years between ages, it was taking fifty seconds. Her face sagged until it came off completely, and her skull protruded from the area where the flesh had once been. At once, Trevor woke up; his sweat still clinging to his chest. He was breathing heavily. He looked around. His dorm room had pictures of sports athletes and famous political leaders as he designed them with his roommate. What was that all about? he thought as he turned his sweaty pillow the other way so he could sleep on the dry side.

Monday morning finally arrived and that meant public schools in New York City were finally open. Blue and green-lined city buses were in full business and commission as the streets were filled with children carrying heavy backpacks. It was easy to separate the public-school kids from the private school kids. Private school kids all wore the same uniform with the school logo printed on their shirts, which was always tucked in nice and neat and ironed out. They took the buses and trains because many of the private schools were located closer to Manhattan. The private scholars generally anticipated the first day of school and walked together in huge, concentrated groups. Public school children, on the other hand, did not show quite the same enthusiasm for the beginning of school. It meant another year of boredom and being in the creative doldrums, going back to the same system that did nothing but prepare the students for guaranteed failure. Although a few of the students attempted to excel in their classes. At this point, school was a place where if the students weren't in elementary school, they barely tolerated it. As Jamal and Omar walked towards the brown brick establishment that was Richmond Hill High School, they were intent on one comment achievement: make their mark as individuals. Jamal already started this by not allowing his mother to walk or drive him to school, which she had done throughout elementary and middle school. Jamal felt that since he was a freshman, he could walk to school. Omar was no stranger to walking to school. Both of his parents worked in Manhattan, so they were not there during the day. Fortunately, Omar lived a block away from Jamal so he just met up with Jamal at seven-thirty so they could begin their twenty-five-minute walk to school.

"Man, it's crazy. Feels like summer went by mad quick, son," Omar said as they crossed an intersection.

"I know. This is a new chapter right here. But I know what I'm gonna do. I'm ballin' this year on that freshman squad," Jamal replied confidently.

He was looking forward to playing on Richmond Hill's basketball team, having heard stories about their success in the past and learning recently, of course, that Trevor McClain played there and was part of the school's success on the basketball court.

"Yo, do you know your schedule already?" Omar asked. Jamal thought for a second.

"Nah, they said we wouldn't get our schedules until we got to homeroom," Jamal recalled. When he signed up for classes in the last month of his eighth-grade year, he remembered the guidance counselor informing him that he wouldn't know his schedule until he arrived at Richmond Hill. "I hope they got us in the same classes this year cuz if they don't, this whole year gonna suck," he added.

Jamal and Omar were not troublemakers, but they did their share of acting up during middle school. Playing small pranks on classmates and making sure they worked together on a group assignment because Omar was very smart when it came to science. Jamal could never forget that Omar helped him with his science project the previous year and he aced the project that helped him secure a B grade in science. So Jamal needed Omar in his classes. If they were separated, there would be no way he could make it through this first year. They saw the throng of kids starting to increase as they got closer to the school and by the time they reached the street across from the school, the throng grew into a mob of hormonally charged teens. Sophomores, juniors, and seniors who had not seen each other over the summer greeted each other and started talking as if they were meeting all over again. At once, Jamal could see that it was a different world. The girls were walking by, and Jamal noticed very quickly there was no dress code, or at least not a strict one because the older girls dressed as if they were still at Panama Beach with small, see-through T-shirts and hip-hugging jeans with brand-name sneakers fresh as if the tags were just removed from them a few minutes ago. The guys were much more intimidating; the more athletic ones wore t-shirts that looked like they could rip at any second with one flex of their pectoral muscles. Then there were the older students, with their baggy jeans that sagged and tall tees and fitted caps.

They hung around the front steps on the school doors cat-calling and hooting the girls that walked passed them; shouting things like, "Damn, baby if you in my class, I'll actually stay in class this time," or "Aye, mami (or mita)" to the Latino girls. Jamal hoped that he wouldn't run afoul of any of the upperclassmen or the older kids. As he and Omar walked up the stairs to the school, one of the stair kids spoke to them.

"Ya fresh blood? Don't even go here, son. You wasting your time hea' man. Find a way to transfer out this bitch," he joked while the other guys laughed.

Jamal and Omar only laughed with them as they entered the school. After asking for directions to the freshman corridor from one of the teachers, Jamal and Omar walked through the busy hallways to get to the proper place. Jamal looked around him. The lockers were huge in this place. Not one of those little middle school lockers, where you had to bring your own lock and could barely fit a full backpack. These were colossal lockers that could probably fit a short kid. As they reached the freshman corridor, there was a chart just outside the double doors. It was the homeroom listings.

"All right, so it looks like we in the same homeroom. C. Canatello, whoever that is," Jamal confirmed.

They walked the hallway, finally reaching Mr. Canatello's classroom. There were a good number of kids who were already at the classroom. Omar and Jamal chose a pair of seats close to the back on the left side. Then the first warning bell rang, indicating that all the late stragglers better make it to class before the second bell rang or they would be listed as tardy. On each desk, there was a folder with the school planner, the lunch forms, and all the health and medical paperwork for the parents to fill out. While Jamal was looking over this information, he heard someone call out his name.

"Jamal! Omar! My two homeboys! What up with you?"

Jamal looked up from his papers and searched for the source of the voice. It belonged to Carlos Collado, one of their friends and classmates from middle school.

"What's up Carlos? You in hea' too?" Jamal asked, as he shook Carlos' hand and Carlos shook Omar's hand as well.

"Yeah man. Ya had a good summer? I know I did. I was kickin' it with my older brother in Puerto Rico for three weeks. I'm telling you….paradise bro," Carlos replied.

"Man, I wish I could've went out of town too. I just spent all summer just going to the park hoopin," Jamal said. Omar agreed by nodding his head, although Jamal was mighty tempted to call his friend out for not coming to the park this past Saturday to put in work.

"Oh ok. Ya gonna try out for the basketball team? Well good luck with that. I heard there are some real monstas on this squad and most of them are coming back for their senior year. Can't wait to see you do work on freshman squad though," Carlos encouraged.

The door opened and at first Jamal thought it was Mr. Canatello, but instead it was a girl. She was wearing a pink shirt with jeans and sandals. She looked Latino as well and Jamal couldn't quite put his finger on it, but he knew he'd seen this girl before. Then the shock registers when he realized that it was the girl from the park, who Trevor called out to embarrass him.

Aww man, this girl's in my homeroom too? What are the chances that she will remember me? Hopefully slim to none. It was a hot day. I was sweating and playing ball and she saw me from a distance. Maybe she won't recognize my face he thought

The girl had a light blue backpack and she was walking toward the back of the class where Jamal was seated. It must have been the first time Carlos saw her because he was already on his game.

"Damn, bro that girl is fine as hell. Watch this and learn from a real playa," he said.

Jamal shook his head. Carlos always acted like a smooth ladies man in middle school, trying to get all the girls and even then, it never worked to his advantage half the time. Carlos approached the girl, putting his sunglasses on.

"Hey baby, allow me to offer you my seat. You so beautiful, it's blinding," he said.

The girl just smirked and blinked twice at Carlos. "Well if you so blind, then you won't see me walkin' past you then," she replied.

Jamal and Omar laughed, their hands covering their mouths to hide how hard they were laughing. It wasn't her fault. Carlos had it coming to him. She sat in the empty seat in front of Jamal and turned to him.

"I remember you," she said, pointing at Jamal.

Jamal looked around to make sure that she wasn't talking about anyone else. "You do? From where?" he asked. The girl's eyes narrowed slightly, although she was smiling.

"Don't play stupid with me. You that dude at the park that was tryin to 'holla' at me," she said, putting her two fingers up and down to represent parenthesis and emphasis on the "holla" part.

Jamal scratched the back of his head, even though it wasn't itching. "Nah, that was just some joke from my boy Trevor. He be playin' too much. Don't mind him," he said.

The girl continued to look at him. She seemed to be studying him. "So you don't think I'm fly? You weren't trying to talk with me?" she said. She seemed to be challenging him. Jamal didn't want it to come down to this. But he decided instead of beating around the bush, he was going to be honest with her.

"I do think you're fly. You ain't lyin'. You do got it goin' on for real and that's just me being real. But I'd like us to be friends first though. Is that cool?" he asked.

The girl smiled. "That's cool. My name is Patricia Cuevas, by the way. What's your name?" she asked.

"Jamal Samuels. Nice to meet you," Jamal replied. As Mr. Canatello, a short stout man, walked into the room and started to call roll, Jamal looked on at the back of Patricia's head and smiled. This year's gonna be a good year he thought.

Sneakers pounded and grinded against the practice court as a group of fourteen elite players ran across the St. John's center court logo in their practice jerseys. With perspiration dripping down their faces and breathing heavily, the players ran cross-court as the coach timed their speed and made sure that they made it across the timeline in thirty seconds. Then they worked on layup lines; some of them touch dunking the ball in the hoop. The layups were fluid, timely and very précised. After that, they practiced their left-hand layups, which were once again flawless and precise. Every time they reached the line, the training coach blows his whistle, and they would repeat the same drill, running to the other end of the court at full speed and back. They were drilled on the three-man weave, which was a running, passing drill that taught how to pass in transition or a fast break situation. Trevor stood as the wingman when his three-man group was set to do the drill and for some reason, his legs wouldn't cooperate with him. The other two players sprinted up the court fairly easily and Trevor was caught a few feet back.

The training coach noticed this and yelled "Let's go McClain! Pick it up!" Trevor nodded only slightly before joining the baseline with his teammates, panting heavily.

Then the college players broke off into individual drills for guards, forwards, and centers. Trevor stood in the forwards' training basket, and they were working on mid-range jumpers; which was normally Trevor's specialty. But he found that he was unable to convert on more than half of his baskets. Every shot that he released hit the back of the basket or got side rimmed. Trevor felt total frustration in himself. He was no stranger to bad practices, but this one had to take the cake for one of the worst practices in which he had ever participated. To top it off, they did a dribbling drill with a defender on them, and Trevor lost his handle a couple of times. A few of the team members shook their heads when Trevor finally made it across the court. The coach finally blew the whistle two times, signaling the end of practice. All the players gathered in a circle around the training coach who explained that they did a good job on the court and to keep working on their games. Practice ended early so that many of the players could get to their class on time. Trevor changed inside the locker room, his mind still clouded with the events of the nightmare he had experienced the other night. He had a plethora of questions about the dream. Why did he have the dream? Who was that woman in the dream whose face peeled off? Who was the baby left on the electric heater crying? Was the lady a heroin addict? Or was she a diabetic patient, who was just taking insulin? Any answer that occurred to him could be the right one. After he changed out of his practice gear and showered in the bathroom adjacent to the locker room, he came out of the locker room and walked past the assistant coach's office.

"Hey McClain, can you step into my office please?" the assistant coach asked Trevor.

Trevor went into the office. Pictures of St. John's alumni were hanging on the wall and there were some plaques hanging on the wall. "Have a seat McClain," the assistant coach beckoned to Trevor as he sat down in the chair facing the coach's desk.

"Is something wrong?" Trevor asked, hoping that the school didn't flub his financial aid or revoke his scholarship for any reason.

"Not at all, son," the assistant coach responded. Trevor breathed an internal sigh of relief. He definitely imagined the worst. It was not every day that players got called to the coach's office, unless they were being cut from the squad or being informed that they would be red-shirted for the year. "No, you're not in trouble sir. I just called you in here because you seemed a bit distracted at practice today. You looked a bit out of it. Normally you would dust my upperclassmen in these drills. It's kinda hard admitting that, actually," the coach said with a smile. Trevor smiled as well. "But today you seemed sluggish, uninterested, and maybe even out of it. I just wondered if things were ok," he added with concern.

Trevor fidgeted in his seat a little bit because he knew the coach was right on all counts but he didn't really want to talk to anybody about the dream that he had the other night. What was he going to say? He had a dream about an abandoned baby and a woman who was supposed to be taking care of it was using so much drugs that her face fell off? As a result, he couldn't perform at the greatest of his ability and potential because of it? Trevor was having a hard-enough time fitting in with the team and just trying to fit into their chemistry heading into the season. He didn't want to disrupt the chemistry with the thoughts that he had when he slept.

"No, coach I'm good. I probably didn't get enough sleep last night, so it was probably fatigue or something like that," he replied. The coach nodded but Trevor had a sinking feeling that he wasn't buying it.

"You hadn't been up partying all night, had you?" he asked with one eyebrow slightly raised.

"Nah, nothing like that. Trust me. I've been focused on putting work for the squad this year and in school," Trevor replied.

"Good. Because I have plans for you this season and I need you to be on point every night, McClain. Bring that A-game every night and every practice," the assistant coach said.

Trevor widened his eyes. For the longest time, he wasn't sure if he would see the collegiate floor as a freshman. He thought for sure the coaching staff would redshirt him for the year.

"Really? So I'm not being red-shirted this year?" Trevor asked the assistant coach.

"Well, it's still too early to decide right now but one thing I know is that we're impressed by your skill set and your work ethic. You are always the last one to leave the gym because you're working on your game. So we may work you in the rotation this year," the assistant coach said. At this Trevor got up and shook the assistant coach's hand. He had feared the worst. As he stepped out of the coach's office, the coach said, "Keep up the good work, son. If something is bothering you or if you need to just blow off some steam, you can come to my office anytime."

Trevor nodded his head to acknowledge that he understood before he walked out of the room, feeling very much better, pushing the horrible images from his previous night into the back of his mind, at least temporarily.

The bell rang at Richmond Hill High School, signaling lunchtime. The students started to file rowdily into the lunchroom talking animatedly with friends, girlfriends, and still catching up on summer events. Shania and Lisa Chen walked out of their fourth period history class and made their way over to the cafeteria. Lisa was a friend of Shania's who was Asian and was very short and petite. She ran track with Shania, and they had been friends for years. Although Shania had known Loree much longer, Loree was not an athlete, so she would not hang out after track meets. Loree's favorite entertainment was the mall; shopping for new handbags, shoes, and clothes. It wasn't as if Shania disliked shopping but to Shania there were shoppers and then there were people with compulsive spending disorders. In Loree's case, Shania always thought she needed professional intervention. Shania and Lisa were the voices of reason for Loree and if it wasn't for the both of them, Loree would probably spend her money into the ground. On their way to the lunchroom, Shania accidentally walked right into Jamal, who was headed the opposite direction to math.

"Oh, my bad, little man! So how's the first day of high school so far?" Shania asked Jamal. The terms Jamal did not like was when anyone called him "little man" or "short stuff." He hated those names.

But because it was Shania and they were well used to each other's company by now he just said, "It's ok. I'm about to go to math class now."

"Oh ok. Who's your teacher in that class?" Shania asked. Jamal took the paper schedule out of his pocket and read the schedule that was provided by his homeroom teacher.

"Let's see. It says my teacher is V. Peterson, whoever that is," Jamal replied shrugging his shoulders. Shania then knew who he was talking about.

"Oh man, be careful with her. I had her my freshman year, and she was one of the toughest teachers I had. She will straight put a zero on a blank sheet of paper if she finds out that you don't do your assignments," she warned Jamal. As they walked in opposite directions, Lisa spoke.

"Ugh I couldn't stand Ms. Peterson either. It always seemed like she was riding me at every term that I had her because I missed a part of an assignment," Lisa said to Shania. Shania shrugged and smiled.

"Oh well. It's not like it's our problem anymore. We are seniors this year. The last year being here, and we are finished. That's all I'm focusing on," she said.

Lisa nodded her head in agreement, and they walked to their table and sat down. Shania looked around. There was no sign of Loree. "Where is she at? She's supposed to me us here," Shania said.

"She's probably still with her man," Lisa said.

Shania did not say it out loud, but she did not trust David Anderson, who was Loree's boyfriend. A quarterback for Richmond Hill's football team, David was strong, well-built, and had a smile that charmed any girl out of her shoes, but Shania was not one to be easily charmed. A lot of guys thought that by talking wise and acting fresh with her, they had a chance of going out with her. Not only was that not true but the opposite made more sense. If any man tried to run any type of fresh words at her, it turned her off and it annoyed her. As Shania looked toward the center of the cafeteria, she saw Loree and David necking.

"Speak of the devil," Shania said as her and Lisa watched Loree kiss David passionately.

Normally Shania didn't care about kissing or other public displays of affection, but what they were doing had to be illegal in several countries. Tongues, lips, and nose all pressed up against each other. It was sickening but Loree couldn't stop bragging about David. Lately since they had started dating, Loree had been talking about how David was not like every other guy. How kind, chivalrous, and debonair he was and how focused he was when he was out on the field. There was not a football practice that Loree missed. She showed up every night. When Loree and David finally stopped kissing, they walked over to the table where Shania and Lisa were sitting.

"Hey ya'll, what's up?" Loree said while her head rested on David's chest.

"What's up, girl?" Shania responded. She wished David was a few steps behind her because she didn't trust him breathing down her neck. As they sat down to talk, before they walked up to get their food, Shania asked Loree, "Are you ok? Is everything fine?" Loree confirmed that everything was ok, but Shania had her doubts about David. By looking closer, Shania saw why she had to continue to keep an eye on David because she noticed something on Loree that made her suspicious. On her left arm, barely visible, was an ugly bruise. If David was doing to Loree what Shania suspected, Shania wanted to make sure it didn't escalate.

CHAPTER FIVE

Wearing a wrinkled white and blue pastel shirt and faded gray slacks, the man stepped out of the bus station at the central terminal in Merrick Boulevard. He walked three blocks to the unemployment office based on a phone call he received regarding a job opportunity. He didn't know the full details of that opportunity, so he made sure he dressed in his nicest suit for a possible interview. The brown shoes he had worn for many years were beginning to show signs of wear and tear. But when there were no alternatives, what other choice did he have? The man who walked in those shoes had been in and out of some serious situations in his life. He had been arrested in the past for drug possession and had watched his future and his life nearly evaporate before his eyes. He watched one of his closest friends die right before his eyes and the images of that horrific night never left him. Every night he slept was another night he was forced to relive the horror that had occurred eighteen years ago. It was an event that compelled him to turn his life around and transform himself into a hardworking citizen. He had lived in Fremont, New York where he stayed with his cousin's family and had worked many different jobs, a handyman, an A/C repairman, and a part-time sanitation worker. He never married, even though he had enjoyed some past exclusive relationships. But they never replaced her.

Life was beginning to improve for the man until one night he was once again confronted by the visions of that horrible night. He decided the only way he was going to put those events behind him was to confront them, and the only way to confront fear was to go back to the very heart of it and then overcome it.

That was the plan and after eighteen years of self-exile, Nathan Reginald Plummer went back home to Queens, New York, his birthplace, and the location of one of the most tragic events of his life. The only word that burned in Nate's mind was revenge. Acquiring a gun license and buying himself a .357 Magnum, he kept it in a special safe in the apartment he had rented near Briarwood. He had never been a huge advocate of violence, but he knew deep down inside that this had to end. He had to finish it. He had to avenge his Nina, no matter what it cost him to do so. Unfortunately his connections and old friends informed him that they did not know where Big Earl had gone. It was as if he dropped off the face of the earth, but Nate did not care. Even though the burning hatred was no longer there, Nate was still convinced that Earl had to pay for what he did. While he attempted to rebuild his life around familiar surroundings, he also had a secret mission: find Earl and eliminate him. He took into minimal account Earl's family, but he didn't care. If Earl valued his life so much, why hadn't he valued the lives of other people? He treated everyone he knew cruelly and expected everyone to do his work for him. He was only looking to get paid by Nate that fateful night and now Nate was going to make sure he got paid.

As Nate walked to the unemployment office, he straightened his shirt collar and rubbed at the trim beard he shaved earlier that morning. Walking into the Department of Labor office, he took a seat to wait until they called him to the counter. After waiting for nearly an hour and a half, the lady behind the counter called his name. Nate stepped up to the counter. The lady gestured him to a small keypad.

"Please enter your social security number here," she said.

Nate entered his social security number. She identified him at once based upon the information presented and handed him a clipboard with various papers.

"Please fill these out and return them to me. Then wait in the area to the far left and one of our representatives for the job posting will call you into one of the interview rooms," she said.

Nate sat down and filled in his paperwork. While filling out the background information, he came across the part he hated filling out the most. Have you ever been convicted of a felony, or have you been imprisoned? If so, explain. Most HR people in the past would read that Nate had been in jail for only a few months, then act as if he was a convicted felon his whole life, costing him the chance at another job. Nate filled the section out the best way he could and waited to be called to the interview. Finally his name was called and he brought the papers over to the lady in the counter and followed the interviewer to a small conference room in the far end of the facility.

"Thank you Mr. Plummer for answering our job post. As you know, the job description is a custodial engineer for the New York City Public School System," the interviewer said. She went on to explain his pay rate and the benefits of working in the New York City Public School System. All of it sounded good to Nate who needed money to make rent payments and get by until another opportunity came up.

"Thank you for the opportunity ma'am. I definitely appreciate it but where do I report for my first day?" Nate asked. The interviewer checked his computer and looked at the schools in the area.

After about two minutes she replied, "Well it looks like you're going to be reporting to Richmond Hill High School number 475 on Thursday morning."

Nate's heart stopped for a moment. His old school? The school where he spent three years playing basketball and the site of his untimely, unceremonious drop out from not only the basketball team but the school? Nate still had his name on some of the basketball trophies and many accolades from those days. Never in all his years did he think that he would return to the place where his whole world began to fall apart. His mind suddenly recalled all the glorious days of the basketball team and the games and his friends and teammates that were more family to him than his actual family members. He was trapped so deep within those thoughts, he nearly forgot that he was in an interview.

"Hello, Mr. Plummer? Did you hear me ok? It'll be at Richmond Hill High School," the interviewer told Nate again as though she had to repeat it many times. Nate stood up. He would have to do his job without thinking of the past. His high school days were over and there was no way he was going to let that get in the way of making money. He shook the interviewer's hand.

"Thank you, ma'am," he said, before walking out of the Department of Labor.

The alarm clock blared loudly Thursday morning as its owner continued to sleep with the covers over his head, unaware that he was supposed to be awake for a significant day at school. As the volume of his alarm increased, the sheets flew off Jamal's face and he sleepily pounded the snooze button on top of the alarm. It was seven twenty-four A.M. and upon realizing the time displayed, he ran toward the bathroom to catch a quick shower. As the water splashed upon him, he couldn't help but feel that today was important for some reason. An event was supposed to take place at school but he couldn't quite put his finger on it. It was the fourth day of school, and it was nearly Friday, signaling the end of a challenging week for Jamal. Not only did he have homework from four of the six classes he had that day, but he had to focus on getting the textbooks required for those classes. Some of them were provided at school but other workbooks he had to order online and have them shipped to him. He was instructed to order them over the summer, but he wasn't aware that he would need those books so soon. He had to remember that he was not in middle school anymore. In middle school, if a student did not have a book or two, he could still be successful because the teacher either printed out the notes or you shared with someone. High school was a different story. If the right books were not purchased or utilized by the beginning of the school term, it would set students back academically. Since Jamal did not have a job yet and his weekly allowance for doing the chores was not nearly enough, his mother would have to help him order the books. What he couldn't do was delay or procrastinate getting those books, because Jamal didn't think his teachers had any patience to wait until he was able to obtain a book for their classes. Especially Ms. Peterson, a cross and stern-faced white woman who established a reputation as a no-nonsense type of teacher. Shania warned Jamal about her and now Jamal could see that she was right. Out of all the teachers that he had in Richmond Hill, he didn't think he had anyone as strict or demanding as Ms. Peterson, who taught Algebra I and Algebra

II. Jamal and Omar were in her Algebra I block, and they thought that Shania's subtle warning was only a joke. Most of the students didn't have to worry about getting homework on the first day due if they had read the class syllabus and general introductions. This was not the case with Ms. Peterson. She ran through her course syllabus and didn't waste any time continuing into the first section for her class on the very first day. She then assigned homework for the whole class consisting of seventy-one pre-algebra questions to complete for the next day in review of their middle school material. Jamal and Omar discussed how difficult Ms. Peterson was on their way home from school that day.

"Yo I can't believe that lady gave us homework on the first day, son," Omar whined as they crossed a busy intersection to get home.

"Yeah, Shania wasn't playing when she talked about this teacher. I got a feeling I ain't gonna like her too much this year," Jamal said in agreement. "I mean, she's giving us so much homework, you woulda thought we had a test to take tomorrow or something," he added. That's when it hit Jamal that Thursday morning there would be a pop quiz based on the first lesson learned in class. Damn I forgot about this quiz he thought as he put on his clothes. He frantically searched his book bag for the one-page review sheet that Ms. Peterson handed out to the class the day before. Where did I put that review sheet? He searched everywhere among his school belongings but there was no sign of the blue-colored review sheet. Feeling defeated, Jamal went to the kitchen to grab a toaster pastry in his way out. He didn't see his mother. Jamal figured she must have gone to work early. First week of school and already I'm about to bomb the first quiz he thought. Unless Omar had it he thought as he walked out of his apartment building and started the walk toward certain academic doom when he saw Omar at the intersection.

"Yo, man what's up? Why you ain't wait up for me when I got out my crib?" Jamal asked Omar as he caught up to him at the intersection.

"My bad bro. I'm probably trippin' over this quiz that Ms. Peterson got fo' us. I ain't tryna' fail my first quiz man. My pops said if I even bring home a C- grade this year, he'll sell all my video games," Omar replied.

Jamal gave a slight snort of disbelief. Omar had to be one of the smartest guys he knew. The last thing Omar needed to worry about was his grades. He has been a straight A and B student in middle school. He never liked to openly brag about his grades because at the end of the day, good grades alone didn't define Omar's character. But Jamal needed his help.

"Yo, Omar you still got the review sheet that Ms. Peterson gave us?" he asked.

A sly smile crept on Omar's face. "Where yours at? You ain't got it with you?" he asked laughing.

"Nah man, I think I lost it and I need that thing. I ain't tryin to bomb Peterson's test either. Lemme see it right quick," Jamal replied.

"All right, hold up," Omar responded when they stopped at another intersection at a red light.

He slipped off his book bag, opened it and handed Jamal the blue-colored sheet. Omar had filled it in with answers and steps on how he figured them out. It was perfect. While Jamal was looking over the sheet, someone yelled out to them.

"Hey, Dumb and Dumber! Wait up!" Patricia had caught up with the boys from the opposite block. "What's up?" she said to Jamal and Omar. She saw Jamal looking at the review sheet. "What the hell's he lookin' at?" she asked Omar.

"It's the review for Ms. Peterson's quiz today," Omar replied.

Upon hearing that, Patricia's eyes widened.

"Oh I heard about that teacher. Everybody I spoke to has her this semester. Thank God I'm not one of them. None of them had anything positive to say about that bitch," she said, taking a look at Jamal's review sheet. "But this stuff is easy though. Jamal, you trying to tell me that you don't know this shit?" she teased Jamal.

Jamal smiled a little bit. It was clear Patricia was trying to rattle him; test his manhood like most girls did to guys.

"Well it's easy to forget and I don't like math that way anyway. I'm more into reading and lit," he replied.

Patricia shrugged. "Whateva', I like math more because when I move out into Hollywood one day and get paid, I wanna be able to count my own damn money! I don't want to hire any agent or any accountant because people be screwing you over in society nowadays," she replied.

"True," Omar agreed.

As they neared the school, Jamal attempted to recall all the information he had read on the review sheet earlier. Algebraic equations, applications to geometry, and other figures were just a few of the calculations he was trying to remember. As they walked to homeroom, Jamal continued to write some of the math problems from Omar's review sheet onto a separate sheet of paper. Carlos came up to Jamal.

"Ok bro, be real with me. How you get Patricia to talk to you? She's like the fourth most finest girl in our class. Let me know the secret, man!" he exclaimed.

Jamal laughed and stared at Patricia while she talked with a female friend about five seats away.

"Man, ain't no secret bro. I'm just being me, man. Patricia and I are just cool. We ain't goin' out or nothing. Let me talk to you later bro, I really gotta study this stuff so I don't flunk Ms. Peterson's quiz," he answered.

Carlos left Jamal to joke around with the other guys while Jamal continued to study the math problems he had written on his paper. Sometimes he wished there could be a life without tests, quizzes, or any of that mess. Why not pass the students who completed more of their assignments? To Jamal it would seem to make more logical sense but that was the way the world worked, he guessed. The only thought in his head was that he knew he couldn't wait for PE class. He had to get his hands on a basketball and quick.

While Jamal studied with the utmost urgency that any common crammer could muster, another person approached the steps of Richmond Hill High School for the first time in twenty years. Nate stepped off the blue-lined bus that dropped him off about a half-mile from his alma mater. He had an appointment with the superintendent and the principal to discuss pay rate, daily duties, and other information that he would need to know for his job. *This place has not changed one bit*, he thought.

He recognized old corners near the school where he used to hang out with his friends in the days before he ever began trapping (dealing drugs). As he was informed at the unemployment office, he stopped by the attendance office to obtain a school visitor tag. All he could think was *please don't let anyone here recognize me.* Thankfully, the more he walked the school, the more his fears subsided. The people he now saw working at the school were new staff workers and had not attended the school in the eighties nor did they recognize him from the streets. He took solace in that because he couldn't bear having anyone see what had become of him: a one-time college prospect who also became a high school dropout in the same year. It had to be some type of record.

As he walked toward the principal's office, he looked past the hallway corridor and saw the double doors that opened to what was once his sanctuary, the school gymnasium. He walked past the principal's office and went to the gym. Although school was in session, the gym was momentarily empty. He looked at the old clock above the wooden court. He knew that a Physical Education course was getting set to begin at any moment, so he began to walk around the gym. He looked at the worn nets and the creaky floorboards, the tinted rims and above him were the gym rafters, where they hung banners for all the school's athletic achievements. He looked past the wrestling, volleyball, and softball banners to the one banner that brought back memories that now began to swim through his head. The banner read RICHMOND HILL MEN'S BASKETBALL 1979-1980 REGION CHAMPS. Looking around at the bleachers where the faded school colors were displayed, he remembered the sights and sounds when the seats were full. Every time his squad hit the floor in this gym, they would put on a show for the fans with quick guard play, solid big men, and athletic forwards who ran like gazelles. The energy that had once filled the building sent chills down his back. Thinking about it twenty-three years later brought those memories back to him because he was a part of it. He was a part of Richmond Hill tradition. He regretted what his parents, the alumni, and the booster club members said about him dropping out. Nate was not proud of what he had done but the regional title couldn't be taken away from him. The contribution he made for the school should and would never been forgotten. He blinked his eyes, and all the cheers came back. The ball was bouncing on the floor and sneakers were squeaking against the courts as players ran hard to hustle after a loose ball.

The year was 1980 and Richmond Hill High School and Cardozo High School were locked in a hotly contested basketball game. The score was 62-61 and Cardozo had possession of the ball after Cardozo guard David Lenny and Richmond Hill guard Nate Plummer dove after a loose ball that rolled out of bounds. There were only 30 seconds left on the game clock. Richmond Hill called a time-out to draw up a good defensive play to regain possession of the ball. The crowd was already yelling themselves in a frenzy, having witnessed Richmond Hill recover from a sluggish first-half performance where they trailed their opponent throughout the whole game on their home court. The lead swelled to 15 points in the third quarter before the coach called the first time-out and then gave the green light to Nate to create for himself and his teammates. Nate had been quiet offensive, running the coaches plays and drawn tactics, but Cardozo was beating them at their own game and Nate felt like it was time for him to take control of the game. He knew Lenny couldn't stay in front of him the whole game and he was ready to erupt. At the huddle, Richmond Coach Jay Osmond called his players in and gave them a pep talk.

"Ok, listen up men. We are down but we aren't out. We are going to start trapping back court and let Plummer create on offense," Turning to Nate, he said, "Plummer, I'm now running our offense through you. You are the captain, the general and the ultimate team player. When you see your shot, take it. Box out and rebound. We need every loose ball from here on out."

After the time-out in the third period, Nate took complete control of the game. He reeled off ten straight points, stopping on a dime and pulling up while Lenny was too slow to contest. He made key passes to Alex Peele and Gary McKey, the forwards of the team for back-to-back baskets and before they blinked, Richmond Hill only trailed Cardozo by one. They also stepped up their defense to hold Cardozo scoreless in the fourth quarter. Then, with thirty seconds left on the clock, Nate wondered if it was possible. He didn't see a clean way out of this situation unless they fouled a player and sent him to the line. It seemed that was the viable option. Coach Osmond stated exactly what Nate was thinking. If they did not get a quick steal, foul to stop the clock.

Both teams went out on the court, with Cardozo inbounding under Richmond Hill's basket. As the ref handed the ball to the in-bounder and blew his whistle to resume play, Nate quickly ran to deny Lenny the ball so he would get a clear shot at the basket. The ball was passed inbounds, amidst a number of Richmond Hill defenders and Cardozo played the passing game until Richmond Hill fouled Lenny with nine seconds left to go in the game. Nate glanced up at the stands. Mike Hillman stood up with the student section and his football teammates. Nina Martin was also standing up and cheering with her class. Lenny stepped up to the free throw line with the Richmond Hill crowd yelling out loud at the top of their lungs, in hopes to distract Lenny's concentration. It didn't work as Lenny sank the first free throw, making it 63-61.

As he shot the second one, Nate, either out of instinct or just part of the distraction himself, yelled, "Short!" as Lenny released the shot.

It fell off the right side of the basket as Gary grabbed the rebound. Richmond Hill called their final timeout and once again decided to put the fate of the game in Nate's hands. Alex Peel inbounded the ball to Nate and Nate dribbled the length of the court, speeding past Lenny who was sticking with him, Nate looks at the clock. 5....4......3....Nate looked around. Nobody was open, so Nate decided to take the last shot, sizing up Lenny as he did so. When Nate put the shot up, he knew it was good. Lenny contested a second later and he was a second too late. The three-point shot sailed through the net, giving Richmond Hill a one-point win over Cardozo 64-63. The crowd celebrated and went crazy as Nate raised his hands in victory as the fans stormed the court and gathered around the players. It was a monumental victory. Richmond Hill retained sole possession of first place in the region. Nina ran down and hugged Nate and ran off to find Mike who was slapping fives with the student fan section and members of the basketball team.

The crowd was filled with chants of 'Richmond Hill!' and 'Nate!'

Reminiscing on one of the happiest memories of his life, Nate knew it was at that point when he truly felt accepted into Richmond Hill and its community. For someone who had a rocky relationship with his parents and grew up being unable or unwilling to trust anyone but himself, that night in 1980 had been total bliss for him. For that one frozen moment in time, people loved him for his accomplishments on the court rather than hating him for the activities outside of it. He had found a sport he was good at and could have made a future doing to support a family; a family he now realized he would never have. Gone were the days of teen innocence and friendly support. What had replaced those dreams was isolation, loneliness, and uncertainty with what the future held for him.

Now standing in the same gym almost twenty-five years later, the force of reality almost doubled him over; crippling him with thoughts of anger, hate, and doubt. There were also so many questions about his potential. Could he have been motivated enough to finish his education and graduate high school on time thus putting himself in a better position for college and scholarship opportunities? If he had stayed away from the drug business, could he have been confident enough to talk others out of joining the street life, potentially saving the lives of others, even that of Nina Martin? Was it possible that he could have preserved the friendship he had with Gary McKey and Mike Hillman if he had stayed clean and lived conservatively rather than indulging so much in drugs that it tore the fabric of the bonds of friendship that had held them together since they were in grade school? Those were the questions that Nate knew no matter how many years he lived his life, he would never get clear answers on them.

The morning bell rang, indicating the start of the next period. Nate began to hear the noise from the hallway, indicating that 'kids were starting to make their way toward the gym, so he exited quietly through one of the back doors and walked out toward the administration office. On his way, he passed a glass cabinet that displayed the school's athletic and academic accomplishments with trophies, small banners, and pictures of some of the school's notable alumni. One of the trophies displayed was the region trophy that had the team picture at the bottom. Nate looked and saw himself as one of the players who sat in the front, due to the fact that he was a guard. As he stared at this image of himself, he looked at his current reflection in the glass and saw what he despised; an over-the-hill middle-aged janitor that could have lived up to his full potential and had all the skill in the world but threw it all away. He couldn't change his past, but he knew the one event he could change was the outcome of it all. He was still intent on finding Big Earl and finishing what he should have finished years ago.

Jamal sat in history class, looking nervously at the clock. Every minute that ticked down to the end of the hour was another minute closer to the quiz for which he was still was not prepared. His history book was open, following the lesson but underneath his history book was his math review worksheet that he would occasionally glance at, to make sure that he knew all the concepts. He continued looking at the sheet intently and then the bell rang. This is it Jamal thought as he walked out of class. Omar joined him as they walked toward Ms. Peterson's class.

"So you ready for this?" Omar asked as they turned the corner of the hallway.

"I don't know, man," Jamal replied. "I'm hoping Peterson cancels this thing and gives us another day because ain't no way I can take this today," he added.

"Maybe she'll ask the same questions that are on the review," Omar said.

Jamal shook his head. If there was one fact that he knew, it was that teachers never asked the same exact questions that appeared on the study guides. Sometimes Jamal thought they did this for their own personal enjoyment; to watch the kids struggle and squirm and strain through the questions they couldn't figure out. The bell rang and the kids filed out of the classrooms. As he thought about it, he felt a tap on his shoulder.

"Hey Jamal, what's up?" Shania greeted him as she headed for lunch in the cafeteria.

"What's up?" Jamal replied, trying to hide his concern.

Shania, seeing that Jamal was distracted asked, "You ok? You look like you about to walk to the electric chair or something," she said.

No, but it's not too far off Jamal thought, but he just replied "Nah, I'm ok. I just got a quiz in Ms. Peterson's class today and I ain't studied for it. I'm over here cramming right now. You wasn't lying about her at all. She ain't no joke."

Shania laughed. "I told you. But her quizzes are easy though. She does base them off her study guides. It's her tests that you gotta watch out for. Just pray about it and go in there. You got this." she reassured him, patting him on the shoulder.

"Thanks. Well I gotta go get this crap over with," Jamal said and he and Omar walked over to class.

When they got into class, they realized there were only six students in there. They must have arrived early.

"Ok, I still got time to look over my stuff one more time. I gotta take advantage, right?" Jamal said smiling as he took out his study guide again.

Omar nodded his head and said, "Yeah whatever man. What you need to do is take advantage of ballin' better. I'm sick of whoopin' yo' ass every time we ball," he joked.

Jamal laughed before replying, "All right whateva, nigga. At least I show up in the clutch unlike someone who ain't even show up to the courts last week," Jamal replied.

"That's because yo' mama showed up In my place that night and I had to make her work," Omar replied, laughing.

Jamal laughed as well. It was good to have a friend who knew him so well that when he tensed up, he would help him relax. Omar was that type of friend to Jamal. They joked about each other all the time because that was who they were. While they laughed, Ms. Peterson entered the class, wearing thick glasses across her stern face.

"Good afternoon class. Everyone clear your desks and have a clean sheet of paper with a # 2 pencil," she said. Jamal cleared his desk, said a short prayer, and prepared to take the quiz.

CHAPTER SIX

"Yes, Mr. Eisner, the estimated price you'll be looking at is eight thousand four hundred and fifty-seven dollars for a total bathroom sink remodel. That includes putting a new medicine cabinet, and a white marble top," Michael Hillman said over the phone.

Pastor Mike was sitting in his office, which was located in the corner of Woodhaven and 91st St. Hillman Marble Company was a large, two-story building built right before the Woodhaven intersection. With over a hundred workers, contractors and foremen, Hillman Marble Co. was at its most productive time of year. Fall was approaching and with it came the rush of people calling to have their kitchens or bathrooms remodeled before the holiday season approached, because many people were expecting visitors during the holiday season and wanted to make sure their homes were in presentable fashion. It also didn't hurt that the company was having a sale that dropped the rates of the remodel work by twenty-five percent, so people jumped on that immediately. He was currently sitting at his desk negotiating prices for Mr. Joshua Eisner who lived in Baldwin, New York.

"Yes, sir, we did apply that discount towards the final price for you," Mike responded when Mr. Eisner wondered why the price was high and if it was because Mike forgot to apply the discount. With a calculator in hand and his reading glasses on, Mike added, subtracted, and divided figures based on the design and the architectural build of the home he had pulled up with the aid of an online satellite map. Mr. Eisner had compared prices with another company, and he found Mike's price to be much lower. As Mike continued to speak over the phone, Stan Jackson, one of the contractors and Mike's employee knocked on his door. Michael gestured to Stan to come sit in the chair facing his desk as he wrapped up the call with Mr. Eisner.

"Ok I understand. No problem, sir. Thank you for doing business with Hillman Marble Company," Michael said before hanging up. Stan smiled as he saw Michael get another sale. One trait that set Michael apart from most owners, managers, and head supervisors was that he never had a streak of pride in him. He was a fair manager who exercised his control, but he would also get on the phones to close some deals. He would even ride to a client's home and do the measurements himself, bringing the tiles with him to help sell his product. His workers trusted him, and he appreciated how diligently they worked for him. Of course, he would enjoy it if some of them came to his church sometimes and he had echoed that sentiment a couple of times, but so far, he had not been successful.

"Hey Stan, what can I do for you today?" Mike asked.

"Yeah Mike, what's up man?" Stan greeted. "I got a customer here who was inquiring about the price for remodeling her kitchen counter. I gave her a price of seven thousand three hundred and sixty-five dollars for the job, but she stated it was too high. So I dropped the price, but she still insisted. Finally, I gave her the best price possible at three thousand three hundred and thirty dollars for her, but she still wasn't going with that amount," Stan explained.

Mike stared at him in thought, his eyes squinting a bit at the sale sheet that hung on a wall in his office.

"Is she just getting her kitchen counter replaced or is she remodeling the cabinets, drawers and cupboards as well?" Mike asked.

"Right now, it's only for a counter job," Stan responded.

Mike couldn't understand it. Stan had virtually given this customer the lowest price available, and yet she still insisted on a lower price?

"Look, I was wondering if maybe you can talk to her. She might understand when she hears you explain the price," Stan insisted.

Mike agreed to assist. Taking the sheet from Stan, Mike looked at the figures. "What is the lady's name?" he asked as he looked over the figures.

"Well, her name is on the top there. Sorry I wrote it that way. I definitely tried to make it more legible, but you know how it is," Stan said, smiling. "Her name is Isis Samuels," he added.

Upon hearing the name, Mike's eyes seemed to do a double-take for a moment, before recognizing her.

"Ok, I know this lady. She and her son actually attend my church. Yeah, maybe if I talk to her, I can get her to agree on a price," Mike replied as Stan stood up and got ready to go back to his desk.

"All right. Thanks man. Try that preacher persuasion on her. Maybe she'll agree long enough to let the sale go through," Stan said with a smile.

Mike sat back and called Isis's number, but the phone just went to voicemail. She must be at work now or something he thought. He decided to go ahead and leave the voicemail.

"Hello, Mrs. Samuels? This is Mike Hillman from Hillman Marble Company. I was just calling to discuss the price for the countertop you are replacing in the kitchen. When you have a chance, please give me a call back at 718-457-9021. Thank you," Mike said in the voicemail before hanging up.

Sitting back on his chair, Mike tried to make out what Stan told him before he left his office. Preacher persuasion? He wasn't sure what that meant, but he couldn't deny that he liked the sound of it.

The bell rang at a quarter past three in the afternoon, ending school at Richmond Hill. As students started to file out of the classroom, Shania walked out of her chemistry class with a huge sigh. Science is definitely not my cup of tea she thought as she waited at the side of the locker corridor for Loree. She finally saw her walking the hallway and Shania waved to Loree so she could see her through the throng of kids exiting the school.

"Girl, Mr. Barnes gave us this huge-ass assignment and I was trying to get details before I came out too late. My bad for the wait," Loree apologized.

"It's ok, girl. I've gotten used to it by now. Unfortunately, I couldn't walk as slow as you if I tried," Shania replied with a wink toward her longtime friend.

Loree took it as a play challenge. "Uh-uh I know you ain't talking, Ms. Decathalon," Loree responded back, laughing.

As they walked out the doors one of the older guys who normally hung out on the school steps spotted them and decided to try his luck at courtship.

"Aye, ain't you on the track team?" he asked Shania.

Shania wasn't interested because she had heard every pick-up line under the sun and to her, those lines weren't flattering, cute, or clever. They were a waste of time and not only were the jokes dry most of the time but the boys who were interested in her were those who lacked any type of discipline or self-control. She thought these jokes were extremely needy and she did her best to ignore them.

The guy proved her right. "Well if you are on the track team, I'd like to run your lane anytime, baby," he cooed.

At this line, Shania and Loree walked away laughing at the top of their voices. Of all the ridiculous pick-up lines, Shania thought that particular one took the cake. She ignored the boy's next come on and kept on walking in silence with Loree next to her. Loree lived in the house across from Shania, so they were headed the same way.

"I don't know, girl but maybe you should've given him some play this time," Loree said.

Shania laughed and nodded her head. Of all her friends, Loree was the most unique while remaining true to herself. In some aspects, Shania was jealous of Loree because Loree looked and dressed like a model and she had a body which boys desired.

"Girl, I was never going to pay him any type of mind," Shania replied.

Loree put her arms around Shania. "Nia, I think it's about time you let that 'innocent preacher's daughter' routine go. I mean, I know you got needs like I do, if you feel me," she said.

Shania thought about it. She couldn't move as fast as Loree did when it came to men, cosmetics, and fashion despite being an athlete. She couldn't help but notice that the guys at Richmond Hill seemed star-struck by girls like Loree and she garnered most attention in the school.

"Well, I'm waiting for the right guy to come by and sweep me off my feet," Shania said to Loree.

"Shania, this isn't a buffet line, and this isn't exactly the land of opportunity. You gotta take advantage of your chances. Finding a good man is almost slim to none. You need to get back out to the game. Come back and join us, boo," Loree replied, laughing as they both continued to walk in the direction toward Shania's house.

"By the way, Daddy caught me wearing the black dress that we bought at the mall last weekend. He wouldn't even let me see the light of day with that on. I love him but sometimes he be trippin," Shania said.

"You mean that dress that I was gonna get but you got the last one before I could even make it to the rack, Ms. Discount Clearance?" Loree replied. "It's all good, I ain't even want that dress anyway, it's more for them skinny anorexic hoes that ain't got no chest or ass," she added in jest, winking.

At this Shania stopped in her tracks and gave Loree an incredulous look. "Hold up, what you mean skinny, anorexic hoes? So what you sayin' I'm skinny now? I thought we was girls, ReRe," Shania shot back, although she was smiling a bit.

Shania knew that Loree could get away with calling her skinny because they were friends; the same way that Shania could get away with calling Loree "ReRe" because Loree normally did not appreciate anyone addressing her by nicknames. She was a pretty girl, but Shania would be the first to let anyone know not to let the pretty looks fool them. Loree was nice when she needed to be, but Shania knew that if anyone pushed her buttons, Loree could get confrontational very quickly. She was not afraid to talk back to anyone, especially boys who enjoyed ridiculing her. The only exception to the way she treated guys was David Anderson.

If there was any boy that had Loree eating off the palms of his hands, it was David. Not that David wasn't good looking, he was strong, athletic, popular, and had a winning smile. But he also had some shady connections that Shania could not confirm as of yet. She knew in the back of her mind, David still had associations with gang members, especially M.O.B. (Money Over Bitches) a gang that was prominent in the 101 Avenue and Jamaica Avenue areas. Largely responsible for small, isolated robberies and domestic disturbances that resulted in serious injury or death, M.O.B. slowly became a rising threat in the community. The police strived to keep the peace in the streets, but they found the gang very elusive. They normally hid in an informant's house or abandoned building to avoid any contact with law enforcement. The leader of the gang, Tadarius Hill didn't just run a gang, he ran an underground operation. He knew all the connections to the big drug kingpins and alcohol distributors in New York and was very business-like in his endeavors and approach but if anyone dared to cross him, he would react violently. M.O.B. also actively recruited young boys who were homeless, abandoned renegades.

The word spread that David Anderson was a gang member and that he was a member of M.O.B even before he got serious in school and football. Shania didn't know him well, but she knew in the back of her mind that he was no good for her best friend. Shania wondered if Loree saw a side of David that she couldn't see. They always had their arms around each other, hugging and kissing each other not only incessantly but publicly. It sickened Shania. As she and Loree approached Shania's house, Shania took out her house key, opened her door, and they went inside. She knew both of her parents were still at work, so she went upstairs with Loree to her bedroom. They always liked to spend time going through her closet and talk about her clothes, and Shania liked to just sit and watch Loree get into her fashion police mode while raiding her closet. They also got around to doing their homework eventually but not before talking about clothes, boys, and future career and plans.

As Loree eagerly looked in her closet, Shania said, "Uh-uh, ain't nobody told you to go inside my closet yet, trick. That's right, step your freeloading behind out."

Upon hearing the boldness of her usually passive counterpart, Loree emerged from the closet with a sheepish grin on her face.

"What you giving me that Joker grin for?" Shania asked as Loree walked out of the closet before she realized that Loree had something behind her back. It was the black dress that Mike Hillman did not allow her daughter to wear to church.

"Don't tell me your daddy didn't approve of this. It's not even that risqué," Loree retorted as she held the dress out for a better look.

"I know girl. I tried telling him that on Sunday, but he wasn't even trying to hear me, girl," Shania said.

Loree nodded her head. "That's crazy though. What is he afraid of? Boys hittin' on you? You ain't gotta worry about that anyway, since your daddy's a preacher and all. Niggas are trying to avoid you like a plague. They ain't tryin to have a size 14 large footprint on their ass," Loree said as she went through the closet to look for more clothes. She pulled out another outfit; a pink halter-top with a short white skirt. "Girl, when did you buy this? I know you ain't holding out on me now!" Loree exclaimed.

Shania looked at the outfit that Loree flaunted in front of her. "Yeah, I got that one about two months ago, but I wasn't trying to wear it in front of Daddy. After the way he reacted to the black dress, I know he would've locked these doors to my room to keep me from going out in public," she replied.

Loree rolled her eyes in exasperation. "Girl, you are basically grown up. You can't always stay Daddy's little girl forever. So is he gonna be there every waking moment of your life? He can't hold you back like this. Imagine how cute you would look walking to school in this and the skirt," she said.

Shania laughed. "I mean, if I made it out the house, Daddy would be the least of my worries. Every dude on this planet would be tryin' to holla at me. Half the time, the dudes that roll up on me got stank breath. Like come on. Breath mints aren't illegal, you know," Shania said while Loree laughed.

Loree then went into the bathroom to change in the halter top and skirt she had taken out of Shania's closet.

When she came out, Shania thought enviously It really fits her perfectly. She got the curves for it.

"What you think, Mami? Do I know how to kill it or what?" Loree asked as Shania took another look at her outfit as Loree flaunted her shapely figure in it.

"Yeah, but if David sees you wearing that and walking around school, he'll probably kill the guy staring at you," Shania replied.

"Leave David alone. He wouldn't hurt anybody," Loree bit back, her tone suddenly becoming serious.

"I'm sorry, girl. I was only joking. You know I ain't mean that," Shania tried to explain but the damage was done. Loree walked to the opposite end of the room, her head down.

"Do you think I don't know what people say about us behind our backs? Do you think I don't see the way people's eyes look at us whenever we walk down the hall?" she asked.

Shania looked on with concern toward her friend. This was the sensitive side of Loree that she never revealed to others, but she knew Loree had those moments, especially when it came to David.

"ReRe, I know you like him but the way you're going about this, don't you think you're rushing it just a little bit? I just care about you, and I don't want to see you hurt," Shania said.

"I'm a big girl Nia. I can take care of myself. It's just that people never gave him a chance throughout his life until he made the football team. He always had a bad rap on him because of his past but people can change," Loree insisted, while unbuttoning the halter top. While she was doing so, Shania saw it. Not just a bruise but a couple of scratch marks.

"Loree, what happened to you under your arm?" Shania asked.

"Oh that? I just scratched myself getting out of the shower or something. It's ok," Loree said, shrugging it off.

But Shania wasn't going to let it slide that easily. "Right, Just like how you got that bruise. You seem to be accident-prone a lot lately, girl. Is he hitting you?" she asked Loree.

"No, he ain't hitting me. Why would you even say that? What would give you the idea that my boyfriend is hitting me, Nia?" Loree replied angrily.

Shania could see that Loree was getting offended and this probably wasn't going to go anywhere. "Look, I've spoken with people who know David. They all said the same thing. David has a temper and when he gets frustrated, he tends to get confrontational. He's even got into fights with his teammates in the locker room, Loree," she said before realizing that Loree had put her regular clothes back on and was beginning to pack up her belongings.

"You know what? I don't even think I wanna stick around to hear this mess right now. You been my girl since ninth grade. Out of all my so called 'friends' that I have, I would've thought that you of all people would support me. Whatever, I'm gonna do me and you go ahead and do you, ok? I'm out," Loree said, grabbing her book bag while leaving the room. Shania just looked on, dazed. What just happened? she asked herself silently.

Mike Hillman came back from work at six-thirty-five, carrying some groceries with him. He put the bags down so he could unlock the door, then opened it, and called his daughter.

"Shania, I'm home. Can you help get some of these bags upstairs in the kitchen for me?" he asked.

Shania came out of her room. Seeing her father with so many bags, she came over to help him carry some of the bags to the kitchen. She helped him take out the groceries and placed them in the refrigerator and cabinet, working in silence. Mike thought her behavior was strange because she was usually so vibrant and talkative. Seeing her head down and hearing her silence did not sit well with him.

"Shania, is everything ok? Did something happen to you at school?" he asked. Please God, don't let it be boy problems. Please don't let it be boy problems he thought.

Mike was fully aware that his daughter was growing into a young woman but to him she was still his little girl. If he found out that any boy had hurt her in any way, he wouldn't know how to react. They would have to lock him in an insane asylum because he knew he would completely lose his mind.

"No Daddy I'm ok," Shania lied. She really hated lying to her father mostly because her father saw right through her lies every time. She didn't know what it was; maybe it was the power of God. Maybe preachers, pastors, and chosen leaders had an anointed sixth sense about those issues. But Shania couldn't discuss the problems with her best friend with her father. Mike didn't know Loree very well anyway and he dealt with enough at work. She didn't want to weigh him down with her problems, but Mike continued to pry some more.

"Come on, baby. You can tell me. Is everything ok?" he insisted.

Shania then sighed a little bit. If she was going to tell her father what was wrong, she was going to have to do it anonymously for her and Loree.

"Ok Dad, let's say I knew a girl at school who was being abused by her boyfriend. She never admits it, but everyone knows what's going on. Although she knows what's going on, she decides to stay with him anyway. What can I say to her? "Shania asked.

Mike's face was deep in concentration, almost stoic. He was trying to see if Shania was referring to herself. Sometimes teenage girls tried to make problems a mystery that one had to figure out. As he started boiling water to add pasta for the night's dinner he said, "Shania, no matter who it is, whether it's a close friend that you know very well or if it's a stranger. If you see someone getting abused, you have to report it to the authorities. It can very well be the difference between life and death," Mike replied.

Shania turned her head toward the staircase and small hallway. Report it to the authorities? Why should I be the one to report it? She should be the one reporting him, Shania thought. "That's easier said than done though. What if the boy that's abusing her has done this in the past? What if he is dangerous? What if I put my life at risk?" she asked.

Michael didn't understand why she was in full panic mode. It had to be a close friend; someone she spoke with every day on a regular basis.

"Shania, are you sure you don't know this girl well?" Michael said as he took the tomato sauce out of the refrigerator to pour it on a pan.

Shania had to keep it discreet. She couldn't leave any clues or obvious signs that Loree was the main focal point of the conversation. Although Mike didn't know Loree, he also knew that Shania didn't have a huge circle of friends so he would eventually figure out who the victim was in this scenario.

"Well I know her a little bit. I just don't want to cause trouble or get in the way," she said.

"Baby, to tell you the truth, the world would be a much better place if people got in the way, especially if it's a friend or family member who was in danger. The biggest trouble that we can get into is when we sit by and do nothing and allow the abuser to continue his ways. By doing that, we are helping the abuser. We are not helping the victim or ourselves," Mike replied.

Shania thought about what her father just said. It made sense and it would be exactly what she would want to do. But crossing with David's "connections" was not too high on Shania's priority list and in order to run track this year, she needed her most valuable asset: her life.

"Thanks Dad. I'll definitely report it when I have the chance," she said.

Mike smiled at her. Super Dad strikes again, he thought.

"So Dad, I see you're cooking tonight. Are you trying to impress Mom again?" she said, laughing.

"Oh come on baby, what makes you say that?" Mike asked quickly.

Shania rolled her eyes and started laughing. She knew that every time her father started cooking dinner when her mother came home late from work, it meant he was trying to get on Robyn's good side. Dazzle her with great cooking, enjoy a good meal, then go to the bedroom for a "reward" that usually took the place of dessert. Shania, being in the room across from her parents, certainly heard her parents make love. Shania, who had long since matured, learned to respect her father's efforts at keeping his marriage strong and the love for Robyn alive. She only wished and prayed that the Lord would send a man like that her way. She knew it would probably be quite a while, but the Bible instructed to wait upon the Lord and that was what she planned to do.

"Here baby, taste that and tell me what you think," Mike said, giving her a taste of the sauce he had prepared.

Shania tasted it. "It's good Daddy. I see you're going for the home run tonight, huh?" she said with a wink.

"Hey, hey, hey, sometimes a man gotta take to the stove. I can't let your mom cook; especially when she's working long hours," Mike replied.

After fifteen minutes, they both heard the front door open, indicating that Robyn had finally arrived home. By this time, Shania had already set the table and was on her way to spray perfume in the room before joining her parents at the table.

"Wow, Mike this smells really good. I'm starved. Work was very brutal today," Robyn said, preparing to sit down.

"Uh-uh. Not till everyone washes up first. Cleanliness is next to godliness you know," Mike stopped her.

Robyn looked at Mike incredulously.

"Cleanliness advice from you?" Robyn asked laughing with Shania as they went to wash their hands.

In a few minutes they were at the table, saying grace and then they helped themselves to spaghetti, sauce, breadsticks, and salad. It was a delicious dinner which Mike secretly hoped was enough to impress Robyn that night. While they were eating, Robyn was telling them about her day at work.

"I spoke with a young girl today, Mike, who everyone called an introvert because she wouldn't play with the other kids or talk with the teachers," she began. "For many days the teachers had a hard time reaching her and finally her parents brought her over to me. She wouldn't talk to me in front of her parents. Finally I asked her parents to leave the office and I asked the girl what was going on. She informed me that every weekend her uncle would come over to visit their family and would sometimes watch over her whenever the parents would step out. I found out that her uncle was sexually molesting her, Mike. She's only ten years old. I couldn't believe the parents couldn't see what was going on with their daughter. I finally told them what she told me and the looks that I saw on their faces were looks of just pure shock and horror, Mike. They had no clue. I thank God I was able to identify that and alert the parents before it got any worse," she added.

Mike looked at Shania and it was apparent that Mike was recalling the earlier conversation that he had with Shania about her friend.

"I'm sorry you had to go through that today, baby," Mike replied. "I'm just grateful that God used you in a mighty way today to save a life. Who knows? Maybe it'll help save the lives of other kids going through similar devastating situations," he added.

Robyn nodded her head in agreement. As they finished their dinner, Shania offered to help clear the dishes and sweep the kitchen floor and suggested that her parents should go to bed early. As Mike went to the bathroom to find his robe to put on top of his pajamas, he heard Robyn from the room.

"Baby the room smells real good. What did you spray here?" Robyn asked.

He stepped in and took a deep breath. With his teeth brushed and breath smelling fresh, he was ready for romance; he just hoped his wife was in the mood. God did instruct Solomon in the book of Proverbs to enjoy the wife of his youth; love her, kiss her, and caress her. He was ready to do all that and more. As he waited in bed while Robyn went to the bathroom when without warning, his bedroom door opened. Mike assumed it was Robyn but it was Shania who poked her head through the crack of the door with a sly grin and flashed him the thumbs-up sign.

"Will you get out of here, already?" Mike laughed as he threw a designer pillow in the direction of the door hoping the pillow would hit his daughter. He missed and the pillow hit the door that she had already closed on her way out. After a few minutes, Robyn came out. She had her usual sky-blue nightgown which accentuated her features and her amazing curves.

Tonight's the night. She picked the perfect night to put that on. God, I love you so much for blessing me with an exquisite woman he thought. "Wow, baby you are breathtaking!" he said as she sat at the foot of the bed, applying lotion to her long slender legs. Mike knew he had to be careful, because he was being a bit too greedy, but he couldn't help it. Her soft hands and applying the lotion to her smooth legs was causing an arousal in him. When she finally turned off the lamp that sat on their nightstand, Mike wrapped his arms around Robyn and started kissing his wife on the shoulders.

"Oh, baby I've been thinking about you all day today. Coming home to you is one of the greatest gifts that God has blessed me with," he said while kissing her shoulders. Robyn started laughing and then turned around on her side of the bed and responded by kissing Mike on the lips. The kiss was passionate, and Mike felt himself getting more and more ready for what was to come. Robyn must have sensed it too.

"Oh baby, is that how much you've missed me today? You've been waiting that long?" she whispered.

"You have no idea, baby." Mike whispered back to her. He started to remove his flannel pants and reached over to remove the nightgown that she had on. But Robyn whispered in his ear.

"Not tonight, baby. I'm really tired and I want to get some sleep. But keep it up for me, ok? We'll do this again later and I promise there will be a sequel," she replied before turning around, pulling her nightgown back down below her knees, flushing Mike's hopes of a romantic evening down the drain.

Sequel? There wasn't even a part one Mike thought sadly.

"Ok baby. That's ok. Get some rest. We can do this tomorrow or something," he said, trying to hide the disappointment in his voice. After all he's done to get to this point, and he was being denied yet again. "Please Lord, give her strength for another day and please give me strength for tonight," he prayed before turning over in his bed to sleep.

CHAPTER SEVEN

The courtroom was filled with silence and apprehension as the convicted felon Gerry Almidor, awaited his fate. His public defender, Arthur Blaylock, noticed the beads of sweat forming over his defendant's forehead. While it was a very hot Saturday morning at the Queens County Courthouse in Jamaica, Queens, Arthur knew that the room temperature was the furthest thought from his mind. The fact that his client's life and future swung on a balance that could very well be severed by the twelve jurors who were in the room deciding the result of the case was quite unsettling. Earlier in the month, Gerry had been arrested on suspicion of armed robbery at a local corner store in Queens Boulevard. The police received a 9-1-1 call from the store clerk who was held hostage at gunpoint while two masked individuals went about stealing groceries and cleaning out the cash register of that day's earnings. Since all the witnesses couldn't identify the men behind the robbery, the detectives were forced to draw out all the clues to make a possible connection. The case went cold for a few days until they received a tip from an anonymous caller who stated that he saw Almidor and another man wearing the same sweaters that resembled what the robbers wore on that night. Based on that tip, the police were able to get a search warrant for Almidor's apartment home on 163rd Street in Jamaica Avenue. Almidor, who was half Haitian and half Jamaican had to sit and watch helplessly as the police ransacked his home searching for evidence that may tie him to the robbery. Growing tired with frustration, one of the officers started to call off the search until the other officer made a discovery. He saw an unlicensed Glock .17 deep in the closet floor where Almidor had attempted to hide it earlier. Coincidentally, the gun was the same model that was described by one of the buyers in the store as the weapon that was brandished during the robbery. The police felt that was enough and Almidor was arrested and booked into the Queens County precinct to await trial. His family fought back by hiring Arthur Blaylock, a headstrong defense attorney who refused to see any type of justice done unless there was enough evidence to support the action that was about to be taken against an innocent man. According to Blaylock, Almidor was nowhere near the store the night of the robbery, having gone to the city of Manhattan with his girlfriend Dominique Winters to see a show at Madison Square Garden.

During the days the case dragged on in court, a number of witnesses were brought before the judges stand; the store clerk, some of the witnesses, Dominique Winters, as well as Almidor's mother, Sylvia. While a number of people identified Almidor as one of the masked gunmen who robbed the store, Almidor's family always testified to his innocence and claimed that the gun Almidor kept in his home was meant for protection due to a recent string of home break-ins that had occurred in his apartment complex. The prosecution then gave a key rebuttal as to why Almidor did not have his firearm licensed or registered. With Almidor's permission and the help of his family members, Arthur went back to Almidor's apartment and searched a specific drawer that the police failed to open during their search. Crumpled up near a pile of old clothes, unseen by anyone but Arthur, were the gun registration papers. Bringing the papers to court, Arthur argued that Almidor did have a right to have a firearm in his home for protection. While that evidence prevented Almidor from serving more time for the unregistered firearm, he still had to wait for the verdict that would either drop the armed robbery charges against him or convict him for up to fifteen years behind bars. During the trial, the police were still searching for the second perpetrator in connection with the robbery, but they had no success. Saturday morning was the final day for the trial and Almidor's family waited anxiously for the jury to reach its verdict, as the courtroom waited in silence.

Arthur reached over to Almidor's ear and whispered, "As soon as they acquit you, I got a couple of Mets tickets in the car, my treat."

Almidor looked at Arthur in disbelief. How did he know they were going to acquit him of this crime? He stared at Arthur's surprisingly smug face. He turned around and noticed his mother, brother, and girlfriend still waiting for the verdict. The look that pained Almidor the most was the look on his mother's face. Across from them sat the prosecutor along with the store clerk who would occasionally throw Almidor dirty looks that suggested he would love nothing more than to see another street thug thrown behind bars. Finally, the door opened, and the jurors walked out of the room. They finished deliberating and were ready to deliver their verdict. Facing the judge, one of the jurors, a middle-aged white man read the verdict loud enough for the courtroom to hear.

"We the jury of the court, find the defendant, not guilty of the armed robbery at One Stop Store due to the lack of evidence tying him to this offense."

The man may have read more details from the verdict but at that point it didn't matter to Almidor or his family who were smiling and hugging one another with pure joy and relief while the prosecutor and store clerk shook their heads in disbelief at the sudden turn of events. I knew they ain't got nothing on him Arthur thought as he shook Almidor's hand and hugged his family.

After they walked out of the courthouse, Arthur said, "Hey man, my offer still stands. If you up for it, game's on Friday night."

Almidor smiled widely, shaking Arthur's hand.

"You got it bro. Thanks for everything man. I owe you big time," he replied as he walked over to his mother's car with his family.

While still celebrating the court victory, Arthur's cell phone rang. Reaching into his pocket, he looked at the small screen of his phone. Not again he sighed as he answered the call.

"What's up man?" he replied while he walked to one of the small offices in the building.

"Hey Arthur, hope I didn't catch you at a bad time. I gotta talk to you about something," the caller said.

Arthur shook his head. He loved his brother-in-law, but sometimes he could be annoying, especially when he was calling while he was at work.

"I don't know, Mike. If by bad time you mean while I'm working, then yeah, I ain't doing nothing important," Arthur replied with a hint of sarcasm. "Just as long as it's not another church invitation cuz you wearing my ear out with that on the real," he added.

"No, it's about something else," Mike Hillman replied.

Good Arthur thought. He couldn't even begin to count how many times he has received calls and voicemails urging him to come to church, specifically his brother-in-law's church that he ministered. Sometimes he didn't understand why his sister married him. He had graduated law school, becoming one of the youngest lawyers in his graduating class. He was the one who had to do all that, not Jesus. If he had a dollar for every invitation that Mike sent to him asking him to come to church, he would have more money than what his profession paid him. He rarely had time to go to church due to his work schedule, but he didn't think that made him any less of a good man. So if Mike wasn't calling about church, there could be only one other reason that he was calling and the next words that came out of Mike's mouth proved his theory.

"It's about Robyn, bro. I don't know what's going on between us. Would she tell you if something was bothering her?" Mike asked.

Arthur laughed. "Man, my sister, and I barely talk about the weather, much less our own problems. But if something was really wrong, then I guess she would tell me. Why? What's going on?" he asked. He heard a sigh on the other line.

"You mean, what's not going on?" Mike corrected on the other line.

Arthur knew what was going on. Robyn was not sleeping with Mike. It's no secret to him. If Mike wasn't so conservative in so many, areas of his life, especially about church, maybe his sister would make love to him once in a while.

"She ain't givin' you none, is she?" Arthur asked with a smirk on his face.

"No she isn't," Mike confirmed. "I did all I could Thursday to get her to, you know," he added.

"I know, I know, you gave her flowers, cooked, cleaned, and was a good father and all that and you still ain't getting any, huh?" Arthur asked.

"I mean, was it something I did? Do you know if she's mad at me for something?" Mike asked, evading Arthur's direct question about not being intimately successful with Robyn.

"Bro, look I'm sure it wasn't anything you did. Maybe she's working too hard or something. I don't think you did anything to her, man. As a matter of fact, you're probably not doing enough," Arthur replied.

Mike, sitting at his desk at work thought about what Arthur just said. How could he not be doing enough? What did she want him to do? "What are you talking about, not doing enough?" he asked. Mike felt like he did what he could to keep the love burning strong in their marriage but like the Titanic, it was sinking fast.

"I don't know man. Maybe it's the fact that you're too...." Arthur paused for a moment because he did not want to use the wrong word. He wanted to tread softly. "...you're too traditional, man. I mean, I know my sister and what she likes, and she likes a little bit of spontaneity now and then. Your problem is that you do everything by the book, bro. You gotta surprise her one day with something that's really dope, sweep her off her feet. I'm just sayin'," he finished.

Mike sat at his desk, thinking it over. But what could he do for Robyn? "Well, she's your sister, man. What does she like the most that I haven't given to her yet?" he asked.

Arthur just shook his head. For a pastor who supposedly described himself as a humble person, he was sure doing a poor job of displaying his humility by insinuating that everything he had done for Robin was enough.

"Well, she does like Broadway shows," Arthur answered. "Find out what's on the billing and get a couple of tickets and take her to the theater. But don't tell her about your plans. Surprise her with the tickets, then when she finds out that you bought them for her, she will throw herself in your arms; in theory of course," he added.

There was silence on the other line for about two minutes. Finally Mike said, "Ok I'll do it. I'll treat her to a night that she'll never forget and go from there. Thanks man, I owe you one."

Arthur laughed upon hearing this and replied, "That you do, my friend. That'll be fifty bucks, cash up front."

Mike laughed and made a derisive sound on the phone. "If I took you serious on that for even one moment, I still wouldn't pay you. Besides, with your legal career you probably got more money than I ever seen," he said.

"Well, we all gotta scrap for ours, right?" Arthur replied, laughing. As he reached the elevator he said, "Anyway, I gotta get back to work, man. Remember what I said."

"I got you. By the way, are you coming to church this Sunday, bro?" Mike asked before he heard a slight click on the other end before a long silence. Arthur had hung up.

The ball sailed through the net-less rim as it bounced on the asphalt below.

"Check it up, boy!" Jamal exclaimed triumphantly as Omar checked him the ball at the top of the key.

The two boys were at the courts in the public park and were currently engaging in an intense battle of one-on-one. Two days had passed since Jamal's math quiz, and he had received his results on Friday morning. Jamal was relieved that he had managed to score an eighty-two on his quiz, since he had not expected it. He knew he hadn't studied the night before and he had crammed the whole morning of the quiz. Omar, of course, scored a ninety-seven on his quiz, which made Jamal a little jealous. He knew that Omar was his good friend but there were times when he couldn't stand Omar being a smarter student than he was; which made his current situation on the basketball court very satisfying. Jamal knew he was a much better basketball player than Omar and when Omar came to the park on Saturday morning to make for missing the previous Saturday, Jamal was already practicing. Jamal couldn't wait for the chance to show Omar up at his own game for a change. So he challenged Omar to a one-on-one game and he knew Omar would accept because he knew Omar wouldn't back down from a challenge. Omar boasted some skills of his own, although overall he was not as good as Jamal.

Currently Jamal had the ball and the lead. The score was four to zero. Omar checked the ball to Jamal and Jamal started to make his move. He realized Omar was guarding his right side, because he knew Jamal was not as strong with his left hand and it would force him to use his less-dominant hand. Omar's calculated gamble paid off, because as Jamal started to cross his dribble over, Omar stole the ball and went to the basket and scored his first point of the match. As Jamal checked him the ball, Omar went to his move, which was a crossover followed by a behind-the-back dribble move that he saw so many NBA players do on television. Jamal did not fall for the dribble move and played defense on Omar. Omar stopped dribbling and heaved a shot that did not have a prayer's chance of going in and indeed it came up as an air ball.

"Ayo what up kid? Ya still putting up air balls?" a voice asked, calling across the courts.

Omar and Jamal turned around to see who had addressed them. Trevor walked toward them. He wore blue shorts and a sleeveless T-shirt. On his left hand, he carried a college-regulation basketball.

"You know him?" Omar asked Jamal as Trevor started putting up shots toward the basket on the opposite end of the boys.

"Yeah, that's Trevor McClain, bro. The dude that played for Richmond Hill and got picked up by St. John's. He's cool," Jamal replied.

Walking over to Trevor, Jamal watched as he warmed up by stretching "What's up man? What's wrong? Not enough open courts in college?" he asked laughing

Trevor gave him the same skeptical look that he gave his friend John whenever John started talking nonsense. "Nah man, college is all right. I just be coming here to clear my head," Trevor replied as he started putting up shots while talking. All the shots he took went in the basket.

He's automatic Jamal thought as he saw Trevor put up shots.

Omar had walked up next to Jamal and Trevor looked at him. Jamal, realizing that the two didn't know each other quickly did the introductions.

"Oh yeah, this is my boy Omar," he said. Omar shook Trevor's hand and Trevor returned to shooting. Jamal looked around. "Where John at?" he asked Trevor.

"Man, I don't know where that fool at. I ain't heard from him since we came back from the park last week. Word on the street is that he been trapping lately. He tried to get me to come join him in getting that money, but I wasn't with it. I got too much on my plate right now," Trevor replied.

Jamal shook his head. Looking at Trevor, Jamal saw anger and a little bit of regret forming on Trevor's face, a combination of emotions that Jamal had seen before. Sometimes the lure of the drug business was far greater than any other call. Jamal didn't know anyone personally who got caught up in any of it but he had heard stories and there had been more than a few young tenants who lived in his apartment that had to deal with the temptation of drug dealing. Some of the drug dealings were by independent dealers and some were by gang members. Either way, it was very clear that Trevor had just ended his friendship with John the previous week. John must have attempted to get Trevor to join him, and Trevor refused.

Jamal and Omar went back to their end of the court to resume their game which they played to eleven points. Within thirty minutes the final point shot dropped, hailing Jamal as the victor. Trevor continued working out, drinking from a bottle of water he brought with him. Jamal and Omar talked between themselves for a couple minutes before walking over to the court where Trevor was practicing his hook shot.

"Yo, Trevor let's play twenty-one right quick," Jamal said. Twenty-one was a street ball game in which three or more basketball players could play on one basket. The rules were very loose. The first person who tallied twenty-one points won the game.

"You gotta be kiddin' me right? Me play twenty-one against ya'll? You do realize that I would beat both of ya'll asses right?" Trevor boasted.

"Nah, I don't think so, superstar. We got this. I'mma break," Omar replied, taking the ball to the three-point line to start the game. He took his first shot and it missed, far right. Jamal jumped in an attempt to get the rebound, but Trevor easily out-rebounded Jamal and dribbled back toward the three-point line to break the game open with his shot. While he set himself to take a shot, he saw movement out of the corner of his eye that caused him to stare. Jamal followed his gaze and saw that Trevor had his eye on a young woman who had running shorts and an athletic T-shirt. The young woman was currently stretching her muscles near the playground toward the walkway. Trevor watched her as her long silky brown arms reached down to her feet. She had a small white headband that was tied over her head while her hair was pulled back in a ponytail. Omar and Jamal suddenly recognized the girl and felt the need to warn Trevor that there was no need to waste his time trying to hook that one. Jamal had known Shania Hillman for years and he knew Shania didn't appreciate guys making passes at her, especially while she was busy stretching. Omar walked over to Jamal and whispered exactly what Jamal was thinking.

"Do you think we should tell him who he's tryin to holla at?" he asked.

Jamal thought about it and went to warn Trevor, but then a smile broke out on his face. After the way Trevor put him on the spot during his first encounter with Patricia the week earlier, Jamal felt that a little bit of a friendly payback was in order.

"Nah, he'll be ok. He's been talkin' a lot about how many girls he pulled when he was still in high school. Let's see if he can back it up," he replied to Omar. Trevor started casually walking towards Shania, who was unaware that someone was approaching her until he stood a few feet behind her. Sensing someone behind her, Shania turned around.

"Can I help you with something?" she asked in a tone of annoyance.

Trevor stood there smiling, admiring her. "Nah, I was just over there ballin' and I saw you stretching and I thought I'd come over and introduce myself," Trevor replied.

Shania rolled her eyes while bending down once again, giving Trevor a great view of her well-toned yet slender figure. "Whoever gave you the notion that I wanted to meet you in the first place?" she responded.

Jamal and Omar were under the basket, their faces unable to fully suppress their laughter. They wanted to hear how Trevor would respond to such a bold statement.

"Well, to be quite honest with you baby, I'm actually giving you the honor of being introduced to me," Trevor replied, leaning against the swing poles.

Shania gave him a look of mock disgust. It amazed her how overconfident these boys were now. They were always so full of themselves and would do whatever it took to obtain what they wanted even if they had to make a complete fool of themselves.

"I know you, Trevor McClain. You played on the basketball team last year at Richmond Hill and recruited by St. John's University. Basketball players don't really impress me all that much," Shania said, while Jamal and Omar laughed at the scene that was unfolding.

Trevor was being given the business by Shania and it appeared he had bitten off more than he could chew. "Ok, so it's clear that you know me so we can both assume that yo' boy's rep travels," Trevor replied. "So what's your name?" he asked.

Wiping the sweat off her forehead with a small towel, Shania replied, "If I tell you, you promise you'll leave me alone? Cuz I'm trying to get ready for track and the last thing I need is a distraction."

At this, Trevor was taken aback. "Distraction? Nah I think you got twisted, baby. I think I provide the attraction," he replied, putting both of his arms behind his head while leaning on the pole, making sure his biceps and triceps showed.

Shania laughed. "Wow. You provide the attraction, huh? I hope your basketball game's not as bad as your social game," she said while she took a drink from her water bottle. Trevor had his hands in his short pockets while he waited for her to finish drinking water. "By the way, my name's Shania Hillman but it's not like you gonna remember it anyways. You probably got a ton of your groupies sweatin' you over in college right now," she said.

Trevor laughed as well. "Nah I ain't got no groupies. I ain't into stuff like that. I'm just tryin to ball right now. But I have been known to draw a couple of college chicks every now and then," he said while he laughed.

"Yeah, imagine what they'd say if they find you wasting time with high school girls in the park. That would probably drop your stock, now would it?" she asked.

Trevor's eyes widened a little. "Oh ok, so you still in high school? I didn't know that, my bad," he replied. Trevor then asked what grade was she in and Shania informed him that she was a senior in high school. "Oh that's cool. I can step back a year or two. Besides it don't look like you still in high school, either," Trevor replied, giving furtive looks to Shania and her slender figure. "But I bet you hear that from every dude though, huh?" he asked.

"Nope, you're the only idiot that has said that to me so far," Shania answered shaking her head.

Even though Trevor laughed, he couldn't believe how abrasive this chick was.

Damn girl I'm just tryin' to talk with you and you throwing shade like it's nobody's business.

Shania started to walk toward the park exit. "Anyway, I have to go. I guess it was nice meeting you, although I already knew your egotistical ass and you never said one word to me when you were still at Richmond Hill. I'm sure we'll see each other again," she said as she walked out the park. Then she noticed Jamal and Omar at the courts still watching the encounter. "Hey Jamal! Hey Omar! Say hi to your parents for me!" she added as she walked out of the park.

Trevor looked quizzically from Shania to Jamal. As he walked back to the court he turned to Jamal. "Yo man, you know her?" he asked.

Jamal nodded his head, laughing. "Yeah bro, I was tryin to tell you but you was killin' it over there and I had to watch the master operate," he laughed.

"Yeah, the master of getting dogged out," Omar chimed in, laughing with Jamal.

Trevor chuckled a bit to himself. "It's all good, though. I think she's feelin' me too. She just playin' hard to get," he boasted proudly as he watched her walk down the sidewalk. Trevor loved a good challenge whether it was on the court or in the game of life. If people told him he couldn't accomplish a goal it just inspired him rather than discourage him.

The illuminating streetlight shone down on the rickety group of fences that lined the small, abandoned homes in 101 Avenue. Big Earl doubled over in pain when his abdomen was ruptured by a powerful fist. As his wide frame rose back up to retaliate against his assailant, another fist flew in, connecting with his chin and he felt his jaw break. Nate backed up, nimble and agile as a young heavyweight, ready to strike again. Big Earl let out a grunt of anger and rage as he attempted to rush Nate, but Nate used his speed to avoid Earl's wide arms. Instead, he thrust his leg up into Earl's belly forcefully, knocking the wind out of Earl. Earl almost fell to his knees, overwhelmed by the sheer force of blows coming from Nate's fists.

"What up now?" Nate yelled. "Get up! Get yo' punk ass up, I ain't through with you yet!" He shouted even louder as he continued to hit Earl in the face, chest, and legs causing trauma and internal injury.

The sidewalk was covered with Earl's blood as Nate continued the assault. Earl tried to fight back but Nate was too quick and too strong for him, and he couldn't avoid the fists and kicks as injuries began to take a toll on his body. After what seemed like fifteen minutes, Nate let up while Earl lay on the pavement, spitting more blood. Nate took out the gun from his pocket and pointed it at his enemy. A grin of satisfaction crosses his face when he saw Earl's fear reflected back to him.

"I should pull this damn trigger and waste you, right here and now but it's too good for you," Nate said in rage before putting the gun back in his pocket and continued wailing away at will, his eyes closed as he released every angry fiber of rage in every swing against the huge body mass.

Opening his eyes and panting, Nate found himself facing the punching bag at 101 Avenue's workout gym. The whole scene that featured him and Earl had been in Nate's head as he imagined a total revision of the night Nina was murdered. He kept flashing back to his feeble efforts in fighting Earl and how easily Earl had handled him. Since then, Nate went to local gyms to learn boxing and did strength exercises to bulk up his body. He would never allow himself to lose another confrontation again and if he ever got that second meeting with Earl, he would be ready. Nate didn't believe in giving anyone an easy way out of what he felt they deserved. Just as he was forced to watch Nina take her last breath in his arms, he would force Big Earl to own up to what was coming to him. He didn't want Big Earl to die quickly, he wanted him to suffer. He wanted him to feel every bit of pain Nate endured during the last eighteen years. Every punch that landed in Earl's body, Nate wanted to cause severe damage. Nate wanted to be sure Earl felt Nate's impact and to be the one delivering the scars for a change. He would never let up, no matter how hard Earl begged or pleaded. No mercy would be shown this time. Just as Earl had shown no mercy to him or Nina, Earl would not receive any type of mercy from Nate's rage. Nina was a mother, a sister, a true friend, and an angel, despite her shortcomings. She was somebody's baby and now she was six feet underground for no reason at all. If taking a life was meaningless to Earl back then, Nate would make sure that Earl's life dangled in the balance before he would take it. Hitting the bag with even more rage and anger than before, the other gym members stopped what they were doing as they watched Nate punish the boxing bag. He continued hitting and hitting until he stopped, sweat pouring in streams down his face. He didn't seem to notice that all eyes in the gym had been trained on him and his primal rage on a seemingly harmless punching bag. He walked over to the water fountain to get a drink of water when one of the gym members came to him.

"Man, that was some of the best displays of punching power I've ever seen. Sure you're not a retired boxer or something?" he asked.

Nate turned to him and shook his head. "Nah. I just get zoned in on my workouts. Gotta go hard or go home, right?" he replied smiling.

The gym member agreed although he had suspicions about Nate and his punching power.

"Yeah, you right. But if I didn't know any better, it sort of looked like you hated that bag or something. I mean look at the dents, man," he said, pointing at the bag.

Nate followed his gaze over to the bag where he noticed deep crater-like dents in the middle of the bag.

"I don't know about you, but I would feel sorry for the dude that pissed you off," the member said before going to the locker room.

Nate took a towel and began drying his face. Could it be that he allowed his anger to escalate him into a different plane of existence? Could that plane somehow be a forecast of the future that remained to be unfolded? Where was Big Earl now? Was he even still alive? Was he still dealing drugs in some unknown city, still making money off poor saps who thought no different than Nate had when he was still a naïve young man? The thought that Earl could be building another covert drug empire was such an unbearable thought to Nate that he suddenly made up his mind. He couldn't sit back and do nothing. Another young girl might have fallen victim to Earl and his violent ways. Earl had to be located and eliminated before the end of the year.

CHAPTER EIGHT

The cell phone vibrated on Loree's night stand early Sunday morning. Loree, still lying in bed, picked up her phone.

"Hello?" she responded sleepily.

"Hey, girl it's me. How you been?" Shania asked on the other line.

Loree took a deep breath and sighed.

"I'm ok Nia, thanks for calling," Loree said followed by a brief moment of silence on both lines.

It had been three days since their argument had taken place at Shania's house, and they had not exchanged words since then. Shania wanted to give Loree time to reflect on herself, even if it meant avoiding her for a couple of days. Loree's popularity in school kept her so busy, she might not miss speaking with Shania as often as usual but as the days passed, Loree realized that she missed her best friend. Still, she hesitated in calling Shania to apologize because she did not want to give Shania the satisfaction of confirming her suspicion about David.

On Friday night, the Richmond Hill football team went on the road to play Flushing High School and they were humiliated by a score of thirty-four to three. David suffered his worst performance as quarterback, throwing several key interceptions that allowed the Flushing defense to pick apart Richmond Hill's offense easily. It also didn't help that Richmond Hill's defense was stagnant for much of the night. Loree attended the game to support David, but she found the task to be more difficult than she expected. David took the loss especially hard, lashing out at his teammates for showing a lack of commitment and passion and threatened to quit the team. When Loree went to see him after the game, she ran up to embrace him as usual. David promptly shoved her aside, refusing to talk to her at all. When Loree tried to comfort him and remind him that it was just a game, David got even more violent and yelled at Loree to leave him alone. After about an hour arguing; spewing verbally abusive diatribes, and filling the air heavy with expletives, each of them walked their separate ways. David headed toward his home on 103rd and Liberty. Loree walked back toward 101 Avenue. They hadn't spoken to each other since that argument and when her cell phone vibrated. Loree's heart skipped a beat, hoping it was David calling to apologize as he normally did after every argument, but she was still pleased when Shania answered because they still had to clear the air, too.

"Look Nia, I wanted to apologize about what I said to you the other night. We've been friends forever and I know you were just looking out for me. I hope you ain't still mad," Loree said.

"Awww, I could never stay mad at you, boo. We girls forever and ain't nothing gonna change that. I forgave you from the time you left my house that night. Guess I was just too scared to go after you," Shania confessed.

"Why were you scared?" Loree asked.

Shania was silent for a moment. "I don't know," Shania answered. "I guess I didn't want to talk you out of going out with David. I just wanted to give him a chance as you have. I still want to give him a chance," she continued.

"Honestly, I don't know where I stand at with David now," Loree confessed. "He lost his game yesterday and he went off at me for no reason. We were shouting for like three hours, Nia. I never hated him as much as I did yesterday. I hate him but...." Loree's voice trailed off and came to a complete halt.

"...But you love him," Shania finished.

There was another moment of awkward silence between the two teenage girls, then Loree heard Robyn's voice in the background on Shania's end, telling Shania to hurry up and get ready for church.

"Well anyway, I won't hold you up with my issues. Boys ain't worth the trouble at all. Girl if I was you, I'd stay married to Jesus. Don't waste your time with these boys," Loree said.

Shania laughed upon hearing Loree joke around again. This was the Loree who had become her best friend years ago. "Girl, who you tellin?" Shania asked rhetorically. "That reminds me, guess who I saw at the park yesterday when I went running?" she asked.

"Hold up, you went running without me? Why you ain't tell me that you went to the park?" Loree asked, disappointed.

"Well, I thought you were still mad at me and last time you went running with me I had to wait for you to catch up for 3 blocks. You slower than special ed, girl," Shania replied. "Nah but guess who I saw for real? Trevor McClain," she added.

"You mean that cute light-skin boy who played basketball last year? I thought he went to St. John's," Loree said.

"Well, he does, but he comes back to the park from time to time trying to talk to all the shorties there," Shania replied.

"You mean he was tryin' to talk to you? Girl if it was me and I wasn't with David, I would've snatched him up before anyone else did," Loree said.

"Girl, trust me, he ain't all that," Shania said, laughing. "So am I gonna see you in church today?" she asked Loree.

"I don't know if I'm going today. I just got a lot of things on my mind right now and I need some time to myself. My parents and Andrea are gonna be there, today though," Loree said. Andrea was Loree's twelve-year-old sister who was in Shania's Sunday School class. She had just about the same model looks as her older sister. "I'm sure 'Drea will tell me how the service goes when she comes back," Loree added. "Oh ok, hey I hope everything improves with you and you-know-who," Shania replied.

"Just keep me in prayer today, Nia," Loree said.

"I will definitely keep you in prayer today," Shania said. "I'll talk to you later, girl. Daddy's on the war path today and I ain't even showered or dressed up yet," she added.

"Ok, I'll talk to you later, girl," Loree said before she hung up.

Loree went to the bathroom to shower and dress in casual Capri pants and a blouse. She went to check on her parents, Amos and Alisha McAfee. Her father was in the room, tying on his favorite tie and her mother had walked in the bathroom to add finishing touches to her hair.

"Good morning, sweetie. How come you're not dressed up to go to church?" Amos asked as he put on cologne.

"Well, I won't be going to church with you today. I'm just not feeling up to it," Loree replied.

Amos walked up to her and looked her in the eye. "Is everything ok?" he asked.

Loree looked at him. "Yeah, I'm fine Daddy. It's just that I got a lot of studying to do for my classes and I got a lot more than I expected, so I'll take a rain check for church today," she answered.

Amos shook his head. He never believed in forcing his daughter to go to church because he didn't think the word of God was something that needed to be forced. Sometimes the individual had to find the Lord on their own.

"Ok, baby, well get some work done and get some rest today," Amos said as he finished putting on a gray suit.

Loree kissed her father. "Ok. Thanks Daddy," she replied as she went back to her room.

As soon as she went back to her room, she checked her cell phone. She had one missed call. When she checked her call log, she saw that David had called her. Rolling her eyes, she pressed the option to call him back, even though she did not feel like calling him. The phone rang a few times before he picked up.

"Yo, what's up baby?" David's low scratchy voice spoke through the receiver.

"I don't know David. You tell me what's up," Loree answered coolly. "Most boyfriends don't yell at their girlfriends after a bad game then call like nothing ever happened. What do you want?" she asked.

"Look, Loree my bad for the way I yelled at you yesterday. I'm just going through a lot right now. I shouldn't have taken out my frustration on you. You've been there for me since day one. I never known a girl who would still ride wit' me after all the stuff I did to you," David apologized.

Loree thought about what David said. Nobody actually knew about the often-explosive parts in their relationship, although Shania's suspicions had grown stronger day by day.

"David, I really care about you but when you hurt me, you really hurt me. There are days where I feel like I deserve better and I know I deserve better, but I give you so many chances," she said.

"I know baby, and I know I don't deserve another chance, but I promise if you give me one, I will never hurt you again. It's just that I'm stressed out a lot from football season to school to college applications. I just want to do something positive in my life. I done did so much shit that I can't take back, but I can change it if you believe in me. Look can you meet me somewhere so we can talk?" he asked.

Loree didn't know how to respond to him. In the back of her mind, she knew it could be a bad idea to go anywhere alone with David at the moment, but David has been known to have a complete change of heart after any abusive encounter. "Ok fine. Where do you want me to meet you at?" she asked. David gave her the name of the local fast-food joint where he wanted to meet with Loree.

Thirty minutes later, Loree walked over to Jon's Burgers which also served as the local teen hangout at the corner of 113th St and Jamaica Avenue. She looked around until she saw David in one of the small table booths next to the window. He wore his Richmond Hill T-shirt with gray sweatpants. His upper body reflected years of conditioning and weightlifting he had maintained to remain in shape for the season. His muscles rippled from his arms down to his chest area. At the moment Loree saw him, she began to feel the butterflies in her belly that she always got whenever she saw David. She loved the way he looked masculine and sexy in anything he wore but she knew that she had no time to dwell on his looks at the moment. She was on a mission to talk with David and set some guidelines in their relationship.

"Hey baby, what's up?" David said embracing her but Loree could only return a half-hearted hug.

She was definitely not in the mood to play nice with David at all. She sat in the chair opposite of him. "Ok David, why did you want to meet me here?" she asked him.

"Well, I just needed a place that wasn't obvious, you know?" he replied. "I wanted to talk to you about the way I treated you on Friday night. I stepped way out of line in the way I talked to you. If there is any reason that I have a second chance in my life, it's because you stuck with me and you believed in me," David said.

Loree rolled her eyes. She was not falling for his apologies again. It was the same story after every strike, both mentally and physically. "Ok whatever David, but why did you come here? Why couldn't you come to my house to tell me all this? My parents already know you, so they weren't gonna trip," Loree said.

David looked in her eyes, holding her hands from across the table. "Well I also came here cuz a brotha hungry. Football players gotta eat too," he said, laughing.

Loree laughed as well. "Well I am a little hungry myself," she agreed.

"Say no more. I'll order for the both of us," David said smiling warmly.

Loree smiled back. It was hard to refuse that smile; from the little dimples that appeared or charm he had with that smile. His smile could reassure and manipulate others at the same time. His smile was the one factor that kept bringing Loree back to him. After six minutes, David appeared with a burger, fries, and a special kind of salad with the drink for Loree.

As they sat eating, David said, "Loree, I got something to tell you. I made a huge mistake on Friday night and I don't think I can get out of it."

Loree's heart sank. Was he at large again? Is he being chased by the authorities? She hoped it didn't have to do with any of the first two thoughts she had in her head. "What happened? You know if you got any type of problem, you can come to me. I want to help. What can I do?" Loree asked.

All of a sudden, Loree noticed that David's mood began to change. He became more evasive, his eyes every so often looking at the windows and doors. It was almost as if he expected someone to confront him. "Well, you can do something for me actually. See, I made a small bet with Tadarius on Friday, hopin' I would win the game. But as you already know, I lost," he said, putting his head down.

Loree felt a sinking feeling at the pit of her stomach. "Don't play wit' me David. What's going on? What were the conditions of this 'bet' that you made wit' that nigga?" Loree asked.

"Actually, you were involved, baby. Promise me you won't get mad, ok?" David asked.

"Well, it depends on what the hell this bet was about," Loree replied.

"Well, you know Tadarius and I go back to since we were in juvenile hall, and I know that sometimes he likes to push his chances. If I won, he would pay me $300. If he won...." David began but stopped when he looked into her face.

Loree lowered her face and glared at David. "Ok, if he won the bet, meaning if you lost the game; would you have to pay him money?" she asked.

"Not exactly," David replied. "Tadarius saw you and he thought you was fine as fuck, and he's heard a lot about you. So he said if I lost, I would have to let you go down on him," he replied.

At that, Loree lost her appetite. "What?" she thundered while patrons sitting around them looked at her. "So you mean to tell me that you betted me over to your boy without knowing or even caring how I would feel?" Loree replied angrily.

"It wasn't like I agreed at first. I don't want anyone putting their hands on you. But Tadarius has a way of....convincing people," David replied hesitantly.

Loree couldn't believe what she was hearing. David was supposed to be her man and stand by her when things got tough. But instead of using his brawn (or brains, for that matter) he signed Loree up to do something vulgar and disturbing just to save his own tail.

"So, you want me to have sex with him?" she asked.

"Nah, don't get into bed with him or nothing like that. Just blow him. Look, Loree, I wish I had never made that stupid bet with him. But Tadarius is crazy, baby and with all the homeboys he got with him, ain't nobody tryin' to mess with him," David replied.

Loree pushed her food tray away. Hunger was not even a factor anymore. It was as if her eyes were finally open to the kind of guy that David was. Maybe he hadn't changed after all. Maybe he was the same old David who was still locked up in juvenile hall as a young gangbanger. With a look that could burn through lead, Loree reluctantly agreed to fulfill the obligations of the bet.

"Ok, I'll do it. But after it's all over, we're done. If I'm so worthless that you are willing to gamble me just to save your ass, then you can find yourself another bitch that can do all your dirty work for you. Shania was right about you, David, you need to check yo' self before you get involved with me again," Loree replied firmly.

"Come on Loree don't be like that. I don't want us to end," David pleaded.

"Then stop rollin' with Tadarius and his crew like his little whipping boy. Stand up for yourself, for once," Loree challenged.

"You right, I gotta stop playin' games like this. I don't wanna mess wit'....aww shit!" David exclaimed. He looked outside the window, his face getting paler by the second. Loree followed his gaze and saw Tadarius standing right outside the restaurant, hands in his pockets. He wore a long white tank-top and his arms, neck and back were littered with tattoos. He wore a blue du-rag on his head with baggy jeans. Although he had a skinny frame, Tadarius was a very dangerous individual who had brushes with the law on several occasions on charges of assault and battery, disturbing the peace, unlawful distribution of drugs, and alcohol to minors. He stood outside with a smile on his face, no doubt anticipating the reward for the bet that David lost.

"Baby, gimme one second. I'm 'bout to go talk with him. Maybe he'll change his mind," David said before he stepped out of the restaurant. Tadarius waited for David to come out of the restaurant.

"Well, well, if it ain't Mr. Heisman himself. So tell me dawg, what went down at that game on Friday?" Tadarius asked in mock curiosity.

"We lost, ok?" David replied angrily.

Tadarius shook his head. "Well you win some and you lose some right? I get to keep my money and yo' girl, too," he said.

At this David stepped close to Tadarius, his jaw taut. "Listen man, I think we need to call this whole thing off. I didn't tell her about the bet and she ain't really down wit' it…." David began but Tadarius cut him off in mid-sentence.

"Trust me, imma make sure she down wit' it. She ain't got no choice in the matter. Look I'm just gonna get this quick head and I'm gone. She's all yours again, homeboy and maybe you'll learn not to gamble with a nigga who knows these streets. Where she at, anyway?" Tadarius asked. "She wastin' my time. Get her ass out hea'," he demanded.

David looked inside the restaurant and gestured for Loree to come out. She came out, the look of disgust still attached to her face. Tadarius suddenly grabbed her arm, pulling her closer to him but Loree wrested her arm free.

"So where we gonna do this at?" she asked.

Tadarius took one look at David, then looked at Loree.

"We going to my old spot on 83rd Street, only a couple blocks from here. You welcome to come too dawg, if you wanna see the show,"

Tadarius said to David, smiling. David shook his head. He couldn't even bring himself to look directly at Loree's eyes.

"Nah, I'm good. Just get it over with and let her go home. Just make sure you don't hurt her. If you do anything to her…" David started.

Tadarius gave David a look that suggested extreme cockiness. "Nigga, you ain't gon' do nothing," he said. "Who knows, I might turn her out," he added as they left David at the parking lot and Loree glanced back over her shoulder at David with a look that had betrayal written all over it.

After the morning service ended at Rock of Jacob Baptist Church Sunday afternoon and the members had begun to disperse, Pastor Mike ran to find Isis Samuels.

"Sister Samuels, can I speak with you for a second?" he asked.

Isis, who had been speaking to one of the other members of the church turned around to face pastor Mike.

"Yes, pastor? That was a great sermon you preached today about remaining in prayer. I know I need to do that," she answered.

Pastor Mike laughed. "Thank you very much sister, I appreciate being able to give you the gift of the Word. That's why the Lord gives us the Bible to read. But this is regarding some work that you wanted done on your kitchen counters and sink. I tried to call you during the week, but I didn't get a response. I guess you were a bit busy," he said.

Isis puts her hand over her mouth, as if she committed a grave sin. "Oh yeah, I did receive your call and voicemail. I'm so sorry I didn't call you back. My work schedule can get a little hectic at times and I get forgetful. But yes, I was meaning to talk to you in regards to lowering the price for the job," she said.

"I know," Pastor Mike said with a laugh. "One of my employees informed me about that when you spoke with him. I reassure you sister, we are giving you the lowest price that we can offer for a kitchen counter remodel," he added.

"Well come on now, you can't give me, a church member a community discount?" Isis asked.

She wasn't angry when she asked. It was actually very friendly, if anything. Mike looked at Isis, and started to realize for the first time, her true beauty. From her summer dress that hugged her curves just right to her warm smile to her eyelashes which batted at him every chance they got; she was intoxicating. Michael shook away those thoughts and remembered he had a job to do, and he was going to accomplish it without being distracted. Besides he was married, so she was off limits.

"Ok I'll tell you what I'll do. I'll come by with one of my contractors and we will do a live measurement of the countertop we will be working on. What day is good for you?" Pastor Mike asked.

Isis thought it over. Her schedule was not very flexible, and she knew that she would be needed during the week unless she called in to let them know she would be about an hour late due to this work estimate.

"Well, I work every day during the week and right now it's really hard for me to schedule anything during the week. But I can call in and let my job know that I will be coming a little late to work. How about Wednesday at eight in the morning?" she asked.

"I don't know, sister. I might be too busy that day, I'll have to get back with you," he said jokingly.

Isis laughed. Mike felt relieved. It was a nice change to be around someone who appreciated his off-hand humor. Not to say that Robyn didn't like his jokes, but she liked to shrug them off, implying that they weren't funny.

"No, but in all seriousness, I will be there," he reassured.

At the same moment, Jamal came up to Isis. "Hey Mom, Omar and I are gonna run over to King's to get some beef patties. Is it ok if I go? I'll be right back," he assured.

"Ok Jamal, you can go. I'm gonna talk to some more people here in church but I want you to come back as soon as possible," Isis replied.

Upon securing his mother's permission, Jamal and Omar walked over to King's Caribbean restaurant, a Jamaican restaurant located about a block away from the church. It was more than just a regular restaurant for the residents of Queens, New York; it was a great hangout spot. Playing non-stop reggae dancehall numbers and known as a popular relaxation spot for all the island men within, King's was once a lounge/pool hall owned by crooked gangsters and mobsters, but the small building strip was bought and owned by Lamar Delroy who ran it with his wife, Sakina. They had done their best to make the store seem like a home environment with rocking chairs for the senior citizens and a movie rental rack where they sold dozens of classic African, Jamaican, and Haitian movies. Jamal and Omar had been eating at the restaurant for over five years, so they were well known regulars at the store and Sakina regarded them as her children at times. They would talk to her while she prepared the patty orders. As they stepped inside the restaurant, they saw a couple of dread-headed Jamaican men playing cards on the table and the small TV was turned on a soccer channel. Sakina was already behind the counter when she saw the boys.

"Aye it's my two favorite boys! My, my, you two are getting so tall! I'm gonna break my neck one day from looking up too high," she said.

Omar and Jamal greeted her as they sat down on the stools that stood in front of the counter.

"So you two going to play basketball in school this year?" she asked.

"Yup we both are going to try out for the freshman team and probably make varsity," Jamal replied.

Omar scoffed sarcastically. Jamal looked at him with a look that said shut up.

"Well, you boys can do anything you set your minds to. Remember, who Jah bless, no man can curse. So what can I get for you two this afternoon?" she asked in her strongest Jamaican accent.

Omar ordered first. "I'll have a beef patty with some cocoa bread and a Coke," he said.

"I'll also have a beef patty and a Sprite, but I don't want the cocoa bread with mine," Jamal said.

"How come you never want your beef patty with cocoa bread?" Sakina asked Jamal.

"I just like to eat my beef patty like that. Don't take it personal, Sakina please?" Jamal asked, smiling.

Sakina smiled. "Ok but one day, I'm going to make you try my cocoa bread. It's some of the best bread you ever had. So do you boys want your patties spicy or mild?" she asked. There was no doubt in Jamal or Omar's minds.

"Mild," Jamal replied.

"Spicy," Omar replied at the same time.

Sakina informed them that their patties would be ready in 10 minutes and while she went to the back kitchen to prepare the food, the boys looked out the window and saw Shania walking past the restaurant.

"Check it out. Wonder where she's going?" Jamal asked Omar who was watching the soccer game on television before realizing Shania walked past them.

While the boys waited for their order, Shania walked over to the park. She didn't know why but her instinct told her to go to the park. She saw him practicing, knocking down jump shot after jump shot. Driving the ball strong to the basket, finishing with strong athletic dunks, his body muscles contracting with every movement he made on the court. He wore a red tank top with black shorts and black sneakers. For the first few minutes, he was oblivious that anyone was watching him as he played alone, taking whatever frustrations he had out on the rim. Trevor didn't know why but he had a feeling that told him to turn around because he felt someone watching him. When he saw it was Shania who was watching, he smiled.

"Couldn't stay away, huh?" he asked as he took a swig from the water bottle, he bought with him.

"Well I was just taking a walk in the park just to clear my head and you just happen to be here. I wasn't looking for you," she replied.

Trevor didn't know whether she was joking or if she was playing with him again.

"Doesn't St. John's have a lot of baskets over in their gyms? Why do you come here all the time?" she asked him.

"I come here to clear my head. It's hard to do that in a controlled environment with sixteen other guys trying to take yo' playing spot," he answered.

Trevor took a good look at Shania. She wore a short orange summer dress that complimented her figure. "Well it's ok. The groupies normally don't come to this part of town," Trevor added, laughing at Shania. "So I see that you're all dressed up today, where'd you come from?" he asked.

"I was in church today, Captain Obvious," Shania replied back.

"Well you look great," Trevor said.

Wow he actually said that I looked great. Not fine, not sexy but great. He might not be so bad Shania thought.

"I like the look," he added.

"What, don't you ever go to church?" she asked.

"Well my parents did go with me when I was younger, but our schedules got so hectic coming up, we just never had the chance to go to church anymore. It's all about working hard and playing even harder," Trevor replied.

He saw the disapproving look that Shania gave him after he stated that he never had time to go to church.

"It ain't that I don't believe in God or nothing like that it's just....sometimes I don't even know If he exists and if he does, why would he care for someone like me?" Trevor blurted before realizing that he stepped into a touchy subject with a girl he found out he liked. Why did he have to say what was on his mind? She probably gonna think I'm the devil or something and try to get as far away from me as possible he thought.

But Shania didn't think of Trevor that way and saw it as an opportunity to lay the groundwork to have the gospel shared with him. "Ok I'll make you a deal. If you go to my church next Sunday, I'll think about letting you take me on a date," she said.

Trevor smiled a bit. "So you bribing me to go now, is that it?" he said. The last thing he needed was to go somewhere he knew he wasn't wanted. He knew that because he felt those stares only too many times in his life. His parents were not religious folk, but they did go to church on the days when it mattered. Christmas and Easter and that was it. Did any other day matter as much? If a person didn't attend every church or Bible study, did that make them a bad person? Trevor was not going to act like he was perfect because he was the farthest from perfect as one could get. From early authority issues in elementary and middle school to being the big man on campus at Richmond Hill where he carved a reputation of being a great athlete but a womanizer off the court. He never actually revealed the number of different girls he had been with but when the rumor mill at the school ran, instead of fighting it, he ran with it. From cheerleaders to homecoming queens and prom dates, there wasn't a popular girl in high school who didn't have an old story about Trevor. Meanwhile, he ignored the other less flashy people including Shania because he liked who he was and what he had achieved. His parents tried to help but he could never quite understand them either. They may have done more harm than good by spoiling him with what he wanted from the time he was little. It was as if they wanted him to be the golden child who loved them unconditionally but sometimes, he felt that there was a secret they weren't telling him; a secret related to how he was and why he acted as he did.

"I'll think about it," he replied.

Shania took out her phone. She wanted to call Loree but all she got was her voicemail. "Where is she at?" she asked herself.

"Who are you trying to call?" Trevor asked.

"My friend Loree. She didn't go to church with us today, so I was just checking up with her," she replied.

"You mean Loree McAfee?" Trevor asked.

"Yeah, you know her?" Shania asked.

"Yeah, every time I went to someone's party in high school, she was always there," Trevor replied. Shania rolled her eyes. It definitely sounded like Loree. "But I did see her with some tatted up dudes earlier. One of them was mad skinny and was only wearing a tank top," Trevor replied.

CHAPTER NINE

Arriving at his parent's two-story red-brick house where he spent the first seventeen years of his life, Trevor pulls up in his mother's old Ford Contour. Reaching for his basketball, which sat next to him in the passenger seat, his head was still spinning from the conversation he had with Shania earlier. He couldn't help but remember the look of concern and fear that crossed Shania's face when he informed her that Loree was with some boys. She had been so upset that she had left without saying goodbye or thanking him for the information. Of course, he knew they weren't the most popular people to hang around with, but he didn't think Shania had anything to worry about. She left him standing there shaking his head, wondering why she was so upset. Trevor didn't know the boys very well, but he had been around the area long enough to know who to watch out for and who wasn't remotely dangerous.

Unlocking the door to his parents' house, Trevor went up to his old room, which was currently being used as a guest bedroom and sat on the couch to watch TV. While watching his favorite TV sitcom, his mother returned from her shift as a daytime nurse.

"Trevor, baby, I stopped by the store to get some things for dinner. Can you help me put some of these in the fridge?" she asked.

"Yeah Mom, I got you," Trevor replied getting up from the couch to help his mother put the groceries in the fridge.

Tiffany McClain was a short, petite beautiful middle-aged woman. With her long hair now tied in a ponytail behind her back and dressed in her nurse uniform, she sat down to rest her feet.

"So were you at the park shooting hoops again?" she asked as she elevated her feet.

"You already know I can never stay away from them courts, Mama. It's like a second home to me," he replied, laughing.

Mrs. McClain laughed. "It's your second home now, huh? So what does that make us now? Your Motel 6?" she said as she checked her phone for any calls.

"No, it's not like that, Mama. You know I love coming here. Ain't nothing like coming back home," he said.

"Yeah, but sometimes I wish that you never went to school in that area. I wish you had let me pay for private school for you. I don't even feel comfortable knowing that you are at the park there sometimes because of the extreme gang and crime activity on there," Mrs. McClain said.

Here we go again, Trevor thought.

Every year they had the same conversation about how dangerous it was at 101 Avenue and Lefferts Boulevard. But year after year, Trevor had proven his mother wrong by not only attending the school and emerging safe and free from harm at every turn, but by spending more time in that neighborhood than both of his parents combined. As a matter of fact, he rarely saw his parents venture to 101 Avenue because they both worked at the Long Island Jewish Hospital which was about an hour away. There were times Trevor wondered if he was even related to his parents, who would never step foot on Lefferts Boulevard, while he had no problem being there. His parents would say that he had a tough temperament.

"So where's Pop?" Is he still at the hospital?" he asked.

"Yeah, your father is still there working overtime. He is a surgeon after all," Mrs. McClain replied.

Trevor nodded his head in agreement.

"So did you meet any cute girls at the park today?" Mrs. McClain asked, completely surprising Trevor with her question.

"Mama, how can you say that? When I go to the park to practice, I do work. I ain't got time for socializing," he lied.

But Mrs. McClain knew her son and his way with girls.

"So, what's her name?" she asked furtively.

Trevor laughed. His mother was not what most people would call a traditional mother. Sometimes she would give some smart-mouthed comments, but it was all in good fun.

"All right you got me. Her name is Shania. She's smart, athletic, and very good looking," he answered while his mother raised an eyebrow.

"I was about to say, none of the first two traits of hers matter to you as long as she looks good!" Mrs. McClain said.

"That's not always true," Trevor countered. "Looks aren't everything. You got compatibility, street smarts, and uh…. other things," he added.

"Wonder what those other things are," his mother said winking at him.

Trevor shook his head before heading up to his room. Sometimes he thought his mother knew far too much about him, which was not always easy during his high school years. On more occasions than not, his mother would come home and catch him kissing a girl with whom he was supposed to be having a study date. He would be embarrassed at first but when a boy was a popular, coveted basketball player sometimes they appeared to be more attractive when they were vulnerable. Trevor chuckled as he thought of that fleeting moment. It was just another day in the life of a high school athlete. Nobody said he had to be a saint. But while Trevor basked in his success in high school, he also had questions stemming from the time he was a little boy. It started when other kids would see him with his parents and ask "Why do your parents look so different from you? Are they even your parents?"

Trevor never took those conversations too seriously and he made sure he kept talking about his parents to a minimum around his classmates and his friends. However the more time that passed, the more obvious it became to Trevor that he was different from the people who raised him.

One day during the sixth grade, he did ask his parents if he was adopted but his parents quickly dismissed the issue by bringing up unnecessary scientific arguments to prove they were his parents. They would give him explanations such as "well my great grandfather was your complexion it's just the gene pool" or "when the XX-chromosome or the XY-chromosome develops into this or that." Although it would frustrate Trevor terribly, he finally stopped asking because he realized he would not get a clear answer. Besides, at the end of the day, Jack and Tiffany McClain were the people who had raised him and to Trevor they were his parents, even if they might be hiding the real truth about his lineage from him.

Sitting on his bed, Trevor reached into his book bag and took out his CD player and his headphones. With tunes, beats, and lyrics swirling in and out of his mind and subconscious, he fell asleep. It wasn't until a few hours later that he felt a gentle shake on his arm. Trevor woke up and saw his father hand him a long yellow standard business letter.

"What's up, Hoop Dreams? You got mail," he said as Trevor received the letter.

"Who's the letter from?" he asked groggily.

His father shrugged. "Not sure but if it's money, let me know," he said winking at him.

"You a trip, Pop," Trevor said, laughing.

After his father went downstairs, Trevor closed his bedroom door and opened the envelope. A small circular item fell out of the envelope onto the carpet floor. Looking closer, Trevor saw that it was a blank CD. There was no name or label on the CD. Wondering what the CD was all about, Trevor reached into the envelope and pulled out a letter that was folded in the envelope. The letterhead was marked with the seal of the Radisson Hotel based in Mount Vernon, New York. Questioningly, Trevor unfolded the letter and proceeded to read the contents within. The letter read:

To: T. McClain, I hope this letter finds its way to you. I've actually wanted to get in contact with you for a very long time but I never got the chance. I know that by now you must have many questions and in due time I will answer them all for you. Unfortunately, I have to keep this letter anonymous because if I reveal my identity to you at this time, you may not trust me to communicate with you again and it will be very difficult for me to sit down with you to explain what you need to know about your mother, your REAL mother. I will continue to give you more information about her as time passes but please take a look at the DVD that is enclosed with this letter. It may not be all that you are looking for, but it will help you get closer to finding out who you really are and who your mother really was.

The letter ended and there was no signature on it. At least Trevor didn't see a signature but when he looked near the bottom of the letter, he did make out to small initials listed as G.M. Trevor pondered over what G.M. could possibly mean. Holding the DVD in hand, Trevor was ready to pop the DVD in the DVD player downstairs when his phone rang. He stared at the screen on his phone. It was Sean Wilson, the starting point guard for St. John's.

"Yo what up?" Trevor greeted.

"What's good man?" Sean replied. "Yo, coach wants all of us to get back to campus for a last-minute team meeting. Where you at right now?" he asked.

"I'm at my parent's crib right now, but I'll be there in about forty-five minutes," Trevor replied.

"Ok cool," Sean said. "Oh and one of the homies is having a party up at his dorm this Wednesday. He's charging $15 at the door so make sure you bring cash. He gotta pay the bartender that's gonna be there. So who you tryin' to roll up there wit', son?" Sean asked Trevor.

"I don't even know right now, man. I ain't even thinking about that right now. But let coach know I'm comin' up there," Trevor replied before hanging up.

He stared once again at the letter and the DVD before putting them in his book bag. Whatever was on that DVD would have to wait until he got back to school. He checked to make sure he was leaving nothing behind

"Leaving so soon? You're not gonna stay to eat with us?" Trevor's mother asked as he reached the front door.

Trevor looked into her eyes. The eyes of the woman he assumed was his birth mother but was now unsure. Should he tell her about the letter and the DVD? He quickly decided against that.

"I actually just got a call from one of my teammates and he said there was going to be a team meeting at school tonight so I gotta head back a little early," Trevor replied.

His father who was already sitting at the kitchen table eating asked him, "So what was in that envelope?"

Trevor stared blankly at him as if he didn't understand what he asked.

"The envelope?" he asked. He thought about it for a moment before replying.

"Oh it's just a letter from one of the hotels that the team will be staying in. They wanted to confirm reservations and make sure I knew my way around things," Trevor lied.

His father thought about it for a moment. "All right son, have a safe trip and don't forget to call when you arrive," his father said.

Trevor agreed and walked over to the car with his backpack so he could drive back up to St. John's. As he waited at the light to enter the freeway under the Grand Conduit Parkway exit, he thought about the mysterious envelope. He felt guilty for lying to his parents but how did he know his parents were not lying to him all these years? What if the DVD somehow confirmed his suspicions that he had been adopted? If his biological parents were still alive, the couple who raised him, whom he had always called his parents, would have to tell him the truth.

Shania left home at about a quarter to eight the next morning. She was hoping Loree had already made it to school. Despite the many times she attempted to call Loree, she had not received a call back or any indication that Loree had received her phone call. A wave of fear started to manifest in Shania because Loree never ignored her calls. Although they had the huge argument a few days ago about David, Loree had forgiven Shania and it seemed all was fine between them.

Shania had received the news from Trevor that Loree was seen with a group of boys and she was sure one of them was Tadarius. Hearing that information set off all kinds of red lights in Shania's subconscious, because she knew Tadarius was a very dangerous character with a terrible street reputation and violent gang influence. The only way Loree could be hanging out with Tadarius is if she was doing some kind of favor or demand from him, like selling drugs or prostituting herself for money. She hoped she wasn't selling drugs and she really hoped Loree wasn't selling herself. Just the thought of it made Shania sick to her stomach.

As she approached school, she passed the same group of boys who did nothing but hang out in front of the school doors and front steps all day. She even noticed the boy who had made the track lane comment to her the other day. Shania made an attempt at hiding herself among the other kids entering the school. She didn't want him to notice her but unfortunately, he picked her out of the crowd.

"Aye what up Flo-Jo? Lemme got out your way so you can get inside this piece," the boy said stepping away from the door path. Noticing someone missing, the boy asked, "Yo, where the other shorty at? Big booty Judy?" referring to Loree.

"I don't even know. Did she come by ya'll yet?" Shania asked.

The boy looked at his friends and they all shook their heads. Shania could feel her spirits drop.

"Nah she ain't walk by yet. If I see her, I'll tell her you lookin' for her, iight?" the boy replied.

"Ok thanks," Shania said and then she went inside to get to her homeroom class.

Out of all the classes that Shania had, she only shared one class with Loree this semester and that was World History in the morning. However, Loree was nowhere to be found and Shania was really beginning to worry. It wasn't like Loree to miss a day of school without telling Shania why she was absent. She could only hope that David or Tadarius hadn't hurt her. When class finally let out, Shania walked to her locker and as she passed the attendance office, she saw Loree walking out with a small yellow slip; an excuse note. Fighting against a throng of kids heading in the opposite direction, Shania made it to her friend. When Loree saw her, she simply gave her a small smile and a head wave.

"Loree, what happened? You ain't checked your phone all day yesterday? I tried calling you and all I got was the machine. What's going on?" Shania asked.

"My bad Nia. I had a lot of studying this weekend and I just never got around to calling you back," Loree answered.

"Studying?" Shania retorted. "Loree you could stop frontin' on me and tell what's going on for real," she challenged.

Loree stared at Shania, a blank, confused expression on her face. "Girl, I have no idea what you're talking about," she replied.

Shania didn't understand why Loree was lying straight to her face like this. "Girl, please tell me that you weren't hangin' with that fool Tadarius on Sunday," Shania said.

A look of quiet shock registered on Loree's face and Shania caught it but it was fleeting and she resumed giving Shania the same expression of cluelessness and confusion. "Whoever told you I was rollin' with Tadarius?" she asked quizzically.

"Don't worry about who told me!" Shania exclaimed. "What are you involved in, Loree and is it something David put you up to?" she asked.

"No Shania, it ain't nothing like that. I was out shopping for some clothes, and I ran into Tadarius and some of his boys. Shania, you know what I was involved in and what I almost got myself into before," Loree said, referring to a time in her life when she slept around on a regular basis. Although Loree had publically denied any involvement in sex with multiple partners, only Shania knew how many men Loree had really been with in the past.

"I know what you were involved in Loree, but that ain't you anymore. You can't be going back to that same mess. You still ain't answered my next question though. Did David put you up to this?" she repeated.

Loree folded her arms in front of her. "Damn, Nia this ain't Jeopardy so you ain't gotta hit me with twenty-one questions. Why don't you mind your business and just keep out of mine?" Loree snapped and with that she turned her back on Shania and walked to her next class.

Shania just watched as Loree walked out of her room and showed the same level of concern for her. If Loree wasn't going to fight for her own life, then Shania would fight for her. Shania knew that Loree was a victim of her past and anyone, including David had the power to use Loree's past against her with blackmail, coercion, and even death. Shania decided she wasn't going to shoulder this burden on her own anymore. She would be going to the police before the situation got worse.

After school ended, a group of fifteen boys made their way to the school gym. Normally open gyms were held after school for a couple of hours so potential basketball players would have a chance to brush up on their skills and prepare for tryouts. On this day, Jamal and Omar decided to stay after school to participate in the open gym after getting permission from his own mother and from Dominique Keaton, who was Omar's mother. Once school finished, they headed toward the locker rooms to change into their shorts and t-shirts they had laid aside for the open gym. They followed the group of boys as they headed out onto the basketball court. The giant logo of the lion, which served as the school mascot, seemed to stare up at the boys as they started taking the basketballs from the rack that stood near the bleachers. Omar ran up to grab a good basketball and ran back to Jamal who practiced on one of the side goals. The gym had six baskets. There were the main basketball hoops which were the baskets that were utilized during the official games. Then there were four more side baskets which were used during physical education classes but were lifted through machinery to the rafters whenever the gym had any other spectator sporting events. However on this day, the side goals were kept low so that the boys could practice.

While Jamal and Omar worked on their jumpers and lay-ups, one of the other boys, Kevin Thomas, who was also in their freshman class called them over to the basket where he was practicing. He was challenged by some other boys to a three-on-three game and they needed 2 more players to round up the game. Kevin picked Omar and Jamal and as Jamal looked at who they would be playing. He gasped.

Wait this can't be right Jamal thought in horror. The other team had a big kid that could scrape a couple door frames. Jamal found out that the boy played on the Varsity basketball a year or two ago.

"Yo Jamal? You got big dude, right?" Omar asked as he ran to defend a player that was his size.

Jamal hated when Omar did this. Omar knew he couldn't defend anyone, so his option during these pick-ups games was to have Jamal guard the other team's best or tallest player. Jamal had good arm-wingspan length for his age but there could be no way that this guy was his age. He looked like he already graduated Richmond Hill and he came back for the fun of it. Jamal knew that he would be exposed defensively because the player he was guarding was about six-foot-five. Jamal was barely five-foot-eleven. He was going to get beaten. Sure enough that was the case and Jamal's team fell behind early and the big guy was having his way with Jamal in the paint. Jamal tried to front him and deny the ball but it seemed as if every pass would sail above Jamal's head and land in the hands of the big man who laid it up with Jamal all over him defensively. The big guy, whose name was Bill Charles, kept posting Jamal up just outside the paint and it proved to be a very poor mismatch.

After the opposing team rang up eight straight points, Jamal finally decided to let Kevin guard Bill and he began to play defense out on the wing, defending another opponent by the name of Alex McCray. Alex was a sophomore who had played on Richmond Hill's freshman team the previous year, so there was no question that he was good. But Jamal did his very best to guard Alex and followed an old defender's trick, which was to watch the player's waist. Never look directly at the player's dribble because by focusing too much on the dribble, the opposing player can make a quick first step and a quick crossover move that leaves a defender trailing. Jamal held his ground for a couple minutes, but Alex's speed and his stamina was beginning to wear Jamal out. Jamal started panting heavily like a winded dog. Alex, sensing weakness, started to jab at Jamal.

"What's wrong, freshman? You gettin' tired already?" he said while making fake heavy breaths, mocking Jamal.

Jamal's eyes creased in concentration, and he started to feel the silent rage coursing through him. Alex knew this and decided to exploit it. With his team up fourteen to three, Jamal knew he must seriously lock Alex down because the next point would win the game. Jamal checked the ball back to Alex at the top of the key. Bill and the other teammate shouted for the ball, but Jamal looked at Alex's eyes and saw that his intention was to take the last shot.

Ok, you ain't goin' nowhere. I got you this time. Jamal thought as Alex started to dribble toward the basket. Jamal had never needed water so badly in his life.

"Damn nigga, you breathing all hard and shit, lemme just drop this in your eye real quick," Alex leered as he began to make his maneuver.

He faked left but Jamal did not fall for the fake and stuck right on him. Alex measured the amount of separation between he and Jamal before squaring up and letting the jumper fly. Jamal jumped as high as his fatigued legs would let him and alter the shot but no such luck. The shot swished into the basket and some of the boys who had finished playing their pickup games and were watching the last few minutes of Jamal's game were celebrating and chest-bumping Alex.

I don't know what the big deal is. It's only a pick-up game. It ain't like we playing for real Jamal thought as he, Omar and Kevin slapped high fives with Bill and the other teammate. But Alex continued gloating.

"Who got next?" Alex shouted to some of the boys watching.

Jamal was then hit with a sudden inspiration of perseverance and redemption. "Play it back!" Jamal shouted over the voice of the other boys.

Kevin and Omar looked at him with surprised reactions. Did Jamal have a death wish?

"You mean you wanna replay them after they just handed our asses to us?" Omar asked.

Alex shook his head. "Nah, I need someone who's worth a challenge," he said.

Jamal was unrelenting in his demand for a rematch until someone stepped into the gym floor. He had been watching the boys play and was watching the last intense pick-up game that was about to get testy. Nate was off the clock since school ended and was headed to the locker room to change when he was stopped by the sight of the sport he loved so much. He watched and he saw the talent. All the boys were ok but none of them equaled Nate's talent. None of them had that fire; that drive to win. Watching Jamal demand a rematch at any cost was enough for Nate to know that he had the fire in the belly. He was not a quitter; not like he once was, walking away from the game before hitting his prime.

"Hey youngblood, hand me the rock," Nate said as he walked onto the court.

The kids looked at Nate, then looked at each other, their faces reddening with laughter. "The janitor?" They shouted with glee. This wasn't during school hours, and it wasn't as if they knew Nate from anywhere, so whenever a middle-aged black man walked up to ask to take a shot, the other boys saw nothing but immediate disaster and embarrassment. Not only were some of the boys taller than him but some were presumably in better shape than Nate. Unfortunately for the boys, they didn't know Nate's past. They had no idea that he once ruled the very courts they were playing on this very day. They did not know he held some of the school records for assists and steals. They were about to find out.

"Lemme see that real quick," Nate asked Alex who was holding the basketball while gloating.

"Bro, shouldn't you be somewhere mopping floors or something?" Alex asked.

When Nate held his hands out to catch the ball, Alex finally threw it to him, almost zipped it as if he expected Nate to be so old that his hand-eye coordination wouldn't be up to par but Nate caught the pass perfectly and firmly.

He started to dribble toward the half court line and took only a couple steps forward. Jamal and Omar were watching intently, wondering where this janitor was going to take his shot. When he squared up, Jamal looked at where he was standing. A couple of the boys continued laughing and scoffing, not projecting what was about to happen in the next few minutes. Nate was past the college three-point line, as a matter of fact he was past the NBA three-point regulation line too. Alex shook his head.

Nah, ain't no way you makin' this, man," he said.

Nate smiled and rolled his uniform sleeves up. He raised the ball in an almost-perfect motion and released the shot. The boys laughed, expecting an air-ball from someone so ancient, but at the next moment, everyone's laughter was silenced when the ball sailed right down the middle of the rim without touching it. The ball landed in Bill's hands, who looked as if he'd never seen a basketball in his life. Knowing the street rules of make-it, take-it, which demanded that if a basketball player made a basket, he would continue shooting until he missed. He passed the ball back to Nate, who shot the ball again, this time from a step backwards from where he originally shot the ball. Nothing but net again and suddenly the boys weren't laughing as much as they were before. Nate loved the silence of his critics when they said something about him on the court. It fired him up even more as a player.

He made four baskets in a row until Alex said, "Yeah, it's easy to do that when you ain't got nobody guarding yo' crusty old ass."

Nate looked at Alex, smirking.

"Why don't you guard my crusty old ass, then?" he retorted, tossing Alex the ball.

Alex was almost beside himself with laughter. "Hold up. You challenging me one-one one?" he asked.

"Did I stutter?" Nate replied, walking to the top of the key. Alex shook his head. This old guy had no idea who he was dealing with.

"I don't care if you can shoot from half-court man. I will shut you out. Game up to three only," Alex said among encouragement from his peers watching.

Alex checked him the ball. Nate began dribbling, his mind flashing back to his many high school opponents that he faced in the gym. Alex, who was a good defender, stuck with him and did everything that he could but Nate rose up and swished the first shot over him. 1-0. Nate took the ball out and began to show his handle. His opponents from Forest Hills, Cardozo, and Bayside were falling under the weight of their fatigue and his sudden change of direction.

"Yo come on Lex, stick him!" one of the boys shouted.

Jamal and Omar were still watching, although they really couldn't believe what was unfolding before their very eyes. Nate shot again. 2-0.

"I don't hear any laughing now," Nate said as Alex, now seething with anger and humiliation, threw the ball at him and started to play more aggressive defense on Nate, even hand-checking him a little bit.

Nate shook him off and blew by Alex and streaked toward the basket. What happened next, even Nate couldn't have predicted it. He dunked the ball with two hands, hanging on the rim for a second, before coming back down and handing the ball back to Alex.

"That's game, boy," he said as he headed towards the locker room.

Alex threw the ball at the other side of the gym in anger as he walked out of the gym with his friends who could only shake their heads in both sympathy and shock while Jamal and Omar walked toward the locker room to change and go home.

"Yo man, who was that janitor?" Omar could only look at him and shrug. There was nothing he or anyone else could say.

CHAPTER TEN

arlier that same day while the boys were in the gym, Shania walked out of her last period class to wait for Loree outside the school doors as the throng of high school kids rushed out to walk home or get to the nearest bus stop. But Loree did not appear and after fifteen minutes passed, Shania took out her cell phone and called Loree's cell phone. After a few rings, the call went straight to voicemail. Shania tried calling again but she still got Loree's voicemail. Where is she? Shania wondered as she started to walk the few blocks to her home. The noisy boys who normally sat on the steps of the school weren't there; not as if Shania cared but she did find it a little odd that they weren't at their usual perch. As she continued walking, she racked her brain trying to figure out where she was at fault in her friendship with Loree. One minute, everything was ok, then the next minute Loree had developed a short fuse in an even shorter period of time. During the course of their friendship, Shania and Loree had their normal share of arguments and disagreements. It was no different than any other friendship as far as Shania was concerned but the last couple of times they had argued, Loree had been extremely irritable to the point that Shania had feared the worst; their friendship was coming to an end. It was as if Loree was covering for someone. Shania didn't understand why Loree couldn't just be honest and tell telling Shania what was bothering her.

Shania remembered a very trying time in Loree's life when rumors circulated that Loree was considered a "cheap 'hoe" because of her supposed relationships with different boys. The stories about her flew high and fast and Loree, who was just a freshman at the time, was clearly affected by those rumors. For a while, she felt the stares of other girls on her and heard all the hushed whispers about her. Nobody stood up for Loree during that time in her life except Shania. Although Shania couldn't prove any of those rumors to be false, she stood by Loree and remained Loree's pillar at school. Loree would reveal to Shania that while she wasn't the "hoe" that everybody made her out to be, she did make a mistake by sleeping with a couple guys from school. They were not actions she was proud of and she wanted to make amends in her life and she confided that to Shania. They had been friends before but after consoling Loree about her mistakes, it drew them even closer than sisters. Shania, who was an only child, never had someone with whom she could laugh, cry, or understand her eccentricities as Loree did. It was as if the void she felt for having a sibling was filled by Loree. Although going to church and having a pastor for a father kept her rooted to the church, it was Loree who kept her down to earth.

As she walked, she heard a honking sound coming from behind her. At first, she didn't know who it was and didn't know if it was addressed to her but when the honking continued, she finally turned around to see who was honking at her.

"Yo baby, we gotta stop meeting like this," a voice said from inside a car. Trevor was driving his mother's old car in the neighborhood and spotted Shania walking alone and smiled as he said it.

Shania rolled her eyes, but she was smiling as well. "Don't you got class today?" she asked.

"Last class I had today was cancelled so I thought I'd stop by and pay a visit," Trevor replied as he slowed his car down to match the speed Shania was walking, even though it caused several drivers behind him to honk angrily and swear behind him as they shifted to the next lane to drive off. "So did you find yo' girl yet?" he asked.

Shania nodded. "I saw her today, but I don't know what's going on. It's like she didn't even wanna talk to me earlier today when I saw her and the next moment, she's gone. I tried calling her phone but no answer," Shania replied.

"Hopefully she's all right. It's too dangerous out here in these streets for a pretty girl like you to be walkin' by yourself. I can give you a ride to your place," Trevor offered, smiling.

"Thanks, but I'm a big girl now and I don't need any handouts," Shania replied.

As they approached an intersection, the traffic light facing them turned red, so Trevor came to a full stop. "All right I'm just offering. Check it, my boy back in St. John's got this house-warming party thing on Wednesday that he wanted me to come to. One catch though, I gotta find a date. You down?" he asked.

Shania shook her head. "Uh-uh. That wasn't part of the deal, remember? You gotta come to church on Sunday before I go on any dates with you," she quickly reminded Trevor.

"I know, I know. I'll keep up my end of the bargain. You'll see me getting my praise on Sunday morning. But when my boy told me to bring a date, I just thought I'd come by and see if you wanted to come," Trevor said seriously.

Shania thought it over. A college party with no chaperones she thought. "What, you couldn't get none of your groupies to go with you?" she asked.

"Well none of the other girls got what you got. Brains, beauty, and athleticism. Triple threat, baby," he said.

Shania looked closer at Trevor to see if he was just pulling her leg and playing around with her but for that split second, she saw the cocky, brash Trevor disappear and replacing him was another man; one more sensitive and gentler. The light had already turned green and drivers were angrily honking Trevor from behind him. One driver even pulled up to Trevor's side on the second free lane and shouted obscenities while flipping him the bird. Trevor ignored it, disregarded this, putting on his emergency lights so the other cars could pass him.

"Come on, Shania. What you got to lose? I'm being for real now. I think you fly and I ain't sayin' it just to be sayin' it, you feel me?" Trevor asked. He didn't know why he was telling Shania all of this. He had dated a lot of girls in high school but he never had the courage to tell any of them how he really felt about them. He always found it difficult to open up to girls, especially when he knew they only liked him for his physique and the fact that he was an athlete. He swore he would never tell any girl that he loved her. Love was such a strong emotion and strong emotions led to attachments which led to commitments which led to wedding bells and Trevor was nowhere near ready to get married to anyone. At the same time, this girl Shania did something to him. She was real. She was down to earth. She was not impressed by his stature or his name. He didn't know or understand why he felt so drawn to her. Maybe it was just the challenge of impressing her. Trevor was never one to back down from a challenge.

"Well I don't know. I mean I be watching how crazy these college parties get. Drinking, pot-smokin', and girls everywhere half naked, I don't know if I'll be feelin' all that," Shania replied.

"You ain't gotta do none of that stuff," Trevor reassured her. "It's just a little get together at my boy's crib. I'm just gonna introduce you to some of my brothers from the squad. If you ain't wit' it, I'll drive you straight home, no questions asked," he added.

Shania thought about it. It sounded like a pretty good plan right now and with the way her life had been going lately with school and practicing for track along with her drama with Loree, she needed to get her mind off of all of it for just one night. She knew there was a huge obstacle blocking the confirmation of her plans: her father. Not only was it a school night but she was absolutely sure her father would forbid her from going to a college party, especially if she was going with another boy.

"Ok, but you know you gonna have to make up a story for where I'm going when you pick me up from my house," she replied.

Trevor wondered why Shania's father would have a problem, until he remembered that Shania's father was a pastor at the church near Lefferts Blvd. So he knew he was going to have to convince her father that he was dependable enough to take care of his daughter and bring her back home safely. Trevor balked internally at the proposition of meeting her father. When he had dated high school girls, he would always have to pick them up from their homes and each time he did, he was met by a father who had that cold look on his eyes that said, So YOU'RE taking my daughter out, huh? You better make sure on your damn life that nothing happens to her or you can kiss your career goodbye." Of course, the fathers had never said any of that out loud but the looks said it all. If looks could kill, Trevor's body would be riddled with bullets from all the other past dates. So he knew Shania was right and they needed to play it safe.

"Ok, I'll tell him that I'm taking you to get a bite to eat, then we'll go to a movie. Sean's party don't start till nine so we could just make a stop and just chill for a few minutes, and I'll get you home. Is that ok?" Trevor asked Shania.

Shania just shrugged at him. "It's the best plan that I could think of right now but don't think I'm gonna make a habit out of lying to my daddy, cuz I don't like to do it," she answered. Shania knew she would have to pray for some serious forgiveness when it was all said and done. Not only was she lying to her father, but she was lying to the Lord. She didn't know what she was getting into, and she could already feel the pangs of guilt stab at her, but she was going to listen to Loree for once. No more sitting on the sidelines and continue shutting everyone out. She was going to have fun and let loose because it seemed that everyone, including Loree, seemed too upset or preoccupied with their own problems to worry about her. Her father had not yet embraced her individuality as a woman. Robyn had, but only to a certain degree. None of them understood what it was like to be in high school or college today, especially her parents. "Ok, pick me up at seven. If my dad answers the door, then just sit politely on the couch and answer the questions that he is bound to ask you. I'm sorry that I'm warning you about this but knowing my father, he ain't gonna take no chances," she said.

"It's all right. He hasn't met me yet. I'll turn him into a believer, trust me."

Good luck. You're gonna need it. I'll be prayin' for you boy Shania thought. She didn't say that out loud, but on the inside, Shania knew the plan they had would have to be enough and they would have to be careful. Trevor agreed to the plan and drove off, turning at the next intersection.

Isis walked out of her bedroom into her kitchen Wednesday morning. Walking to the counter that she had every intention of replacing, she walked over to the coffee maker she had received as a gift the previous Christmas. Brewing herself a cup, she sat down at her kitchen table and blew into the cup before taking a sip. Facing the double-barred window reflecting back at her, she took in the view of the bustling people and cars filled with people on their way to work. She didn't remember the last time she had a quiet morning like this. Normally she would be on her way to work at Jamaica's African Queens Beauty Salon, located on Jamaica Avenue, about a block away from Jamaica Coliseum which was a stretch of three blocks that had a series of shops, outlet stores and restaurants lined down a street paved with red brick. Sometimes performers or famous artists would make appearances and entertain the throng of people shopping in the Coliseum. The beauty shop was regarded as one of the most popular places on Jamaica Avenue. Business was never slow, as women from every corner of the borough came to African Queens Beauty Salon for signature hair styles and discounted weaves. It had become more than just a hair salon; it was a hangout spot for women where they felt liberated and could speak whatever was on their minds. Subjects would often get a little risqué at times when many of the clients and stylists talked about men, favorite foods they cooked, men, favorite television shows, men, and favorite guilty pleasures (that included men) Isis loved working at the salon, it was a way for her to get her mind off of her ex-husband and mingle with similar strong-minded women. Her manager, Karina Stacy, was a laid back middle-aged black woman who acted less like a manager and more like one of the clients. Her attitude made it easier for her to excuse Isis for one morning; especially since Isis had planned to assist Pastor Hillman and his fellow contractor measure out the length of the marble counter she was planning to replace. Isis promised to arrive at work as soon as she could and would work until closing time to make up for rescheduling some of her client's appointments. Jamal already left for school. She was very proud of him and impressed by how much Jamal had grown. Sometimes she would think how despicable it was that Robert, Jamal's father, was not present in Jamal's life. He rarely even called to see if the family was doing ok. Mike Hillman had been more of a father to Jamal than Robert had ever been. His church, the ministry, and his encouragement of Jamal's age group and demographic meant the world to Isis. Robert's small mind believed that Jamal would be stronger without his father's involvement. He couldn't be more wrong. Boys who were Jamal's age needed a father because the early teen years were when peer pressures, temptations, and mixed emotions played such a pivotal role in their lives. Isis could only play the role of mother and father for so long because she couldn't teach Jamal how to be a man. That took a courageous, confident, well put together man who admitted to having flaws of his own to pave that road for him. No one came closer to that image than Pastor Mike. She also gave thanks to the Lord because only He knew what kind of trouble Jamal would get himself into if he didn't have that strong church support system and fellowship. Finally, she heard a couple of knocks at her door. Looking through the fisheye in the door, she saw it was Mike and his co-worker. She unlocked her door, top and bottom, and undid the little chain that connected the door to its post before opening it.

"Hello, guys. Thank you so much for coming again," Isis greeted them as they walked in with the folder of their marble samples and their measuring yardsticks to determine how much marble they would need to re-surface the counter.

"Thanks, Sister Samuels I promise this will not take long. Jerry and I will just measure out the length of your counter, then we'll discuss what countertop you want to use before giving you the final price run," Mike said as he walked to the kitchen with Jerry.

Isis followed them. "Can I get you guys something to drink? Coffee, maybe?" she offered.

"Yes, that would be wonderful. Thank you," Mike said as he took out his measuring kit with Jerry to prepare to measure the counter.

Isis went to her coffee maker and placed it on the kitchen table as she plugged it in an extra outlet. Mike and Jerry helped clear the kitchen counter so they could get a clear measurement. Mike took the measuring tape and bent down and asked Jerry to hold one end of the tape. While the men worked, Isis knew she should be focusing her attention on which one of the patterns she wanted to use for her countertop, but she found herself focusing elsewhere. Isis had never realized it before, but Mike was actually quite well built. Dressed in a work T-shirt and some fitted jeans and work boots, she realized how broad his shoulders were and how strong his hands were. It was never easy to see those physical aspects of him on Sundays because he wore a suit that covered his physique. Besides, her mind wouldn't be focused on his body at church. Yet in this setting she saw a big, brawny, brown model of manliness. Isis was actually a little jealous of Robyn. She not only had a man who loved the Lord and loved serving his community but she had a man who was a strong father and a great husband. She often found herself wishing she had a man who resembled Mike. She continued to pray about it and let God work but it was difficult to turn away from the Greek god-like man who was measuring in her kitchen and she was not referring to Jerry, who looked ok but was nowhere near the physical prowess of Mike Hillman.

He had to have played some kind of sport in high school like basketball or football Isis thought. A man couldn't be that well-built without playing sports or lifting weights. Either way, Isis found herself envying Robyn more and more by the minute. If Mike ever walked by the salon or in the salon, he would probably be surrounded by twenty of the thirty women there. She needed to keep Mike to herself. What are you doing, Isis? The man is married and you over here sweating him like he your man. Put your eyes back in your head Isis told herself internally as Mike continued measuring the counter.

She had to be careful not to make it so obvious that she was watching Mike because she risked getting found out by Jerry and no doubt Jerry would not withhold that information from Mike, who would probably think she was crazy and would keep his distance. It wasn't as if Robert hadn't looked good or hadn't been a gentleman, but he never had Mike's physique and if he did he would probably flaunt it incessantly. Mike was extremely humble and did not like to brag about his physical strength. Finally Mike stood up and rolled his ruler tape measure back up.

"Ok, so looking at the dimensions here, your countertop is twenty-three inches high with a depth of about eighteen inches, so it's not too bad to work with," he said.

"Great! So how long do you think the process will take?" Isis asked.

"It actually shouldn't take long. We should be able to get this done in two days for you, which won't result in too much delay in your normal kitchen activities with you and your son," he replied.

Isis led them to the small living room where he opened his binder with the different countertop samples. Isis stared at the samples that he and Jerry laid out before her. There are so many to choose from she thought. Finally Isis went with the synthetic solid countertop as she felt that it would blend with the current silver/gray background of the kitchen. After Mike gave her the price for the job, she agreed to the terms and created a payment plan. Mike informed her that he would schedule the workers on Friday morning. Isis looked at the clock that hung just above her kitchen doorway.

"Wow, I really need to be getting ready for work. Thank you guys so much," Isis said as she walked Jerry and Mike to the door.

"No problem, sister," Mike replied. "By the way, can I expect to see you at service this Sunday?" he asked with a sly smile.

Isis rolled her eyes. "Of course, pastor. I would have to be dead before I don't attend service. I'll see you there," Isis laughed as she closed the door behind them before she went to put on her work clothes.

The bell rang at Richmond Hill High school, signaling the end of third period. Students filed noisily out of classes to head to their lockers or talk to friends in the hallway. Jamal and Omar emerged from world geography class with sullen faces. Their teacher, Mr. Barker, had just assigned a report on the growth and developmental culture of Western Europe. Along with the usual workload their math teacher gave them, it made for a stressful day.

"Yo, but for real, what's up with Barker?" Omar asked Jamal in frustration as soon as they were a safe distance away from Mr. Barker's classroom.

"I don't even know, son. I got so much damn homework, I don't even know when I'm gonna be able to ball," Jamal said and shrugged.

"Speaking of that, did you ever hear from Alex? I swear dude's been running scared since that janitor did him up," Omar said laughing. Jamal laughed as well.

This rumor was true, however. Alex, who had been slated to make the varsity team, had been beaten on the court by a school janitor and that news had spread quickly. The word was that Alex never heard the end of it from his friends and fellow teammates who had spoken endlessly about it. Even his teachers would jokingly mention it at random points in the class. Alex tried to laugh it off, but the more people talked about it, the more his frustration grew. Alex was known to shoot off at the mouth and brag about his basketball skills, so he was perceived as being arrogant by those who knew him.

"That's what he gets for talkin' so much crap," Jamal replied.

While walking through the hall, they passed the corridor where the lunchroom was located. The janitor was there replacing the trash bag in one of the large trash containers in the cafeteria. Jamal looked at him. He didn't get it. This guy was slightly tall and, based on what he saw Monday afternoon, strong and athletic.

"Come on," he gestured to Omar while walking to the cafeteria. Omar shot Jamal a quizzical look. They needed to get to their next period before the bell rang but he followed Jamal to the cafeteria. Nate had just finished replacing the trash bags in each of the containers in the cafeteria. Now he had to do his normal bathroom evaluations before lunch, but he looked up and saw two boys walking towards him.

Not again Nate thought. For the past two days since he had humbled that high school player on the court, he had been bombarded by high school students who either wanted to know who the "ballin' janitor" was or to get pointers from him about their game. This was not his plan. He began to regret playing against that kid now. When he looked closer, he saw it was the boy who had been chastised by the aggressive ball player who he challenged with his friend.

"Hey sir. I don't know if you remember me, but I never got a chance to tell you how nice you was on the court Monday," Jamal said.

Nate laughed. "Appreciate it, youngblood," he replied.

Jamal stood there in silence, not knowing what to say next. Fortunately Omar asked the very question that was on Jamal's mind.

"How'd you know how to ball like that?" he asked.

Nate smiled. "Well I just picked up a few tricks from playing in the streets. No big deal," he said and shrugged as he began walking to the custodial closet.

Jamal and Omar followed. "Did you used to play in high school or something?" Jamal asked, but by that time, to Nate's relief, they reached the custodial closet where no one except for authorized personnel could enter.

"Sorry fellas, I got a lot of work to do. Maybe we'll talk again some other time. Ya should hurry up on to class before the late bell," Nate said before closing the door behind him.

Jamal took one look at Omar. The hallway was emptying with kids filing into their classrooms. They both took off running, not wanting to be tardy. As they approached their Sociology class, Patricia came from the opposite direction with another girl who Jamal remembered seeing in his math class, but he didn't know her name. Omar, however, knew the girl's name, which was Tania Goodwell. The only reason he knew was because he has tried to work up the nerve to talk to her, but he didn't know how to approach her on his own. Sociology was the only class that the four teens shared together.

Jamal had no idea how Omar felt about Tania and Omar hoped it would stay that way. Omar didn't want to be ridiculed for his lack of savvy with girls. There was a natural way Jamal spoke to girls, not shy or overbearing but relaxed in his approach. Omar was pretty sure Patricia knew Jamal's reputation because when Jamal wasn't paying attention during class, Patricia would stare at Jamal for several minutes. She sat two seats to his right and Omar sat 3 seats away from Jamal, so he watched what was going on. Patricia liked Jamal but Jamal was oblivious to Patricia and her feelings towards him. Omar couldn't understand it. Jamal had the luxury of having one of the most beautiful girls in the freshman class check him out and he didn't even know it. But Omar was not about to put Jamal on the spot because Jamal was doing him a favor by not telling the whole world he was pursuing Tania. On this day, Patricia had some news.

"What's up Omar?" Patricia said in greeting. Then when she saw Jamal, her voice softened. "Hey Jamal, I heard that Jamaica Lanes has a Bowl for Five day today. You free tonight?" she asked.

Jamal thought about it. Jamaica Lanes was the bowling alley located right by the movie theater on the corner of 160th Street and Parsons Ave. He wasn't sure if his mother would let him go. Not only was it a school night but everyone knew that Jamaica Avenue was not a safe place to be at night. Although Jamal's mother worked there during the day, she never liked staying there until nightfall and tried fervently to get home before dark. On the other hand Jamal thought of the opportunities; a night away from homework, school, bullies from the basketball team, and most importantly, a potential date with Patricia could be the start of a relationship. She could see that he wasn't the bumbling klutz assumed by everyone else on the court.

"Cool, I can meet you there about six o'clock. Is that, ok?" he asked. He wanted to be sure because he knew if he met them by six, he would ensure there would at least be a little more sunlight out there before it got dark.

"Yeah, that's cool. Tania and Theresa will be coming too," Patricia replied. Upon hearing this, Jamal's heart sank. He had half-hoped that this would be an exclusive event and that he would spend more time getting to know Patricia.

"Yeah, that's ok, as long as Omar rolls with us too," Jamal added. Patricia rolled her eyes jokingly, but she did agree that Omar could join them. They both looked at Omar who was already seated at his desk and pulling out his books for class. Patricia leaned closer to Jamal, so close that he could smell the sweet lotion on her face she had just applied. It was clear that whatever she was telling Jamal, she did not want anyone else to know.

"Ok, I'm tellin you this straight up. Tania likes Omar but she too nervous to talk to him. She told me this in confidence, so don't be runnin' your mouth to your boy about this. I'm still tryin' to make sure her head on straight cuz she be trippin," she whispered to Jamal. Jamal laughed a little bit. He always thought there might have been something there but he really didn't think too much of it. "I'm serious Jamal. Don't tell him nothin'. I don't think I was even supposed to tell you about it. Hopefully if all goes well tonight, she'll tell him what's up," she said.

Jamal raised an eyebrow. "So what's up with you and me?" he replied with a sly smile.

Patricia laughed and playfully hits him on the shoulder. "Shut your thirsty ass up. You'll never find out what's up," she replied before heading to her seat a couple rows to Jamal's right side.

Jamal joined Omar at his desk. "So what was she whispering to you, dog?" Omar asked.

Jamal just shrugged. "Nothing. Just some bowling thing she wanted me to go with her on," he replied.

Omar nodded his head, smiling. "You mean a date? That's my boy," he said, grinning slyly.

"Not really," Jamal answered. "See she's bringing a couple of her friends over so I thought I would bring my boy along. You ain't busy tonight, right?" Jamal asked.

"Damn son, on a school night? I don't know how I'm gonna swing that," Omar replied.

"Well, I know how you gonna swing it. You're gonna go and meet me and a couple of girls there," Jamal said.

"Did you say a couple girls?" Omar asked. When Jamal nodded his head in agreement and confirmed the event, Omar said, "My schedule just cleared up," he said with a smile.

CHAPTER ELEVEN

After school let out on Wednesday afternoon, Shania waited outside the school steps as she normally did for Loree but as long as Shania waited, Lorie never walked out of the school's double doors. Shania had continuously attempted to call Loree's cell phone number but was still unable to reach her. Shania was at the point of desperation. She knew the habits and the tendencies of her best friend. She also knew about the moral weaknesses that plagued Loree throughout her life. Shania's greatest fear was that Loree would be tempted to go back to her old ways of doing favors for boys with whom she had no business associating. Earlier in the day, Shania even asked David about Loree's whereabouts but to her surprise, David was just as clueless as to Loree's whereabouts. She also thought he was a bit defensive, which frightened Shania even more.

"How should…., where the hell she at?" he replied angrily. "She broke up with me Monday. She said she couldn't see me anymore because of what she did in the past and she needed some time alone," he added.

Shania didn't believe a word that had come out of David's mouth. "You guys broke up? She never told me that. I thought you guys were still together," Shania replied.

Although she had advised Loree against dating David and prayed for their eventual separation, this was particularly sudden. "Look I never wanted it to go down that way. Unlike the other dudes she done been with, I thought me and her had something, but I guess I'm wrong," he said, shrugging before walking away from his locker, leaving Shania.

There she was, waiting for Loree to walk down the steps so they could apologize to each other and move on to some semblance of normality when out walked Loree's friend and track teammate Lisa Chen.

"Hey girl, what's up?" she asked Shania.

"Lisa, I don't even know anymore. Have you seen or spoken to Loree today?" Shania asked in exasperation.

Lisa shook her head. "I haven't seen her all day. I heard that you got into it with her the other day in the hallway. I hope nothing is wrong," she said.

"I don't even know anymore," Shania said with a sigh. "We did get into a bit of an argument because she practically lied about what she was doing Sunday. I thought she was at home, but I found out that she's been hanging around with Tadarius," she added.

Lisa gave a little gasp. "Tadarius? That boy is cracked, Shania. Everyone knows that he's crazy. I hope Loree isn't with him now," she said.

"I don't know though. After all, we know how fragile Loree is when it comes to these roughnecks out here, but sometimes she acts like she knows it all when she really doesn't," Shania replied in anger. She felt so upset that she felt a lump starting to form in her throat and her eyes watering. She feared it was her overprotection that pushed Loree into Tadarius's arms. Lisa came and patted Shania's shoulder.

"Shania, I know what you mean and how you feel. Loree's my friend too and I can't even bear to think what could have happened to her. But we can't live her life for her. She has to make the decision to get out of the situation she's in," she said.

Shania turned to her. "What if she's incapable of getting out on her own?" she asked.

Lisa shrugged. Shania walked Lisa over to her bus stop and offered to stay with her until the bus came. "Do her parents know she's been skipping school?" she asked.

Shania wasn't sure if they knew or not but if she knew anything about Loree's parents, she knew they would be mortified if they found out their daughter was skipping school. "No I don't think they know and I really want to tell them, but she wants me to butt out," she answered.

"Even if their daughter's life is in serious danger?" Lisa blurted.

Shania thought about it. She really should tell Loree's parents but what if Loree had a perfectly good reason for not being in school? What if there her phone was broken and she just couldn't return her calls? Every time she has overreacted to any of Loree's situations, it drove them further and further apart. Besides she had somewhere to go that night. "I will see her parents but maybe tonight. I got this...thing I gotta go to," Shania said.

She had promised Trevor that she would go with him to the party, and she did not want to break her promise. Lisa didn't know about her plans with Trevor but somehow, the look on her face was one of genuine concern.

"Ok, but afterwards I would call her parents just to make sure she's ok," Lisa said.

Just then the bus turned around the corner and rumbled its way towards the bus stop where Shania and Lisa were standing.

"Ok I'll call her parents as soon as I can," Shania said.

As the bus pulled up next to them, Shania gave Lisa a hug before she got on the bus. Shania began to walk the few blocks to her house, still thinking of what she was going to do. She found that she wasn't in a very festive mood and had half a mind to call Trevor and let him know that she wouldn't be able to make it after all. Then she remembered what Loree had said a couple weeks ago about putting herself in the game when it came to dating. Looking at it from a peripheral point of view, she shouldn't be attracted to a guy like Trevor. The guy was so brash, overconfident, and full of himself that it made her sick. But there was another side she noticed about him and maybe she was a little crazy for seeing it but she noticed sensitivity in Trevor that she had never seen in other guys. He had shown concern for Loree even though he didn't know her very well and he had acted like a gentleman when he drove back to ask her to the party instead of bragging that he was going to take her, like most guys tried to do. She took mental notes and although they weren't much to go on, they were enough to at least give him a chance at impressing her. Wherever Loree was, she was sure she was fine. After all, Loree was the one who had told Shania that she could take care of herself. If she wanted to go out and have what she defines as fun without her, why couldn't Shania have fun too? Two can play this game, she thought as she walked home.

Several blocks west of Lefferts Boulevard on the other side of 101 Avenue near Briarwood and Hillside Avenue, Tadarius and his companion, Terrance Stone, sat in a Toyota Camry. Parked in a secluded area near a deserted parking lot and some abandoned buildings facing a dark alley, the two gang members had been counting money that was earned through alcohol and drug selling. The Camry was old, and the paint was rusted on it. Stolen from a businessman who worked near Cambria Heights, the car had been reported stolen to the NYPD the previous week and the police were looking for the car, based on its license plate and color description. Thanks to one of Tadarius's followers who worked part-time at an auto shop in Astoria, Queens the car looked aged, and the license plate was removed and replaced with a fake temporary license until Tadarius could replace it with a more legitimate license. Eventually they would give the car a good paint job to throw off the police indefinitely but at the moment Tadarius and Terrance had more pressing matters to talk about.

After receiving more sexual favors from the "school hoe" as Tadarius often liked to address Loree, he was thinking about what to do next. The previous session hadn't gone well. The girl had tried to escape and had threatened to call the police, but Tadarius's comrades were able to suppress her and led her back to one of the buildings where his members lived and held her hostage. Her phone was out of battery power, so no matter how many times friends and family tried to call her there was no way anyone could reach her. As she sat there under the surveillance of the other gang members who sat around smoking, drinking, and playing cards, Tadarius started to plot his next move inside the car.

"That bitch damn near bit my dick off and she thought her ass would get away with it," he said angrily.

Terrance, who finished counting the profits of their day, looked at Tadarius. "So what you gon do? You gonna let that bitch walk?" he asked.

"I ain't got no choice, son. My ass already been in juvey and upstate. I ain't tryin to go back to the pen. I ain't got no choice but to let her ass walk," Tadarius replied. As much as he did not want to go back to prison, it was almost certain that he would be returning there because he was sure the girl was going to open her mouth and expose them all to the police. He knew he didn't have any alternative.

Terrance looked at Tadarius. "Nigga, if we let her go, all our asses gonna be thrown back in the pen," Terrance said.

Tadarius thought about it. He knew Terrance was right. As long as the girlfriend of his stupid quarterback friend David was still alive, their own lives could be over in a matter of days because there was no doubt that she would report not only the crimes committed against her but every other crime she knew about.

"Light me an L," Tadarius asked as Terrance reached over to the back seat to grab a small shoe box. Opening the shoe box, there was still some marijuana in there. Terrance rolled up a blunt and lit it before giving one to Tadarius.

"Good lookin' out dog," he said as they both puffed in silence for about seven minutes.

What was he going to do? With prior offenses on his record, Tadarius knew he could not afford to be convicted of any more crimes. Forget about murder. If he even stole a chocolate bar from the corner store and got caught, he knew he would be looking at least eight to ten years in federal prison just for his past record. He would have to get rid of her but somebody else would have to do the job. He couldn't afford any blood on his hands. As he smoked his marijuana, Tadarius turned to Terrance. He had an idea.

"Ok, so here's how it's gon' be. Have da crew take her out to eat. I don't care where it is. Just take her somewhere away from 101. Bring two of our homeboys and have 'em strapped. This is their first test. After she's finished eating, take her to the outskirts and waste her. Make sho' the gatt ain't got ya fingerprints on it. After you finish, make sure ya come back ASAP. Don't give five-oh any clues or evidence. It gotta be a clean hit, in and out. You feel me?" Tadarius instructed.

Terrance nodded in agreement. As the smoke from their joints filled the inside of the car, Terrance asked, "What about her man and the home girl she be hangin' with?"

Tadarius made a sound that resembled the sucking of teeth. "You mean Mr. Heisman and Ms. Decathalon? Nah leave 'em alone for now. Besides, that ole hulk-lookin' nigga don't know shit about her and neither does her home girl," he said. "But this hoe saw the whole operation and she dissed us. She got too much information and if she gets to the cops, it's lights out and game over for us. I ain't worked my ass off this long to lose what I built. I still run this shit. I needa protect my rep and send a message. Get Antonio and Terrell in here so I can let em know what it is right quick," Tadarius added.

As Terrance started to get out of the car, he turned back to Tadarius. "You sho' bout this, dog?" he asked.

"Hell yeah. People die in the streets every day. She was just in the wrong place at the wrong time. They know what it is. Now get them two lil niggas in here so I let em know what time it is," he demanded as Terrance closed the door. That's the way it's gotta be. Never trust nobody. You the only one that got your own damn back, he thought as he rolled his window down and let the smoke out.

"I don't like it. Not one bit," Mike said as he paced back and forth in his room while Robyn took her shoes after just arriving home from work.

"Honey, she's just going on one date and it's the movies. I don't see what the huge deal is," Robyn replied.

Mike was reacting to Shania telling him that she was going out to the movies with a boy. This did not bode well with Mike at all because he was always of the mindset that girls should not look to date or pursue any type of serious relationship until they completed high school. It wasn't because he didn't trust Shania, it was because he never trusted the boys. They should have been regarded as young men who could act responsibly and be mature in their everyday decisions but what he witnessed every day were not young, upstanding gentlemen but immature boys who sagged their pants so low that you could see what color underwear they wore. They were boys who acted purely on impulse rather than thinking before they acted. That was the danger with this generation and Mike did his best to advise Shania to be strong and wait until she accomplished her high school goals before she dated and even if she was in college, not to look too much into dating until she met the man who would be the one for her. Shania may not agree with his views immediately but someday she would thank him for it. When he was told that a boy wanted to take his daughter out on a date, Robyn and Shania conspired against Mike in his own home.

"Robyn, I have half a mind to tell Shania to call this thing off. I can't believe you're agreeing with this nonsense. Did she even tell you his name?" Mike asked.

"Not yet but Shania speaks very highly of him. He doesn't sound like a bad guy," Robyn replied. "Besides he's coming here to pick her up. It's not like she's meeting him somewhere. At least we'll know who he is," Robyn added but it still wasn't good enough for Mike.

"I don't care who he is. Robyn, all boys are after one thing in girls and it sure ain't the perfume they wear," Mike said. He walked toward his room door. "Where is Shania now?" Mike asked looking out across the hallway.

Shania's door was locked. "She's getting ready for her date tonight. So how was your appointment with Mrs. Samuels?" Robyn asked randomly, catching Mike off guard. Mike found himself searching for words to say. His mind was still trying to grasp the fact that his daughter was going on a date for the first time.

"The appointment was ok. We're scheduled to start working next week. But that still doesn't make me feel better about all this. As a matter of fact, I...." Mike started but then he heard his doorbell ring.

"Daddy, it's him. Can you get the door for me and let him know that I'll be out in three minutes?" Shania said from inside the room.

Grudgingly, Mike walked down the hall and walked downstairs to answer the front door. As soon as he opened the door, he saw a tall young man dressed in a Polo shirt and casual jeans with new sneakers.

"Hello sir, my name's Trevor McClain. I'm here to take Shania to the movies. How are you?" he greeted with his most winning smile.

Trevor held out his hand to shake Mike's hand. Reluctantly Mike shook his hand and while he shook Trevor's hand, he looked into Trevor's eyes. Trevor's eyes were sincere, yet there was a smug, confident look about his brown eyes that reminded Mike of someone. It was as if he was looking at the ghost of someone he hadn't seen in a long time. He saw her again. The smug look she gave him when she was in his arms many years ago but was secretly sleeping with one of his friends behind his back. He saw Nina Martin again. He didn't know why this boy reminded him of her. This boy might not have had anything to do with her at all and maybe he was going off the deep end. Maybe he was suffering a mid-life crisis. During his introspection, Shania emerged from her room, dressed in a small college t-shirt and jeans with high-top sneakers of her own.

"Daddy, you didn't even invite Trevor to sit down?" Shania asked, snapping Mike out of his thoughts.

"It's ok, really. I don't want to impose," Trevor replied.

You are imposing enough by taking my daughter out Mike thought.

Robyn came into the room with a smile on her face. "Hello, Trevor. I'm Robyn, Shania's mom. How are you?" she greeted, shaking Trevor's hand.

"I'm doing good, Mrs. Hillman," Trevor replied. "I promise I'll bring her back right after the movie ends tonight," he added, looking at Mike.

"Ok son, I'll take your word for it. Make sure you take care of my little girl. If you get into any trouble, I want to be your primary point of contact," he added, although Trevor was sure that he was addressing his daughter rather than him.

Walking out of the door, Shania said goodbye to her parents and Trevor opened the passenger side of the car, letting Shania enter in his car before closing the door for her. Mike watched as Trevor entered his car through the driver side. As they backed out of the driveway, Mike watched them. Robyn walked up beside Mike.

"Oh Mike, stop worrying. She'll be fine. God's watching over them both. If there's anything I know, it's that we raised our daughter right," Robyn said.

It was true. Mike was worried and he knew that fear was nothing more than an emotion brought on by the spirit of discouragement but that wasn't all that was bothering Mike. The strong resemblance that Trevor had to his ex-girlfriend from high school was uncanny. Everything from his complexion to his eyes to the confident way he carried himself reminded him of Nina. Then again, it could be him thinking too deeply into it. After all, Mike wasn't looking to re-open old wounds from the past. He was a different man from that time and the boy who had once Nina dated was nowhere close to the man he was today. It was only after he returned back home from Nyack that he learned Nina had passed away, having been a victim of gang violence. Hearing such news was so unsettling for him that he almost didn't move back near 101 Avenue. Despite his fear, God had given him a heart to give back to his community and to change lives. In order for him to lead his flock, he had to think beyond himself.

"Your parents are cool. They ain't as bad as you make 'em out to be," Trevor said to Shania, laughing as he drove the highway to get to St. John's University campus.

"Yeah I love them, but you know they was frontin' for you, right? They're not always this nice," Shania replied.

"I beg to differ. They seem laid back. Especially your dad. Didn't you say that he was a pastor? If you never told me that, I wouldn't have believed it," Trevor said.

Shania looked at him. "Really?" she asked.

Trevor looked at her for a split second before turning his eyes toward the road. "Yeah, for real. He's kinda big too. Did he used to play sports back in da day?" he asked.

"Yeah he used to play football for Richmond Hill. He was the quarterback back in the late seventies and early eighties," she answered.

"What happened?" Trevor asked.

"What you mean, what happened?" Shania repeated back to Trevor.

"I mean, a dude as big as your father probably had a ton of scouts coming after him. He probably could've gone pro," Trevor replied as they passed under a bridge overpass.

"Maybe, but he had a different calling. Sometimes when God calls you to do something for others, you gotta listen to what He's saying too," Shania responded.

Trevor shook his head. He was sure being a pastor was great and all but this was a man with immense talent that passed up playing in college football and the professional league. To Trevor, that was guaranteed money and financial security for life. He couldn't see himself passing up the opportunity to possibly go pro, even when it came to church.

"Doesn't he ever regret not playing professional football? He could've set your whole fam for life," Trevor said.

"Maybe, but he wouldn't have been happy. He always said the best decision he ever made was becoming a born-again Christian. That was more important to him," Shania replied.

Born again? Trevor tried to make sense of the words that were coming out of Shania's mouth. How can someone be born again? Unless science and evidence was wrong, a person could only be born one time, live life, and die.

"So what do your parents do?" Shania asked.

"They're both doctors at Long Island Jewish Hospital. Neither of them really had an athletic bone in their body," Trevor replied. If you ever need an operation done in your brain or something, they got you," he added. As they approached the campus, they looked for parking and as soon as they parked their car they stepped out to look for Sean Wilson's dorm hall.

"What took you guys so long?" Patricia asked Jamal and Omar as they made their way inside the crowded bowling alley.

Jamal easily had the answer to that question. First and foremost was getting permission from his mother. Isis Samuels debated on whether she would let her son go to the bowling alley with his friends because she did not trust Jamaica Avenue after dark because even though the streetlights came on, other characters came out. Isis and Jamal argued for the next five minutes before she finally gave in and let him go as long as he and Omar came straight home. With the remainder of the allowance money Jamal had left for the week, he and Omar pooled up their money, took a Q9 city bus which dropped them off about a block away from the bowling alley. When they paid the discounted amount to enter the bowling alley, they were confronted by Patricia and Tania, who waved at Omar, batting her eyelashes. Omar waved back as Jamal stared at the two of them.

"We were about to start without you two," Patricia continued as they walked over to the counter to get their shoe rental to get their bowling shoes.

"So how many times have you gone bowling?" Tania asked Jamal and Omar, although it was clear that she was talking to Omar.

"Well I've been bowling for a couple years now. I'm still working on that perfect game," Omar replied before Jamal could even get a word in.

Jamal looked at his friend. When and how long have you been bowling? he asked himself. Jamal didn't know much about Omar's bowling skills but the one time he went with him in middle school, he must have rolled at least ten gutter balls. There was no way he knew bowling as much as he bragged. He's frontin' for Tania. My boy's got it bad Jamal thought with a shake of his head as they went to their bowling lanes. Midway through the game, the three girls were beating the boys handily. Jamal stared at Omar with a look of disgust.

"So, when were you gonna work on that perfect game? Cuz if you can keep count, these girls are workin' you right now," Jamal asked.

"Shut up, man," Omar replied. "Check the score. They smoking both of us, fool," he added while the girls slapped high fives and laughed at the little spat that was developing in front of them.

As Patricia took her ball from the rack and prepared to roll, she bent down in concentration, giving Jamal more than enough rear view. That girl's gifted with that body Jamal thought

Omar noticed him staring and started laughing silently. "You know, bro if you gonna stare so much, you might as well get your swerve on. Stop playing and get with her already. She doing this on purpose," Omar said.

Jamal knew Omar was right. Patricia knew very well what she was doing and Jamal was being held hostage with his eyes as they feasted on Patricia's shapely curves. As Patricia bowled, she added to her score, which was higher than her friends. Jamal dreaded to even look at the screen at the moment. His score, along with Omar's was pitiful, to say the least. The screen arrow pointed onto Omar's name, indicating it was Omar's turn to bowl.

"It's all good, dog. I'll get us back in this," he boasted confidently at Jamal.

"Just shut up and go already!" Jamal exclaimed, exasperated by his friend's big time talk and little show. Omar took his bowling ball out of the rack and took his time before letting it go. It rolled right down the middle and for a moment Jamal thought Omar finally had a decent turn but his hopes were dashed as the ball veered to the left and hit only two pins.

Omar turned and shrugged sheepishly at Jamal while the girls roared with laughter. Omar sat next to Jamal.

"Remind me never to go bowling with you again," Jamal told Omar.

Walking up the stairs of the St. John's room hall, Shania and Trevor encountered some of the party guests gathering outside; boys and girls who were talking and drinking bottles of beer, wine coolers, or shots of tequila. From the inside the hall, the reggae music blared and as Shania and Trevor entered the house. Shania was shocked to see the number of people inside. Many of the partygoers were on the floor dancing and the DJ was standing off to the side managing the turntable and switching the music every which way as the air was filled with the sound of laughter, shouts, and merriment from students who had been waiting for an opportunity to unwind.

"It's probably not what you expected, but it's something," Trevor said to Shania, although he had to raise his voice a tad bit so that she could hear him.

"Are you serious? I knew it would be crowded," Shania replied but in the back of her mind she was thinking *I didn't think it would be this crowded.* She had only been to a couple parties in her sophomore and junior year with Loree and none of those parties had the same guest magnitude as a regular college party. Sean walked up to Trevor and Trevor introduced him to Shania.

"Yeah, Shania this here's my boy Sean. We both play for the squad," he said. Shania shook Sean's hand.

"Hey, girl what's up? Trevor did tell me that he was gonna bring a date over but he never told me that he was gonna bring someone like you here," he said, looking at Shania with a look of lust.

Five seconds was enough before Trevor stepped in. "Aye, aye man go get you one of them shorties over there. She's with me, dog," he said, pushing Sean away roughly.

Shania laughed as she watched this brief scene unfold. Was it possible that Trevor was more into her? As Sean went back to mingle with the crowd, Trevor turned to Shania. "Sorry about that. He can be a little physical sometimes," he said.

Shania watched as Sean made his way through the throng of people. "It's ok," she reassured him. "So I held up my end of the bargain, Mr. All-Star, now it's all on you. Am I going to see you at church on Sunday?" she asked him.

Trevor nodded confidently. "Oh no doubt, I'll definitely be in there getting my praise on and what not," he replied. Damn I can't believe I said that wack-ass line to her again. She probably think I'm mad lame Trevor thought.

At the same exact time, another one of Trevor's teammates, Joey Malone came by with a serving dish of what appeared to be tiny cups of vodka shots.

"Yo Trev, you want a shot? I got you right hea'," Joey said in his strong Jersey accent.

"Nah man, I ain't takin that right now," Trevor replied.

Seeing Shania next to him, he made the same offer "What about Ms. Foxy over here? You want a shot?" Joey asked Shania.

"Nah man, get that shit outta here. She ain't gonna wanna drink that…" Trevor started but it was pretty clear that he did not know Shania very well because before he finished his statement of refusal, Shania had already grabbed a shot glass and gulped the warm, cool liquid down her throat.

"So are you gonna stand there or are you gonna ask me to dance?" Shania asked as she laughed at Trevor and Joey, who looked dumbfounded. She only had one goal on her mind and that was to party as hard and as long as possible. Her parents didn't trust her and she wasn't sure if her best friend was even her best friend anymore and Shania did not wish to dwell on those thoughts. After Trevor stared without giving her a response, Shania spoke again. "Well, I didn't come here to stand against the wall. You comin' or what?" she asked, walking out to the center of the floor where the dancers were.

Trevor took Shania's hand and allowed her to lead him to the dance floor. She ain't gotta ask me twice he thought as he held her soft hands and walked to the floor.

Then it was as if everyone else disappeared and it was just them and the music. There were no noisy party guests, no food or drinks on the floor. As the blue and neon lights flashed across the room, the music continued to play and Shania danced even closer to Trevor. Trevor felt his temperature rising as Shania gyrated closer and closer to his midsection. Her moves were hypnotic, causing him to enter into a trance of lust. Her hips were shapely and her long slender legs seemingly hugged his.

Ain't no way this girl is a church girl. She don't dance like no church girl at all. Trevor thought as he stayed on beat and his hand wrapped around her midsection as she proceeded to grind against him. He lifted her shirt up just a little bit so her belly would be exposed just below her belly button. Shania knew what was going on but she couldn't stop. She didn't want to stop and she didn't want Trevor to stop either. With the temperature rising up in the room, the sizzling chemistry in the bodies of Trevor and Shania were reaching sweltering levels. They were slaves to the music, slaves to their senses and slaves to each other.

Twenty-eight-year Cindy Crofton turned at the corner of Guy R. Brewer Road in her four-door Honda Accord. She had just returned from picking up her three-year- old son, Ashton, from the Early Head-start Education Academy. Heading toward Baisley Park, she looked in her rearview mirror. Ashton was playing with the small toys she had bought for him over a week ago. She couldn't even begin to explain the depth of her pride in her son. The professors at the school said that Ashton was developing quicker than they expected, listening to rules and showing signs of early artistic creativity.

It made Cindy reflect on her humble background when she was born in Paterson, New Jersey and grew up underprivileged and always reminded how she would never amount to anything because she came from nowhere. Cindy eventually used it as motivation and ended up receiving her Ph.D. in Psychology and became a full-time working psychiatrist in Elmont, New York. She ended up marrying to her high school sweetheart, Cecil Crofton, and she gave birth to Ashton not long after. Her road to adult life had not been marred by any traumatic events or controversy. Little did Cindy know she was about to enter a world from which she thought she had escaped.

While driving down Guy R Brewer through the deserted alleys, she was waiting alone at a red light. Nothing could have prepared her for what happened next. A young woman collapsed on the top of her car, her clothes stained red with blood, startling Cindy. She had appeared to appear out of nowhere, yet Cindy's windshield was stained with the woman's blood.

"Oh my God!" Cindy exclaimed as she got out of the car.

"Mommy, what's that?" Ashton asked.

"Honey stay in your seat, ok?" Cindy replied.

She stepped out of her car and looked at the motionless figure lying on the side of the road. As she stepped closer, she saw the color drained from her once-beautiful complexion and her clothes were torn in various areas. Cindy then heard a voice coming from the bleeding young lady who was breathing short breaths.

"Help me," she said in a voice barely above a whisper, pointing to her chest.

Cindy looked and saw an exit bullet wound in her chest cavity, just above her heart. As Cindy frantically called 911, she looked at the ground where she noticed different pieces of paper and cards that had spilled out of her pocket when she collapsed. Cindy shifted through the cards to look for identification. Her eyes fell on a Richmond Hill High School ID, which had the name: LOREE ANNE MCAFEE.

CHAPTER TWELVE

Relieved that the night was coming to an end, Jamal resorted to playing some of the arcade games in the bowling alley. His favorite was the car racing game because to him, it was an early introduction to driving. He knew he was at least two years from being eligible to apply for a driver's license, but he was determined not to take the bus for the rest of his life. While he played, he occasionally turned around and saw Omar talking with Tania in a table booth, but he didn't see Patricia sitting with them. He wondered where she was, before drawing the conclusion that Patricia might have just gone to the ladies room. As he made his last lap in the car racing game, he sensed someone standing behind him. He turned around; expecting it to be someone who was waiting for their turn to play, but it was Patricia, grinning from ear to ear.

"Who were you expecting? Yo' boy Omar?" she asked.

Jamal laughed. "Actually, I didn't think it was him. I see him over there with yo' girl, Tanya," he replied.

Patricia looked at them. "Yeah, it's about time they started talking to each other. We make good matchmakers, don't we?" she asked laughing.

"Yeah we do," Jamal agreed.

Figuring that Patricia wanted to play the car racing game, he said, "I'm almost done. I can give you a turn if you want."

Patricia shook her head. "I don't want a turn after you." she said.

Of course she wouldn't want to play. Who was I kidding? he thought.

"I want to go at you. Your score really sucks at this," Patricia finished, laughing.

"What you mean my score sucks? What was your highest score playing this?" Jamal challenged.

The car game was set on highest scores based on speed and number of checkpoints passed during the race. Usually before a player began the race, it would show the highest scores of players from the past.

"You know the name 'Sexy Chica89?'" Patricia asked.

Jamal vaguely remembered seeing that name on the score display near the top of the score list, but he didn't think twice of it. "Yeah, I remembered seeing that name. You're not gonna tell me that's you now, is it?" he asked, laughing.

Patricia stopped laughing momentarily. "That is me, El Stupido. I stay killin' people all day in this. You wanna try me? Or is you scared?" she challenged.

This girl loves proving she's boss over everyone. I'm gonna have to shut her mouth he thought. "Nah, I ain't never scared. You're on," Jamal replied confidently. "Unlike Omar, when I say I'm good at something, I can actually back it up," he added.

Patricia sat down on the second car seat for the two-player race. "Shut up, so I can beat yo' ass in this like I beat ya' in bowling," she countered, laughing as they put in a quarter apiece to begin playing the two-player race. Jamal chose a nice, snazzy black car with white lightning streaks down the middle.

"You see my ride, right? Probably wish you had a pimp car like this huh?" Jamal gloated.

Patricia, in turn went for a hot pink number with three stripes down the front and back of the vehicle. "Please. My ride looks more fresh than that wack-ass knight rider you got there," she replied as they prepared to race.

As the race began, Jamal noticed she held the steering wheel differently than most people. It was as if she had been playing for years and rightfully so. She was at least a couple hundred feet ahead of him and although he tried to pass the other cars and other obstacles that got in the way, he was unable to overtake Patricia in the race and she ended up winning by more than two miles. Jamal couldn't believe it. First she beat him soundly at bowling and now she beat him at video games.

"Ok you got it but be for real with me. You gotta be a dude in a woman's body, right?" Jamal asked.

Patricia laughed. "Nah, I just got a couple older brothers at home and they always challenged me to this game when I was younger. I would always get my ass whooped by them. Then one day, I challenged them both to race me in this and I ended up dusting them both and they were the high scorers before I was," she recalled.

"You could've told me you was boss at this game, otherwise I wouldn't have challenged you," Jamal said.

Patricia smiled the most mischievous smile that Jamal had ever seen. "I really could have but it wouldn't have given me the satisfaction to see to the look on your face after beating you again," she said.

Jamal laughed. He was really having fun with Patricia. More fun than he'd had in a long time. She wasn't like other girls. There was a real quality about her. A down-to-earth personality that made hanging out with her really entertaining. Jamal was almost on the verge of asking her if they could go out together but before he could gather his thoughts to ask her, he heard the cell phone in his pocket ring. It wasn't his phone, it was his mother's phone she had lent him so he could call in case of emergency. Jamal had been asking his mother for a cell phone for a long time but due to Isis's house and bills, the money for a new phone had just not been there. Looking at the caller ID, Jamal realized it was his house number. Asking Patricia to excuse him, Jamal walked toward the exit doors of the bowling alley where he answered the phone.

"Hello?" he answered.

"Jamal, it's Mom. I need you to come home right now," Isis said over the phone. She sounded really frantic as if his life depended on it. Jamal looked at the clock. It was thirty minutes after ten. It wasn't that late but Jamal didn't want to argue.

"Sure, Mom I'm coming home now. Is everything ok? What's wrong?" Jamal asked.

"I'll tell you when you come back but I want you and Omar to come home right now. Don't stop anywhere in Jamaica, don't talk to anybody. I need you back home as soon as possible," his mother said before hanging up without saying goodbye.

Perplexed, Jamal walked back to Patricia at the arcade site. "Yo Patricia, Omar and I gotta bounce. We can walk you back to the bus stop since we're going the same way," Jamal said.

Patricia's face fell. "Aw, you're leaving so early? Why, does Mommy need her little boy back home?" she asked.

Jamal didn't want to tell her it was exactly what she thought. "I just gotta get back. I ain't start my homework yet or anything," he said.

Patricia had a look that suggested she didn't fully believe the reason why Jamal had to leave but she took it just fine. "Ok that's cool. My older brother's actually gonna come pick us up. I guess I'll see you at school tomorrow," she said.

Jamal waved goodbye and went to get Omar, who he practically had to drag away from Tania since they were having a good time together.

"Man, what's up?" Omar asked, annoyed that he had to cut his alone time with Tanya short.

"My mom said we have to come back home," Jamal said.

Omar looked at him, shaking his head. "Yeah, your mom said that you had to go home. She couldn't be talkin' about me too. She ain't my momma," Omar replied.

"She said you and I both had to go home, bro," Jamal said. Omar shook his head, clearly not agreeing with what Jamal said but grudgingly followed him out of the bowling alley.

At the college campus party, Shania finally sat down, tired from dancing. A couple of other college boys had tried hitting on her while Trevor was talking with the other members of the basketball team, but Shania clearly and firmly let the other boys know she was not interested in either of them. She looked at her watch. It was a little bit after ten. She knew she had to ask Trevor to drop her off back home before her parents started to worry about her. In the scheme of it all, she felt a wave of regret for what she had done. Growing up in a Christian home, Shania hated lying to her parents about where she was going.

But I'm still a teenager who's going to have fun and enjoy my time as much as I can she thought. She was having good responsible fun, and it was needed after her day and especially after her fallout with Loree. Oh no Loree! Shania thought. She completely forgot about checking with her. She had barely pulled out her phone, when she saw it ring. It was her mom. She walked outside, away from the noise of the party.

"Hey Mom," she replied over the phone.

"Honey, I know you are at the movies right now, but I need you to come home now," Robyn said, her voice filled with frantic concern.

Shania's heart skipped a beat when she said "movies." She felt the stab of guilt, but it still didn't explain why Robyn sounded so strange.

"Sure Mom I can come home. What's going on? Is everything ok?" she asked.

There was a long pause at the other line. Then Robyn replied. "No. Everything is not ok, Shania. I have devastating news. Loree is at Queens Hospital Center in Parsons. She had two gun-shot wounds to the chest and she's in critical condition,"

At that moment, it was like the world had melted away. Nothing seemed to make sense to Shania anymore. There was just no way her mother just told her that Loree had been shot and was currently fighting for her life at the hospital.

"What?" she asked in disbelief.

"I got a call from her mother a few minutes ago. Mike and I are going to the hospital right now to visit with her family right now to await further information," Robyn said.

"Then I'll meet you at the hospital," Shania told her mother.

"No, Shania I want you to go straight home. These streets are not safe right now at all," Robyn said and even through the phone, Shania could tell that Robyn was trying very hard to fight back the tears.

"Mom, she's my friend! I knew I should've checked on her. This is my fault!" Shania exclaimed, fighting back her own tears. "I'm coming to the hospital too," she repeated before hanging up the phone.

It was as if every step she took, her senses became more and more numb. She went back into the frat hall and desperately looked for Trevor. She found him sitting in the couch talking to his friends and basketball teammates. As soon as she came up to him, Trevor could see by the tear streaks on her face and distressed look that something was wrong.

"Trevor, I need you to take me to the hospital!" she said frantically.

"Why, what's wrong?" Trevor asked.

Shania didn't feel comfortable explaining the details in front of Trevor's college friends, so she pulled him from the couch and took him outside. Once they were a few yards away from the party site, she told Trevor what had happened.

"It's Loree. My mom called me and told me that Loree's been shot twice in the chest. She's at the hospital right now and I don't know how she's doing but I gotta be there," she explained, sobbing.

Trevor did not hesitate. "All right I'll take you to the hospital. Which hospital is she at?" he asked while he searched his pocket for his car keys.

"Queens Hospital Center in Parsons," she answered. "It's my fault. I knew I should have told her parents or the police what was going on. I was afraid something like this would happen," she added.

As they walked toward the parking lot, another college student noticed Trevor walking to the parking lot.

"Yo Trev, leaving so soon? We bout to hit the pool with the honeys in about fifteen minutes, you coming?" he yelled.

"I can't, son. I gotta get up out of here. I'll talk to you later," Trevor replied.

He got into his car and Shania got into the driver seat. Trevor drove as fast as he possibly could to avoid any traffic lights or slow-moving vehicles. He glanced at Shania next to him. He could see her starting to cry again. Although he didn't know Loree very well, he wondered how and what Loree had gotten herself mixed up with to get hurt badly. Certainly he didn't want to ask Shania at the moment, so for the first twenty minutes that they drove, it was in uncomfortable and awkward silence; except for the little rack of sobs that would escape Shania's lips. Then, guilt started to enter Trevor's mind. After all, the only time he had seen Loree was that day in the park when he was playing ball and he had seen her with some boys. Could Trevor have suspected something wrong and was it possible that he could have called the police then? Not only was his night cut short, but Shania might be so stricken with grief, she might start lashing out at those people around her who she felt could have prevented this from occurring. Trevor would most likely be on the top of that list.

"Can't you go any faster? God, I hope it isn't too late," Shania said.

"I'm doing the best I can. We're almost there. I just hit Sutphin right now," Trevor replied, referring to Sutphin Boulevard, which crossed Jamaica Avenue and Parsons Boulevard. In less than five minutes, they reached the hospital and Trevor dropped her off in front of the emergency room. While Shania rushed inside, Trevor searched for parking within the visitor section of the hospital. Shania went to the waiting room and saw her parents, Loree's parents and Andrea, Loree's little sister. They were all sitting together, holding hands waiting for any news. According to Mike, they responded to a distress call made to 911 by a lady named Cindy Crofton who saw Loree barely clinging to life. If Loree somehow pulled through, Cindy would be the hero for her quick response. Shania looked around for Cindy but Mike said that Cindy left the hospital shortly after Amos and Alisha McAfee arrived. Although they had taken the news extremely hard, Amos and Alisha poured out their thanks to Cindy who rode in the ambulance along with her son to make sure Loree was promptly attended to as soon as possible. Her little boy was very tired and hungry, so they understood that she had to take him home. She left her phone number with them so they could keep her updated on her condition. Amos then called Pastor Mike and his wife who both arrived as quickly as they could. At first Mike couldn't believe what he heard. A feeling of numbness and doubt over the validity of the report came over him. He always knew the risks of living in an inner city environment where there was little regard for education and young people who were all too eager to get in trouble with the law by meddling in drug dealing and street violence. It was a reality, but it never had never hit so close to home. This was the daughter of one of his members and a close friend of his own daughter. He had so often seen Loree in church, sitting next to Shania. Her little sister was very bright, as Shania would gush about her every Sunday afternoon about how well she was doing in Sunday school class. His initial thought was for the McAfee family until it turned over to his own daughter. He told Robyn to call Shania at the movies to inform her to go home. In light of what happened, Mike was not going to put his own daughter's life at risk.

The doctors emerged to let the family know that Loree had been taken in for emergency surgery to remove one of the bullets which was still lodged in her chest cavity. They feared it might have hit her aorta so they were very quick to perform the surgery. While it was happening, all everyone could do was wait.

The hospital doors swung open again and to Shania's surprise, Trevor walked in. He found Shania sitting next to her family. He went over to them to get more information on Loree. Mike stood up from his chair when Trevor approached Shania. He was still not comfortable with Trevor and he wasn't sure if Trevor had outside connection with the people that shot Loree. He still, however, couldn't get over the fact that Trevor reminded him of Nina. He couldn't shake off the feeling. He couldn't shake her off every time he saw Trevor.

It was October 1980, and the seniors at Richmond Hill High School were approaching the last year of school. Mike was walking out of the gym, having just talked to the coach about an upcoming playoff game against Forest Hills. As he walked out into the hallways, he saw Nate and a couple of other guys he didn't know. Based on their haggard appearances and hazed eyes, he could tell right away that they were potheads. Mike walked up to his friend.

"Hey man, what's happenin'?" Nate greeted Mike as they both leaned against the locker.

"Nothin much, man just getting ready for the next game. Yo Nate, you seen Nina lately?" Mike asked.

Nate shook his head. "Nah man, I ain't seen her around today," he said.

Mike looked at Nate. His story had to be one of the most tragic he had ever heard. The previous year Nate had been in the running to be one of the best basketball players in the state. Now he had left school to deal drugs but he still came back every once in a while to talk to his friends.

"You good, man?" Mike asked Nate.

"Never betta' brotha'. It's all about the cash game to me," Nate replied with his head cocked to the side and his eyes in an almost dream-focused state.

Then the school doors opened again and Nina, along with two of her friends from the cheerleading team walked in. She wore the same cheer outfit as the other cheerleaders but being the model of promiscuity, she had modified the look so her naval would show and her legs would show even more. She saw Mike and walked toward him, kissing him deeply and embracing him.

"I missed you so much, baby. How was practice?" she asked, looking up at him with her soft brown eyes and even softer lips.

"Practice was ok. Coach is working on a game plan for Forest Hills so I gotta get my throwin' arm ready," Mike said confidently.

Nina looked up at him with those eyes that melted him. The rest of her body seemed perfectly sculpted.

"You can't forget about your good luck charm, though," she cooed as she started touching his strong chest under his shirt.

It was almost too much. Mike and Nina wouldn't exactly call themselves sex fiends but at least four times a week they would have sex before his upcoming games. It had become part of an unwritten ritual for them. While Mike kissed Nina passionately, her girlfriends giggled as Nate looked on with mock disgust.

"Can't even get 'em a room," Nate said to the girls. "Well I'm out, folk. I'll catch you in da 'hood," he added as he walked out of the school.

As they broke apart from the kiss, Mike said. "Look I'm about to shower but if you wanna wait till I get out the locker room, we can go to my place and just relax,"

Nina agreed to wait for him and Mike went inside the locker room showers and took off his clothes, his muscles rippling back and front as the water from the showerhead came down. He grabbed the bar of soap he always brought with him and started to scrub his body. Suddenly he felt a hand on his shoulder and on his lower regions. He turned around and realized it was Nina, standing there. She wore no clothes.

"I couldn't wait," she said as she kissed him, her hand moving more vigorously on his manhood and his hands holding her in an embrace.

"You know you gotta get out, right?" Mike asked. "If coach finds you in here, we can get in some trouble," he added.

Nina smiled that very mischievous smile that drove him crazy saying, "Then I better work fast seeing how I don't have much time," before kissing him some more and they participated in one of their weekly rituals.

Her body felt so good when it was wet and they were joined together, he felt himself connected to her in a way he knew no other girl could. It was more than lust, he thought. It had to be love. No other emotion could make him feel the way he felt with Nina.

"I love you," he whispered in Nina's ear as their water-soaked bodies intertwined.

"I love you too, Mike," she whispered back to him.

Mike found himself back in the Queens Hospital Center waiting room. Shania stopped sobbing but was reduced to looking out the window in a hypnotic trance, completely oblivious to the world around her. Mike didn't feel it was prudent to check on her at the moment because he knew how empty she felt. It was the same pain he had felt at her age, but he had no one at whom to turn in his grief. All he had were the memories of what once was and what might have been. He could only pray and hold steadfast that Shania would rely on her faith to get her through. Surveying the room, he also saw Amos consoling his wife as best he could. Mike knew that no amount of pain that either he or Shania felt could compare to the pain that Amos and his wife were feeling. Loree was their flesh and blood in the emergency room fighting for her life. Mike dreaded the additional burden he was expected to carry all over again. The last time he carried heavy responsibility that reflected negatively upon him, he had almost drunk himself to the grave, sacrificing a once promising sports career. God had been able to pull off a miracle in his life. Could He pull off one more miracle? It was possible. Mike had to believe it. Not only for himself to justify his own faith but he would have to be strong for Shania. He would have to be strong for Robyn and the McAfee family. Andrea had been crying for a quite a while, but her grief had caused her to fall in a deep sleep where she stretched over two of the waiting room chairs. He walked over to Robyn.

"Hey baby, I'm gonna go get some food for us and Loree's family. Do you want anything?" he asked.

Robyn said that she couldn't eat but a cold drink would be good. Mike walked over to Amos and informed him that he would be going out to bring some food. They thanked the pastor for remaining with them and assured him that he didn't have to stay through the night because they knew he had a business to run and did not want to compromise him, but

Mike shrugged it off, saying that it was no problem and he and Robyn could stay there as long as they were needed.

The police department was seriously investigating the identity of Loree's shooter and they knew they had a tough road ahead of them. Queens was such a large city and even knowing where to start would take at least a day or two. They had questioned Amos and Alisha McAfee at the hospital about any of Loree's potential enemies, whether at school or anywhere else. As soon as Shania arrived at the hospital, they interrogated her as well. Shania did not seem to know who was responsible but then she remembered her ex-boyfriend, David. She also mentioned Tadarius with whom the police were already extremely familiar, so the police had two leads. They immediately went to David's house, where he lived with his grandmother. When his grandmother responded, she stated that David went to the city of Rosedale with some friends, and he wouldn't be back for a few hours. The police left a business card and told David's grandmother to inform David to contact them when he returned so they could speak with him.

Ten minutes after Mike had gone to buy food, the doctors came out of the emergency room and informed the family that Loree was out of surgery but was still in a comatose state. Shania and Trevor went inside the room and it broke Shania's heart to see her best friend lying there, all but lifeless with what appeared to be a hundred tubes sticking in and out of her. Shania sat down in the seat next to Loree's hospital bed.

"Hey girl, I don't know if you can hear me, but I wanted to let you know that I'm sorry I left you alone. I should've been there with you tonight," she said, her voice starting to crack.

Trevor wished he knew what to say. He had never been in a situation like this before and wanted to hug Shania and to tell her everything would be all right but even Trevor did not know if Loree would pull through. All he could do was to stand by in silence while Shania tried to reach her friend.

"I want you to know that even though I wasn't there for you tonight, I'm here for you now. When you wake up, we are going to go shopping and you can steal my clothes anytime you want," Shania said with a smile.

She turned around at Trevor, who was smiling as well. Just by witnessing this scene, Trevor knew the girls had been more than friends; they were more like blood sisters. Trevor didn't know if God truly existed but if He did, he hoped that He would revive Loree.

CHAPTER THIRTEEN

Jamal arrived home a few minutes after Omar crossed the street toward his home. Jamal reached into his pocket for his keys, and he had a little difficulty locating his keys until he found them at the very bottom of his jeans pockets. Walking up the stairs, he was still thinking about the bowling alley. He had chuckled a bit when he had seen Omar making headway talking with Tania, but he was still wondering where he stood with Patricia. Did she like him, or didn't she like him? It seemed like every time they were on a track to hit it off and maybe develop some kind of chemistry, they would end up either arguing or competing against each other. Was this norm for relationships? He remembered the saying that opposites attract, so that might be the case with him and Patricia, but he wasn't sure. He knew if he stayed unsure for too long, Omar and his other friends would start getting on his case about taking too long to make a move.

As Jamal reached his apartment, he turned the lock on the top of the doorknob, before turning the lock on the bottom of the doorknob that opened his door. The moment he opened his door, Isis came running out of living room to hug her son. It wasn't as if Jamal didn't appreciate the love, but his mother was hugging him so tightly. If she didn't let go soon, she might cut off his air supply.

"Hi Mom. I missed you too," Jamal said in a strangled sort of voice. Isis finally let go of Jamal and when Jamal looked closer at his mother's face, he could tell that she had been crying. "Mom, why are you crying? Are you ok?" Jamal asked.

Isis sat down on one of her dining room chairs before responding to Jamal. "I'm just happy God brought you back safe and sound. I received a call from one of the church members. There was a girl that was shot tonight, Jamal," she explained.

Jamal couldn't believe the words that had come from his mother's lips. "What? Someone was shot? Who was it?" Jamal asked in a voice that expressed disbelief.

"I don't remember the name of the girl, Jamal. You might know her. She goes to Richmond Hill and she's the same age as the pastor's daughter," Isis replied, tears still falling from her face. Jamal's world came to a crashing halt as the identity of the victim became clear to him.

"You mean Loree, Mom? Was Loree the one who got shot?" Jamal asked frantically as he sat down trying to process the information.

Not Loree, not the girl who had been nice to him at church at times and who he had mistaken as Shania's sister when he first started attending Rock of Jacob Baptist Church. It couldn't be true.

"Is she going to live? I mean, she ain't dead yet, right?" Jamal asked.

Isis shook her head. "Baby, I don't know. They found her on the side of the road off of Guy R. Brewer and took her to the hospital. But from what I heard, it ain't looking too good," she replied.

Jamal just sat there, across from his mother in stunned silence. Now he understood why his mother had rushed him out of the bowling alley and why she hugged him as if she didn't think she would see him again. The most numbing part was that Jamaica Lanes was not too far from Guy R Brewer. Of course, he hadn't heard the bullets fly across the cool New York night but how could he have heard anything if he was in that noisy bowling alley? What if he had found out while he was in there that the gunman was close by? So many questions left unanswered. He got up to go to his room, when his mother called him back to the table.

"Jamal, in light of what happened, I don't want you outside the house after seven o'clock and I think I would like to start dropping you off to school in the mornings before school begins. Right after school, I want you to come straight home and call me as soon as you get home," she said.

Jamal understood her concern, but he certainly didn't agree with all of the new rules his mother established. "Come home after school? But Mom, I have basketball conditioning on Mondays and Thursdays after school," he argued.

Isis would hear none of it. "I don't care, Jamal. Right now I'm concerned about your safety more than I am about your after school activities," she said firmly.

"But Mom! Basketball tryouts are a month away. I already don't have time to go to the park that much anymore because I have a ton of homework. There's no other way I can practice!" he argued, voice becoming slightly elevated.

"Don't you raise your voice to me, young man!" Isis shouted. "A girl is fighting for her life right now. That could've been you Jamal. It could've been Omar. It could have been anybody that you see in school. You are my only son and I will not risk losing you out there in these streets," she added.

"Mom, the open gyms are chaperoned and no one's going to be bringing any guns there. I don't see why I can't stay after school in the open gyms!" he shouted.

"Can chaperones stop a crazy boy from coming in the school and shooting everyone up?" Isis asked. "Can chaperones ricochet the bullets for you so they won't hit your body when they fly your direction? I don't want to hear it. It's gotta be just school and home, at least until they find Loree's attacker," she said.

Jamal hit the wall in frustration on the way to his room. "That ain't fair, though! You know if Dad was still here, he wouldn't hold me back like this!" Jamal countered before going into his room, slamming the door behind him, leaving Isis standing alone in the small hallway corridor.

Jamal spent thirty minutes pacing back and forth in his room, trying to calm down. He felt his mother could never see eye to eye with him at all. He was hurting just as much as everyone else but he shouldn't have to put his dream on hold just because his mother told him to do so. What Jamal had learned from this moment was that he needed to work even harder to succeed at playing ball because he suddenly realized life was all but temporary. The next day was never a guarantee and Loree's situation was just another example of how cold the world had become and how society didn't give two cents about the lives of others. He had to think of a he could still play basketball without his mother worrying about him being shot. Logging onto his computer, Jamal accessed his instant messaging chat online under his log-in name, which was HolyBaller14. He waited for a few moments. He knew Omar would be logging on sooner or later. All of a sudden, he heard a bell sound that indicated that Omar had logged on and right on cue, he saw the chat name TheOman14 appear on his chat screen. Jamal began to type.

Yo son, did you hear what happened tonight? Jamal typed. He waited a moment to see how Omar would respond before the following words came up a few minutes later:

No. What happened? Omar replied.

Shania's friend Loree was shot tonight. My mom told me that someone from the church called her and told her about it. Jamal typed to Omar. Again he waited for a response which took a little longer than the previous reply.

Are you serious? Is she dead?

Jamal replied back, making sure that he used the right words, so he wouldn't twist the story. Nah man, she still at the hospital right now. But from what I heard, she barely hanging on. he replied.

Damn I know Shania must be losing her mind right now. They like sisters, Omar replied after a pause.

Yeah I know. She was cool. I don't know why anybody would wanna try to kill her. Jamal typed his answer and waited for another response.

Do you think her boyfriend got something to with it? I heard that he used to roll with M.O.B. Maybe he had a hit put out on her. Omar replied.

Jamal thought it over. He had seen Loree with her boyfriend walking around holding hands. She definitely was not the shy type. But Jamal, just like Shania, did not know or trust David at all. Could it be possible that they broke up and because he felt upset, David decided to take his anger out on Loree by trying to get rid of her? He didn't know but it was certainly possible.

Maybe. I don't know but I never trusted that dude so I wouldn't be surprised if he did it. Jamal replied.

Jamal wasn't sure though. He had seen TV shows with situations where ex-boyfriends or ex-girlfriends would break up with their partners only to have their lives taken so violently shortly after. The worst part was that every time they would investigate or interrogate the lover, they would deny it but eventually they would turn out to be be involved.

I don't know bro. Anyway, my mom trippin big-time over this. She ain't letting me stay in the open gyms after school to get ready for bball season. Jamal typed back and waited for a reply. Finally he received a response from Omar.

What? Come on, man. You gotta be there. We gotta get right for tryouts and I'm trying to get some PT cuz ain't no way coach leaving me on the bench all season.

Jamal couldn't believe the arrogance of his friend. Here he was, sweating over the future of the sport that he loved and whether he would play any time soon and Omar was already scheming not only to make the team, but also getting playing time which Jamal knew was never guaranteed.

Whateva, son. You'll be lucky if you even see the floor. Anyway I'm still tryin to ball, yo. What am I gonna do? Jamal answered and waited for Omar to reply. Finally he received an answer.

Why don't you ask your mom to drop you off to school early? Maybe you can work on your game then.

That actually was not a bad idea. Jamal had to hand it to Omar. Sometimes he talked too much and was so cocky to the point where you wanted to glue his mouth shut but there were moments when he actually had some good ideas. This was one of those moments.

Yeah I might do that. I'll bring my ball and meet you there at 6:30, Jamal typed.

Um, who said anything about me being there with you, bro? I like to sleep in, you already know, Omar replied. Jamal rolled his eyes as he read the message.

I thought we was boys man. Ok whatever that's iight Jamal replied back. This time Omar took even longer than every other time to respond to his post.

Yo my mom's about to use the phone, so I gotta get off this. I'll catch you at school tomorrow. Peace.

Jamal then saw Omar's chat indicator turn gray and disappear. He closed his computer and went to his mother's room to ask for a favor. He found her lying down on the bed, reading a book.

"Hey Mom, I wanted to apologize for the way I talked to you earlier," he said.

Isis looked up, her reading glasses pushed a little forward to her face. "It's ok, sweetie. I'm sorry too. I know how much you wanted to prepare for basketball this year but you're my only son and after I heard what I heard tonight, I just can't envision life without you," she replied.

"I know, Mom. But everything is going to be ok. She'll make it. I'm sure they're gonna catch the guy who shot her," Jamal said.

"I'm sure they will too, honey," Isis reassured. Sensing that there was another purpose for Jamal's entry into her room, she asked "Is everything ok?"

Jamal took a few seconds to gather his thoughts so he could ask his question in the best way possible to ensure the best response available. "Well Mom, I was in my room, and I was just thinking. I know you didn't want me to stay after school anymore to practice basketball, so I was wondering if you could drop me to school before seven in the morning so I can at least practice alone?" he asked.

Isis sat up in her bed and took her glasses off. How could she respond to a question like that? Someone they were very close with was lying in a hospital bed with bullet holes in her body; flirting with life and death. Could she trust her son being out in the wee hours of morning at school before anyone else got there?

"Jamal, I don't think it would be a great idea," she said but Jamal would not give up easily this time.

"Aw come on Mom, please? There'll be teachers there and the janitors will be there, so they'll open the doors to the gym so I can practice. Please?" he begged.

Isis gave a small sigh. She was his mother and whatever she said was final but she dearly wanted to prevent distance between herself and Jamal. If there were teachers that were at the school and as long as the doors were open to let Jamal inside, maybe it wouldn't be such a bad idea.

"Ok, we'll do it your way this time but if there are no teachers there or if I don't see any adults there, I will remain there with you until the doors open, because I will not leave you by yourself," Isis said.

Jamal lunged forward to hug and kiss his mother. "Thanks Mom. I'll go set my clock right now," he said as he walked out of his mother's room.

"But either Janice or I will pick you up after school, do you hear me?" Isis said. Jamal halted for a moment, groaning. Janice was their neighbor who lived in the apartment directly across from them. She was an older lady who was like a grandmother to Jamal. She had a grandson named Kyle who lived in Philadelphia, Pennsylvania and visited her every summer. Kyle always had the latest video games and whenever he was in town he and Jamal and sometimes Omar would be playing for hours. Jamal loved Janice but he was not crazy about the idea of her picking him up after school. The whole point of being in high school was to be – or at least appear to be – independent, which included walking home without having Mommy or Daddy or a babysitter pick him up and walk him home.

"Come on Mom!" Jamal protested but this time Isis would have none of it.

"Don't 'come on' me, boy," she replied. "I compromised with you and I expect the same respect in return. Is that clear?" she asked in a stern voice. Jamal hung his head. He knew he had no choice but to agree.

"Oh all right then, I'll wait for her after school," Jamal grudgingly agreed before walking out of the room, closing his mother's door after him.

The alarm clock blared at six AM, waking Jamal quickly from sleep. He prepared for school as usual, bringing his shorts, basketball sneakers, and an extra T-shirt. After a quick shower and applying deodorant, he tossed the deodorant and his body lotion in the same plastic bag in which he carried his basketball, spare jeans, and T-shirt. He walked into the kitchen and ate a small bowl of cereal. His mother was already dressed in the kitchen, none too pleased about having to wake up early to drop Jamal off to school.

"Good morning, Mom. Did you hear anything on how Loree's doing?" Jamal asked.

Isis shook her head. "No I haven't heard anything. I can only pray and hope that God can work a miracle," she replied as she took her car keys and house keys and prepared to leave her apartment. Without warning, she turned back around to face Jamal.

"Can we say a prayer before we leave?" she asked.

Jamal didn't see why not so they both bowed their heads in prayer and Jamal started praying.

"Dear Heavenly Father, I thank you for waking us up another day. I thank you for the food on the table and the clothes on my back. I thank you for my mom and my dad and my friends. Lord I come before you to ask for your healing touch on Loree today. We don't know what's gonna happen but you know what will happen so we leave it in your hands. Please work a miracle, in the name of Jesus, Amen." Jamal prayed.

Jamal didn't notice that while he was praying, the eyes of Isis were open wide, watching her son pour out his heart to the Lord. She was very proud of how much he had grown. She didn't know what she would do if Jamal was taken from her. She couldn't bear the very thought of it. When they arrived at the school, Jamal was nervous because for a moment, the school grounds looked deserted. He knew if there were no cars present, Isis would not risk leaving Jamal outside on his own but as they approached the school, he saw two cars there.

"See Mom, I told you there would be people at the school already," Jamal said, smiling.

Isis chuckled. "Yeah, yeah whatever. Get out of the car," she laughed.

Jamal waved goodbye to his mother and walked to the doors of the school. He was delighted to find the doors open. He made his way over to the gym. Please God let the gym be open he thought because if the gym wasn't open, it would have defeated the whole purpose of him even showing up so early. He pushed the gym door handle down. To his surprise, the gym was open. He slipped off his book bag and laid it off to the wall. Then he began to dribble the ball but seconds later he heard a second ball dribble. Realizing he was not alone, he turned around to the opposite end of the court to see who was dribbling the ball. At first, because the gym was not fully lit, he wasn't sure who shared the court with him. After the mysterious person took his first jump shot, the form and the way the shot was taken was all too familiar to Jamal. It was the janitor who could do no wrong on the court. Jamal was transfixed with the skills of this janitor, almost as transfixed as he was the day he displayed his skills to numerous members of the student body just a few days ago.

"What you doing here so early, son? Ain't it a bit early for school?" Nate asked as soon as he realized he wasn't alone in the gym.

Jamal looked back at him, still dribbling the ball. "I should be asking you that same question, sir," he replied smartly.

Nate shook his head and laughed. This kid standing in front of him may not be very tall, but he had guts.

"Now I see why your shot's so nice all the time," Jamal added.

Nate laughed some more and continued to shoot on his own side of the basket. Jamal dribbled to the top of the key and took a shot that barely grazed the rim. Gotta shake off that morning rust he thought. As he grabbed his own rebound, he dribbled toward the left elbow and took another shot, which rattled in this time. He continued to shoot from different areas around the basket.

"You know," Nate said helpfully, "if you spread your fingers more and place your hand under the ball, you'll raise your shooting percentage."

Jamal stopped shooting for a moment and looked at Nate. He placed his hand under the ball, just as Nate instructed, and attempted to spread his fingers more but when he put his shot up, he came up with nothing but air.

"Damn!" Jamal yelled in frustration as he chased the ball down. Nate walked over to the side where Jamal was shooting.

"Here, pass me the rock. I'll show you," he offered. Jamal passed the ball the Nate. Nate caught the ball and began to dribble toward the three-point line. "Ok, stand by me right quick," Nate said.

Jamal ran over and stood a few feet from Nate on his right. Once he made sure Jamal was standing next to him, Nate continued. "What you always want to remember is that your shot is always defined through your legs and your arms. When you first rise up to shoot the ball, the first thing that you want to remember is to make sure your elbow is pointed at the direction of the basket. If you close one eye, your elbow must be aligned with the basket," Nate instructed. Then he took a shot with only one hand. The shot sailed through the basket.

I wish it was that easy for me Jamal thought as he attempted to straighten his elbow to release the shot with one hand, just as Nate had done but had a terribly different result from Nate's. His arm moved out of the straight line and it affected the shot, causing it to hit the side-back of the rim.

"Don't worry, it takes practice. It's all about repetition," Nate reassured Jamal as he passed him the ball to shoot again. Jamal concentrated and made sure his fingers were spread before he released his shot. He was surprised by how comfortable his shot felt when it released and the ball sailed right through the net. Nate smiled at Jamal as if he knew the shot was going in all along.

"Ok so let's step back a little bit now," Nate said, backing up toward the three point line.

Jamal stared at the line, hesitating. Three point shots were not his favorite shots in the world.

Nate noticed his hesitation "What's wrong, man? Ain't nothing to be afraid of," he said as Jamal stepped back toward the three point line.

Applying the same shooting techniques Nate taught him at the mid-range location, Jamal attempted his shot. It hit the front of the rim.

"Remember to hold your follow-through," Nate instructed.

Jamal took another shot, making sure he followed through. Unfortunately he leaned forward and his foot went over the line, technically making it a two point shot but Jamal was able to sink it. Nate and Jamal continued to shoot the ball for about twenty more minutes until they noticed through the gym windows that the sun was beginning to shine brighter than before and more people were starting to file into the school.

"Well, I gotta get ready for work, son," Nate said as he shook Jamal's hand but Jamal was not going to let him go that easily. Nate had just taught him more about the fundamentals of basketball than anyone else had ever done. This janitor had true skills and Jamal had to figure out why.

"All right, for real, where did you learn to play like that? A guy with mad skills like you should be doing more than just mopping floors," Jamal said.

Nate looked at the clock over the gym. He had a little over 15 minutes left before his shift started, so he might as well show the kid.

"All right follow me, man," he said. Jamal followed him out of the gym into the hallway corridor which led to the locker room. Along the corridor were trophies, plaques and team pictures from what Jamal saw were taken from the seventies and eighties. Nate pointed at one of the team pictures. When Jamal read the picture that read: 1979-1980 CITY REGION CHAMPIONS he noticed that the edges of the photo was frayed and chipped but what he focused on was the squad that he could see. They were the last region champions in Richmond Hill's history and what took Jamal by surprise the most was the boy in the center of the picture. He had a mini-Afro and broad shoulders, smiling at the camera. Suddenly Jamal knew who that young man was and when he read the name description at the bottom of the photo, it confirmed what he knew: #21-NATHAN PLUMMER: GUARD.

"So you did play here?" Jamal asked.

"Yup, for 3 years. I led the school in steals and three point percentage," Nate said.

Jamal looked at the photo, transfixed. "If you were so good in high school, why didn't you play in college or the pros?" he asked.

Nate knew Jamal would ask that question. It was a question he would ask himself every now and then. "Well, I screwed up and made some bad decisions in high school that caused me to stop playing. It's not something I'm proud to admit but if I can use my story to prevent you kids from making the same dumb decisions I made, then I would repeat the story over and over again," he answered.

Jamal had his suspicions that Nate had played before but never knew it until now. As Nate started to walk toward his personal room to get changed, Jamal asked Nate one more question. "Hey, I'm planning on coming by tomorrow morning. Are you gonna be there?"

"Yeah, I'll be there. Listen, that picture I just showed you of me, I need you to do me a huge favor and not tell that to your friends," Nate said. "The last thing I need is rumors with my name attached to it. I'm flying on a low profile and another thing, you might wanna consider showering. Your girl will thank you for it," Nate added, laughing as he walked out of earshot.

Jamal smelled under his armpits. Oh yeah, he's right. I stink right now he thought. But as he remembered that he didn't bring any soap to shower in the locker rooms. A box of soap came flying out of nowhere, landing next to him at the hallway corridor.

You're welcome," Nate said. Jamal looked at the bar of soap, before looking back at the corridor from where it had flown directly into his hand. Nate had already disappeared into his office. As kids started to make their way to class, Jamal headed inside the locker room to shower and change into his spare clothes.

Shania and her family continued the agonizing wait at Queens Center Hospital for any news about Loree's condition. After Shania visited Loree in her room and sat by her best friend's side for a few minutes, the doctor came back into the room and asked Shania and Trevor to leave the room. Shania left the hospital room but she quickly broke down uncontrollably sobbing. Trevor did all he could to comfort her and even offered to stay at the hospital with her until some news came out. Andrea was not faring much better through the ordeal. Her sister was everything to her; her best friend and her role model. Whenever she felt ostracized or isolated and her friends didn't want anything to do with her, Loree was always there to be an extra ear for her. Loree was savagely protective of her little sister.

Being aware of her own past and her own shortcomings, it was always Loree who advised Andrea not to embark on any relationships and to focus on her school and her goals because she would never know when she would get a second chance.

"You'll never have another chance or an opportunity to make a difference in the world," Loree would tell her little sister.

Many older sisters were either too self-absorbed or beguiled by the company they kept to remember there were younger kids who looked up to them. Andrea never thought Loree had that type of selfish character. Andrea was also a student in Shania's Sunday school class and one of the brightest students in the class. Shania would look at Andrea and every day she would see flashes of Loree in her. Her individuality, her drive, and her wit were just a few of the attributes Andrea shared with her sister. For the whole night, Andrea stared blankly out the window; out of touch with reality and unable to keep a thought in her head other than the health of her beloved sister.

Loree's parents also waited with Robyn and Mike Hillman. During the night, there were no limits to the prayers that were lifted up to God for the health and recovery of Loree. As the night progressed, a few other members from the deacon department at Rock of Jacob Baptist Church came by and prayed for Loree and her family as well. As people came and went, there was still no update on the condition of Loree. Not until four o'clock in the morning did a doctor come out to inform the family that Loree's condition had worsened and she was still in a coma. Alisha broke down into tears and Amos held her, unable to control the flow of tears coming down his own face. Shania sat next to Andrea and Trevor was sitting next to both of them.

Turning to Trevor, Shania said, "I know you got to get back on campus. You don't have to stay," she started to say but Trevor waved his hand in front of her.

"It's ok. I can stay some more if you want me too. My coach and teachers will understand," he said, even though he knew this wasn't wholly true. School or practice meant nothing to Trevor at the moment. It seemed that life and death carried a much larger significance than his personal issues.

"No, Trevor, it's ok. You've been by my side this whole night. I can't thank you enough but I don't want to interfere with your life," Shania replied.

Trevor didn't want to leave the family in their time of distress but he didn't want to be any more of a burden either.

"When you hear anything, give me a call, all right?" he asked.

Shania agreed and they exchanged cell phone numbers. Mike didn't notice this because for the moment, he was still talking to the McAfee family. Trevor said goodbye to Shania's family and Loree's family before heading out of the hospital. Shania walked over to Andrea.

"How are you holding up, sweetie?" she asked her.

Andrea turned around from the window where she had been staring and Shania could see the dry tear streaks on her face.

"I'm ok. Thank you for staying here with me," she said.

Shania reached over and hugged her tightly. "No problem," she said.

At the same time, the doctor, a middle-aged Hispanic woman, walked into the waiting room and from the downcast look, the trembling lips and the way she immediately held Mrs. McAfee's hand and sat down with her, Shania already knew what she had revealed before a word was spoken. Loree Anne McAfee, aged eighteen, was pronounced dead at four twenty-three in the morning.

CHAPTER FOURTEEN

The first thought that echoed in Shania's head when she saw the doctor enter the waiting room was please God, don't let Andrea hear it too soon. She wanted Andrea's family to break the news to her gently but that would be impossible. Andrea couldn't help but see the tears well up in Shania's eyes and her gaze automatically followed Shania's eyes toward the doctor.

"Shania, what's going on? What is that doctor telling Mommy and Daddy?" Andrea asked Shania before reality dawned on her face and she felt the first wave of nausea.

Sitting in their own corner, Amos and Alisha were having trouble accepting the news of their daughter's death. Alisha let out a loud yell of anguish, tears flooding her face as the doctor and families of other patients' in the waiting room attempted to comfort her, but it was to no avail. She was inconsolable.

Shania got up from her chair and for the next few minutes she was numb; far removed from this world. She felt like she had entered the Twilight Zone. It just wasn't possible that her best friend was no longer alive. It wasn't possible that her best friend had just left this world; had left her alone to deal with the pressures of her life. Where would she go with her secrets and her problems when she couldn't go to her parents, and she wasn't sure what to do? When she needed a shoulder to cry on, whose shoulder would she cry on?   Shania kept on walking. She didn't know where she was going or what the heck, she was going to do but she had to leave.

"Shania, where are you going?" Robyn asked, her tear-filled eyes pleading, as she did her best to comfort the McAfee family. Shania didn't answer her mother and walked quietly away.

At that very moment, nothing mattered. School didn't matter and track meets didn't matter. Church didn't even matter anymore to Shania. I don't get it, God. Haven't we done everything we can to keep her alive? Didn't we pray hard enough to you to spare her somehow?

She opened the door of the hospital and walked out, deaf to the world. Robyn ran out after her.

"Shania!" she yelled out but Shania broke out into a run.

Shania felt like she was in one of her track meets, racing as she raced against a rival school. She didn't know the name of her competitor and she didn't know how she would win but she kept running at the same speed. Her opponent now was life and Shania had to run as fast as she could to get away from reality. With the wind whistling in her ears and countless yards of pavement behind her, she continued to run. Pedestrians and motorists stared at this lovely young woman who appeared to be running without a care in the world, oblivious to the streets around her. Shania could still see Loree at the other side of the street, her arms opened wide enough for Shania to run into them so she could comfort her.

Back at the hospital, Andrea was inconsolable in her grief. She had just lost her best friend, her idol, and her older sister. She was buried in her mother's arms as she sank deeper in her embrace in attempt to escape the somber reality of her sister's death. There was no amount of comforting words that could appease the pain that both mother and child felt at that moment.

Shania ran until she reached the corner of Hillside Avenue and Parsons Boulevard. Crying and panting, she walked around the block, still questioning in her mind why her friend had to be the one killed. God, why couldn't it have been me? Why didn't you take my life? Loree was just starting to get her life back together and now she's not here.

Shania's mind was running with different thoughts on how this could have been prevented. She knew Loree had gotten herself involved with David, Tadarius and their crew. She should have taken that as a red flag and immediately called her parents or the police. Loree was the kind of girl who always wanted to take care of business on her own without pulling others into her own problems but that didn't make Shania any less guilty. The only issue Shania had with Loree's mentality was that most of the time people who lived and thought that way ended up hurting the ones most close to them, especially family. Did Amos and Alisha deserve this cruel twist of fate? Shania blamed herself more than anyone for Loree's death; so much so that she might as well have been the one who pulled the trigger.

Suddenly, Shania's phone rang. It was Trevor. Shania couldn't answer the phone initially. She just did not feel like she could talk to anyone, not even Trevor. No one understood how she felt and if no one related to her pain, what good would it do to talk to others who had never experienced the agony that she was now enduring? The phone stopped ringing and Shania thought for a second that Trevor had given up on calling her but no more than a few seconds later, her phone rang again. Once again it was Trevor. This time, Shania decided to answer the phone.

"Hey, what's up? Why didn't you answer my call the first time?" he asked.

Shania didn't know what to say. "I….just couldn't do it. I don't know what to say right now," she said, her voice cracking.

It took a moment for Trevor to get a hint on the situation. "What's going on? Is Loree gonna be all right?" he asked.

Shania tried to keep herself composed but she couldn't control the overwhelming emotion that washed over her. She broke down over the phone. It was in that moment Trevor realized that Loree was gone and he knew Shania was going to need some time alone.

"Yo, I'm sorry, Shania. I can give you some time. I'll call you later," he said.

"Ok," Shania managed to choke out before she hung up the phone.

After he hung up, Trevor just fell back on his bed in his college dorm room. He realized it was only when the gift of life was taken away from a person that it became more precious and yet, it was constantly taken for granted every day. Trevor played basketball and he went to school in one of the top colleges in New York but there were times when he knew it could all be taken away in the blink of an eye. This was why Trevor always had his doubts about the existence of God. If God was real, why did He allow death in the world? If God was such a loving God, why was there bloodshed wherever he turned?

As he laid back in his bed, his eyes fell upon the small package that was delivered to him at his parent's residence. The package had a letter attached to it. He opened the package, bending the small box that contained a silver CD case. Inside the case was a CD or DVD. It didn't resemble any of the music CDs he was accustomed to purchasing, the ones with song titles or subtitles with the names of the song. The cover was blank, and the disc only had one word written on it and it was scrawled in a red marker with the word MEMORIES. Obviously, it was a DVD. A look of confusion crossed Trevor's face. What did this guy mean when he said memories? Trevor decided the best way to find the meaning was to watch the DVD. He didn't have a class until later in the afternoon so he figured he would have enough time.

Trevor walked out of his dorm room and made his way over to one of the computer labs on campus. He put the DVD inside the personal computer and waited for the loading sign to stop running. Finally the full contents of the DVD were made known to Trevor and as he stared at the movie, his head continued to run for a good while. What he was seeing on the computer screen seemed impossible for him to fully comprehend.

There were outtakes of a baby, no more than a few months old, playing with a small toy. The boy seemed to be enjoying himself thoroughly with his small stuffed animal. The baby was preoccupied with his toy and didn't look up at the camera until he heard his mother's voice.

"Peek-a-boo! Peek-a-boo, I see you!" a young woman's voice said.

The baby boy looked up and seeing his mother talk to him, looked up and began laughing, showing mostly gums and two baby teeth pushing through the gums. Trevor didn't know it but somehow he felt that he was somehow connected to this little boy who he saw laughing without a care for the world. The woman sounded so familiar but Trevor couldn't pinpoint the connection. After a few minutes the woman who addressed the little boy finally came into view and it was there that Trevor felt as though the cat took his tongue. The mother had handed the baby a small basketball. The mother was the same woman Trevor had dreamed about when he had awoken in a cold sweat. The boy enjoyed throwing the ball on the ground repeatedly while laughing. But Trevor's mind was still on the mother who he has seen only in his dream.

"Are you gonna be my little basketball player, Trevor?" the woman asked.

Trevor always had an idea who it could be but when this woman on the video had used his name to address the baby that gave it away. The woman on the DVD had to be his mother, his real mother and it wasn't difficult to see where he received his love for the game. The young woman had a slight build but by the way that she was talking, she deeply loved him. So if these were his real parents, why had the McClains keep the truth from him all those years?

How could they not tell me who I was and who my real mother was? Trevor thought.

All those years, the McClains had not been very truthful at all. He watched as the young woman came back in the scene and continued to talk and kiss the baby boy.

"Mama loves you very much. One day you are gonna grow up and you will be a big man and play basketball, yes you are," the young woman said to the baby.

Trevor was trying to prevent it, but he couldn't hold back his emotion as a couple of tears rolled down his face. It was as if his mother was predicting the future because he had become exactly the man she had created. The young woman started to talk toward the direction of the person holding the camera, who Trevor guessed was his father.

"Baby, he is gonna be a big-time ball player like you were, don't you think?" she asked.

"I absolutely think he will be a big time ballplayer. He might end up being better than me, to be honest with you," his father said.

Trevor watched the whole video straight through to the end. He didn't know how he did it while still being able to hold his composure. Finally the DVD presentation stopped. Trevor took the DVD out of the computer and placed it right back in the case. He had a bevy of questions swirling in his head but the most pressing question was: were his parents still alive? He could accept being privileged because that was basically the story of his life but he couldn't accept his adoptive parents keeping a secret as monumental as this one. It wasn't right and it wasn't fair but the blame had to go to someone. As he walked back to his door, he took the DVD with him to the room. It all made sense. From the way his parents always avoided conversation about why he looked different from them to the way they had always acted like they acknowledged talking about their differences. With what he had seen on the DVD they could no longer deny that the eye color of the baby matched his own. The baby's skin complexion matched his own. Even the woman in the video matched him in looks, displaying the same dimples when she smiled and a nurturing character. There was no question that he was watching his biological mother. From the moment the DVD stopped, Trevor came to a crucial decision. Life was too short and the death of Loree had proven that.

Trevor decided to go on a personal mission to find his birth parents and get questions answered. He wouldn't let anyone get in his way or let anything stop him. He went back to his dorm room and looked at the letter. Since there was no signature on the letter, only initials from the writer, it really didn't give him much information with which to start his quest for answers. The letter had been the first step, and the DVD was a second step in the direction of fulfilling his mission.

Two buses and a couple of blocks later, Shania was finally home. Unlocking her house door, she walked inside and walked up the stairs, almost zombie-like. Her cell phone had been ringing for God knows how long and she knew it was her parents wondering where she was but at that very moment, Shania didn't want to talk to anyone and she most certainly didn't want to hear her father start with all the "death is a part of life" monologue. All she wanted was to be alone in her room; to shut out the world. As her eyes found their way to the closet, she could still see Loree's smiling face as she had rifled through her closet and tried on some of her clothes. She remembered Loree's jokes and exuberant personality whenever they were in school and most of all, she remembered how Loree was always with her at to church. Shania would be the first to admit that it wasn't always easy being a Christian girl growing up in a world where promiscuity was heralded and appreciated by society and people looked upon her as an oddity because she didn't act as her peers did.

Young women in her society were being treated as objects by men and most of them didn't mind being treated as such. Boys who were raised in the slums and in rough environments didn't know any other way to live because they were only following the examples of those who had come before them. Girls didn't know their worth as young women who deserved and demanded a level of respect because they were so used to being treated as property by weak-minded young men who knew no way of expanding their mental and educational horizons. Shania was one of the few girls who went against the grain and she was determined to become more than what the government was offering. With visions of becoming an elementary school teacher in the future, Shania was thankful for her early training as a teacher in her father's church. She felt it had been preparation for what the Lord wanted her to do in the future. Loree, on the other hand, was a girl who was conflicted. Part of her had tried to fit into a mold of women who accepted favors from men, while her conscience had itched to be an individual who could think for herself. Shania reminisced about the first day that they officially met and became friends.

It was the fall of the year 2000 and the kids were filing inside Richmond Hill High School on the third week of school. Standing only five-foot-four and barely weighing one hundred pounds, Shania, who was a high school freshman, walked tentatively through the halls of the school. Her hair tied in two long braids behind her and Shania acted the way that she looked; a small lost nervous freshman who had few friends. She walked to her locker and on the way, she saw various members of the school's basketball team gathered in the hallways. There were four players and Trevor McClain was one of the boys talking to girls and different admirers. Shania couldn't stand those rich, pretty boys. It seemed all the guys were totally conceited all because they could bounce a stupid ball around. Ok, so maybe it wasn't totally stupid because in all honesty, she respected all athletes because she was an athlete herself. She ran track and field for the school but she never flaunted her status just to get people to appreciate her. When she had watched Trevor and a couple other boys saunter around in their warm-ups, it made her slightly ill. Shania was looking for Amber Freeman, her friend from middle school who had some classes with her. Stopping by her locker, she prepared to open it when she heard some catcalls from some of the upper classmen boys not too far from her.

At first, Shania thought the catcalls were aimed at her but that thought quickly dissipated when she saw them. The group of girls; nicknamed the 'Black Barbie' girls, consisted of three senior girls and two up and coming freshman girls who strove to be a part of that group. The 'Black Barbies' had a reputation that followed them. They were notorious as girls who knew how to please the boys in the school and even in their neighborhoods, in more ways than one. Dressed in clothes that would make strippers blush, they showed more skin, more appeal, and more desire. Trevor took a look at them as they passed the halls and a confident smirk emerged on his face. There was no doubt in Shania's mind that he had been with one of these girls. Most girls in Shania's age group actually envied these girls but Shania did not envy them at all. As a matter of fact, she felt sorry for them. She believed that if they portrayed themselves as tarts, there was no way they would be respected for any other achievements in life and they surely would not get the respect they sought. Shania recognized the oldest of the group, Kim Lane, who was the prettiest but also the rudest. Shania knew her because on the very first day of school, she made the critical mistake of accidentally stepping on Kim's very expensive pumps and Kim ended up embarrassing Shania.

"Can't you watch where you goin', girl? Lookin' like a black Marcia Brady with them pigtails…" she said while the other kids laughed.

Shania turned slightly red and walked away so the whole incident could be avoided. What she didn't know at the time was that one of the hopefuls did not laugh and when Shania walked away with her head down, the girl had rallied to her side.

"Kim, leave that girl alone. She ain't mean to do it."

Kim looked down at the girl, raising her eyebrows at the freshman who had dared raise her voice to challenge her.

"Then why don't you tell her to move her big-ass feet a lil faster so it could be avoided?" Kim asked.

After that incident Shania was especially careful to avoid any type of bodily contact with Kim or any of her girls. As she passed them in the hall, the girl who had spoken up in Shania's defense gave her a quick head nod. At least it looked like a head nod to Shania. Shania wasn't sure. Did one of those painted up dolls actually say hi to her? Shania thought it over for a split second but not too soon after that, the warning bell rang so she took her books and went to class. After school Shania walked down the steps and started on her way home. Barely a block away from school Shania saw the girl who had acknowledged her in the hallways earlier while walking with the "Black Barbies". She appeared to be crying. Shania was conflicted because her mind was telling her not to talk to this girl because she was part of a group that was shallow as they appeared and as promiscuous as they dressed. Shania had once heard through a classmate that all of those girls had been sexually active with at least one guy. Shania later learned that freshman girls were no exception because having sex was a prerequisite to joining that elite social class. Kim must be a pro because Shania was almost positive Kim had sampled every type of dude who was worth her notice. But Shania did what most people didn't do when approaching someone who was conflicted; she used her heart.

"Hey are you ok?" Shania asked the girl.

The girl turned to look at Shania and Shania could tell from her pained expression that she didn't want to talk to anyone and initially she was correct in that assumption.

"I don't want to talk about it, ok? Why you even talking to me?" she asked Shania as though Shania was a different species; not human and certainly not worthy of talking with someone like her.

"Well, I just wanted to see if you were ok, that's all," Shania replied.

The girl just shook her head. "No I mean why you even talkin' to someone like me? Especially after the way my friend dogged you out that day. If I were you, I wouldn't want anything to do with us," the girl said.

Shania came up next to her. Shania might have been quiet, but she wasn't shy or tentative and that enabled her to make friends and relate well with others. "Well, I'm not you. I can't pull your style off with them shoes, that's for sure," she replied.

The girl looked at Shania, unsure if she was making a joke or if she was being genuine. "You like them?" the girl asked Shania.

"Yeah girl, them shoes are fly, and with the gear you got on, it's on point," Shania replied.

The girl laughed. Shania felt relieved that she had finally broken the ice with her. The girl stopped laughing and sighed.

"It's just this boy that I was going with earlier. I just found out that he was sleepin' around wit' this other chick. What an asshole. I gave that nigga the best he ever had," she said.

Shania hadn't asked for all of that information of course but it did bother that this girl was sexually active so early. Shania knew immediately that she would have to look out for this girl because it was pretty obvious that the" Black Barbies" didn't care enough to be consoled.

"Don't even sweat that, girl. That nigga didn't know who he had and before he knows it, he's gonna realize what he missed," Shania replied and after that she instantly regretted it.

She hated using that word and she hated that other people used it in the 'hood so frequently but she was starting to make a connection with this girl; a girl with whom she had nothing in common. The girl also seemed to realize that Shania had stepped out of her comfort zone verbally as well.

"Hold up, ain't you a pastor's girl? Where you learn to be raw like that?" the girl asked.

Shania laughed because she would get the same reaction from all her friends. Yes, she was a Christian girl but when she wanted to speak her mind, she would speak her mind and not hold back what she said. "Yeah, I'm a pastor's girl but that don't mean I'm perfect. It just means that I got two strict daddies who won't let me do nothing but school, church, and track" Shania replied.

The girl raised an eyebrow. "Two daddies, huh? I wonder how that works," the girl replied.

Shania laughed at the girl's obvious confusion. "I meant God and my father. Please don't get it twisted. I don't roll like that," she laughed.

The girl laughed as well. She found that Shania was easy to talk to and they had more in common than she thought.

"My name's Shania by the way. I'm over here running my mouth and I didn't even introduce myself," Shania said.

"Yeah, how rude of you," the girl replied before she laughed. "Nah I'm just playing. My name's Loree. Where you stay at?" the girl asked.

Shania told Loree where she lived. "Oh wow, you stay literally across the street from me. Let's go," Loree said, and both girls started to walk the same direction toward their homes. "I'm sorry for the way Kim messed with you. She my girl and all but sometimes she be treating people like they're nothing," Loree explained.

Shania looked at her. "Don't apologize for Kim. She just don't know any better and if you want my opinion, you can do a whole lot better than Kim or her crew," she said and at that moment she knew she meant it.

Loree was a pretty girl who wasn't always rough, she was misunderstood at times. "I think I am doing a whole lot better now with picking my friends now though," Loree said as they both walked home.

The ceiling stares back at Shania as she reflected on that chance meeting with Loree. They could not have been any more different from each other in character but the more they got to know each other over the course of their high school years, the more their friendship grew to the point where people really thought they were related. If anyone had just moved into the neighborhood and saw Loree and Shania, they would assume they were sisters. Shania couldn't even imagine what her life would be like now. Loree's sister Andrea, who was basically Shania's little sister as well, was going to endure the most excruciating pain of her sister's loss for a great deal of time.

I have to be there for Andrea. She's my sister now and I have to be strong for her, Shania thought as she turned over in her bed.

She saw her Bible sitting on the nightstand where she had placed it after church on Sunday. Opening the Word, she did her very best to remember that dying as it was described within the sixty-six books that comprised the Bible was a journey and a passing from one life to another.

Shania knew Loree had been far from perfect; she certainly had her shortcomings and she's done shameful acts. She may have made some terrible choices in her life but if God flipped the mirror and showed Shania her reflection in His eyes, she probably had no better soul than Loree. Sure, she had taken Loree to church, explained the Gospel as it was written, and had done what she could to help Loree depend on the Lord but Shania was not perfect. Suddenly she heard the turn of a key against the lock of the front door.

"Shania, are you here?" Shania!" her mother's voice rang out downstairs.

Robyn walked into the house, followed by Mike. Mike was only half-listening to his wife; he was still trying to gather his thoughts as he looked ahead to what would be a very trying week. Not only was he compelled to work and keep his own family going but he would have to break the news of Loree's passing to his church and help the family make funeral arrangements to lay her to rest.

My job is never easy and now it just got much harder Mike thought as he imagined of the tough road that lay ahead of him. He walked up to Shania's room door and knocked on the door.

"Shania? Baby, can we talk?" he asked through the door.

After a couple of minutes, Mike sensed that his daughter wanted to be alone. He began to walk away from the door but before he could, the door swung open and Shania stood at the doorway, motioning her father to come in. Mike stepped into her bedroom. He looked around the room and saw the wall covered with old pictures of Shania as a little girl, showing various school trips, Girl Scout pictures, and newspaper pictures of her victories in track and field meets at her school. Sometimes Mike had forgotten how much his daughter had grown up. He sat at the edge of the bed with her.

"Hey Shania, I know you're going through a very difficult time right now. Loree was your best friend, and she was taken from us way too soon. I just wanted to see if you wanted to talk," he said.

Shania thought it over. "I don't know Dad," she replied shaking her head. "It's just…. I still can't believe she's gone. I thought I did everything to protect her," she said, tears streaming down her face.

Mike puts his hand on her shoulder. "Shania, sometimes we can do everything we can to save those we love, but our efforts may not be enough. I don't want to pretend that I knew Loree as well as you did but I know based on our conversations that she was struggling with her relationship and with her life. I know you tried your best to be a positive example to her," he said.

"Dad, the thing that bothers me the most is that she never understood what she learned at church. I just wish I had more time to effectively reach her. I wish there was more that I could have done," she lamented.

Mike tried to understand what his daughter meant. He didn't want his daughter to take the burden of Loree's death on her shoulders.

"I believe you did all you could. Besides, who are we to judge where Loree's soul went after death? Only God knows where her journey ended," he said. "That reminds me, Shania. I wanted to tell you to be extremely careful with who you associate and who you befriend. Not everyone who shakes your hand or hugs you has your best interests at heart. Especially these young men out there today," he added.

Shania gave her father a glowering look. She knew exactly why her father was saying that. It had to be because of his fear of Trevor.

"Dad, he's not a bad guy at all. He just works hard in school and on his basketball team. I have a right to like who I like don't I?" she asked vehemently.

"You may have a right to like who you like, but I have a right to protect my family. I don't want what happened to Loree to happen to you," Mike replied. "I don't know this boy too well. Loree put her faith and trust in a boy that she didn't know too well and look where that got her," he emphasized before realizing that he might have gone too far. Shania lay down on her bed, her back to her father. Mike hung his head. "I'm sorry, ok? I just care about you too much and I can't bear to lose you," he said before he stood up and left Shania lying on the bed.

CHAPTER FIFTEEN

After school Jamal and Omar walked out of the school double doors. Jamal knew he couldn't walk home with Omar as he usually did. Omar asked about his early practice session that morning.

"It was good. I got a lot of work done on my dribble and jump shot," Jamal replied, leaving out the fact that the school janitor had helped him. He sure he didn't want it leaked that he was getting basketball lessons or else ninety-five percent of the school male student body wouldn't let him hear the end of it. "You need to consider coming early one of them days, for real," Jamal added.

Omar appeared to be thinking about it for a moment before he replied "Nah you could keep that. While you work on your own, I'll be getting mines with the JV and varsity squad. We'll see who ends up makin' the team," he challenged jokingly.

Jamal laughed. It would be Omar who would turn this into some type of contest. At the same moment, they saw Patricia making her way out of the school.

"Here's your chance, dog," Omar said. "You be playin' around with her emotions, now you gotta handle yours before some other dude steps in," he added.

Jamal looked at Patricia. He had been trying to keep it friendly between the two of them, but she had been making it harder by throwing subtle hints that she was interested in him. There had been more than one instance when he would be innocently taking notes in class, and he would look up and find her staring at him. Their eyes would meet for a split second before she turned her eyes to her own work as if she had never looked at him at all. Then, when he was at his locker, he would look up and she would mysteriously appear; telling Jamal about her day, her teachers, and gossiping about her friends and new relationships. None of those topics interested Jamal but he would nod and pretend that he was interested. Then there were the clothes she would wear. Carlos had not been lying when he talked about her beauty, and she made sure everyone was keenly aware of it. Short skirts, low-waist jeans, and tight blouses were just the tip of the iceberg in terms of the fashion choices she made. Jamal didn't have a problem with what she wore to school, but he suspected she was wearing these clothes for a reason other than making a fashion statement.

"Do it, man," Omar said, winking at Jamal before starting to walk home.

Jamal started to say something to Omar, but Patricia caught up to Jamal too quickly.

"What's up, Jamal?" she greeted. Jamal smiled at her.

"What's good?" he asked.

"Care to walk me home?" Patricia asked.

"Actually, my mom's coming to pick me up in a few minutes," he replied.

"Why?" Patricia asked, looking puzzled and confused. "You live so close to here. What? She don't trust her little baby Jamal walking home on his own?" she asked, mocking Jamal for what seemed like the hundredth time.

Jamal didn't know what to say. He didn't feel like explaining that his mother was worried about his safety after a friend had just been shot and was fighting for her life at the hospital.

"Nah she don't trust me cuz she afraid I might get into trouble," Jamal replied, grinning.

"I wonder what trouble you be getting into after school?" Patricia asked, raising an eyebrow.

Jamal decided to tease Patricia for a little while. It was about time to turn the tables on her for a change.

"Oh don't worry about what I be doing. I'm a regular renegade," he replied coolly, putting his hands in his pocket and leaning against the wall.

The boys who normally hung out on the front steps in front of the doorway stopped talking amongst themselves and started watching the interaction between Patricia and Jamal.

"So are you saying you a bad boy now?" Patricia asked.

This is it. I'm bout to blow her mind Jamal thought.

"You'll find out lata'," Jamal replied, in his best Brooklyn accent.

Patricia seemed a little taken aback by Jamal's sudden confidence. "Is that so? Well here, Lemme give you this and we can find out sooner instead of later," Patricia replied and took   out a pen to write her phone number on his hand.

Jamal looked at the ink on his hand. Patricia came close to Jamal's ear and Jamal felt his heart skip and suddenly he felt warm but he didn't let Patricia know it.

"Call me anytime and trust me, I can be bad, too," she whispered in his ear before kissing him on the cheek.

The boys, watching on the doorway started to laugh and gave each other fist pounds and congratulatory handshakes as Patricia made her way down the steps of the school to walk home. As soon as Patricia walked out of earshot, one of the boys walked to Jamal and gave him a fist pound.

"Yo I gotta give it to you, dog. You got game," he said to Jamal. Turning to his friends, he said, "Ya need to take notes from my lil nigga ova hea'. Ya see the way he put it down?"

The other boys nodded their heads and shouted in agreement. They all came to give Jamal handshakes and fives but Jamal made sure he did so with his left hand. He did not want to smudge or smear the phone number until he got home and wrote it down on paper so he could call her.

Suddenly a car horn blared. Unbeknownst to Jamal, his mother had arrived a few minutes early to wait for Jamal and had seen Patricia write on Jamal's hand. Growing impatient, Isis had honked her car horn to get Jamal's attention. Jamal ran to his mother's car and his mother unlocked the passenger seat door.

"I see you no longer need my help adjusting to your new school, Mr. Big Man on Campus," Isis said as Jamal got into the car. Jamal didn't know what she meant, until he gazed down at the phone number written on his hand.

"Oh, I guess you saw that, huh? How much did you see?" Jamal asked sheepishly.

"Oh, I saw Ms. Thing write on your hand and kiss you on the cheek. Is there something you wanna tell me, Jamal?" Isis asked, in a voice that Jamal wasn't sure was sarcasm, anger, or disappointment.

"Well I'm making new friends," Jamal replied grinning.

The stern look never left Isis's face. "Jamal you really need to watch who you associate with. You two are much too young to be involved in anything right now. I really wish you would slow that down," Isis said.

Jamal stopped grinning and looked at his mother with a look of confusion. "I know what I'm doing Mom. Trust me, I won't force anything," he replied.

"Do you?" Isis replied, her voice rising, alarming Jamal. "Kids nowadays are going to abuse your trust, baby. Don't trust anyone out here, especially in this area. As a matter of fact, I don't think this school is the best one to be going to right now. It's filled with drug-dealers and kids being hurt for no reason," Isis added.

Jamal looked at his mother again. His mother was losing it. "Mom, what's wrong with you? Why you talking like this?" he asked, surprised by his mother's sudden outburst.

His mother was silent for a moment. Relaxing for a moment, taking a couple of deep breaths, she said, "Loree didn't make it. She's gone, Jamal."

If the words had not come out of his mother's mouth, Jamal would not have believed it. "What?" he asked in complete disbelief.

Tears began to fall down Isis's cheeks. "Honey, the doctors did everything they could but they couldn't save her. I got the phone call from Pastor Mike this morning. As you know, his crew will be coming tomorrow to start work on our kitchen counter and he broke the news to me," she replied.

Jamal sat back in his seat, stunned. Loree McAfee, Shania's best friend as well as a friend of his, was no longer in this world. "I thought she would make it, Mom," he said. "I didn't think it would be serious. I thought she would make it…." he repeated but found himself unable to finish his statement. When they arrived at their apartment building, Isis reached over and hugged her son as tightly as she could.

As soon as the last staff member left the school grounds at six o'clock in the evening, Nate made his way over to his small closet in the janitor room and changed to his gym clothes. He planned to hit the gym right after work, but he knew he wasn't going to arrive at the gym before seven o'clock as he originally planned, mostly because of the city's public transportation. In order to reach the gym, he normally had to wait fifteen to twenty minutes for his first bus at the stop which was just a block away from the school. He had to ride that bus for another fifteen minutes before getting off to catch another one to arrive at his destination nearly thirty minutes later. It was annoying and inconvenient to go through this on a daily basis. He had given some thought to purchasing a car so he wouldn't have to wait continually for buses or even worse, worry about riding any of the subways. A car would shave at least twenty-five minutes off his hour-length commute to go to the gym from Richmond Hill High School. He took out his duffel bag and started to put his work clothes in the bag when a photo fell out of his bag. Nate was the only person who knew this particular duffel bag was the same one he had used during his playing years and it was considered something of a memento to remind him of the memories of happier days he had enjoyed. Besides keeping warm-ups, practice clothes, and sneakers in that bag, he also used to carry photographs in the bag. It was just a habit to some but Nate was a man who believed that players had certain good luck charms that they brought with them before games. He had continued this tradition until he had stopped playing basketball; ultimately dropping out of school to sell drugs. The bag had been stored away for some years and was not used again until very recently when Nate started working and going to the gym again.

As he picked up the photo that fell on the floor, he took a look at it and grinned. Mike Hillman and Nina Martin were staring right back up at him and there was Gary, who joked around all the time, raising his head in between Mike and Nina, with his tongue hanging out in a silly gesture. It was the last photograph Nate had of his friends when they were still part of each other's lives. Since then, he never really knew what became of them. From what he heard through old sources, Gary moved to Jersey and Mike Hillman went to some college and of course Nina was no longer around. Big Earl had seen to that. Nate was convinced that it wasn't over yet and if it was the last act he ever did on earth, he was going to find Earl and make him pay for what he had done to Nina.

As he walked outside to wait for the bus, Nate looked across the street and saw a couple of boys walking the sidewalk carrying paper bags that suggested they had returned from the corner store, laughing and joking around as if they had never known tragedy or pain.

So carefree is the life of a child. I wish my childhood was carefree like that Nate thought as he watched.

A few minutes Nate's bus pulled up and Nate entered. He swiped his Metrocard on the kiosk and Nate quickly saw the bus was very crowded. Fortunately there was an extra seat in the middle of the bus, so Nate made his way over and sat down. A couple of bus stops later, he reached the gym and walked inside to get to work. As he began to lift weights, his friend Rob Curry, the man who had marveled at Nate's punching power a few days earlier, walked over to help Nate out.

"Hey man, I thought for a second, you weren't coming," he said as he spotted Nate.

Nate smiled as he continued lifting. "What made you think that my man?" he asked as he strained to get the huge barbell up.

"Normally you get here a bit earlier and get right to work. Seems to me you're slacking some," Rob joked.

"No never. I ain't never slacking bro," Nate laughed. "It's my job. Cleaning up after some rowdy kids takes a lot of time and patience and right now that patience is cutting into my time," he added.

"I hear you," Rob agreed. "That can't be easy doing what you're doing. But I gotta give you this though, you're relentless at it and it's about the dinero, right?"

Nate couldn't agree more. He needed money but there wasn't a lot of it, especially at his current job. As the realization dawned on him, he stopped lifting and sat up on the benching area, looking Rob straight in the eye.

"I need another job," he said seriously, although Rob took it as a joke and started laughing. Nate started laughing as well. "But first I need to get me a car. Doing this whole bus and subway thing ain't me man," he added.

Rob looked at him questioningly. "Well, what's stopping you from getting a whip, bro?" he asked.

"Well for one thing, my credit's jacked up right now and the way my paycheck's set up, I can barely afford anything right now. Hell, I can barely even afford to pay my rent, much less a car note," Nate replied.

Rob appeared to be in deep thought for a moment. "Tell you what, I'm gonna refer you to my boy Antoine Sparks. He works over at that new spot, Distinct Auto Dealers over in Astoria. They specialize in selling used cars for really low rates. They might be able to hook you up," he said.

Nate shook his head. "I appreciate it, homie but I'm not trying to drive no car that's gonna break down on me after one- or two-months man. I'm tryin to get something that's gonna have decent mileage and probably hold me over for a couple seasons," he said.

"Trust me man, this dude will get you a nice ride. Antoine's the same guy that sold me the used ninety-six Acura for four-fifty down man, and no additional payments. You ain't gotta worry about paying no car note. Antoine is one of the salesmen that works there and trust me, he'll give you a nice lil' deal," Rob insisted. "As a matter of fact, hold up," he added before running over to the locker room in the gym to retrieve his bag. He emerged from the locker room after five minutes with the business card for Distinct Auto Dealers in Astoria, New York. "I knew I still had one of these lying around," he said, handing Nate the card. "Don't take my word for it bro. When you get a chance check 'em out. All the cars on the lot still run good and he can give you an estimate on how long you can run before any type of oil change or adjustments," he added.

Nate looked at the card. The more he thought about it, the better he thought getting a car, even if it was a used car; would be to his advantage. "All right, I'll try 'em out. Good lookin out, man," Nate replied, putting the card in his pocket. He made the decision to make the trip to Astoria, Queens on Saturday when he was off. I can't do it this week, gotta clean up some messes and watch them rowdy kids he thought as he got back to working out.

Staring at the empty side of her room at the bed where her late sister had once slept, there were moments where Andrea expected Loree to waltz into the room with the swagger in her step, talking animatedly on her cell phone to Shania or another friend. She waited for Loree to come into their room so she could reveal her innermost feelings about boys and dating. She expected Loree to walk into their room with a new outfit from the mall, asking Andrea for her opinion. Maybe the most painful expectation was to see Loree sitting next to her in church on Sunday. After the service they would have brunch with Shania and they would discuss the message that was preached that morning, what it meant to them and how they could start to apply it to their own lives. She remembered the slumber parties when Loree and a few of her friends would come over and do each other's nails and talk. Of course, the conversations would always veer toward boys. Instead, Andrea paced the room as she waited to join her parents to accomplish chores she dreaded. She and her parents were going to find a funeral home to bury her sister, sign the large life insurance policy that had to be withdrawn from the bank under Loree's name, and they had to set a date for the actual funeral service. Andrea closed her eyes. She wished she could die. She wished she could've taken the place of her sister that night.

God, why her? Why my sister? Why couldn't you have taken me instead? I thought I did everything for you. I went to Sunday school, I prayed every day, and yet I'm the one that ends up suffering at the end of it all.

She wished there was another bedroom so she wouldn't see the memories, the pain and the death but it didn't matter; the whole house had pictures of Loree. After a few minutes, the house phone rang. There were two receivers, one out the in hall near Andrea's room and the other in her parent's room. Andrea didn't bother answering but her mother picked up the phone and after a few minutes, she came to the room, the sorrow still washed on her face.

"Honey, it's for you." Alisha told Andrea, holding out the cordless phone receiver. Andrea took the phone.

"Hello? Who's this?" she asked.

"Hey sweetie, it's me," Shania replied on the other end. "I was calling to check on you and I wanted to apologize about running out of the hospital the way I did. I wanted you to be strong for Loree but I guess I have to learn to be strong too," she said.

Andrea sighed. "It's ok, Shania. I would've been running too and kept on running until there's nowhere else to run. I just want this to be over," she replied.

"I know how much it hurts Andrea but I just wanted to let you know that I'll be there for you whenever you need me and if you want to talk, we can talk," Shania said. "Loree was like a sister to me and just as she learned from me, I've learned from her. To tell you the truth, I don't even know if I could go back to school. Everywhere I go, I'll be reminded of her," she added.

Andrea felt her eyes watering again. "I know, but I'm gonna keep praying, Shania. You taught me that during the rough times, I had to depend on God. Even when I don't know or understand why some things happen, I have to trust Him even if it's hard," she said.

Through her sorrow, Shania couldn't conceal how proud she was of Andrea. She had grown so much and she had already started to develop the strength that her late sister had shown.

"You know, in some ways you remind me of Loree. How strong she was and how smart she was. I know you're going through a tough time now but maybe we can hang out this weekend, maybe Saturday?" Shania asked.

"That would be great. I'd love that," Andrea replied.

"Great!" Shania exclaimed. She felt the best way to forget the sorrow of death was to reach out to Loree's sister and life. Too many times, Shania had seen situations where younger brothers and sisters lost their siblings in unexpected accidents and unfortunately too many of them, because of uncertainty and isolation, had turned to other forms of relief, whether it was alcohol or drugs. Shania knew how young and impressionable Andrea was and if she didn't reach out now, Andrea could begin seeking other means to cope with her sister's death. Shania wanted to be an older sister to Andrea and although she knew she could never take the place of Loree, she would watch over Andrea and continue to train her and prepare her for life.

"There's this new pizza place spot that just opened up on Lefferts and 102 Street. Maybe we could check it out," Shania said.

"Ok cool," Andrea replied. "By the way, is he coming?" she asked.

"He who?" Shania asked, clearly confused.

"You know who," Andrea laughed. "Yo' man, Trevor," she added.

Shania laughed. "First off, he is not my man, ok? Let's get that straight and when has that been any of your business anyway?" she said, laughing.

"I've known you for a long time, Shania and I saw the way you looked at him when he fell asleep on the chair at the hospital. It's ok, I think he likes you too, or else he wouldn't have stayed with you as long as he did. I would definitely hold on to him before someone else snatches him up," Andrea replied.

Shania laughed. It was amazing how much of Loree was in Andrea. Shania could hear Loree saying the same exact words.

"I don't know right now, ok? It's complicated between us. Besides you know my father don't want me going out with anyone right now," she said.

"But what does your heart say? What does your soul say?" Andrea asked.

Shania didn't know how to answer those questions directly because she really didn't know what her heart or her mind was trying to say to her. With her upbringing, she had grown to learn about herself and her relationship with the Lord and the way her father raised her told her that this guy could be bad news. On the outside, Trevor was a self-centered, selfish, impulsive boy who had accomplished all of his goals since he had started high school. He was a star basketball player who was very talented on the court, and he had been somewhat of a playboy off the court. She could never erase the image of Trevor as a young sophomore in high school smiling as the "Black Barbies" walked down the hall letting it all hang out, no doubt intending to poison and manipulate young, naïve minds like Trevor's. He epitomized all that was wrong with young black men today. He had a world of ability and opportunity at his hands but he was quick to waste it by hooking up with girls who wanted him for reasons other than love. Yet Shania knew there was a different side to Trevor that she knew was present the more she spoke with him.

He was a gentleman, very sweet, and generous. Nobody had asked him to stay at the hospital when they were waiting on Loree's outcome, yet he spent all night at the hospital. Only someone who deeply cared for another would do a kind generous act. It was that side of Trevor that she was attracted to and it was that side of Trevor that she wanted to get to know better. But at this time, it just didn't seem ideal, especially dealing with a tragedy that hit so close to home. There was also the physical aspect of Trevor that Shania considered. Trevor took very good care of his body, which was obvious when his muscles rippled under the T-shirts he wore. Shania was in great shape herself because she ran track. The biggest revulsion to her was a guy who never worked out. To Shania, it showed a complete lack of discipline and dedication and Shania had to admit that those were two traits Trevor that were sacred to him.

"Only God knows where we stand Andrea," Shania finally replied. "I don't really know what's gonna happen, but he is a great guy, and he is very strong and smart," she added.

"I know. I saw him with you, and I was hoping you two would hook up," Andrea said. Shania laughed. It was time to end the call.

"Ok Andrea, I'm done with you right now. We'll talk later about Saturday, ok?" she continued.

"Ok, Shania, Bye," Andrea said, before hanging up. Shania hung up as well, shaking her head, laughing. She wondered if Loree had really passed away or if she had taken over Andrea's body because the similarities in the conversation were just too uncanny to those that she would have with her late friend.

Earlier that afternoon, Trevor drove to his parent's home in Jamaica Estates. He drove with a determined look on his face, searching for answers that he knew his parents would attempt to deny for the millionth time. First he had received the letter then it was the DVD with the mother and the child. The revelation of his beginnings had started with the questions he had about his skin tone, his eye color, and even his facial expressions. Maybe when he was a child those traits weren't as obvious but after watching the DVD and seeing the child who he now suspected was himself as a baby with a woman who he surmised was his mother, he was in the middle of a puzzle. Who was his biological mother and why had she disappeared? Why had she left him to the McClains? Where was his real father? Although he did not see his father's face on the video, he was positive that it was his father the woman was addressing; the man who held the camera. Was it a case where the responsibility of having a child was too much for him so he walked out on her, leaving her with the job of being a single parent? Could the abandonment be what led her to drug abuse? Was it due to the overall stress that she had finally snapped and gave him up to the McClains? So many questions ran through his mind, and he had been patient throughout his elementary school years. He had been patient through his middle and high school years. Now he was at the beginning of his college career and starting his adult life. Trevor's patience could only be pushed to a point before it broke. He no longer wanted to wait. He wanted the truth.

Trevor arrived at his parent's house, parked his car on the side of the street instead of in the large driveway where he normally parked. He knocked on the door. Mrs. McClain opened the door, in apparent shock. She had not expected Trevor to visit during the week.

"Hey, honey, how you doing? Is everything ok?" she asked.

"No Mom, we need to talk. Do you have a minute?" Trevor asked, entering the home abruptly without waiting for Mrs. McClain to invite him inside. He saw his father sitting at the kitchen table. Good thing he's off work now cuz he's involved in this too he thought.

His father looked up from the newspaper he was reading. "Hey big baller what brings you here? What can we do for...." He started but never got the chance to finish his statement because Trevor cut him off.

"What do you know about my real parents?"

Tiffany and Jack looked at each other for a moment before turning back to Trevor.

"Um, where is this coming from?" she asked Trevor who stared at them with a look of deep intent and determination.

"Don't be givin' me no riddles or jokes or anything this time. I need ya'll to tell me straight up. Who am I and where am I from?" he demanded.

"Whoa, I think maybe you need to ease up on the way you talk to your mother," Jack replied.

"My mother?!!" Trevor exclaimed, infuriated. "Are you sure?" he asked them.

He knew he was over-stepping his boundaries but what boundaries were there when the people who set them didn't even abide by their own rules?

"I always tried to figure out why I could never get a straight answer whenever I asked that question or even mentioned it," Trevor said, shaking with fury. "I mean, I don't know why you thought you could keep it from me all this time. You think I wouldn't find out what was up?" he asked.

Jack had never been known to raise his voice at his son for reasons other than disciplinary when Trevor was a boy, but as far as Trevor was concerned, those days were over. Jack, however, was still determined to make his authority known.

"Look, boy we took you in and took care of you. We put clothes on your back, and we put food on that damn table for you. You best be thankful for what we did," he said firmly.

But Trevor wasn't backing down easily this time. "You gave me everything... everything but the truth," he bit back. "All you had to do was be real with me, clear some things up. If I don't know where I came from, do you think whatever I did up to this point means anything?" he asked.

Tiffany tried to embrace Trevor, but Trevor wouldn't allow his mother to embrace him.

"I want to know the truth, Mom," he demanded again, putting emphasis on the word 'Mom'. Tiffany looked at him with eyes that expressed her pain and hurt.

"I wish it was easy to tell you honey but...." She had not finished her statement when Trevor reached into his pocket and took out the letter with the DVD and put both of them on the kitchen table.

"Seems like it was easy for somebody else to tell me, so why couldn't you? Don't believe me? Don't take my word for it then, just watch the movie," he said.

Tiffany read the letter and when her eyes reached the very last sentence on the letter, she closed her eyes, which started to weep. She turned to Jack.

"Honey, we have to tell him the truth. We can't keep nothin' from him, anymore," Tiffany said. Jack opened his mouth, as if to protest but kept his mouth closed as if he had nothing more to say.

"Ok, I'm listening," Trevor said, sitting down.

Tiffany sat down as well. Without caring to watch the DVD, Tiffany said, "Trevor, the woman that you probably saw in the DVD was Nina Martin. She was your biological mother. Before I became your adoptive mother, I was actually your babysitter and I used to help her watch you while she went to work." she added.

"What do you mean, she 'was' my mother? Where is she now? Can't I visit her?" Trevor asked.

"I'm sorry, but Nina's no longer here. She passed away," she replied.

CHAPTER SIXTEEN

The kitchen was silent for a full three minutes as Trevor stood still, while those devastating words flowed inside his ears, his mind, and his conscience. So his birth mother was dead without any possibility of finding her. She was gone without a chance of reconciliation and reunion. Trevor was not sure if his so called "parents" had told him the whole truth. How could he know they weren't lying to him just to pacify him? How could he ever trust them again after they had lied to him for so long? Trevor, who had been standing at the opposite end of the kitchen table across from his parents, dropped into his chair upon hearing the news that he had been adopted. He had always held out hope that his mother was still alive somewhere, waiting for him to return to his home; his real home. Away from this painted, fancy lie he had been living in for the last seventeen years. How would he ever know why this happy mother had given up her only son. Then he remembered the chilling nightmare he had a few days earlier in which he had seen a woman shooting heroine up her arm while the baby lay crying his eyes out; crying for attention, crying for nourishment, crying for love that he would never know or feel. The bitter truth was not only sickening but somber. Trevor needed more answers because despite what Tiffany had told him, he still didn't fully trust her or Jack.

"How did she die?" he asked in a tone that was hushed, although he felt enraged inside at the people who had the gall to call themselves his parents.

"Honey, it's best if we don't give you that information. I don't think you'll be able to take it," she replied.

Trevor's fist hit the table with such force that it startled his parents. "What happened to her? Did she get sick? Did she get shot in the streets? What happened?" he demanded of his parents.

Jack finally stood up from his chair. He had enough of Trevor acting as if he was a boss in his own home. "If your mother thinks it's too sensitive for you to hear, then that's the end of that. She don't have to say nothing else do you hear me!?" he yelled.

"That's not good enough. I wanna know what happened to Nina Martin. I have the right to know!" Trevor exclaimed.

His mother stared at him, somber as ever. "Trevor I'm so sorry we kept it from you all of these years, but we only wanted to keep you safe, to protect you," she replied.

At that point, Trevor knew she was telling the truth because her eyes began to fill with tears again. Nina did not die of any sickness or natural cause, she had either overdosed from doing too much drugs or she had met her end in the streets by either gang violence or a drug deal gone wrong. Tiffany was afraid that Trevor would go looking for the culprit, thus endangering his own life in the process.

"So what you tryna not tell me is that she was murdered, is that it?" he asked Tiffany.

Tiffany and Jack continued to look at each other, both unable to properly answer Trevor's assumption. Tiffany walked over to Trevor's side and rubbed Trevor's left shoulder.

"Honey, Nina was a very beautiful girl. I first met her at a Duane Reade pharmacy store, where we both worked at. She was generous, charismatic and driven to make something of herself in life," she said. "But she had her demons, Trevor. You see, Nina was a heroin addict and at first she hid it, but I can't count the number of times I would walk in a back room or the loading area and I would see her shooting up. She became the way she was because she associated with people who didn't care about her. She was hanging out with drug dealers and low lives," she added.

Trevor did not like where this story was going. If Nina was so generous and well liked as everyone said, why didn't anyone step forward to keep her from the streets?

"She never stopped believing that she would conquer those demons one day because the most wonderful thing happened to her. You were born," Tiffany continued. "She would always tell me that she would turn her life around and do better for herself because she didn't want you to be trapped the same way she was. She went to rehab a few times, if I remembered correctly, and attempted to steer clear of drugs but she would eventually relapse. That's what happened to her, Trevor. She couldn't stay away from the streets and from the drugs and the temptation and lure of it all. Then one night, she went to the streets one last time and the streets finally claimed her. You were not even a year old, Trevor. I was watching you that night and she told me she would return but she never did come back that night," Tiffany explained.

Trevor shook his head, his face in his hands. There were so many emotions running through him, he couldn't even function.

So my dream has been right all this time Trevor thought. His mother was nothing more than a drug-using floozy who didn't give a damn about her son or their future. If she did, maybe she would have tried even harder to quit using drugs. But something else bothered him. He had been putting all the blame on Tiffany and Jack for concealing this from him and he had been putting the blame on Nina for not letting go of the drugs, but someone else deserved some of the blame. That had been his biological father.

"So, where was my father at?" Trevor asked roughly.

Tiffany continued to pat his shoulder. "Your biological father didn't even stay a month with Nina. He never even called her periodically to check on her or you. He was one of the biggest disappointments in being a good father to you, Trevor. I would see him whenever he came to pick her up from the pharmacy. His name was Greg or Gary or something like that. I don't remember. I never spoke to him then and I haven't spoken with him recently," Tiffany said, almost defiantly as if she held bitter memories of Nina's relationship choice.

"Ok I got all that but is he still alive? If so, where does he live?" Trevor asked.

Tiffany shook her head. "I don't know where he lives, to be honest with you. But I know he's alive because we did receive a letter from him a few years ago, asking us to visit him so he could see you. I decided that I didn't want to do that just yet," she explained.

Trevor rubbed the sides of his head. He tried to understand the way his parents thought. They had tried their very best to blot out any memory or any information about his roots or background, but Trevor wasn't going to give up this time. Not without speaking to his biological father.

"I'm gonna find him. I bet he was the one who sent the letter. I bet he was the one taping my mother that day," he said, rising up to leave the home.

Tiffany ran to detain him before he left the house. "Trevor, promise me you won't go looking for this man. It's been years since you've seen him. If he really wanted to see you, he would've came here and visited you on his own, instead of writing letters from God knows where," she said.

It was too late. Trevor has made up his mind. "I don't care. I gotta go find him and I will find him, with or without your help," he said before he left the house.

Tiffany went outside and watched Trevor get into his car and drive away. Tiffany closed the door and walked over to Jack, who was staring at Tiffany as she shook her head.

"You still think it was a good idea to tell that boy anything?" Jack asked. "Now he's gonna go out there and visit his good for nothing father and find out personally what a loser he is," he added.

"Jack, if there's anything I know, it's that Trevor won't go out there and get himself in trouble. He may have said a lot of things, and he may have done a lot of things, but he'll think it over. Just watch," Tiffany reassured Jack.

Jack sighed. "I hope so," he said.

Later that afternoon, David Anderson walked about six blocks to Ozone Park, which was at the corner of Lefferts Boulevard and 117th Street. The small row of houses that faced the park was dilapidated and rundown, giving the area the aura of being abandoned and vacated. As he walked through the park, David looked nervously behind him. He was extremely nervous because he knew the police were still investigating Loree's shooting. The past couple of days had been nothing short of a nightmare for David and his grandmother, with whom he had since he was a small boy. The NYPD had been relentless in attempting to get a confession out of David to implicate him and his involvement in the shooting but David maintained his innocence. His grandmother had been nothing short of supportive; never giving David away because she was one of the few people who knew David's past.

David had been a young gangbanger and had started heading down the path of destruction in the streets at an early age. Tadarius had been more than Davis's friend, he had been like a brother to David. David's parents had abandoned him when he was young and he had bounced around from one foster home to another, looking for acceptance. The courts finally granted custody to David's grandmother on his father's side. Although he lived with his grandmother, the trouble never ceased for David, who had anger and aggression issues from the beginning.

When he had been thrown into a child juvenile facility for nearly killing a man, David met Tadarius, who had been locked up at the time for grand theft auto and assault and battery. A brotherly bond developed within the two boys and when they were both freed from the juvenile facility, they kept busy running the underground operation of M.O.B. David eventually built muscle and acted as a bodyguard to Tadarius. Whoever came at Tadarius the wrong way would have had to answer to David and the person who dared challenge Tadarius would be out of the picture. David never saw Tadarius as others did because Tadarius was the older brother David never had, so he would mimic whatever Tadarius did. David smoked cigarettes, drank endless amounts of alcohol, robbed various stores, and continued to stack money with Tadarius. The two had been partners – until David saw a way out. Football became his escape.

The gridiron and the field and the promise of a scholarship lured him more and more out of the streets.

David had been going to school but was performing poorly in his classes. He eventually pulled through enough to make it to Richmond Hill and the first time he played football, even if it was on the freshman squad, he fell in love with the game. Due to his grades however, he was ineligible to play until his senior year when he had completely left Tadarius's ranks and made a promise to his grandmother and to himself to perform better academically so he could play football. His play in the summer leagues and training camps drew scouts from NCAA Division I colleges and David continued building the momentum. It was extremely hard work and he certainly had days when he wanted to give up but two people believed in him. The first person was his grandmother, who was proud of the effort David was making to succeed on the field. The other person was Loree who went to every game, patched up all his cuts and massaged his shoulders whenever he needed a massage. Loree had definitely been his number one fan, until the argument at the fast food restaurant when Tadarius had won the truly stupid bet David had accepted with his surrogate big brother. Now Loree was lying in the hospital, no doubt fighting for her life, and David was fighting to stay out of prison. The more the police pressed him, the more difficult it was for him to save face and maintain his innocence. Loree's words at the restaurant echoed in his mind.

"Stop hanging around Tadarius and his crew like his little whipping boy. Stand up for yourself, for once," she had said.

With those words ringing loudly in his ears, David walked toward his familiar haunts, to the area where he knew Tadarius and his M.O.B gang would be hanging out. He looked across Ozone Park. The park was mostly deserted, other than just a couple of kids who were on the jungle gym playground.

Where they at? David asked himself as he looked around.

Giving up all hope that they were at the park, David headed toward the lobby of an old apartment building on 123rd Street. Sure enough, he saw plenty of evidence that his old crew was in the area; broken beer and malt liquor bottles, hundreds of cigarettes and joints on the sidewalk and the stream of marijuana smoke emerging from the lobby of the apartment building. David walked inside the lobby and saw two members of M.O.B playing craps on the lobby floor, three more guys playing cards, and three other members playing dominoes. He walked up to one of the members, a heavy brawny guy posted up next to the doorway of the apartment building acting like a club bouncer or security.

"What set you rep, homeboy?" he asked in deep tones, his hands reaching inside his pants pocket.

David didn't back down. He knew this guy. "Malik, stop playin' nigga. You know who I be. Where Tadarius at?" David asked.

Malik's facial reaction remained stoic for a moment, before breaking into a wide, toothy grin. "Yeah I know you, my nigga. I was just fuckin' with you. Tadarius's skinny ass is in hea' wit' a couple bitches. Work hard, play even harder, you know what it is," Malik laughed.

David faked a laugh to avoid any suspicion. He didn't want to give the impression that he was going to rejoin the group. Normally when a gangbanger left his crew, the crew labeled him a traitor and the banger was dealt with seriously. Nobody left Tadarius but since Tadarius and David had more history than anyone else who followed him, he had allowed David go out on his own to be a great football player. David knew there was an ulterior motive and although Tadarius didn't speak it out loud, the fact that he let David play football had an underlying motive.

If you killin' it in high school and college, you definitely headed for the pros which means a million dollar contract and a million more in endorsements. If I allow you to go that far, I expect to be reciprocated. If you win, we all win. If you rich, we all rich. Take care of us and we'll take care of you, was Tadarius' unspoken motive.

David had been in the streets long enough to know that as long as he was still playing football, he was playing not only for himself, he was playing for Tadarius and M.O.B as well. Anyone else might feel trapped but David was determined to end his gangbanging when he left for college. As far as he was concerned, he didn't plan to give Tadarius a dime. The moment he got that contract he was going to move his grandmother out of New York; away from danger and away from M.O.B. David didn't have any time to waste. He knew his home could possibly be under surveillance by the police who still suspected him in the shooting.

"Yo, Malik, I gotta holla at him right quick, I ain't got much time," David said.

"All right, hold up," Malik replied as he walked up to the first apartment door that he guarded.

David heard laughter and moans from inside the room. Malik knocked on the door with three heavy knocks.

"What you want? Can't ya hear that I'm busy?!!" a loud voice yelled from the inside.

"I got yo' boy David lookin' fo' you, man." Malik said in his deep voice.

After a few minutes, the door opened and Tadarius came out smiling, wearing an overlong t-shirt and jeans that sagged so low, his drawers showed.

"Yo, what's good Heisman? Gonna show them boys up this Friday night?" he asked.

David didn't smile one bit. "We need to talk, dog," he said.

Tadarius gestured him out of the apartment building and David started to walk around the block with him. David didn't waste any time.

"Tadarius, I need you to be real wit me man. Did you shoot her?" he asked.

Tadarius gave David a look of bewilderment. "Shoot who? Nah, it's been pretty slow lately. Ain't nobody been shot, at least not by me," he laughed.

David turned to Tadarius; his face deadly serious. "I ain't messin' around wit' you man. This shit ain't no joke. I know you, dog. I know your style," he said. You got any idea the type of hell you put me through? Police goin' all up in my grandmama's house, searchin' through her shit, thinkin' I got something to do with it, and why her, Tadarius? Why Loree? What did she ever do to you?" he asked angrily.

Tadarius laughed. "What difference do it make, son? In a few years, you'll go pro and you'll be swimming neck deep in so much coochie, you won't remember your own damn name!" he exclaimed.

Losing his temper, David gave Tadarius such a hard shove and he staggered back, hitting a trash bin behind him. "I really cared about that girl, man!" David exclaimed angrily. "She was the only one that stood by me when nobody else gave a shit about me," he added.

Suddenly Tadarius's eyes narrowed. "When nobody else gave a shit about you," he repeated, stepping closer to David, pointing at his chest. "When we were in juvey together and them big ass boys were pickin' on yo' small ass, who fought them off and saved yo'ass? I did. When you decided to go back to school and left my crew hangin', my boys wanted to blast yo' weak ass, who spoke up and made sure they never blazed you or your grandmama if you made it to the damn NFL? I did. You go out and you start messin' around with that bitch and you let her poison your mind. You musta' forgotten who yo real fam is, nigga. She was gonna expose you and us to five-oh. So I handled it for us. I didn't do it just fo' me, I didn't do it just fo' you. I did it fo' us. Nobody comes between blood. I thought you knew by now. I gave more than I should to save yo' pathetic ass," Tadarius ranted, his eyes gleaming in the twilight and moon that was peeking out of the remaining clouds of the dark blue sky and blanket of night.

David shook his head. "I don't give a damn about this no more, you got me? I wanna be out of this gang shit. I ain't tryin' to get my ass thrown back in the pen," he said with his head bowed.

Tadarius approached him and put his arm around him as if he was comforting him. "Man, don't you see? You need us, dog, and we need you. One hand washes the other, you feel me?" he asked. He put his hand in his pocket and pulled out a small cloth which contained an object the size of a small handset and handed it to David. David had a sinking feeling that he knew what was concealed in the cloth. As he unwrapped the cloth, his stomach sank when he saw that it was a .38 handgun. David, who was no stranger to firearms, took the weapon and looked at it as though he never seen it before.

"Ain't been burned yet, man. It's all yours, just come back to da crew. We need more dudes like you and Malik to apply some force if anyone else gets in our way," Tadarius replied.

David looked at the gun, then shoved it back towards Tadarius.

"Nah man, I don't want any part of this anymore man. I can't cosign to murder people. I'm going to the police and I'mma turn yo' ass in," he said, before he instantly regretted it, with Tadarius holding the gun. He could just shoot David and get on with his life, but David knew, in the back of his mind that Tadarius needed him. He needed David because of his future investment and promise of inclusion into his future life of luxury. To his surprise, Tadarius put the gun back in his pocket with the cloth wrapped around it.

"I don't think that's a smart idea, nigga," he replied, and David did not appreciate the tone of Tadarius's voice. It was full of mock confidence that David would not go to the police; almost very smug. "If you go to the police, someone might let slip the truth about how David Anderson keeps his game up," Tadarius said, reaching in the small side pouch of David's school book bag and taking out a small bottle of what seemed to be medicine pills but to David, they were so much more.

He hadn't been using them until the last couple of years, but David found out the performance-enhancing drugs increased his stamina, his speed, and his aggressiveness. David reached up to grab them out of Tadarius's hand, but he held them out of reach.

"Imagine if the Richmond Hill football team found out you were using PEDs, man. Wouldn't look too good on that scholarship, right? They might even use it as evidence if they charge you in the killin'," Tadarius said smugly. Before David could even ask, Tadarius read his mind. "That's right, yo' girl's dead, dog. The police are gonna keep lookin' and lookin' for the murderer, but they ain't eva gonna find him, ain't that right, David?" he said with a sinister smug to his tone.

David knew that he was trapped. Only Tadarius knew he was taking PEDs. He was well aware that it was illegal in every athletic committee in America and if word ever got out that he took PEDs, he would be banned from playing football for life. If that happened, he would be expendable to Tadarius and M.O.B. Family and blood would be irrelevant at that point to him or his crew. If he failed to live up to his street reputation and his hype, he would lose football and his life. David knew he had no choice.

"Nah man. They won't know nothing. I'll make sure it stays that way," he promised regrettably.

Tadarius threw the pills back to David. "That's my boy," he replied and David felt his heart sink at the mention of those words.

He was indeed Tadarius' whipping boy and the reality was unsettling but what was even worse was that there was no way out of it. He immediately regretted ever meeting Tadarius at the juvenile facility where they had been incarcerated years before. When he took his book bag and walked home, David never felt worse than he did that very moment. He should have listened to Loree and dropped Tadarius when had the chance. He also realized on the walk home that he should have treated Loree better. He wished he could take back every time he had verbally and sometimes physically abused her. David wasn't stupid; he knew his ill temper was usually brought on by the drugs he'd been taking but that didn't ease his conscience.

Mike went to the grocery store and he walked through the store, he could think about his relationship with Robyn. Their relationship was already strained from an emotional standpoint and the death of Loree had done nothing but complicate matters even more. During those tough moments, Mike relied on the word of God through the Bible for the answers he sought. He asked the Lord how he could keep his family morale positive through such a devastating tragedy. Although there were plenty of verses to choose from that could comfort him, he found himself almost in denial. Apathy was a better word to describe his mood. He felt he was being tested so severely and the Enemy was striving to break him by dividing his family. Shania barely came out of her room during the day. Robyn, who still had to work, was only going through the motions at her job; her mind drifting off at times. The lethargy that had attacked Robyn had certainly affected her relationship with Mike.

It was nearly dinnertime, but the pastor's home was teetering on borderline awkwardness and uncomfortable silence. Mike abruptly decided to go to the grocery store to ease the tension in the home. Maybe if he left, Robyn might take the opportunity to speak with Shania. After all, who understood the mind of a teenage girl better than another female? Mike was so busy in his thoughts that he didn't notice the other man who was shopping in the same aisle. When he pulled his thoughts to the present, he was standing next to his old friend. Nate had to do a double-take to make sure he wasn't dreaming.

"Big Money Mike, is it really you?" Nate asked.

Mike looked up from the can of beans he was holding and was jolted by the nickname he hadn't heard since high school. At first Mike didn't recognize Nate. Gone was the nappy-headed white-lipped basketball player-turned drug pusher that used to hang out with him in the early days.

"I'm sorry, but do I know you from somewhere?" Mike asked.

Nate looked at him with mock amusement. "You mean you don't remember me, kid? Maybe you'll remember me if I was bouncing a ball or holding powder," he said.

Then the light of realization dawned on Mike's face. "Nate, is that you?" he asked.

"The one and only, bro," Nate replied as the two came forward and shook hands.

"It's been a long time, man," Mike said as he continued to walk the store aisle with Nate.

"Well, that's what happens when nobody calls after twenty-four years," Nate replied smartly.

"Man, I'm so sorry about that," Mike said. "After I finished high school, I went away to college and lost touch with everyone from our class. When I came back, I heard that Nina passed away," he added.

The scene at the old house with Nina and Big Earl replayed in Nate's mind. He then felt indignant that people said Nina simply 'passed away'. "Mike, Nina was murdered," Nate corrected somberly.

Mike put his hand over his mouth with a look of sorrow and anguish. "I didn't know that, Nate. I'm sorry to hear that. We are just getting over a gang-related death in our area right now. It seems like this violent trend of early death will never end," he said.

Nate couldn't believe what he heard Mike say. Out of anybody, he would've thought Mike would be more emotional, given their past relationship.

"It wasn't gang violence. It was just one man and I intend to find that man and make him pay, Mike," Nate said.

"Nate, I understand how you feel, but you can't take this into your own hands. You've got to let the authorities handle it," Mike replied.

Nate looked at Mike. "You understand," he repeated. "How can you possibly understand it if you weren't there to begin with?" he asked. "You were the one that left her alone. It's been eighteen years, Mike. The authorities have been on that guy's trail for eighteen years and still he runs around free while my friend lies six feet under," he replied.

"She wasn't alone. Last time I heard, she was with Gary. Whatever happened to him?" Mike asked.

"What do you think happened?" Nate asked as if Mike had just asked the stupidest question on earth. "He ran out on her and she relapsed. Gary was too busy to be bothered with her, I guess," Nate replied.

Mike stepped closer to Nate, as though two men were ready to square off and duke it out. Mike didn't like Nate's flippant responses to him. It seemed Nate had changed in physical form but he was still the impulsive, lazy-eyed drug dealer he had always been in Mike's eyes.

"Nina cheated on me, Nate. What was I supposed to do? I was young and I was depressed. I gave up playing ball because of how my so called "friends" did me and you couldn't tell me anything," Mike replied.

"But that didn't stop you from pickin' yourself up and actin all brand new now did it?" Nate asked. "Word on the street was that you a pastor now and all. Lemme ask you something since you a lot holier than me. How does it feel to know that Nina's death was your fault, too? Do you think God or your Holiness or whatever the hell you serve could've helped you out?" Nate asked.

Mike's temper suddenly flared. "I'm not part of whatever you got involved in. She made her choice; the same way you made your choice and I made my choice. The choices we make determine the outcome of our future. You're not gonna hold me responsible for her death, because that's another burden that I absolutely refuse to hold. I got enough burdens to worry about now," he replied firmly as he stepped up to the register to pay for his items and Nate paid for his as well. As soon as they walked outside, Mike began walking toward the car and Nate made his way back onto the sidewalk. "Look Nate, I'm sorry for what happened, but you have to forgive and let go, as I have," Mike said.

"I can't do that," Nate said as he walked away. Then he turned back to Mike. "She left her son behind."

CHAPTER SEVENTEEN

It was before sunrise when Nate found himself back at the Richmond Hill's High school gym running shooting drills with Jamal again. He figured that since this young buck had invaded his sanctuary, he might as well teach him the tricks of the game. Jamal showed not only the desire and enthusiasm to be a better ball player but to have tenacity and work ethic. Nate noticed that on this particular day, Jamal didn't seem as engaged in his shooting drill as he had been previously.

Boy's probably tired. It is really early, and I know none of them kids like to get up early he thought. But as they played, Nate began to eliminate the initial thought that fatigue was the cause for Jamal's disinterest. While they were working on shooting drills at the top of the key, Nate started to get impatient with Jamal. His shots were aimed in the right direction, but they were either falling short or hitting the side of the basket.

"C'mon man, put some springs under them legs! What's wrong with you?" Nate asked as Jamal shot and missed shots repeatedly.

Nate was right; Jamal was distracted. The death of Loree hit him like a heavy blow to the chest that had knocked all the wind out of him. Added to his grief, his father had not called him to patch up the difficulties between either him or mother. Jamal was positive that he was trying to avoid the family altogether. Not to mention the fact that the contractors had begun working on replacing the kitchen counter, so the sink was inaccessible for the next couple of days. Isis had to buy bottled water and all their dishes would have to be washed in the bathroom sink. It was all a bit much for Jamal to take in but the death of the girl whom he had known and spoken with occasions seemed to weigh more on him. Basketball just didn't seem important to him, but he still came in early because grief or no grief, the world still moved. He was still competing with the boys who were trying out for the same team and the same position as he was himself and competition wouldn't stop due to his grief.

"C'mon man, rotate that ball! Get that shot up even higher!" Nate exclaimed, losing patience by the minute. Finally he had had enough. "Ok, stop man, obviously something's bothering you. Wanna talk about it?" Nate asked as Jamal put up his final jump shot.

With sweat pouring down Jamal's head and face, he went to the restroom and washed his face with water and dried it with a paper towel before he joined Nate, sitting in the stands.

"I don't know man. I guess I'm not feelin' this today. I just got a lot on my mind," Jamal replied.

Nate patted Jamal's shoulder. "Tell me about it, son," he said reassuringly.

Jamal didn't know where to start. "It's just a lot of things right now, man. School work is getting harder, one my friends, Loree, was killed, and my father not caring for me or my momma," Jamal answered.

Nate thought about it for a second. Mike had mentioned that a girl was murdered but he hadn't paid much attention. He might have heard it on the news that night, but it seemed like hundreds of kids who were murdered appeared on the news and it got to be so depressing and redundant that Nate decided to avoid watching news altogether. It was just too repetitive, and the psychological effect didn't help either. It always reminded him of Nina's death and how he had been too late to save her.

"I'm sorry to hear about your friend, man. Sometimes things happen in life and no matter how hard we try, we just can't avoid all the wrong that goes on in this world. I know you shook up by this, man and I hope they find the slime bag that did this to your friend," Nate replied.

"Thanks," Jamal replied.

"So what's up with your father, man? Did he leave you and your moms or something like that?" Nate asked. He didn't want to sound like a psychologist because he wasn't. However, through his own experiences he had learned that when people expressed themselves, it created a sense of relief and release. Of course, in his situation, the only way he would ever feel that of relief would be if Nina's killer was dead.

"I don't know, Nate," Jamal replied. "He left my mother a long time ago and he always promised that he would come back and make things up to her but it's like he never keeps his promise. I really want my parents to get back together, man," he said.

"We all want our parents to be together but we gotta let nature take its course on that, man. If they were meant to be together, then it'll happen. If not, then you can't let it prevent you from being your own man," Nate said firmly.

Jamal shrugged. "I guess I gotta let God handle it," he said.

Nate made a small sound. Not too obvious a sound but it had escaped his lips without realizing it. The sound suggested that he didn't fully buy the last sentence.

Jamal heard it and turned to Nate. "What? You don't believe in God?" he asked.

Nate had hoped it wouldn't come down to this. Now he was going to have to hurt this boy's feelings. "I don't know, to be honest with you man. I mean, if there is a God, why did He let your friend die? Why does He let a lot of good people die, like Martin Luther King Jr., Mother Teresa, all them people? They believed in God and look where it got em. God or not, we all die and go underground bro. It's part of life and we gotta move on from it. We can't rely on religion to do it, the power is within you," Nate replied.

Jamal shook his head. "God doesn't allow people to die, Nate. We brought it on ourselves when Adam and Eve sinned at the Garden of Eden in the beginning," Jamal explained.

"Who and who at the garden of what?" Nate asked. It was clear that he did not know the Bible and the origin of sin. Jamal didn't know if he was the right person to do it, so he thought of something else.

"Why don't you visit my church on Sunday? It's Rock of Jacob Baptist Church, only a few blocks from here," Jamal asked.

Nate shook his head and laughed. "Sounds like you gonna be a pastor just like my boy Mike," he said.

Jamal looked at him, surprised. "The pastor of our church is named Mike," he said, unaware that Nate was referring to the same person.

"It wouldn't happen to be Mike Hillman, would it?" Nate asked. Jamal looked at him quizzically.

"Yeah it is," he answered. "What, do you know him or something?" Jamal asked.

Nate laughed out loud; so loud that Jamal had to look around to make sure no one heard his hyena-like outcry. "Yeah, I know him, man," he laughed. "We go way back to them I.S. days, bro. We went to Richmond Hill together man. It was me, Mike, and Gary Mckey. We were boys, tight as anything man," Nate reflected. "While I was doing my thing on the court, Mike was handling business on the field, being quarterback for the squad," he added.

"Quarterback? You mean just like David Anderson right now?" Jamal asked.

Nate shook his head, yet again. "Mike was way better than that brotha'. He had a way of passing between the pocket and he had crazy athleticism. He had college scouts coming over trying to recruit him almost every week," he explained. Jamal couldn't believe what he was hearing. It was the first time he had heard about Pastor Mike in this light. Never once did he imagine that Mike and Nate were once best friends and they played sports in their time at school.

"But what happened? Why didn't he keep playing football?" he asked.

Nate scratched his goatee beard in thought. "Your guess is as good as mine. Gave up, I guess, just like I gave up playing ball," he said.

Jamal couldn't believe it. Pastor Mike had the ability to play football at an elite level and instead of pursuing that profession, he settled for being a pastor instead. He didn't know if he could have made the same decision if he was in the pastor's shoes, but knowing this now made him love the pastor even more. Nate decided to get much deeper with his knowledge of Mike.

"How well do you know Mike, man?" he asked Jamal.

"Until now, not much until you dropped all that history on me," he answered.

"Well, Mike was also quite a ladies' man too. See, I bet he don't even like to mention that to you boys at the church house. Money Mike, as we called him, was one of the biggest playas of his time. He could snag five to ten honeys in a minute without blinking. Before he started going with this one girl, he would receive all types of letters from Linda, Keisha, Elizabeth, and every other female you could think of," Nate said, chuckling.

Jamal laughed as well. He definitely couldn't imagine Pastor Mike being the Rico Suave-type guy as Nate described him. Pastor Mike never presented himself that way.

"Better check that pastor of yours before you go about listening to his 'better than thou' type stuff bro," Nate said. The sun had already started peeking through the windows, indicating that school was to start soon. "Anyway, keep your head up man," Nate reassured Jamal as he walked toward his locker room. "Same time tomorrow morning?" he yelled through the hallway corridor.

"Yeah, I got you," Jamal confirmed.

"Good. Make sure you bring that A game tomorrow morning," Nate instructed.

The feelings that surrounded the students attending Richmond Hill was a mixture of sorrow, anger, confusion, and fear upon the news of the death of their classmate. Loree's locker was decorated with a small memorial wreath and her picture, smiling at some long forgotten joke, sat at the center of the wreath. A few of Loree's classmates went by and dropped flowers and cards that expressed their grief over her untimely passing. Some students were crying in the hallways, unable to hide their emotions and love they had for Loree. Most of the students who grieved were grieving were female. The male students on the other hand, were struck more by fear and by suspicion. Who could have committed such a heinous crime? There had been many murder cases but to many students it was the first time it had affected them directly.

Many parents who saw the news coverage wasted no time withdrawing their students from the school. They even began speaking with realtors to plan moving away from the area. There were a few students, however, who felt no pity for Loree. They didn't see her death as an accident. Loree's death was surely brought on herself. She had many friends, but she also had a few enemies. The attitude of too many people, whether they were within the halls of Richmond Hill or outside the school, was that this girl could not have been widely respected by her peers. The police continued their investigation to find clues that would lead them to Loree's murderer. Mike had driven Shania to school that morning. The whole ride to the school was silent and uncomfortable. Robyn had attempted to talk to Shania to remind her that if she wasn't ready to return to school yet, there was no pressure, and nobody would hold it against her but Shania chose to go to school.

"It's ok, Mom. I already missed a day of school. I have to face this, even if I don't want to," Shania had told her mother that morning.

"Ok, but if you don't think you could make it through school, give me a call and I can ask my boss to leave early to come get you," Robyn said, kissing her daughter on top of her head.

As Shania prepared to step inside the car, Mike could see the expression painted on her face, which was one of uncertainty. She had never dealt with this before. Shania was going to the place where she was accustomed to seeing a person every day and that person was gone.

Surely walking those halls would re-awaken the grief and sorrow for Loree. Mike couldn't allow his daughter to go to school with a spirit of hopelessness and sorrow.

"Would you like to say a prayer before we take off?" he asked.

Shania looked across the car to her father. "Okay," she agreed.

They both stepped inside the car and once they were inside, Mike held his daughter's hands and closed his eyes. "Heavenly Father, I thank you for giving us the gift of life for another day. We are not worthy of it but you have granted it to us anyway. During the last few days, we have dealt with a very terrible ordeal with the passing of one of our sisters, friends, and daughters. Only you know, Lord, why it happened, and we know we cannot put the blame on you because you did not cause this to happen. I pray for the spirit of protection, comfort and strength to cover all your children not only this day but for the rest of the days moving forward. Please forgive our sins and help us start anew every day in your grace and loving kindness. I pray all this, in the name of your son Christ, who shed His blood on Calvary for our sins. Amen," he prayed.

Then he started the car and shifted it to gear before he took off. Shania remembered why she loved her father so much. Despite the sorrow and lack of faith of those around him, he was still a rock and he had stayed faithful and sturdy throughout the tragedy. His ship was still solid through storms of adversity, and she only prayed that one day she would develop the same strength that her father had developed over the years. As they arrived outside the school, Mike slowed.

"Remember, if you can't do this, give us a call. Today may be a challenging day only if you let it be challenging. But you can go through this. Philippians four verse thirteen," he said.

"I can do all things through Christ who strengthens me," Shania answered, laughing at the reference of the verse drill they would do every Sunday morning. She stepped out of the car, took a deep breath, and entered the double doors that led inside the school.

Mike watched as she entered the school. He was impressed by how strong his daughter was, dealing not only with the tragic death of a friend but choosing to continue living. Many people fell apart by losing their friends. Mike recalled that dark moment in his life when he himself had nearly fallen apart when he learned his best friend and girlfriend were seeing each other behind his back. In recalling that moment, Nate's words from the supermarket as he drove away were still glued in his mind.

She left her son behind, Nate had said.

He thought about the boy that Shania had been seeing lately, the boy with whom she had gone to the movies with and to the hospital. He admitted that he could have been a little more polite to him. After all, he had done nothing wrong other than date his daughter who he thought was too young to dating. Mike couldn't shake off the fact that this particular boy had such a strong resemblance to Nina; from his eyes, to his smug, almost relaxed expression, to his height. Nina had not been tall but then he remembered: Gary was six foot six because he played on the basketball team the same years, he played football. Could it have been possible that they both had a son together after high school? Mike quickly pushed the thought out of his mind. What Gary and Nina had in high school couldn't have been more than a fling. He didn't think they would have purposely decided to raise a family together. It just wasn't in their nature. Then again, anything was possible. As he drove to work, he couldn't allow those thoughts to ruin his day. That was the past and he has become a new person now. Unfortunately he couldn't say the same for Nate. He hoped that maybe someday Nate would catch on and change his way of thinking.

Shania walked to homeroom, but on the way, she stopped at Loree's locker. The locker was already overflowing with flowers and cards and the locker still had a worn look about it as if it's owner would be coming back to place more books in it. For a moment, Shania expected to see Loree glide down the stairway and join Shania at her locker. She knew it was her mind playing tricks with her. A small group of students gathered around the locker and saw Shania. As if on cue, they began to walk away from the locker as though they knew Shania was the best friend of this dead girl and she deserved to have her time alone with the locker and the photos holding the memories of her late friend.

"Hey girl, it's me," Shania whispered to the photo, as if it could hear her. "You always talked about wanting people to appreciate you for who you were and the sweetheart you were on the inside. I wish you could see how much people loved you. I always remembered how much you wanted to wear this dress one day. Here you go, girl," she said, reaching down and opening her book bag.

She took out the black dress that was in her closet, the one Loree wore when she visited her house no more than a week ago. Maybe she was crazy for doing this. It was a brand new dress and some other selfish girl might come by and steal the dress from Loree's locker. But at the moment, Shania didn't care who saw her and she didn't care what happened to the dress. She carefully placed the dress under the flowers and cards and wiped a tear from her right eye. The warning bell suddenly rang, and all the students rushed to get to class. Shania placed her hand on her lips and placed them on the picture of Loree smiling. Then she walked toward her homeroom.

Jamal sat at his desk in his own homeroom as all the kids filed in the classroom. Jamal's mind remained as distant as it had been on the basketball court earlier. He had also walked by Loree's locker and saw the love she had received. He could only hope that her family and her little sister would be able to recover from it all. Finally all the students filed into class and the PA system rang aloud with the principal's voice.

"Good morning faculty and students. Before we begin morning announcements, let us have a moment of silence for one of our students who was gunned down in a random act of violence two days ago,"

Normally the morning announcements never carried much weight with the students, so they would continue to talk through the announcements. Not so on this particular day. Every student turned quiet and respected the moment of silence that was given for the fallen student. The principal went on to explain the safety guidelines and the prohibition of weapons or any firearms within school grounds and that grief counselors were going to be at the school for the next week to comfort students who knew Loree personally. During those announcements, a boy sitting two rows on Jamal's left raised his hand. He actually shot his hand up so quickly that it was a blur to Jamal.

"Can I go use the bathroom, Mr. Canatello?" the boy asked.

"Sure thing, Antonio. Don't forget to grab the hall pass on your way out," Mr. Canatello replied as Antonio stood up to go to the bathroom.

Jamal wondered why Antonio was so jumpy. "Aye, man you all right?" he asked Antonio.

"Yeah, I'm straight," Antonio answered as he walked out of the room.

Antonio Franks was a tall, gangly black kid who normally wore a careless face every day to homeroom. Jamal rarely spoke to Antonio but Antonio was so chill that it didn't matter. That's what made his sudden outburst even more perplexing to Jamal. Before he could dwell on Antonio's mysterious behavior, he felt a tap on his shoulder. He turned around and saw Patricia looking at him, one eyebrow raised.

"Hey what's up," Jamal said casually.

Patricia pretended to be tapping her foot on the ground. "I don't know, I'm still tryin' to find out since you ain't call me or anything last night," she said with edgy tone that Jamal knew only Patricia can deliver.

"My bad Patricia, I had a really tough night yesterday. I really didn't feel like talking to anyone because of all this," Jamal confessed.

Patricia sat down in Antonio's vacated seat. "You knew that girl who was killed, didn't you?" she asked.

"Yeah, she was a friend of mine. We went to the same church and I actually know her fam. She was so cool and laid back, I don't know who could have done this," Jamal said.

"Nobody knows, I guess," Patricia confirmed. She then leaned closer as if she didn't want anybody else to hear. "But, word on the street is that her ex-boyfriend probably did it," she said in low tones.

Jamal couldn't believe what he was hearing. "Who, David Anderson? Nah I don't believe that," he said.

"Then maybe you still sleep," Patricia bit back. "It's not a secret that when they were together, David would beat her like she stole something. I personally never saw it but I got friends who are juniors and seniors and they all tell me the same thing. David got some issues," she said.

Jamal shook his head. He didn't know David as well as he knew Loree but David didn't seem like the type to hit girls for no reason. Sure he was big and had muscles on top of muscles, but that was because he played football. "I don't know, I don't think he did it. I mean, if he did it, then why is he in school today? Wouldn't he have been arrested already?" Jamal asked.

"Unfortunately he's in school but if I was him, I woulda stayed my ass at home, cuz we don't do murderers around here," Patricia said, before noticing Antonio had returned to the class and stood up to return to her desk.

It was true. David had decided to go to school despite the warnings of his grandmother and the experience could not have been much worse. Eyes that once emitted obvious praise on the field were now hostile glares as he walked the halls. Some kids just kept their distance from him altogether.

As one freshman walked by David with his friends, he said "Don't look him directly in the eye. He might smoke you next."

David clutched the sides of his book bag in anger. He could easily snap that kid in half but that certainly wouldn't help to prove his innocence which he was determined to maintain. He didn't arrive at school until the middle of the day, while most of the students were in class. Only a few were out in the hall. David walked by Loree's locker and saw the flowers, cards, and the black dress that decorated the locker. Steely-eyed he walked past the memorial.

"Yeah that's right, keep walking," a voice said behind him.

Shania had emerged from the girl's bathroom and was staring at David. David looked at the ground as Shania walked toward him.

He better be thankful that I don't have a gun on me, because they would have to put me in jail Shania thought. "You got some nerve walking back in here like it's all good," she said, stopping a few feet short of him.

"I don't got to say nothing to you. Leave me alone," David warned, the silent rage coursing through him. He tried walking away from Shania, but she persisted.

"Just tell me why you did it?" she asked. David continued to walk toward his fourth period class, ignoring Shania but Shania wasn't going away easily. "She really cared about you. Do you think she would've gone out with your abusive ass if she knew you was gonna do harm to her?" she asked.

That was just enough to set David off. "I didn't kill her!" he yelled across the halls, causing a couple of teachers to walk out of their classes to see the commotion. Shania looked closely at David, unable to take him at face value. She glanced into his eyes. There was no smug reaction, no absence of emotion. For a split second, David actually looked like he hadn't committed the crime, but Shania was not born yesterday.

"So now you're yelling huh? Wouldn't it be easier to take out your piece and shoot me too?" she asked.

One of the teachers stepped forward between the two. "Ok you two, that's enough. Anderson, go to class right now. Same for you, Ms. Hillman," the teacher added. Shania turned around and with one last glowering look at David, walked back to class. David punched the locker closest to him in frustration before walking to class. The students had walked out of their classes to see what the commotion was about before the teachers had regained control and ordered the students back in the classroom. Back in their math class, Jamal and Omar heard the buzz of students who had walked outside and were also wondering what was going on.

"Yo, did you hear David? That dude got a deep voice. Shania betta' chill or she gon' get shot too," one of the students murmured.

Jamal sat and wondered what was going to happen next. Until David was actually charged with the murder of Loree, he was not convinced that David was the one who had pulled the trigger. Jamal's mother told him that Loree had been found in an alley miles away from the school. That it told Jamal that it was a gang-related hit. Loree might have known a couple of the gang members and maybe she had run her mouth about them. Then they took her to a secluded area and killed her. Jamal had heard about the heavy recruitment of M.O.B and their initiation methods. Known to be one of the most raw, inhumane practices, M.O.B would recruit younger members and test them by forcing them to take a human life and remain silent about it. If anyone broke down by either confessing to the murders or by turning any of the members over to the police, the informant would be dealt with, permanently. It was the sad but painful truth and Jamal knew that every day he walked on the streets he could be a target; a target of the police who could mistake him for a gang member or a target of an actual gang member or gang leader looking to recruit. Jamal heard it mentioned that David had been a member of M.O.B but left them after his last house arrest. Jamal wasn't sure that David would throw all that away by killing Loree only months later. It just didn't add up. Patricia along with countless others, were more than convinced that David was the murderer because of his known arguments with Loree and physical confrontations and evidence of abuse; bruised arms and thighs.

Later on that day, after school, the students began to file out. Shania and Lisa walked out through the double doors. The boys who normally sat out on the steps were still there. Nothing had changed.

One of the boys who had previously referred to Loree as "Big Booty Judy" earlier in the year said, "Ayo, sorry about yo' girl," he said.

Shania normally didn't like to talk those boys but she thought the boy was very considerate to offer his condolences.

"Thank you," she replied as she walked past them.

Before Shania started on her way, a sophomore cheerleader ran up to Shania, Lisa, and the group of boys sitting on the steps.

"Yo, ya need to come ova to the football field. Five-oh rollin' deep on the field," she said.

Without saying a word, the whole group ran over the football field, which was located at the right backside of the school. They followed the cheerleader who ran toward the site. Shania thought the girl was crazy and might have been talking nonsense but when she finally arrived at the field, she realized that the girl was telling the truth. There were about four police officers walking onto the field where the football team was preparing to practice. Shania, Lisa, and the boys watched the whole scene unfold from the fence that surrounded the football field. The police walked up to the football coach.

"Good afternoon coach. Is Mr. David Anderson here?" one of the officers asked.

"Yeah, he's in the locker room. No trouble I hope?" the coach asked.

"Well, we have a warrant for his arrest in the involvement of the shooting death of Loree Anne McAfee," the officer answered showing the coach the warrant.

The coach took the warrant from the officer. Turning to the police, he said, "No, this can't be right, this has got to be a joke. Anderson is my starting quarterback. There is no way he could've shot that girl," he argued.

The police disregarded the coach and asked that David be brought out onto the field. One of the players ran to retrieve David. David came out of the field, still dressed in his practice gear and cleats.

"What's goin' on?" he asked when he saw the police officers.

"Mr. Anderson you are hereby under arrest for the third-degree murder of Ms. McAfee," the police replied and while he read David his rights, David looked at the coach. "Coach, I didn't do it. Please tell them," he pleaded as they handcuffed him.

One of the officers took David's book bag and unzipped it. When the contents spilled onto the ground, there was a small white folded cloth that David recognized. The officer unfolded the cloth and concealed inside was a gun.

CHAPTER EIGHTEEN

Trevor found himself at the St. John's University school library. He had logged onto one of the computers and began a search for his biological father. He was terribly frustrated because he didn't really know where to start. The only clue he had was the initials on the letter he had been sent. 'G.M.' appeared as a signature. That was hardly much of a clue. Trevor had searched for what seemed like hours trying to find the identity of G.M. He had started his search for a family tree by using his own name. Groaning with impatience and frustration, Trevor tried almost every name combination that started with both G and M with no success. He remembered his mother telling him that his father's first name was either Greg or Gary.

That answers my question for the first name but what the hell's his last name? Trevor thought.

Trevor didn't know and it seemed as if he had tried almost every combination of last names beginning with M as well: Mitchell, McStay, McCall, Martin. That's when it hit him. Martin. Martin. That was his biological mother's name. He might have better luck if he searched Nina's name through the records. Surely there must be a record of her. Trevor typed Nina's name in the search engine bar. What he saw was one of the most significant clues that would lead him to his destination. There was an old archived school paper with a picture of Richmond Hill High School and an old sports section story. Trevor read the report. It was the moment when Richmond Hill High School won their region by narrowly defeating Cardozo High School. There was a picture printed above the article. As much as Trevor would have enjoyed reading about that thrilling win, the basketball story was not what drew his interest. Underneath the black and white photo were the descriptions of the people who were in the photo, Trevor took a closer look at the photo. The whole team appeared to be getting mobbed by their classmates and fans at the end of the game. Trevor instantly recognized his mother who was in the far right, wearing the cheerleading outfit.

He saw the names and descriptions of their positions in the photo. Oliver Whitehead. Stanley Nicks, Amanda Ford, and finally his eyes fell upon the picture of a basketball player who stood six-foot-five or six-foot-six who was hugging Nate Plummer who had apparently made the game winning shot. Nate Plummer….why did that name also look familiar? But Trevor looked at the name of the player hugging him…Gary McKey. Gary McKey. G.M. Trevor's face broke into a smile when he finally saw the picture of his biological father. Now he knew the source of his height. At the same moment, Trevor's cell phone started to ring. The ringtone wasn't loud enough to be a disturbance to other people in the library, yet it distracted him to where he needed to shut it off and continue working. He searched Gary McKey's name through the yellow pages and found out that Gary lived in Carlstadt, New Jersey. He quickly wrote the address on his pad of paper and left the library. Trevor made up his mind that he was going to visit Gary on Saturday and get some questions answered. He needed to know how his mother had passed and why Gary had never taken responsibility for Trevor. As he walked out of the library, he noticed his phone began to ring again. This time he picked it up.

"What's up?" he answered.

"Where were you at? You didn't see me calling you the first time?" It's not good to keep a girl waiting, you know," Shania replied on the other line.

Trevor laughed. "You right. My bad. So what's up? How you holding up?" he asked her, knowing she was still recovering over her friend's death.

"Taking it one day at a time, I guess," Shania replied. "You're not gonna believe what happened today though. The police came by and arrested someone at school today in connection with the shooting," she added.

"For real? Who'd they catch?" Trevor asked, interested because he would like to see whoever committed the crime pay for it.

"Her ex-boyfriend, David Anderson. He was at school today and I confronted him in the hallway," Shania explained.

"Are you crazy?" Trevor asked, alarmed that Shania was even remotely close to the guy. He couldn't bear to think of the same tragedy happening to Shania.

"Yeah, I stared him down. He ain't scare me. He almost had me convinced that he didn't do it, Trevor. Then they found a gun in his book bag," she continued.

Trevor didn't say a word and Shania thought he had hung up for a moment. But after a minute, he said in a quiet voice, "You could have been killed."

Shania was very surprised to hear Trevor's sudden concern for her well-being. She really didn't know where she stood with him but it felt great knowing that he did care.

"I'm ok. Anyway I hadn't heard from you in while and thought I'd hit you up. I was planning to take Loree's little sister, Andrea out to eat this Saturday and I was wondering if you wanted to join us," Shania offered, hoping that Trevor would accept to join them.

The answer she received was not what she expected. "Actually, I got plans this Saturday. I'm sorry I won't be able to go wit' you," he said. Shania's heart sank.

She didn't want to openly admit it but she was starting to have feelings for Trevor and the rejection had hurt more than she expected.

"Oh, ok I understand. That's cool," she said in a flat tone.

Trevor, sensing her disappointment, attempted to explain his situation. "It's not that I don't want to go," he replied quickly. "I just....I gotta go visit my father, ok?" he said.

"Your father? Doesn't he live in Jamaica Estates?" Shania asked.

"No, not him. I gotta go visit my father; my real father. I just found out that I was adopted," Trevor confessed.

He hadn't wanted to tell anyone about it and he actually felt ashamed that he just told Shania. What would she think of him now?

"How do you know you were adopted?" Shania asked.

"Well my actual father sent me a letter and a DVD of some home video with my actual mother. I just found out my biological mother died, so my father is the only one who can clear some things out for me," Trevor explained.

"I'm so sorry to hear about your mother, Trevor," Shania replied and she really sounded sincere about it.

"Yeah me too, I never got enough time wither her before it happened," he said.

"How did she pass?" Shania asked.

Trevor didn't know how to answer that question because Tiffany had never really given him a straight answer. "I don't know. I guess that's why I'm hoping my pops can answer that for me," he replied.

They sat over the phone in silence. Finally Shania spoke first, breaking the awkward silence. "How about if I came with you?" she asked.

"Thanks, Shania, but this is my problem. I don't want to drag you into it too. Besides you're still dealing with Loree's death and all," Trevor answered.

"It's ok, I still want to go. We can just take Andrea out to eat and then we'll drop her back home and after that we can go visit your dad," Shania said.

Trevor started to crack a smile. He was happy that Shania understood his situation. "So this must be what it feels like to be married. The woman gotta plan every move," he said, laughing.

"Hey, if I don't do it, who will?" Shania asked, although she laughed as well.

"All right cool. So I'll pick you up at your place and we'll get Andrea afterwards," Trevor said.

"Um, what about if Andrea and I meet you at the park where you normally practice and where I normally run and stretch?" Shania asked. She offered the idea of Trevor picking her up from a different location because she wasn't too sure her father had warmed up to Trevor just yet. She hoped Trevor picked up on this subtle message and gratefully, he did.

"Ok that's cool. We'll meet at the park and we'll take lil ma' out to eat and then we'll go to Jersey. Deal?" Trevor agreed. Shania thanked Trevor and hung up. He still sounded like a moron but he was a very cute-sounding moron.

Saturday came and Nate took the bus and two subway trains on the way to Astoria, Queens where he followed his gym partner's instructions. The last two days of the week had been pretty much uneventful not counting of course, some football player who had been arrested for the shooting of the girl. No matter what year it is, it ain't ever gonna change he thought.

Violence just bred more violence, and it was worse in the streets. Nate had to admit that during his brief reunion with Mike, he wasn't lying. Loree's death brought back memories of Nina's untimely death. They had both been girls who had died way too young, cut down in the prime of their lives.

As he approached Distinct Auto Dealers, a medium sized car lot with a variety of used automobiles, he was impressed by what he saw. Before he stepped inside to front desk, Nate wandered over to look at one of the car models. It was a blue 2001 Ford Taurus. He walked around it, checking the tires, the alignment level, and the headlight and tail lights. At least Rob didn't send me to a cheap garage location he thought.

The cars looked to be in good condition and when he finally met with Antoine Sparks, he couldn't wait to ask him about how the cars ran, if they were properly filled with enough oil, and how frequently they had been tuned up. Nate had signed his name at the front desk where he noticed there were quite a number of people in front of him. The place was full of activity but then again it was Saturday, so he figured it was always busy Saturdays. The girl behind the counter smiled up at him when he signed the register.

"Is this your first time visiting us?" she asked.

Nate smiled as well. "What gave me away?" he asked.

"Well, we normally have the same window-shoppers come in from time to time and after a while you start memorizing the faces of the people who normally come here and I don't remember seeing you here before," she answered.

"Well it is my first time coming here. I was actually referred to you guys by a friend of mine. He wanted me to speak with Mr. Antoine Sparks. Is he working today, by any chance?" Nate asked.

"Yeah he's here, he's just busy with another customer right now, but he will be with you in just a moment. Would you like to have a seat in our waiting area? We got coffee, snacks, and television available," the girl offered.

Nate thanked the girl and went to sit down in the waiting area. So far he has been pleased with the customer service he was receiving. Normally car dealerships were not so courteous, and the salesmen were usually in a rush to get you out quickly when they realized you weren't a buyer. If they couldn't coax the customer into signing on the dotted line after conveniently forgetting to mention all the problems that would come with their automobiles, they showed no interest. Nate didn't receive that type of vibe from this place, and he knew he would find a car that suited him. He wasn't sure he would be able to take the car out of the lot, but he would ask Antoine if he could drive the car over to his house and they could discuss contract and paperwork there. Sitting in the waiting area, he saw that the television was broadcasting the news. It was airing the events from Thursday, when the football player had been arrested for the murder of the girl. The girl's parents were interviewed, and it was clear that the parents were relieved that justice would finally be done. Nate was not too sure about the details, but it definitely seemed like a messy situation that did not reflect well on the Richmond Hill area. He knew from personal experience that if certain precautions were not taken on that side of town, anyone could find himself on the wrong side of the law. While he reflected on those events, he heard the girl behind his desk finally call his name from the waiting list. Nate stood up and started to walk toward the desk, expecting to see Antoine but he was met by a tall, skinny white man who wore an eccentric-colored tie and a wide smile on his face.

"Hello, Nate Plummer. I'm Derrick Stafford, your vehicle ambassador. Antoine is still extremely busy with his customer, so he asked me to fill in for him," Derrick said.

Nate shook his hand politely, although inwardly he was slightly disappointed. What kind of salesman refused to make time for his clients? He had waited for almost an hour to see Antoine, yet Antoine was too busy to meet him? Nate didn't overreact but Distinct Auto Dealers already had one strike against them on the service scale.

"Ok, no problem. So what have you got here, Derrick?" he asked.

Derrick walked through one part of the lot and explained the different types of cars he had. They were all still in very good condition and most of them already had an oil changes prior to being placed on the display floor. Nate looked at many of the cars in the dealership and three cars caught his eye. There was a red 2000 Hyundai, a dark blue 2002 Honda Civic, and a dark blue 2002 Nissan Camry that interested him. Derrick showed Nate the inside of the cars, the brake function, the durability of the gear shift, and the anti-lock brakes. Nate explained that he wanted a burglar alarm. He didn't want to overstate his fears but living in the city, he was used to unpredictability and having a car in the city never guaranteed its safety. Many of the young kids out there might try to steal the car and Nate wasn't going to tolerate it one bit. At least if he had an alarm, he would be ready. Derrick turned out to be a much better sales representative than Nate had originally assumed. He answered any question Nate had about each individual car and even told him the mileage of each car Nate was pleased overall with the demonstrations that Derrick showed him.

Ok this definitely makes up for Antoine being late he thought.

As they went inside Derrick's office to discuss the finances, Derrick took a moment to run a credit check on Nate. After he ran the credit check, he informed Nate that his credit was in good enough condition to buy a car from the lot if he so desired. Nate explained that he wasn't sure if he would be able to come back to the dealership once he had the money to pay it.

"That's not a problem," Derrick explained. "Either I or any one of the sales representatives would be happy to drive the car over to your home."

"Thanks, man. I'll keep that in mind," Nate answered.

As Nate prepared to wrap up the price negotiations with Derrick, he heard Derrick's office door open behind him and a tall, heavy-set man walked through the door.

"What's up D-man?" he greeted Derrick happily.

"Ah, speak of the devil. There he goes. Nate, I would like you to meet Antoine Sparks," Derrick said.

Nate turned around and he was initially smiling, ready to finally greet the man about whom Rob had been bragging but the moment Nate saw the face that stared back at him, his smile disappeared. Staring back at Nate Plummer was the man who haunted his nightmares for eighteen years. The man who had a round impassive face, the face that had once void of any remorse or regret when he had committed an unforgivable crime, looked at Nate right in the eye. The beard on his face was now gone. The booming voice was now gone but his voice still remained deep. Nate had to blink because he needed to be sure the man who was currently staring at him was accurate. He wasn't completely sure if it was really him or not. But it had to be him, because Nate had seen that fateful night in his head so many times, including feeble attempt at fighting the very man that stood in front of him. Nate was finally seeing Big Earl face to face after eighteen years. The bigger mystery was that Big Earl didn't seem to recognize him at all. He probably thought Nate was just another customer with whom he dealt on a daily basis. Nate finally knew why he hadn't seen Big Earl in a long time.

So you went all the way to Astoria and gave yourself a new name, got yourself a new job and even cleaned up your act to fool everybody around you. But you ain't nothin', you fuckin' bastard, Nate thought.

Derrick didn't seem to realize that Nate was staring at Mr. Sparks with so much intensity that heat beams could be coming out of his eyes. "Mr. Plummer, I'd like you to meet one of our top salesman in this dealership, Mr. Antoine Sparks," he said.

"Nice to meet you, Mr. Plummer. I hope you liked what you've seen today," Antoine said.

Nate looked at the hand reaching for his, then after hesitating, he finally shook it. Nate didn't want to believe it was Big Earl; that maybe he had been thinking about Big Earl so much and had been so possessed by thoughts of revenge for Nina that he was starting to go crazy. But the moment Nate shook Antoine's hand, he looked up and saw the confirmation of Antoine Sparks' true identity. He saw three small scar lines that ran from his jaw line to his neck. Many people had scars over the years but not many people had scars that reflected the final attempt of a victim who died at their hands. Nate vividly remembered the night when Nina had scratched Big Earl moments before her death. The nightmares were recurring. So many sleepless nights came back to haunt him while he shook this man's hand and as a result, Nate's internal anger began to build. The fact that his best friend lay in a grave and her murderer was standing just a few feet from him had Nate steaming. Antoine seemed to notice the conflicting emotions reflecting in Nate's face.

"You ok, brotha?" he asked.

Nate took a quick look around. There were too many people in the dealership. If he was alone with 'Antoine Sparks', there would be no telling what Nate would be capable of doing, so Nate decided to keep his emotions in check.

"Yeah, I'm good. Probably ate something funny this morning or something," Nate replied in a weak attempt to explain his strange grimace.

Nate wanted to continue to look deeply into the eyes of Big Earl. He wanted Big Earl to remember who he was and what he did to ruin his life. Yeah I'm ok now, but one day you won't be he thought.

"I see Derrick already showed you all our recent models. Find anything you liked?" Antoine asked.

I'd like to see you with a bullet in yo' brain Nate thought but once again he considered his surroundings, so he played along.

"Yeah, I was feelin' that Honda Civic," he replied.

"The Civic, huh? Great choice, I've actually been tryin' to get her off the lot for a while now," Antoine said, chuckling.

Yeah, keep laughing. You better be thankful that you still got all yo' teeth in your mouth Nate thought as he grinned. He couldn't do this anymore. Every minute he stood there he envisioned sixty ways of killing him. He had to get out of there.

"Gentlemen, I thank you so much for your help, but I must be going now," Nate said. He knew that he had to leave, because if he didn't, there was going to be some violence in the room.

"Ok, well here's my card Mr. Plummer. Feel free to come back and visit anytime. If you need me to bring it over to ya, just lemme know and I'll bring it up to ya with the keys," Antoine offered, handing Nate his business card.

"Ok, great thanks," Nate replied quickly before leaving the dealership.

As he headed straight for the subway station, his mind trained and focused on the huge punching bag at the gym that he was going to punish within the next hour.

David Anderson sat in a dimly lit room with only one transparent window, showing the view of the NYPD precinct. The past two days had been the worst days he could remember since he had left the juvenile hall. After the police publicly arrested him, they took him downtown for processing.

They fingerprinted him and took his mug shot. He felt like he had already been convicted. Once they processed him, he was put in a cell inhabited by more criminals and David was filled with a sense of fear he had never felt before. With his experience, David knew better than to show his fear. When he told the other prisoners that he was a member of M.O.B, they pretty much left him alone. David's grandmother, who didn't know what had happened until she saw the news, ran as quickly as only a wizened old lady could and spent what seemed like hours arguing with the police that David was not Loree's killer. Of course, she couldn't convince them. Earlier that week, the police had received an anonymous tip from a caller who claimed that David was the murderer and that he was assisted by two other gang members. While the identities of the other members were unknown for the moment, they still had David as the primary suspect because of his past relationship with Loree. Every student the police had interviewed recalled the Friday prior to the shooting, when David was seen shouting at Loree. There was also evidence of domestic abuse in the relationship, given David's violent past. Although the police had David earlier, they hadn't had sufficient evidence until the day of the arrest and found the murder weapon. The gun that had been used in the murder had been found in David's backpack, exactly where the anonymous caller told them to look.

David was being held without bond and awaiting his trial. His grandmother could barely manage to scrape up enough to keep their small house, much less afford a lawyer, so there was nothing she could do. As David sat in the room, he heard the door open, and Detective Isaac Sands walked into the room. A tall, black imposing figure, Detective Sands had an aura that made most people, especially suspects, highly uneasy around him. Coincidentally it wasn't the first run-in he had with David. He had served in the juvenile facility for troubled young men in the past and was in the same facility in which David was incarcerated when he had met Tadarius. He stood across from David, his right hand, clutching a rather thick folder.

"I gotta tell you David, you really messed up this time. You told me you promised you would straighten up and stick to the books and the field. What happened man? Why am I seeing you back in this room?" Detective Sands asked.

David looked at him and shook his head. He didn't have anything to say. What could he have told him? Oh I was framed somehow and the guy that really killed Loree is still out there, and you've got the wrong guy. To prevent any further incrimination, David did not reply. Detective Sands decided to begin the interrogation.

"Where were you on the night of September fifteenth between eight and ten PM, Mr. Anderson?" Detective Sands asked.

David decided to break his silence and comply with the detective. "I just came home from football practice. I caught a shower, and I lied down to watch TV, ok? I was nowhere near where Loree was found," David insisted.

The detective began to pace the small room. "I really want to believe you, David, but let me tell you what you're looking at here. If you're found guilty under the court of law, they will not charge you as a minor, because your birthday's coming up in a couple months, is it not?" he asked.

"Yeah," David replied grudgingly. He did not want to disclose anything else to Detective Sands.

"So that means they will charge you as an adult, David, if they find you guilty. You'll be looking at twenty to forty years behind bars and that's not even the worst case-scenario," he continued. David crossed his arms. It wasn't in his nature to look intimidated by anyone, even though deep inside, he was terrified. "David, if you don't confess, what you've endured the last couple of days will be nothing compared to what you will potentially go through for the rest of your life. Please cooperate with me," he asked.

David looked up at him. Of all the police officers and detectives he had known in the past, Detective Sands had been the most reasonable and sympathetic towards him. Regardless, it still didn't manage stop the rift that existed between young black men and police officers. The detective continued the questioning.

"How long have you known Ms. McAfee?" he asked.

"We met in August when I was practicing for the season. One of her friends from the cheerleading squad introduced me to her," David replied.

"Had you two been intimately involved during the relationship?" Detective Sands asked.

David started to get a little nervous, although nobody would be able to tell if they didn't know him well. On the outside he seemed cool, methodical, and composed but on the inside, he was a wreck.

"Yeah," he replied, recalling the many times they had sex. Sometimes they would be at his place when his grandmother wasn't home or they would go to a small overnight motel after a night of partying.

"Eyewitness accounts claimed that on the Friday prior to Ms. McAfee's death, you two were in a heated argument. You said some things and she said some things that might have shaken up the relationship, is that true?" Detective Sands asked.

David put his head down as he recalled the night arguing with Loree after his poor performance on the field that night. "Yeah we did say some things. But couples argue all the time, though. Just because I argued with her don't mean I killed her," David said.

"I know it doesn't. You're not going to jail because of an argument claim. This is why you're going to jail," Detective Sands said placing a couple pictures on the table in front of David.

One of the pictures was the .92 Glock that had been the murder weapon, and the other picture was one David didn't want to see. It showed Loree's bare shoulder from picture taken during the autopsy. Just above her right breast was a bullet hole; the exit wound where the bullet had done its lethal damage. David shook his head.

"Man it wasn't even necessary to show her pictures to me now," he said before Detective Sands took the photos from the table.

"It was completely necessary to see that photo, Mr. Anderson, and the reason why it was important is because you're tied to all this," Detective Sands pointed out. "The kids who saw you argue in the lot after the game and more importantly the gun," he said.

"What does that gun got to do with anything?" David asked in frustration.

"They found your fingerprints on the gun," Detective Sands answered.

The room was silent for a good three minutes. David just stared straight at the wall shaking his head. How could his fingerprints have been on the same gun that killed Loree? It couldn't be… unless… unless he was framed by his comrades.

When he had met with Tadarius, Tadarius had handed him the gun on purpose, knowing he would get his fingerprints on it. He lied about the gun never being used before, when in truth it had been used to commit one of the most horrible crimes in the city's history. David didn't understand why Tadarius would set him up because he had kept up his end of the bargain by not snitching to the police. So why would they betray him, especially with the vision of the NFL becoming a reality. It was in that interrogation room that David finally realized the truth. Tadarius never trusted David from the beginning. Although David had not said a word to give himself away, Tadarius must have come to the realization that David was going to drop him and his crew. Knowing that, Tadarius proceeded to plan to betray David himself. That way he could ensure David would not talk because he knew if David spoke, the secret of his use of PEDs would destroy whatever chance he would get playing football at the next level. Tadarius didn't care who he hurt as long as nobody crossed him and that apparently included his so called "brother," David. David had been living under the false assumption that street loyalty was deeper than family but now he knew he was wrong about that as well. Still, no matter how long Detective Sands persisted in knowing the facts, David was equally intent on not revealing the person who had plotted the murder. He had worked extremely hard to get the second chance he desired, and he couldn't let that go. Eventually he would stop using the PEDs but not before ensuring that his grandmother would be well cared for in the future. He didn't see any other avenue.

"I don't how the prints got there, but I didn't kill her," he insisted.

Detective Sands sighed. These kids and their stupid hood loyalty he thought.

CHAPTER NINETEEN

Trevor sighed deeply as he turned the corner on a green light on the way to the park where Shania and Andrea were waiting for him. If he had his way, Andrea wouldn't be tagging along with them. He was glad Shania would be with him all day. He really couldn't understand it, but Shania brought out feelings he never felt with any other girl he has dated. There was a real quality about her that he admired and her resilient spirit in the face of tragedy made him admire her that much more. He hadn't known Loree very well, so he didn't know her sister or any of her family members. To Shania, however, she was a second sister and if Shania saw Loree's family like a second family, then Trevor couldn't argue with her, even though spending the day with a snot-nosed little kid was the last thing he wanted to do. He didn't hate kids, but he just never had the patience to deal with them.

As soon as he picked up Andrea and Shania at the park, he started to have a change of heart. Andrea was very quiet, almost shy; never spoke unless spoken to. She was actually very mature for a twelve-year old girl and while Trevor drove them to the pizzeria, Shania would brag about Andrea's performance in school and how she was one of the top students in her class. If Trevor's admiration was high for Shania, he would be proud of what Andrea was able to accomplish in school in light of the tragedy. Many kids who lost their siblings or dealt with an early death in the family never recovered from the mental and psychological damages that it caused, but Andrea found a way to remain strong and keep working despite it all. As they entered Tony's Pizzeria on Leffert's Blvd, underneath the train overpass where the 'A' train normally ran, Trevor decided he would pay for the girls as well as himself. It would be a crime to have them pay for their own food. As they took orders on the toppings they wanted on their pizza, Trevor noticed that Andrea chose the combo slice, which had its share of olives, peppers, onions, and other vegetables he didn't particularly like.

"You like all that stuff on yo' pizza, Andrea?" he asked jokingly.

Andrea nodded her head approvingly. "It's good, though. I can't believe you don't like extra toppings on your pizza, Trevor. You need to try it," she said teasingly.

Trevor shook his head. "Nah, you could have that. I'll stick with my regular cheese slice, can't go wrong with the original," he said.

"Don't worry bout him, 'Drea," Shania said. "He only wants a plain because it's boring like him," she joked, and Andrea laughed.

"Hey, hey, hey I eat what I like, all right? Besides, boring is the last thing that I am," Trevor bragged.

"Yeah, what was that you told me when we first met? You provide the attraction?" Shania asked in jest as Andrea continued laughing.

"Don't hate the playa baby, hate the game. Andrea knows what it is, right?" Trevor laughed as Andrea smiled at him.

After a few minutes, their pizza orders were brought to their table. As they heard the rumble and sound of the subway train running above them, Trevor started to eat his pizza, when Shania and Andrea started to look at him strangely.

"What ya lookin' at? Pizza too cold for ya?" Trevor asked.

"No, we just can't believe that's the way you eat your pizza," Shania replied.

Trevor stared at his half-eaten pizza. "What's wrong with the way I eat my pizza?" he asked curiously.

"You eat it weird," Andrea answered while Shania laughed.

"What you mean?" Trevor asked Andrea. He was starting to get confused before finally understanding what they were talking about. "Nah come on, don't tell me ya fold yo' pizza before eating it," Trevor said, rolling his eyes.

"Well duh, how else are you supposed to eat your pizza?" Shania asked.

She took her pizza, folded the sides closely then proceeded to eat. Andrea, as if on cue, copied Shania, folding her slice; onions, peppers and all, before eating the slice. Trevor shook his head.

"I don't know how ya can eat your pizza like that. I don't think it makes a difference," he said.

"Trust me, it makes a huge difference," Andrea replied.

Trevor looked at her. "How so?" he asked, testing how smart Andrea could be at an intricate subject such as pizza-folding.

Andrea shrugged. "I don't know. It just does," she answered.

Trevor and Shania laughed. He liked this kid. After they finished their pizza, they looked at desserts. Trevor ordered the mini chocolate cake while Shania and Andrea ordered the cheesecake.

"Don't tell me you don't like cheesecake either," Shania said.

"Nah, I like cheesecake, but I like chocolate cake better. Ya are missing out," he replied.

Shania and Andrea looked at Trevor's chocolate cake with a look of mock disgust.

"I don't think I'm missing too much," Shania said. After leaving the pizzeria they went to shop at Green Acres Mall near Rosedale, Queens. This was the part of the day Trevor dreaded the most. Shopping with not one, but two girls and who knows how long he could be waiting?

"Ok, if ya gonna go shopping, make sho' ya don't try everything in the whole store," Trevor called out after them before they entered a department store dressing room.

After forty-five agonizing minutes for Trevor, the girls finally emerged with the clothes they wanted and Trevor, the gentlemen, paid for their clothes.

They better be happy that I'm on scholarship and I'm getting money or else they'd be paying this all on their own he thought as all three of them emerged from the store, each with 2 bags of clothes, shoes, and hats.

At three o'clock in the afternoon, they dropped Andrea back home. As Trevor pulled up to the side of the apartment, he glanced at Andrea's face and although she tried to hide it, he knew Andrea didn't look forward to returning home. Trevor couldn't blame her for feeling anxious upon returning. Every corner in that home had to remind her of her sister. Trevor looked at Andrea and Shania.

"You wanna come inside and watch a movie or something?" Andrea asked.

Trevor thought she was primarily addressing Shania until he realized Andrea's eyes were fixed on him as well.

"Sweetie, we would love to, but see…" Shania started to explain but Trevor cut in.

"We'll come back next weekend. I gotta visit some family and Shania says she's coming with me. Is that cool?" he asked.

Shania looked at Trevor in complete shock. She may not have known Trevor completely, but she knew that a guy like him normally had low tolerance for spending time with kids. She looked at Trevor with narrow eyes, wondering if he was giving Andrea a false promise or if he planned to keep his promise for visiting next weekend. She couldn't bear to see Andrea's heartache because of a broken promise. Andrea seemed to understand, maybe more so than Trevor thought, because she started to shift her eyes side to side; from Shania who sat in the passenger seat to Trevor who sat in the driver's seat, with a sly grin.

"I get it. You two want to be alone," she said, batting her eyelashes at Trevor. Shania grinned embarrassingly. She hoped Trevor hadn't noticed the blush that started to rise in her cheeks. Trevor also smiled sheepishly, unsure of what to say at that moment. "Ok, you two crazy kids, have fun. Shania, are you gonna call tonight?" she asked.

"You bet," Shania said while hugging her.

Surprisingly, she reached over and hugged Trevor as well. Trevor was stunned for a quick moment, but he returned the hug. After watching to be sure Andrea was safely inside her apartment, they drove off. While driving, Shania reached over and kissed Trevor on the cheek. It was quick and fleeting, but Trevor still felt the heat rise up in him. That was the first time, other than the dance floor at the college party, that Shania had made any type of romantic advances toward him.

"What was that for?" Trevor asked, smiling.

"That was for being so sweet and nice to me and Andrea, even with all the drama going on in your family. You didn't have to do all this," Shania said.

Trevor's hands started to tense up on the steering wheel. Was he becoming a bit nervous? "I know I didn't have to do it, but I wanted to," he said, even though he was lying. He had no intention of spending the day with Shania and a twelve-year-old kid, but he'd had a good time. "She's dealing with a lot right now. She's a pretty cool kid. Pretty smart for her age. Pretty flirty, too," he added, smiling a bit.

Shania looked at Trevor, rolling her eyes. The ego machine was about to explode. She made one compliment, and his head would swell up faster than the Goodyear blimp. "Ugh, so what are you trying to say? She likes you, or something?" she asked in mock disgust, laughing.

"Hey, you know Trevor luhhs the kids, so the kids show him some love too," Trevor replied, referring to himself in the third person, a trait that normally turned Shania off with other guys, but Trevor knew how to joke about it.

"Really? So what other kid luhhs you?" Shania asked, mocking the distorted way Trevor said the word 'loves'.

"Well, plenty of kids. Like yo' boy Jamal that I met at the park a couple weeks ago. I'm a hero to that boy all day," he said, laughing.

"Please," Shania said, rolling her eyes. "Jamal has a level head on his shoulders, and he is not a little kid. That boy is fourteen years old," she corrected.

"He still a kid to me, though," Trevor said, laughing. "He's a smart kid though and I see a lot of myself in him," he added.

Shania shook her head, laughing. "Jamal is nothing like you. He's quiet, gentle, likes to keep to himself a lot, and he's not a big talker like some people," Shania said, obviously referring to Trevor.

"Look, what I'm sayin' is there was a time when I wasn't always who I am now. I was quiet like him once," Trevor insisted.

"Please! Don't give me that. You were one of the most popular boys in school by your sophomore year. I can still see you in them hallways, posting up with yo' boys, scopin' out girls," Shania said laughing.

"That's not always true," Trevor countered. "We also talked about who we was about to play next, discussing strategy and plays and....stuff," he stammered struggling for words to say. He had to admit Shania showed more patience with his hard-headedness than any other girl he remembered.

"Right. Because most of you guys were standing in the hallway discussing stats and game plays. Who were ya studying? The Black Barbies?" Shania asked.

Trevor lifted an eyebrow upon hearing the name of the exclusive group of girls who walked the halls of Richmond Hill a few years back. "Actually I didn't like any of them girls. One of them did try to make a play at me but she passed after she learned that I was only a sophomore. See, folks got this tendency where they think I'm older than I really am, cuz of my height," Trevor said.

"I can see why," Shania said. "So where we headed off too?" she asked, realizing that Trevor just entered the nearest expressway.

"Well according to the directions I printed online, it says that my biological father lives in Carlstadt, New Jersey wherever that is," Trevor answered.

"Oh ok," Shania answered, currently at a loss for words.

How could she address a situation as delicate as an adopted son who was about to go visit his biological father for the first time? She could never imagine growing up with a mystery as paramount as who her biological parents were. She could sense the tension and nervousness emanating from Trevor because there were long moments during the car ride when there would be nothing but silence between them. During those times, she stared out the windows at passing trees and highway medians they crossed. She knew she should call her father to inform him that she was still out but why bother? She knew her father would not approve of her being alone with Trevor, especially with the sun beginning to descend from the sky, painting it with a swirl of orange, yellow and light blue remnants of daylight. It was at that moment, Trevor asked what she was thinking.

"Does your dad know that you going to Jersey with me?" he asked.

Shania shook her head. "Nah, he doesn't know but the way I figured it, he probably doesn't even know I'm still with you and I don't really want him to find out right now. My mom knows I'm with you though," Shania confirmed.

Trevor laughed a little bit. "Your mom's cool with me. I don't know about your pops though. He probably wishes he had a shotgun every time he sees me," Trevor joked as they crossed under a bridge overpass.

"Well that's not true," Shania countered. "He's leery of any boy my age that comes around me, but he'll warm up eventually," she reassured.

"Yeah, like it warms up in Christmas," Trevor said sarcastically.

Shania gave him a play punch on the shoulder, laughing. Shifting emotional gears, Trevor asked about the investigation, even though he hesitated for a moment, because Shania would unfortunately be reminded of her late friend.

"So when you called the other day, you said they arrested some football player for the shooting?" he asked.

"Yeah. It was actually her boyfriend David. They were still dating when she died. It should be over, right? But for some reason, I don't feel like justice has been done, you know what I mean?" she asked.

Trevor nodded his head in agreement. "Yeah, like someone else could be involved or something but didn't they find his gun inside his book bag?" he asked.

"Yeah, they did but it doesn't add up though. David might have been a lot of things. Careless, reckless, even dangerous but to be capable of murder, I don't know. What do you think?" Shania asked.

Trevor sighed because just like Shania, he was clueless about the whole case. "Well, I actually think there's more to this than just him. Was he ever a banger?" Trevor asked, referencing to any gang history.

"Well there are rumors that he knows members from M.O.B but I don't know if he ever was one himself. He could've been one, though," Shania reason.

"True but there were a few guys I saw on Sunday when I was hoopin' at the park and a name I heard. Tadarius or whatever his name was. I did see him with Loree that day," Trevor reminded Shania. Her eyes widened in recognition.

"You're right. I did remember you mentioning that to me that day. Do you think Tedarius shot Loree?" Shania asked.

"Well I'm positive that if David was involved, ain't no way he acted alone. Most of these old gangbangers don't come out and kill their victims directly. Normally, they send other members to go out there and smoke 'em. If Tadarius is the guy in question, then we know he ain't act alone. He probably had some help," Trevor pointed out.

Shania looked at him. "So you don't think that Tadarius hired someone to kill her and frame David, do you?" Shania asked. Trevor didn't know how to answer that question directly. He had always believed that people were innocent until proven guilty but knowing how the gangland world worked, he wouldn't put it past Tadarius to hire someone from his crew to do the job, especially if Loree was a liability to them.

"I'm almost bettin' that's exactly what happened," he replied.

Shania took a moment to let it all sink in. So the wrong guy was caught, and the real suspects were still free. Poor David. He had worked so hard to clean up his life and become regular high school kid. Then just like that, his world was shattered. All because someone else was trying to save his own backside. The thought of it made her sick. She had to do something to get people to believe David could be innocent. But knowing how due process went, he would probably have to stand trial soon for the shooting. So until a surprise witness was found who had some new evidence to clear David's name or until Tadarius turned himself in, an innocent boy's fate would be in the hands of the judge and jurors. Unfortunately, since they were not even in the city at the moment, there was not much she could do. Meanwhile Trevor saw the sign welcoming them to Carlstadt, New Jersey. They passed public locations, such as the police station, fire station, and some hotels. It was a small town; the perfect place into which a man could flee and blend. After a few more minutes of driving, they finally arrived at the address they sought. It was a small, single-story house. Just looking at the house got Trevor agitated.

So he left me and my mom in the hood to fend for ourselves and he ran to this clean town. Why couldn't he have brought us along? Maybe my mom would still be alive today, he thought as he parked on the side of the house and went to ring the doorbell.

At first there was no response. Then after Trevor rang the doorbell again, he heard a voice from inside.

"Yeah, who is it?" it asked in a sharp, gravelly voice.

"It's Trevor McClain. Is this the home of Mr. Gary McKey?" he asked tentatively.

Again, there was no answer. He looked at Shania and shrugged but before he could decide to leave or try again, the wooden door opened. Standing in the doorway was a tall, thin man with curly black hair with specks of gray in it and the emergence of a bald spot. Trevor took one look at his eyes and that was all it took to see that he was finally looking at his biological father. The man opened the door.

"It's finally nice to meet you, son. Please come on in," he offered them and both Shania and Trevor walked inside the home.

As they walked inside, Trevor looked around and saw pictures of Gary throughout the years; a portrait of him at the hardware store where he worked and a picture of him with a woman and a small child. Gary turned around and shook Shania's hand.

"Who is this beautiful young lady? Is she your girlfriend?" he asked smiling.

Trevor's mind went blank. He didn't know how to describe his relationship with Shania, so being called his girlfriend might be a bit premature but Shania shocked him with her answer.

"Yes, I'm his girlfriend, Shania Hillman. Nice to meet you," she greeted.

Gary's eyes widened as he heard a familiar name that he hadn't learned in so long. "You wouldn't happen to be related to Michael Clark Hillman by any chance, would you?" he asked raising an eyebrow.

Shania's eyes widened as well. "Yes, he's my father. Did you know him?" she asked.

Gary laughed deeply. "Young lady, Mike and I go way back to the Richmond Hill High school years. He was my boy, a very good friend," he answered. "One of the best high school quarterbacks I've seen in a long time," he added.

"Yeah he was, but he doesn't play anymore," Shania agreed.

Gary shook his head. "I know. Unfortunately, I might have had something to do with that. Please sit on the couch so I can bring you both something to drink," he offered.

Shania started to accept the offer, but Trevor wasn't about to accept it. He was determined not to let his father sucker him back in with a winning grin he must have used to his benefit every so often.

"I'm not really thirsty. We need to talk. I think it's been way overdue," Trevor said sharply, and Shania kept her mouth closed. Gary then sat down on the other side of Shania and Trevor. Trevor knew he didn't have much time because he was looking at a two-hour drive back to town and he had to drop Shania back home before her father worried too much. As a result, he cut to the chase. "Why now? Why after all these years you picked this year to reach out to me?" he asked.

Gary took a moment to allow Trevor's words to sink in before he continued. "I made a lot of mistakes in life, Trevor, and giving you up as a young child was the worst mistake I ever made. I just wasn't ready yet," he explained.

"Ready for what?" Trevor asked, demanding an answer.

"Ready to be a father. I thought I could handle it when I first got together with your mother, but the truth was that I wasn't ready yet," Gary replied.

"So you left me with my junkie mama and decided to live here. Very convenient," Trevor finished sarcastically.

"No, it wasn't like that. Please hear me out," Gary pleaded. "Your father, Mike," Gary started, pointing at Shania. "We were best friends, tighter than anyone, along with my boy, Nate. But I'm sure you've seen him," Gary said.

Shania and Trevor looked at each other, unsure who Gary was talking about.

"You mean, you don't know him?" he asked. "He works at Richmond Hill High School now as a janitor. I was able to reconnect with him recently," he explained.

"In case you've forgotten, Dad, I graduated from Richmond Hill last year," Trevor answered with emphasis on the 'Dad' reference.

Shania, seeing the tension between the reunited father and son, said "Oh ok, I think I've seen him a few times. I haven't spoken with him too much though. Rumor has it that he used to play basketball there too," she added.

"The rumors were true," Gary answered. "Nate was one of the best basketball players in the city. Dominated from the point guard position, where he would make plays that even his own teammates wondered how he did them," he said.

Trevor looked at him, still not impressed or convinced. "You played with him?" he asked.

"Yeah, we were teammates for three years on that team. He helped lead us to the top of the city standings," Gary answered.

Trevor remembered seeing the picture in front of the gym on the way to the locker rooms. How could he not have known that his father was on the team that made history at the school? Sure, he had great individual stats but Trevor's high school team was never a stout team collectively and they hadn't won the region in his senior year there.

"Everything was good. Then Mike met her. Nina Martin. She was one of the most baddest sistas out there. Head cheerleader, smart, and very ambitious, Mike couldn't resist her," Gary said.

Shania and Trevor listened although part of them really couldn't help but doubt Gary's account. Were their parents really involved once? As if he read their thoughts, Gary continued.

"Their relationship was steady but then the drugs kicked in. Mike didn't know that Nina was selling and addicted to heroin at the time he started dating her. But the more she used, the more their relationship strained," Gary explained. "It also didn't help that Mike had a reputation of being....well to put it quite frankly, being a player."

Gary finished, hesitating because he did not want to use too strong a word to offend Shania. Shania still listened but she couldn't believe what she was hearing. Her father, the uptight, straight-laced, good pastor, had been a womanizer? She knew he had demons when he was a teen because he often referred back to his younger years during his sermons. Not once had he ever told her that he spent high school chasing women.

"Women loved Mike and Mike loved women. When Nina felt she was no longer being loved, she came to me for comfort. At first we were only friends, introduced through Mike. But the more they drifted apart, the closer together we came," Gary continued. "We hooked up and concealed it from Mike for a few months, but eventually Mike found out about our secret relationship and he felt betrayed. He was hurt and ever since that time, the close bond we had as friends started to tear. Nate and Nina drifted further out into the streets. I was doing all I could to prevent Nina from living that lifestyle, but I was caught up myself. After high school, Nina and I were still together and she was living with me in a pad just outside 101 Avenue. At that point, I didn't know what happened to Mike since we had stopped talking. I still spoke with Nate, even offered him a place where I was living because he had been kicked out and disowned by his own parents," he explained.

Trevor didn't want to hear any more of this. Time was wasting and he felt his father was trying to hold back the one answer he drove so long and desperately to hear.

"Ok, so throughout all of the drug game, what happened to Nina? How did she die, then?" Trevor asked.

Gary sighed and Trevor could see it was becoming more and more difficult to continue. "Well, a few months after you were born, Nina discussed marriage and being a full-time father. Selfishly, it wasn't the future I anticipated with her. Her constant drug use and my desire to leave the area factored in my decision to leave her. I didn't wanna go, but I knew I just couldn't be there anymore. She wanted to keep you with her though. She promised to clean herself up and be a better mother and eventually a wife. I made the very tough decision to leave 101 Avenue to pursue a career in logistics. It was only a few weeks later that Nate called me and told me about Nina's passing. There was a botched drug deal, and the dealer went after Nina. Nate tried to fight him but the man overpowered him and he ended up pushing Nina onto a row of sharp gate spikes. Nate couldn't stop him in time and Nina was killed almost instantly," Gary said as a tear rolled down his eye.

Trevor, who had also shed a couple of tears as the story unfolded, got to his feet almost immediately. He had heard enough.

"Let's go," he said to Shania and they both headed for the front door.

"Please forgive me, son," Gary pleaded to Trevor.

Trevor whirled around on Gary. "All you had to do was stay with her. Because you was too damn scared to handle yo' business, I lost my mother. You ain't got nothin' to say to me now," he said, reaching into his pocket, pulling out the letter and the envelope. "Take yo' shit back. I don't wanna hear nothing from you, I don't wanna see nothing from you, you feel me? I ain't yo' son," Trevor said, enraged as he walked out slamming the door behind him.

Shania turned back to Gary. "He probably just needs some time to cool down," she reassured Gary.

"Yeah, I'm sure he'll come around. It was very nice meeting you, Shania. Please send my regards to your father. I know that it's been years, but I would like to talk to him again, just to catch up," Gary said.

Shania agreed and as she walked out of the door, Gary watched as she got into the car, joining Trevor as they both drove away without looking back.

Sitting on the living room couch, Mike looked at the small clock hanging above the hall doorway. Here it was, after eleven-thirty at night and Shania was still not home. Robyn was in the bedroom, getting her work clothes ready for the next day.

"Honey, where in the world is Shania? Didn't she step out this morning? I thought she was just going for a lunch with Mr. McAfee's daughter," he said.

Robyn came out of the room in her bathrobe. "Yeah I know that. They dropped Andrea off a while ago. She said that she had to help Trevor take care of some family business," Robyn replied.

At this answer, Mike stood up from his chair. He did not like where this was going. "I was under the impression that she went out to lunch with Andrea. Nobody ever mentioned that she would be out with that boy. How come I was not told about this?" Mike asked angrily.

Robyn rolled her eyes. Here we go again she thought. "I'm sorry I didn't tell you but I was sure you wouldn't have a problem with it," Robyn answered. Mike hit the arm rest on the couch in frustration.

"You thought I wouldn't have a problem with what? Our daughter is out with God knows who and I'm supposed to just sit here and tolerate it? Didn't anybody consider what happened during the past few days?" he asked emphatically. "There is a girl Shania's age, who has been murdered, most likely by the hoodlum she was dating, and our girl is out there?" Please explain what's wrong with this whole picture," he said.

"Oh stop it, Mike!" Robyn snapped, just as emphatically. "Unlike you, I trust my daughter's judgment and I trust that she's not getting into trouble. I don't see what you're all worked up about," she added.

"Worked up? You think I'm worked up?" Mike asked. "Where does Trevor live? What time did Shania tell you she would return? If you don't have any answers to those questions, then charge me for being worked up," he countered.

Robyn walked up to Mike. "Why don't you like that boy, Mike? It's not like they're breaking laws, and he seems like a nice boy, in whom you're not giving a chance whatsoever. Why is that?" she asked.

She had asked him the same question so many times that Mike nearly blew his top when he shouted, "It's because I think I know who he is, ok? He's not a positive influence on our daughter," Mike answered.

Robyn looked at him quizzically. "What do you mean, you think you know who he is?" she asked.

Before Mike could explain, they heard their doorbell ring. Running downstairs, Mike shouted, "I bet that's her now," Opening the door, he looked at a person who was neither Shania nor Trevor.

CHAPTER TWENTY

An elderly lady, leaning on a walking cane for support, stood outside the door. Mike looked at her closely. He didn't think she was one of his church members. Even though it was only a slightly cool night, she wore a black shawl around her shoulders that covered the long flowery dress she was wearing.

"Good evening, ma'am. How can I help you tonight?" Mike asked kindly.

"Yes I'm looking for Pastor Michael Hillman. Does he live here?" she asked in a voice that cracked several times as she spoke.

"Yes, I'm Pastor Mike. Please come inside," Mike offered as the lady made her way inside. He held her hand lightly to help her walk up the stairs. While assisting the lady up the stairs, Mike turned to ask her name but before he had a chance to open his mouth, she spoke again.

"My name is Willamena Anderson and I have a very important matter to discuss with you tonight. I just hope I haven't caught you at a bad time," she said.

Mike nodded with a dismissal wave of his hand. "Oh no, don't worry about it, Mrs. Anderson. We were just turning in for the night," he said.

Robin came out of the kitchen just as they were reaching the stair top. "Honey, is everything ok?" she asked Mike.

"Yeah everything is fine. Mrs. Anderson just stopped by to discuss an important matter with me," he replied.

Robyn smiled at Mrs. Anderson. It wasn't unusual for Mike to have visitors come into his home, especially if they were from his church or just wanted some prayer and encouragement. Mike always believed in being hospitable, no matter who came to visit and it warmed his heart whenever the visitor left in better spirits than when they had walked in. The woman distracted them from their own worries about their daughter.

"Would you like anything to eat or drink, Mrs. Anderson? We have juice, water, tea, and I believe we have a few snacks in the pantry," Mike offered.

Mrs. Anderson politely refused the snacks but accepted a glass of water. While Robyn went to get the glass, Mike sat down on the couch but not before offering Mrs. Anderson a seat on the couch first. Mike saw that she traveled a long distance to see him because her cheeks were still slightly red from the cold night and Mike heard the way she grunted slightly prior to sitting down on the sofa.

"If you don't mind me asking Mrs. Anderson, to what do I owe the pleasure of your visit tonight?" he asked. It was never in Mike's nature to ask a person why they came to his residence and what they needed. He was aware that it was a rough area and everyone couldn't be trusted in society. But if Jesus could sit at a table and communicate and dine with sinners, why couldn't he? Mrs. Anderson looked at Mike with a pained look in her eyes.

"My grandson David Anderson brings me here tonight, pastor," she replied.

Mike's heart skipped a beat, although he didn't allow the full shock to register completely on his face. He had only heard that name one time and that had been on the evening news when he had been arrested at Richmond Hill High school in connection with the shooting. David was the boy Loree had been seeing before her untimely death. He was the reason Mike didn't want his daughter to be out after dark. Now here was his grandmother, sitting only a few feet from him.

"Pastor I didn't know who else to turn to but I came tonight to ask if you can help clear my grandson's name and pray over him," Mrs. Anderson requested.

Mike felt nothing but love and sorrow for this courageous lady that sat before him. Her grandson was lying in a cold jail cell and instead of sitting idle and watching the law take action, Mrs. Anderson had gotten up and walked through a windy and potentially dangerous Saturday night. In certain neighborhoods a person could easily be mugged and beaten in the blink of an eye. She had bravely trooped to Pastor Mike's home to see if she could intercede for her grandson. Despite the admiration Mike felt for her, he also felt a stab of anger. Seeing the love she had for her grandson, Mike almost felt enraged that David would be in a situation that would leave his grandmother and whatever family he had left in tears. Mike was sure these young boys didn't appreciate the enormous obstacles that their loved ones had gone through to give them a better, productive life. Instead of repaying their families with gratitude, they repaid them with gang activity, drug-dealing, and underachieving in school. Mike felt that he couldn't have higher respect for anyone than he did for Mrs. Anderson but he didn't know how he could help David.

"Mrs. Anderson, I must first say that while I'm very encouraged and blessed by your company tonight, I don't see how I can help David. He was arrested and he had the murder weapon in his possession. I know you believe the best of your grandson but sometimes kids do make bad choices that can affect their future," he said.

Mrs. Anderson nodded as if she understood but she wasn't going to give up easily. "Pastor, I know for a fact that my grandson did not kill the girl that night. He called me while they were holding him and he has been telling me how terrible it is for him there," she explained, unable to control the racked sobs that were escaping from her.

Robyn brought the glass of water over and Mike offered it to Mrs. Anderson. She stopped crying long enough to take a sip of water and then she continued to talk to Mike.

"Pastor, my grandson made a lot of mistakes in the past. When he was only four years of age, his parents abandoned him and left New York," she said. "My lazy son and his wife just felt that he was taking up too much of their time. So I took the responsibility of raising him. But he got himself caught up in the wrong crowd and he has been in and out of juvenile facilities and boy's reform schools and it was just one thing after another," she explained while the tears spilled, and Robyn offered her a tissue. She took a moment to wipe her eyes before she continued. "Prior to attending this here school, when he was in juvenile hall, he met this one fellow who I did not trust, the moment I laid eyes on him," she said. "I knew he was up to no good all the time, but to David, he was something of a hero and he fooled my grandson into getting involved in all this gang activity. But once he started going to school and started playing football, I saw a change in his eyes, pastor," Mrs. Anderson explained. "I saw him starting to take school more seriously and he was taking football more seriously. He never did get that girl out of his head sometimes. He would talk about how great she was and how she was always there for him. She provided the love that I didn't think I provided to him at times. When the news of her death hit television, I knew for a fact that my David could not have committed such a horrendous crime," Mrs. Anderson said.

Mike thought about what Mrs. Anderson just said to him. In his mind he vaguely remembered when Shania had tried to explain Loree's relationship problem in which she was being physically abused. If David was such a good guy who would not commit such a crime, then why were there abuse reports following him? Why was the murder weapon in his book bag? Who else had he planned to kill that day? It could have been anybody who was associated with Loree, maybe even his own daughter. Just the thought of it frightened him. Maybe David should stay in jail for his own good, because the evidence stacking up against him did not help and his own daughter could still be in harm's way.

"Mrs. Anderson, I really want to believe you but how well do you know your grandson? Do you know who he hangs out with every day? Is he completely innocent here? Sometimes we have to look at all the facts and make decisions based on logic rather than emotion," he said.

As soon as Mike had he uttered those words he realized it was not the response Mrs. Anderson needed. Mrs. Anderson stood up and started to walk toward the staircase.

"Pastor, I come to you with absolutely no money, no way of compensation, and no fancy talk but I come with an earnest heart of a loving mother and grandmother. I only asked for your help, from one parent to another. Just remember this: what if it was your daughter or son? They are all we have left of us in this world. David is all I have left right now because even though my son has left me, David has never left me and I don't plan on leaving him," she said as she slowly descended downstairs.

Mike got up to help her walk down the stairs. Robyn watched as she slowly made her way down the creaky wooden steps, wishing there was more she could say but she couldn't come up with any words. Mike was just as much in the dark as his wife was because here was the grandmother of the suspect asking him to speak up and defend her grandson. She could have been simply pleading on David's behalf, knowing that he was guilty of shooting Loree but on the other hand, there was a pain and suffering in her eyes that cut Mike to the heart. He always believed the Lord had put him in a position to help His people and lead them closer to Him. The Christian faith in Mike would not allow him to just sit by and watch David's grandmother fight the jury, the court, and the state alone. She would have to fight all the people who were sure to charge David with the crime.

As she walked out of the front door, Mike turned to Mrs. Anderson. "I'll do whatever I can to help your grandson through this," he promised her.

Mrs. Anderson broke down into tears of gratitude and hugged Mike tightly. As Mike watched her make her way through the dark streets toward 101 Avenue, he felt a sense of accomplishment, yet he also felt the burden of a task he had promised perhaps too prematurely. How in God's name was he going to be able to help prove David's innocence? Not only was he facing the charges against David, but he also had to face Loree's grieving family. Mike had spoken with them on several occasions and there was no doubt the loss weighed heavily in their hearts. When the news flashed the night David was taken into custody, they had felt a sense of relief because they had no doubt that David had murdered Loree. They had never trusted David and were only too convinced that the weapon found in David's backpack sealed his fate. Mike realized that his reputation and his name would be at risk because Amos and Alisha both attended his church and if they knew he was helping David, it could permanently fracture their trust in him, his family, and his church.

While he thought about those things, Robyn called him from the top of the stairs. Mike walked up to join her.

"Why did you tell Mrs. Anderson that you'd help her?" Robyn asked with a disapproving edge in her tone.

Mike turned to Robyn. He couldn't believe she could ask him that question. Then again, in the back of his mind, he'd always known she would ask it.

"Ok, you want to know why I promised to help her? I did it because what if she's right? What if that young man was arrested for something he didn't do?" he asked.

"How would you know if he did it or not?" Robyn asked back defiantly.

"I have to see the good in people, Robyn. That's who I am. That's how God created me. I mean, what if that boy's innocent?" he asked.

Robyn shook her head. "What if he's not?" she asked back, angrily. "I spoke to Alisha last night, Mike, and she still cries over her daughter's bed. A part of her has died. Aren't you concerned about how they feel?" she asked.

"Of course I'm concerned!" Mike stated emphatically.

This attitude was very uncharacteristic of Robyn. They always disagreed on certain ideology but they never disagreed about helping others. She appeared to be completely blinded. Why couldn't Robyn stand with him this one time?

"I'm very concerned about the McAfee family but I'm also concerned about the young men out there. Do you have any idea how many innocent young men lie in jail for a crime they did not commit?" Mike asked. "If he didn't commit the crime, I can't just sit there and watch his grandmother suffer," he added.

"How do you know his grandmother isn't lying or covering up to save her grandson?" Robyn bit back.

"I just have a feeling that she isn't lying, ok?" Mike replied.

Robyn scoffed at what sounded like nonsense flowing out of her husband's head. "You have a feeling? That's great," she replied sarcastically. "But the police have proof, Mike. There's evidence that David was involved. The gun found in his backpack and the bruises they found on Loree. Shania also said that she believes David physically abused Loree. How do you know he didn't go too far?" she asked.

Mike shook his head. "David may have made plenty of mistakes in life, but murder is not one of them," he replied, secretly hoping that he was right.

Sensing the fight leaving his wife, Mike started for the bedroom door. As he walked, he remembered Shania had still not returned. He attempted to call her cell phone but she didn't pick up. Robyn stepped into the bedroom.

"The question you need to ask yourself is how much deeper do you want to get involved in this?" she asked him.

Mike honestly had no answer for Robyn because he didn't know how deep he wanted to be involved in it. Since it affected the community, it also affected his family and therefore him as a person and a leader. "I have to do this Robyn. I got to show this community a message that not every young black man is a hoodlum. Not every man of color is prison-bound. We only imprison ourselves and our mindset. By God's grace, if a testimony can come out of David's trial, whether innocent or guilty, I know that it will be for the good of those who still remain forgiving, hopeful and faithful," he replied.

Trevor's car pulled up outside of Shania's home at nearly one o'clock in the morning. Shania was sleeping in the passenger's seat, exhausted from the day's events. The ride back to New York had been nothing short of uncomfortable. Trevor certainly hadn't been in the best of moods after the brief reunion with his father and each time Shania had tried to start a conversation, Trevor's responses had been short and terse. After thirty minutes on the road, Shania finally gave up on brightening the mood and entertained herself by watching the trees, the land, and the ponds go by as they headed back to the borough. Eventually, a drowsy sensation overcame her and she fell asleep as soon as they crossed over the state line. At first Trevor was oblivious to the fact that Shania was fast asleep but once he heard her steady breathing and the slow rise and fall of her chest, he realized she was fast asleep. A look of remorse crossed his face as he glanced at her peaceful slumber as night fell. He should have been more polite and open to her on the ride back home but he hoped that one day she would understand why he had reacted the way he did.

It just wasn't easy finding out the way his mother had met her end. She didn't deserve to die that way. Nobody deserved to die the way Nina Martin had died. Nobody deserved to die the way Loree did either, but life dished out cruel, unfair punishments. These deaths, among other reasons, were why Trevor couldn't believe that if God existed, he would allow these tragedies to happen. If God really existed, there wouldn't be wars that tore families apart. There wouldn't be children starving in third world countries. There wouldn't be people on this earth wondering what they were going to wear on their backs to keep them warm. If God really oversaw the world, then how did He allow mass murder and tragedies such as the Holocaust or the Rwanda genocide? Certainly a loving God wouldn't allow such atrocities, just as he wouldn't allow Trevor's mother to be brutally murdered in the dead of night over some busted drug deal. It just didn't make sense to him. Nothing seemed to make sense to Trevor anymore.

When he had gotten the Van Wyck Expressway exit, he had glanced once more at Shania, who turned slightly to the side, curling her long slender legs as she slept in peaceful bliss. He still couldn't get over her beauty. How did he ever overlook her when he was still in high school? Girls like Shania were basically overprotected by their fathers and Trevor had a feeling that the pastor didn't take a particular liking to him at all. He couldn't explain his feelings because this was the first girl who had been real to him. She wasn't prideful like most of the girls he had dated in the past. There was a quality about her that drew him in. Shifting into park, he watched her sleep for the next five minutes. Then he gently nudged her.

"Wake up, sleepyhead," he whispered gently in her ear.

Stirring slightly, Shania's eyelid's fluttered open. "Hey big-head," she whispered back smiling. "Are we already at my place?" she asked as she sat up.

"Yeah we're here," he confirmed while looking out of the widow. He knew Mike would still be awake, wondering where his daughter was at this time of night. "Look, I wanna apologize for not talking to you back in Jersey. I just had a lot on my mind, you know," he explained.

Shania nodded to confirm that she understood and completely forgave him for shunning her. "I understand. It can't be easy finding out what happened to your mother. I should've been more considerate, especially after Loree's passing," she replied.

Trevor looked out of his widow into the starry night. "For so long, I always wondered if I was living a dream or some type of fantasy. Being raised in a nice house, both parents got nice jobs, and playing ball for Richmond Hill," Trevor said. "Finally there's getting the scholarship to play the sport that I love. Then in one month, the dream turns into a nightmare. Finding out that I'm adopted, my dad never wanted me, and my momma was a junkie who died cuz some fool ain't get paid. I just wish it could all end," Trevor sighed.

Shania massaged Trevor's shoulders affectionately, trying to relate to his feeling of hopelessness even though he knew she couldn't. "Well, anytime you wanna talk or just hang out, just let me know," she said. Trevor turned to her and smiled. No sooner had he smiled than Shania brought up the one subject that he didn't want to talk about. "Which reminds me, I did spend the day with you and we did go out on a date one time. So am I gonna see you tomorrow morning at church, right?" Shania asked.

Trevor sighed deeply. He had hoped she wouldn't bring it up. With all the doubts swirling in his mind, he didn't think it would be any benefit for him to go to church the next day. "I don't know. I don't even remember the last time I've even stepped in the doors of a church building. It's been so long. Besides what if your father doesn't want me in there?" he asked.

"Oh come on, he's not gonna say anything negative to you if you come. Please?" she pleaded.

Trevor sat and thought about what it would be like to step into church for the first time in probably twelve years. He could already see the faces of the regular church patrons who would scan him and see him as nothing more than another young black man who needed Jesus and then some. But a promise was a promise. He didn't have basketball practice until two-thirty in the afternoon.

"Ok I'll come to your dad's church tomorrow but if he points at me and calls me out in public, I'm walking straight out," he said as firmly as he could without cracking a smile but it didn't work. A smirk pushed through his facial features. The next thing he knew, Shania grabbed him and hugged him hard. "Ok, all right I need to be able to breathe if I'm gonna come tomorrow, ok?" he asked laughing.

Shania let him go and her next move was so impulsive, even she couldn't explain why she did it but she reached up and kissed him on the lips. Although it was only for a split second, it was evident. Trevor didn't expect the kiss and he could have sworn his lips lost feeling temporarily. Her lips felt soft and warm.

"What was that for?" he asked amazed and taken aback by the moment.

"Well it's for a lot of things. One being a great guy and being there for me," Shania said, with their foreheads still pressed together. Trevor closed his eyes again. He longed to kiss her again; to feel that warm sensation on his lips once again but at the very last moment, Shania opened the passenger door and started walking toward her door. Trevor watched her to make sure that she was able to get inside. As soon as he saw her take out her house key, he slowly shifted into reverse to leave and made his way back to the comfort of his dormitory at St. John's University.

The moment Shania stepped inside her home, she saw the stairway light was turned off and so was her hallway light. As she started to walk up the stairs to her room, she thought her parents were asleep, until the hallway light suddenly turned on and there was her father, dressed in his striped pajamas and bathrobe.

"Miss Shania Elyse Hillman, do you have any idea what time it is?" he asked with a stern look on his face.

"Sorry Dad, on my way back from visiting Trevor's family, I fell asleep in his car and lost track of time. I'm sorry. It won't happen again," she apologized almost sincerely but her Mike sensed the indifference in her tone.

"Shania it is almost one in the morning. Where in the world did you go? Kalamazoo?" he asked, attempting to make a weak joke in a serious situation as he so often did.

"No Dad, I told you I went to visit Trevor's family with him after we spent the day with Andrea. No big deal," she replied.

"Not good enough," Mike countered.

Shania sighed. Sometimes it was like her father didn't even want to listen to her. She couldn't wait until she graduated high school so she could move out of her parent's house. She had just about had it with her father's overprotective attitude. Mike stepped closer to Shania; too close for comfort.

"Where did you go with that boy?" he asked. Shania started to walk toward the room, attempting to ignore her father. "Don't you turn your back on me, young lady!" he snapped at her. Shania turned around to face her father, a look of anger on her face as well. "You best fix your face before I fix it for you," Mike warned. Shania relaxed the scowl on her face "Now, I ask again, where did you go with that boy?" he asked again.

"Do you really want to know where I went with him?" Shania yelled. "I went to New Jersey with him to visit his real father. Turns out he was really adopted, cuz his daddy didn't want him and his momma was killed by some drug dealers," Shania continued. "Shame on me for actually being the only one who really cared about him when he thought nobody else did," she added.

Mike stood in complete silence because he was in shock from the words that had just spewed from his daughter's mouth. Could it be true that his suspicions were right and this Trevor boy was the son of his old high school girlfriend? He had wondered if maybe he had gone crazy or off the deep end but his daughter may have just solved the mystery for him.

"Who is his real father, then?" Mike asked in low tones.

Shania took a minute before answering her father. She wasn't too sure if Trevor wanted his business out there but on the other hand, she had learned a great deal about her father that she never knew, so she felt the need to jog his memory. Mike however, had the sinking feeling that he already knew who Trevor's father was because the similarities were all too familiar.

"His name's Gary McKey, and he lives in Carlstadt, New Jersey," Shania answered and Mike closed his eyes as the arrow of truth pierced him.

He couldn't help thinking that if he had remained with Nina, Trevor might have been his son. His name might have not been Trevor and he may not have been as tall but Gary would never have been in the picture.

"His mother's name was Nina Martin, wasn't it?" he asked in confirmation. Shania didn't answer but she nodded her head to confirm exactly what Mike had suspected the whole time. So the kid is the spawn of the two so called 'friends' who betrayed me back in high school Mike thought.

These were the same people that had driven Mike to alcohol and down a path of depression that had permanently ended his football career...and nearly ended his life. Seeing the look on Shania's face described a different story. If Gary told her about Nina, there was no doubt that he also told her about their history together. Shania walked past her father without saying another word.

"Shania," he began as she prepared to enter her bedroom. "I'm sorry you had to find out that way. I wanted to tell you and your mother about it but..." Mike explained before his voice trailed off.

"But it just slipped your mind and you held a grudge because of your insecurities against a boy who did nothing but try to respect you," Shania finished. She went inside her room and shut the door.

That could have gone a lot better Mike thought.

Sunday morning brought an uncharacteristic sense of gloom in the Rock of Jacob Baptist Church. Right away when service started, Mike noticed that a few members of the church were missing. He noticed while preaching at his pulpit that Isis Samuels was not in attendance and neither was Jamal. Amos and Alisha McAfee did attend service but their faces were still fresh with sorrow as the members of the church did their best to comfort the grieving family.

Before starting his sermon, Mike made the announcement, per request of the McAfee family, that the funeral service and burial would take place the following Saturday morning at Linden Blvd Funeral Home. It didn't help the emotional gloom that it was also physically gloomy because of the scattered rain showers and dark sky. Mike even felt like hiding but he prayed to the Lord and delivered the message as best he could. As he scanned the congregation he noticed Trevor; dressed in old slacks and an old dress shirt from his high school days. Trevor purposely sat in the second level of the church, not wanting to draw attention to himself. He also left before final prayer so he could make it back to school for his team practice. As Mike greeted people after service, he saw Amos and Alisha and knew it was vital to address them.

"Amos, can you and your wife please come into my office? I would like a few words with you," he said. He asked Shania and Robyn to wait for him and that he would not take too long. By this time, the church benches were empty; everyone having left for the afternoon. Mike led Amos and Alisha to his office, which was located on the level below his sanctuary. It was a small office facing the three Sunday school rooms. Mike held the door open for Amos, Alisha, and Andrea to enter. They sat in chairs that faced the pastor's desk. Mike took his seat at his desk as well.

"I called the family in the office today because I wanted to discuss the court details with you. Speaking to some people earlier today, they informed me that you were going to press charges against Mr. Anderson. Is this true?" he asked.

Mr. McAfee cleared his throat. "It's true pastor," he replied. "It's actually good timing that we talked about this because we were wondering if you could testify on our behalf to help bring justice for Loree," he continued. Mike looked down guiltily, avoiding their eyes. "Pastor, you are a very revered individual in this community. You've prayed with us and you've been with us throughout this tragedy. We feel that if you can help represent us in court that day, it will give us a better chance of convicting that murderer," Amos said.

Mike knew they were going to ask this of him because Alisha had called Robyn nearly every day to ask if Mike would support them in convicting David for the crime. Mike had not called to respond but today he knew what he must do.

Looking directly at Amos, he said "Amos, you know that I have nothing but love and respect for you and your family. However, I called you all in here this afternoon to say that unfortunately I cannot testify against David. As a matter of fact, I was hoping that I could persuade you to drop the charges against Mr. Anderson," Mike replied.

He expected an emotional outburst but he was unaware that he had actually opened a Pandora's Box. The whole family stuttered and stammered, not knowing what to say. Had the pastor really asked them to drop the charges against this killer?

"Pastor, with all due respect, I cannot adhere to what you want me to do. That boy killed my baby girl. She is now lying lifeless in some morgue and you're asking me to drop the charges against that thug? That's out of the question," Amos stated, highly upset at the request Mike made.

"Amos, please hear me out on this," Mike pleaded. "There is no concrete evidence that David committed the crime," he added.

Amos narrowed his eyes at Mike. "So the murder weapon found in his bag and a prior history of physically abusing my daughter ain't concrete enough for you?" he asked angrily.

"Amos, that's circumstantial evidence and you know that," Mike argued back.

Amos stood up so quickly, Mike feared that Amos would punch him or inflict some other type of bodily harm, but he stopped nearly inches away from Mike's face.

"What if it was your daughter, huh? What if it had been Shania who was shot that night? Would you accept anyone telling you that you shouldn't retaliate by charging the sick bastard? I don't think so," Amos replied angrily.

Mike sighed. He knew the family would react this way and he understood that it was all out of grief and emotion. "If it was Shania, there's no doubt that I would want justice, too. But we cannot throw another innocent boy in jail," he said.

"Says who? You?" Amos asked, his face turning redder and more maniacal by the second. "I never trusted that thug ever since Loree introduced me to him. One look at this boy and I knew he was no good. I should've done my job and ended that relationship right there. Maybe she would still be here," he added.

Mike decided to explain the late-night visit. "His grandmother visited me last night and said herself that David was not at the scene of the crime, and she believes that David was framed by his former gang friends," Mike started to explain but Amos wasn't having it.

"Yeah, and how do you know his grandmother ain't stickin' up for him? I don't care what he was or what he ain't. None of that concerns me. They're all the same to me. Worthless, ghetto thugs," Amos replied. "Let's go," he said firmly to his family as they got up and walked out of Mike's office.

Mike put his head on the desk. It was apparent that Amos would not drop the charges on David and that only added to the stress and grief Mike felt for the family and more importantly himself.

CHAPTER TWENTY-ONE

Mike was sure his day couldn't get any worse. When he told Robyn and Shania about the disastrous meeting with the McAfee family, Robyn scolded Mike for his lack of tact and sensitivity. She bawled him out for telling the McAfee family he wouldn't represent them in court. Mike knew the only way he could have possibly diffused the anger and rage in Amos was to agree to testify against David in open court.

"What would you have done differently?" he asked Robyn in a challenge as the turned-on Liberty Avenue.

"I don't know but I would've said something else. Mike, you're more than a pastor to these people, you are like their advisor and confidant. If they feel hurt or uncared for, that could hurt any chances of reconciliation in dealing with their grief," Robyn argued.

Mike couldn't stand it. He felt it was becoming impossible to please his wife. They didn't seem to be able to agree on any issue anymore. Not even the way to handle a family who was grieving over the loss of a loved one.

As they finally arrived at home, Robyn said, "I warned you that you're getting in too deep. Now what are you going to do about this mess?" she asked.

The question stumped Mike as it had his wife. What could he possibly do? Amos seemed intent in using the court and state prosecutor to charge David not only for this crime but to use his background against him to lengthen his sentence. Unless...unless David was defended well and proven innocent. The only problem was that Mike was fairly sure that David's grandmother wouldn't be able to afford a good lawyer. That thought gave Mike the initial direction he needed to find someone capable enough to prove David's innocence.

"What about Arthur? Do you think he'd be able to help prove David's innocence?" Mike asked, referring to Robyn's brother. Mike saw that Robyn was mulling the idea over but she doubted its effectiveness.

"You could try to call him, but the fact that you're family doesn't guarantee a free ride. Believe me when I say that he'll charge for this," she warned.

"That's all right. As long as he could help, I'll take care of it," Mike declared.

Mike told Robyn and Shania that he was going to his office to grab some supplies from his desk. As he drove back toward town he dialed Arthur's number.

"Hey, what's up?" Arthur greeted through the receiver.

"Hey, man what's up? Hope I didn't catch you at a bad time again," Mike replied.

"Actually I was busy closing out a couple cases but I can always make time for family," Arthur said. "By the way, did you take my advice on your little situation with Robyn? How'd it go?" he asked.

Mike shook his head. "Still working on it," he replied. "But that's actually not why I'm calling, Arthur. I need a huge favor from you. Have you heard the news about the girl who attended Richmond Hill High School being shot to death?" he asked.

"Yeah, who hasn't heard about it? It was all over the news," Arthur replied.

"Ok, well here's what's going on. There's a young man currently sitting behind bars, connected to the murder of the young lady but I have reason to believe that he didn't commit this crime. The only problem is that nobody else believes him. He has a court date coming up and he doesn't have a lawyer to defend him and his grandmother can't afford one for him. I need you to help prove the boy's innocence on court day," Mike said.

There was silence on the other line as Arthur tried to digest the information. By that time, Mike had arrived at his office. He grabbed his notebooks, rulers, and a couple of lunchboxes he had left there during the week. He heard a sigh on the other end after a few minutes.

"Mike, I am so swamped here man. Just finished handling ten other cases and now you want me to take this one too? I'm surprised you're even involved in this to be quite honest with you. Shouldn't you be on the sidelines praying for an outcome to this or something?" Arthur asked, chuckling because that's all he ever expected Mike to do. Pray for the best in every situation. Wife leaving him high and dry every night, pray on it. Hoping that he would someday come to his brother-in-laws church, pray on it.

Mike had never seemed to be a man of action until today. So Arthur reluctantly agreed to help Mike defend David on the court date and Mike breathed a huge sigh of relief. "But tell me this though. Has this young man been associated with any type of gang affiliation whether it be this year or in the past?" he asked.

"I'm not sure," Mike replied. "Why? What difference would it make, especially if he's no longer in a gang?" he asked.

"It doesn't change anything much, except it makes the job of defending him more challenging. I'm almost certain that the prosecution is going to use every bit of that boy's past against him," Arthur said.

"Really?" Mike asked. Robyn was right, after all. Shania had reservations about David long before the murder, yet Mike still didn't know if David had been involved with any gang activity. So on top of his own pressure, he was adding to his brother-in-law's workload.

"Yes really. But I'll see what I can do. I'll have to see him face to face and introduce myself to this David. Then come court-time, I'll take care of it," Arthur said.

Mike took a breath of relief. "Thanks man, I really do appreciate this," he said in gratitude.

"Oh don't thank me yet," Arthur said quickly before Mike could end the call. "This is definitely coming out of yo' tab," he said.

Mike responded by saying he understood, before hanging up the phone. Relieved that he finally had some type of reinforcement coming his way, he decided to head to the grocery store on the way home to get some milk, juice, and vegetables. As if it wasn't enough that Robyn was giving him grief over getting involved with the legal case, she had been chastising him for letting it distract him from his daily chores and responsibilities at home. As he walked out of the store, he heard the constant revving of a vehicle as it was desperately trying to start. The car was parked only a few spaces from Mike, so he put his groceries in his own car and decided to see if the driver needed any help. He watched so many people walk and drive by without any concern for the driver. Mike quelled the anger that brewed inside him and instead, went to the driver's side. The windows were tinted and rolled up initially so Mike couldn't see who was in the car. He knocked on the window of the driver side.

"Hey, do you need help?" he asked.

The windows rolled down and Mike was surprised when he saw who was behind the driver's wheel. After attempting to start her car multiple times, Isis grew weary and impatient but she was relieved when she saw it was the pastor at her window.

"Yes, I might need a jump start on my car. It was working fine earlier today, then it just quit on me while I was running to get a few groceries," Isis explained. "I hope it's not too much trouble," she added.

"Oh it's no trouble at all, sista. Give me one second and I'll pull up right next to you and give you a jump start," Mike said.

"Thank you so much, pastor," Isis said smiling serenely.

That has got to be one of the most beautiful smiles I've seen on any woman Mike thought dreamily before remembering what he had to do. Oh yeah that's right. I gotta get the jumper cables to jump-start her car he thought. He got into his car and drove directly next to Isis's car. Once he had his car parked, he turned his own engine off and popped the hood open. He opened Isis's car hood and connected the jumper cables to each engine. Getting back into his car, he started the ignition while Isis started hers. She gave a loud whoop when her car finally started. Mike ran to remove both jumper cables from the car. As he removed them, Isis once again found herself looking at Mike's strong biceps as they contracted when squeezing the cable handle to release them from the engine.

"Every time I need help, you are always there to save me. How can I ever repay you for this?" Isis asked.

Mike chuckled. "It's ok, really. I've been through that situation a couple times before, myself. You might want to get your alternator and battery checked out pretty soon or else it's going to keep happening," Mike advised.

"Yeah you're right. I really do need to look into it. Hey, do you have any free time later on? I wanted you to come over to see the new countertop," Isis said.

Although it was not protocol to return to the customer's home unless there were problems, Mike agreed to come to Isis's home to look at the counter. He got into his car and followed her over to her apartment building. All in the while, Mike's head was ringing out silent alarms, informing him that going to her house was not part of the night's plan and that he should turn back and go home as soon as possible. Unfortunately another part of him thought It's no big deal. I'm just accepting an invitation to go to a friend and fellow church member's house. Pastors make house visits every day.

When they finally arrived at her apartment building, Mike parked his car directly behind Isis's. There were no parking lots or driveways, so cars normally parallel parked next to the building. Isis opened her trunk and started to pick up the bags and Mike quite naturally, offered to help her. With both of their hands full of groceries, Mike waited until she unlocked the door and followed her up the stairs to the third floor of the building. Her building had an elevator, which would have made the trip much easier but for some reason Isis elected not to use it. Mike didn't question it nor did he bring it up in conversation.

"So I noticed that you didn't come to church today. Is everything ok?" Mike asked as he followed Isis up the stairs.

"Yeah, everything is fine. I actually visited Brooklyn Tabernacle today with a friend of mine and Jamal. She invited me a couple weeks ago and I just did her a favor and visited," she answered as they finally reached her floor. Setting the bags down, she reached into her purse and took out her apartment keys. After a few seconds, they were inside and Mike set the grocery bags down on the kitchen table.

"Do you need me to help you put these in the fridge or cabinet for you?" Mike offered.

"No that's ok I got it, but thank you so much," she replied as she led him over to the couch and asked him to sit down and make himself at home.

Mike thanked her and sat on the couch. He had been to this apartment before but because he was working, he hadn't taken the time to look around her living room. Framed pictures covered half the wall, some of them pictures of Isis and others were of her family. Mike saw one family portrait that had Jamal, Isis and another man, who he assumed was Jamal's father.

"So is Jamal home?" Mike asked, suddenly realizing how alone they were.

"He's at his best friend's house. He won't be back until tonight. He always goes to his friend's house after church on Sundays and they normally hang out and play video games. You know how young boys are," she said, laughing.

"Yeah, I can imagine," he replied. Then he remembered why he had come to her apartment. Getting up, he walked to the kitchen to inspect the work his employees had done in the kitchen. The acrylic marble counter top was shining in the kitchen light and it still had the new smooth feel to it. No cuts, no knife grooves or blades leaving marks on it. The counter looked fabulous.

"The boys really did a good job over here," Mike comp-limented as he examined the counter.

Isis looked at the counter too. "They did a masterful job, pastor. I can't thank you enough for the deal you made for me to get this done," she gushed.

"Oh, don't worry about it. It was the least I could do," Mike replied.

A split second passed before their eyes met and Mike once again saw the beautiful brown iris that reflected back at him and Isis saw the warmth, strength, and kindness that were reflected in the brown staring back at her. Snapping herself back to reality, she asked Mike once again to make himself comfortable on her sofa.

"Would you like something to eat? I can whip something up for you. Jamal normally eats at his friend's house anyway," she said.

Mike didn't want to put Isis through the trouble. "No, that's ok I don't want to impose," he said.

Isis felt her spirit drop and she couldn't understand why. Why in the world would she feel hurt that Mike refused to eat dinner? "Ok, but let me at least offer you something to drink," she offered.

Mike thought it over. He figured he could stay for a beverage. After all, he was starting to feel a little thirsty and he assumed Isis would offer him some water or juice or soda but what she brought to him was none of the above. She held a bottle of white wine with two long wine glasses. She couldn't possibly expect him to drink that, could she? Especially since he had a troubled past dealing with alcohol. Getting off of that proverbial wagon was the last action he wanted to take; he couldn't take that downward spiral again.

"Umm, thank you sista for your kind offer but I really can't drink that. Do you have any water?" he asked, gently refusing the wine.

Isis persisted. "Oh come on, pastor. It's just a little wine. It's not like I'm asking you to drink shots or a keg of beer. Simply one glass can't hurt you, right?" she coaxed.

No, one glass wouldn't hurt me now but all it takes is one glass for me and that's what I'm afraid of. All it takes is one he thought to himself but instead of saying a word, agreed to have a small amount of wine poured into his glass.

Instead, Isis poured the wine up to the tip of the glass, which was exactly what Mike didn't want. He didn't want to wear out his welcome so he accepted the glass and proceeded to take a sip. He hadn't tasted wine in nearly twenty years but the familiar taste of it made him feel like it was glass yesterday. It was far too familiar. Isis poured herself a glass and sat next to Mike. He started to get a bit nervous. Isis wore a lovely cotton blouse and a knee length skirt but when she sat down, the view changed. The skirt had slits on two sides, so when she sat and crossed her legs, her shapely thighs and legs were fully visible to him.

Wow she is making this real hard Mike thought and he tried to stay focused by looking at the photos on the wall. Conversation. I got to start a conversation. This silence is way too awkward. But it was Isis who started talking.

"I'm sorry to hear about Loree, pastor. How are her parents taking it?" she asked.

Mike shook his head as he once again recalled the meeting with Amos and his wife and second daughter that went horribly wrong. "Well, they're not taking it too well. They just lost their daughter in the worst possible way and there's nothing I can do to console them," he answered.

Isis put her hand on Mike's shoulder. There's nothing you could've done pastor. Don't put the blame on yourself. You didn't cause her untimely death," she said.

Mike wasn't so sure. If he had only listened when Shania had tried to confide in him about Loree's relationship with David, he might have been able to prevent the awful tragedy. He could stand at his pulpit and preach the message of grace and forgiveness all day long but to a grieving family who felt only vengeance, his words were meaningless. It was a message that would fall on deaf ears. Just like Nate, who was on his own vigilante mission to find Nina's murderer. What good was a message of kindness going to accomplish when people were so determined to see justice done?

"I don't know, Isis. I feel like it is my fault somehow. I'm not doing enough and maybe I'm not speaking up enough about the glaring shadow of violence in our community. God has always managed to keep us safe and out of harm's way and now this hits so close to home," he said.

Isis continued to pat his shoulder in an attempt of comforting him. "You couldn't have possibly seen it coming. A lot of families in this community still believe in you and your ministry and you still have an enormous amount of impact on the young men today. My son is a prime example," Isis pointed out.

Mike smiled a little bit. Did he really have an impact on Jamal the way Isis described him? "I'm happy to hear that but I don't know if Jamal would want to be where I'm at now. I have families doubting me, the grieving family doesn't want anything to do with me anymore, and it just seems that all of the enemy's forces are piling up on me. All I can do is pray and hope that some good can come out of all this bad," Mike said.

"Well, for what it's worth, I believe you are doing an exceptional job and despite what anyone thinks of you, just remember that God's opinion of you is the only thing that counts. Loree's death was such a tragedy and believe me, I miss her too and I know your pain," Isis reassured. "All I need is for you not to give up on Jamal, Omar, or any of the young men in this community," she added.

Looking at the predicament that David was in at the moment, Mike wasn't sure if he was of much help to anyone, let alone the young men in the community.

"I mean, look at Shania. You've raised her to be a very independent, well-behaved young woman. There are many girls now who are confused and lost in their way of life and they don't have the positive male guidance. Shania's development speaks volumes as to what type of father you are," Isis continued. "I definitely know I wasn't like that when I was her age," she added.

Mike smiled at her. "Really? How were you when you were eighteen?" he asked.

"Ooh honey, I was a hot mess. I gave my parents attitudes all the time. I wore these barely-there outfits and dated a lot of guys. It wasn't until after I met Jamal's father that I started to clean my act. Robert was more than my boyfriend who became my husband, he was my best friend, someone who I spoke with and who listened to me whenever I needed an ear," Isis replied.

"What happened to you and Robert? I mean, why aren't you still with him?" Mike asked.

Isis stared at the family portrait as though she longed to return back to the moment when she was unencumbered by stress, arguments, differences, and divorce. "We just didn't connect anymore. He was offered a higher position at his job in Florida and he was promised three times the amount of money that he made working at his old job. I wanted him to turn it down and stay, primarily because of Jamal," Isis explained, "but he argued with me, stating that it was the best opportunity of his life and he would come back and move us down with him. But it never happened," she added and Mike felt it was best not to mention any more questions about Robert. "So what about you?" Isis asked, her hand now having migrated from Mike's back and she began massaging his shoulders. "Word around this area was that you were a great football player once," she said admiringly.

Mike felt himself getting nervous again and although Isis's apartment building was well air-conditioned, he felt beads of perspiration start to form in the back of his neck. Isis's hands were so soft and her hands were working magic – no a miracle on his tense back and shoulders. Why didn't his wife offer the same relaxing massages?

"Yeah but that was in high school a very long time ago. I really haven't touched a football since then," he replied. "Where did you hear about my football exploits?" he asked.

Isis laughed. "You'd be surprised how many times the women at the salon talk about you. How athletic you were, how quick you were on the field, and then they would mention other things too," Isis said slyly.

Mike's interest was suddenly perked, in more ways than one. "What else they would say about me?" he asked.

Isis rolled her eyes upward, trying to think, resembling a shy school girl trying to keep a secret from the boy she admired. "They also said you had a nice toned ass," she said, laughing.

Mike laughed too, even though in the back of his mind, a very small voice was telling him that it was time to go home. Unfortunately, the louder voice in Mike's head was that of his self-esteem. He enjoyed talking to Isis; the way she laughed at his jokes and how she stroked his masculine ego. Then there was her striking beauty. Her hands were driving him crazy, as well as her eyes. He was never close enough to see her lips before but he saw them today. They were soft and full which made them more appealing.

Ok that's it. I got to go. I have to go back home to what's-her-name, he thought, his mind a scrambled mess as Isis continued to work on him. He couldn't even remember his wife's name.

God, what am I doing? I want to stop but I can't, she thought. She leaned closer to Mike, her thin blouse revealing her cleavage. "So are all the rumors about you true?" she asked. Subtlety had flown right out the window as Mike's eyes made their way back to her lips, only to prevent them from staring directly at her breasts.

"I....I don't know," he stammered.

Isis placed one of her legs on Mike's legs and Mike was desperately hoping she didn't notice the activity going on between his own legs. As he fell under her gaze, he could've sworn he heard her say, Let me find out...

"Bro, shut up or I'll deck you, fo' real," Jamal replied to Omar as they crossed the street to get back to Jamal's apartment.

They had been discussing why Jamal's father had no interest in coming back to visit him. Omar was under the delusion that Isis was interested in someone else and Jamal refused to believe that. His mother being interested in anyone else other than her father was completely absurd. It was true that his parents were divorced but Jamal's father had always promised he would try to work it out. Jamal's mother hadn't been dating because she was too busy at work, home, and going to church.

"I'm tellin you yo," Omar insisted. "Yo' mama got her eyes on somebody. You'll see. She probably gonna meet someone at work, fall in stupid love, then before you know it, you gonna be a big brother," Omar said.

Jamal sighed in exasperation. He wished Omar would shut the heck up because he didn't want to discuss it anymore. "I don't even know why you talkin' about my momma so much all of a sudden. You act like you tryin' to get at her or something," Jamal said.

"Well, she do got some qualities men like and I am a man so..." Omar laughed but trailed off while Jamal pretended to chase him and fake-punched him.

As they arrived at Jamal's apartment building, Omar asked, "Yo, whose car is that parked behind yo' momma's car?"

Jamal shrugged. "I don't know, man. This is a public street, you know. Anybody can park here. Doesn't mean nothin'," he said with exasperation as he opened the front apartment door and walked up the three flights of stairs to his apartment.

He unlocked the door and walked inside, followed by Omar, oblivious to what had been going on inside. He walked into the living room and the scene that unfolded before him was inexplicable. Jamal's mouth dropped open.

He saw his church pastor lying face down on the sofa on top of his mother. Pastor Mike was shirtless with his pants nearly pulled off and he was kissing his mother all over her face, neck, and chest. His mother's eyes were closed, no doubt relishing the bliss she felt from the powerful adrenaline that was driven by his testosterone. Her breasts were fully exposed, with her bra lying on the floor and her legs were spread, with two of her hands clutching the pastor's bare bottom as she began sliding off his underwear.

Omar entered the living room only a few seconds later. "Yo, Jamal what's good man, what's…?" Omar started to ask before his words came to a screeching halt upon viewing Jamal's mother and the pastor.

The moment Mike heard Omar's voice, he looked up and saw Jamal's face which appeared to be frozen in time; clearly stunned by what he was seeing. Mike already saw Jamal's expression before had a chance to react. He saw the look of betrayal, disgust, and embarrassment all rolled into one. Here was the pastor, beloved by many, including Jamal himself, caught in a compromising position with his mother.

Isis, realizing that Mike had stopped kissing her, sat up and saw her son's distraught face. Neither of them had heard the door open, nor were they aware that Jamal had been watching them in bewilderment. Isis barely whispered Jamal's name before he whirled around and left the apartment, flinging the door aside in anger, fully intending on slamming it. Omar caught the door just in time, as he attempted to call Jamal's name, as he bulleted down the stairs.

"Jamal, Jamal!" Isis shouted as she covered herself with the blouse she had worn up. She quickly pulled her skirt back on and without even bothering to put on her bra, she ran after her son.

Mike quickly put his tank top and shirt on and buttoned his pants. He knew Isis was not the only church member who lived in the area, so he quickly fixed his shirt and collar, grabbed his keys from the coffee table, and left the apartment. Isis and Omar were still at the end of the block, calling to Jamal who had walked to the next block, unwilling to hear what his mother or Omar had to say.

So this was how his mother chose to treat his father. Just dump him and move on to the next guy, and not just any guy, the pastor, Jamal thought. Why did it have to be the pastor? How could she do that to him and break his family apart? As he tried to understand it, Mike attempted to drive away unnoticed, unaware that he was being watched.

CHAPTER TWENTY-TWO

Mike pulled into his small side driveway at eight o'clock in the evening. He shifted the car into park and buried his face in his hands. He could still smell her perfume and feel her delicate skin on his own, his lips on her lips and his body on top of her body. He had made a devastating mistake. What he felt and what he had just experienced should have been reserved for his wife, who sat at home alone with his daughter, no doubt wondering where he could be.

"Mike, what the hell did you just do?" he asked himself as he sat alone in the car, trying to digest what had happened.

All these years, he believed he had a burning love for Robyn that he would never have for anybody else. Her humility, her support for him in his ministry, and her community efforts were just a few of the attributes that always attracted him to her. She was also very beautiful and a great mother to Shania. What made him do what he did with Isis and probably would have continued doing; had Jamal not shown up when he did? How could he possibly be expected to lead his church and talk about fighting those urges when he himself had not been successful fighting them? He only wondered how Robyn was going to react. Should he just break down and confess his infidelity to Robyn. How could he be sure Robyn would forgive him? He looked at the thin wedding ring on his left finger as thoughts bombarded his mind.

I promised you for better or for worse, Robyn and this ring were signs of the promises I made to you and I broke them tonight. I know I messed up but is there a way we can try to talk about it and move on?

Mike knew it would break her heart for sure. Just knowing he had been out there giving the love that was reserved for her, to another woman. A huge part of Mike wanted to blame Isis for her strong sexual advances, all the while knowing he was married, he was in a committed relationship with another woman, and had a daughter with her. Isis herself should be ashamed, being the mother of a teenage boy who thought the world of her. Now what was Omar going to think of his mother? What kind of light would she portray to him after this? Then there was the issue of how Jamal would see his pastor after what he had seen. Isis had told Mike several times that Jamal looked up to him as a male role model and a spiritual leader. He could only imagine how that image had changed in Jamal's eyes; snake, imposter, liar, cheat, manipulator, player... all those words came to mind to describe himself so he could only imagine the strong words that were running through Jamal's young mind.

Taking a deep breath, Mike stepped out of his car and locked the door. Mike reflected on how much of an emotional rollercoaster his day had been. It had started with being chewed out by his friend and regular church patron for defending a boy who had been judged guilty without a trial. Then he had found a successful lawyer to defend that same boy. His day had culminated in helping a woman he barely knew, only to have her seduce him. It resembled Joseph in the Old Testament of the Bible, when he had been tempted by the wife of the chief steward of Egypt under whom he served. Apparently, the temptation was very strong and was in favor of Joseph, a beautiful woman who had money and power. Yet Joseph had stayed true to God and even though it got him imprisoned, he was strong enough to withstand the temptation. Why couldn't Mike do the same when Isis deployed the same tactics and why couldn't he escape her gaze? That look she gave him whenever he looked at her. It was at this moment of anguish and soul searching that a terrible thought crossed his mind. Could it be that he was not as righteous or as innocent in the Lord's eyes as he thought? Could he have mistaken the call he received from God so many years ago to pastor and lead his people?

He opened the door and stepped in the house. As he walked up the stairs, the hallway was dark, so he knew his wife and daughter were both in their bedrooms. He stepped into his bedroom where Robyn was lying down, reading the Bible. Just looking at Robyn made the stab of guilt worsen for Mike.

"Hey honey, where have you been?" she asked. Mike thought about how he was going to respond to that question. "It seems like you've been gone for the whole night. What did my brother say?" she asked, while a flood a relief washed over Mike, realizing he might not have to confess just yet. She was only wondering about the case.

"He said he'll represent David. So I thanked him and he'll give me a price eventually. I'm not sure of it yet," Mike replied.

"That's good," Robyn said as Mike changed out of his clothes and put on his robe. As he got into bed, Robyn noticed that Mike didn't make his normal nightly advances, nor did he attempt to start any conversation. "Is everything ok?" she asked.

No, everything is not ok. I just came back from a woman's house where I had no business being at, and I was caught with her by her own son he thought. He just couldn't bring himself to confess to her just yet. "Yeah, I'm fine," he lied. "Just got a lot on my mind today, that's all," was all Mike could say.

"About the McAfee family?" Robyn asked.

Yeah sure we'll go with that he thought. "Yeah, I guess I never thought how upset Amos would be when I spoke with him today. I'm just thinking, when all is said and done, will it all be worth it?" he asked.

Robyn put her arm around Mike, causing Mike to wince a little bit, out of nervousness. Robyn didn't seem to notice. "I know it will be worth it. Making sure David doesn't go to jail and proving him innocent is the most gallant thing you've ever done," Robyn said as Mike knelt down and prayed as he did every night. His heart was still heavy about not telling Robyn the entire truth about his visit at Isis's house.

Early Monday morning, Jamal walked out of his apartment building to wait at his mother's car. Normally they would walk downstairs together, while talking animatedly about how school was going and how she was going to try to work through the issues with his father. After what Jamal had witnessed, he couldn't care less about talking to his mother. She had managed to catch up to him Sunday night, nearly three blocks away and frantically apologized. She swore she didn't know what had come over her and that she made a grave mistake.

No shit Sherlock Jamal thought cruelly as his mother gently coaxed him to come back into the apartment. Jamal had ended up walking back to the apartment but he did not speak to his mother for the rest of the night. Isis went to her room and cried herself to sleep.

On the afternoon Mike had come over, she had just gotten over a heated argument with Robert, which had left her feeling inadequate and unwanted. After she had visited her friend's church, all she wanted to do was to lie down and sleep the day away, since she normally didn't work on Sundays. Later in afternoon she had remembered she had to buy groceries for the week. She grudgingly went to the store and when she got back into her car full of groceries her car wouldn't start. That had lead to the chance encounter with Mike. She knew full well that he was a married man and he not only had a family to lead but a church to lead. He was an influential person and many people regarded him as a powerful spiritual leader but he was also human. A part of Isis forgot that he was struggling as well. She was so angry at Robert and wanted some type of comfort – any type of consolation – that night. Just having Mike at her house; his humor, his attentiveness, and his kindness had been exactly what she needed. His great physical shape had added to her confusion, as she fell in love all over again without thinking. In retrospect, she knew it was wrong to act on those needs and the worst part of what she had allowed to happen was putting her relationship with Jamal in jeopardy.

When Isis made it outside to the car, she saw Jamal with his basketball waiting for her. Without a word, she opened the car and unlocked it so Jamal could get inside. As they drove to Richmond Hill High School, she broke the awkward uncomfortable silence between them in a feeble attempt to start a conversation.

"Looks like it's gonna be a sunny day today. Better than yesterday, at least," she said.

Jamal continued to look out the window without responding to his mother. In essence, what did he have to say to her? He thought about the excuses she had given him. She had said that 'it just happened' and 'she didn't know what came over her'. Unbelievable, he thought. If she liked Pastor Mike so much, why had she given him false hope that it could ever work out with his father? As they pulled up to the school, Isis placed her hand on her son's head and started caressing it, lovingly.

"Please talk to me, Jamal. I'm so sorry that I hurt you yesterday," she apologized.

Jamal stepped out of the car without another word. Before closing the door, he said, "You're only sorry that I caught you." Turning his back on his mother's car he walked toward the gym entrance.

Isis wiped a tear away from her face before driving to work. Jamal walked toward the gym and as he opened the doors, his anger began to abate. Maybe he had been a bit too cruel towards her but what else could he do after she and one of his heroes had both betrayed him? Jamal decided that he wasn't going to dwell on it. Basketball tryouts were fast approaching and he needed to get to work.

The gym was open, but empty. Surprisingly, Nate wasn't there yet. Jamal turned on the gym lights and began shooting. The last time he had felt this emotional, he couldn't hit the broad side of a barn. With the image of Mike and his mother lying half-naked on top of each other fresh on his mind, he was hitting his shots. The more he thought about the pain, the more intense he was and the more he concentrated. Hitting two jump shots in a row, then three, then four, the flood gates opened as he used all the fundamentals that Nate had taught him. Amazed by his improvement, Jamal stopped practicing for a moment and ran to the custodial room. He found Nate sitting at his desk. He seemed to be writing or at least he looked busy. Jamal knocked on the door. Nate looked up.

"Hey man what's up? My shot's falling today, come check this out!" he exclaimed.

Nate smiled as his pupil explained how he was showing improvement in his game. After Jamal finished speaking, Nate stood up. "Sorry for not being there when you first got here. I was busy with something. But it looks like I got some time left before school starts. Have you worked on your defensive slides yet?" Nate asked. Jamal looked at him blankly. Nate shook his head. "Basketball's more than just scoring, boy. You gotta be able to stop folks. Here I'll show you. Come on," he said, running out to the gym.

Nate couldn't explain it, but there was an inexplicable rush that he felt when he was teaching Jamal the finer points of the game. He felt like he was passing knowledge down to a younger generation that played the game differently than he had; felt the game differently than he had. Jamal also had a willingness to learn. Many young people did not have the same enthusiasm and passion that Jamal showed whenever it came to learning something new in basketball.

As Nate walked out to teach Jamal defensive slides, the paper Nate was working on, remained at his desk. It wasn't a letter or any important document. Nate had drawn a diagram of his ploy to draw a certain Mr. Antoine Sparks to the park that upcoming Saturday with the car he believed Nate would purchase. Nate didn't want him to think for a second that just because he had changed his name, he could get away with murder. Nate drew a line around the gazebo and toward the back of the park where he was sure there would be no one present but him and Earl. This time he would make damn sure Earl didn't get away.

Walking out of his sociology class, Trevor headed back to his dorm. He was grateful that it was his last class of the day and he had nothing else on his mind but to get back into his room and relax while playing basketball video games. He found out very early in his life that video games acted as a release for him from the real world. There had been times when he wished he was anywhere else but in reality. Life was so much simpler when he was in a fantasy world in which he wasn't adopted. A world in which his mother was still alive and his father stayed with them instead of fleeing like a coward. A world in which his biological parents came to all his games, mend his injuries, and be comfortable with who he was outside the court. As he made his way back to his room, his phone rang. Sighing, he picked up after the third ring, not even bothering to look at the caller ID on his phone. Somehow, he knew it was Shania. The previous night, after he had gone to church for the first time in a decade, Shania had called him demanding to know why she hadn't seen him. Trevor was at a loss for words initially because when he went, Pastor Mike was preaching so intensely and very convincingly, that he felt like a fish out of water. He was totally out of his comfort zone. So he had made a quick exit from the church, although he had regretted it later because he didn't want to hurt Shania or cause her to lose trust in him. Since Saturday night, he hadn't been able to get her out of his mind. It wasn't easy for him to admit that he was falling for her, because the first rule on his guy code was never fall in deep with these girls. He had always been the type of man who tried new rides and if he wasn't feeling it, he moved on to the next one but the more time he spent with Shania, the more he started to believe that she might be the one. He might actually settle on this one...if he could find common ground with her father.

"Hey what's up?" he answered.

"What's up, baby?" Shania replied with her best soft, seductive voice.

"I'm actually getting out of my final class right now," he replied. I'm bout to go chill at my spot right now. You probably still in school right?" he asked, snickering.

"Yeah, I'm at lunch right now," Shania confirmed and sure enough, Trevor heard the buzzing of a hundred school kids in the background. He laughed, sensing Shania's pain.

"That's the part of high school that I don't miss. Actually, come to think of it, there are a lot of things about high school that I don't miss," he said.

"Ugh, can't wait till I graduate and move on. I'm so over this," Shania said with exasperation.

"How's Andrea doing? Did you speak to her?" Trevor asked.

"Yeah I spoke to her before school. She's holding up ok," Shania replied. "She asked about you, by the way," she added slyly. This made Trevor smile even more. He was such a great influence on children.

"Really, what did she say?" he asked.

"Well she wanted to know if you were down for a movie on Saturday with her and another dope chick by the name of Shania," Shania replied.

Trevor laughed. "Tell her she's on. I'll see ya Saturday night," he replied, before saying goodbye to Shania and hanging up.

He arrived at his dorm building and walked inside, taking the stairs to the second floor to his room. He tried to turn the key but surprisingly his door was already open. Damn, Al must've left the room open again. I don't know why he be forgetting to lock up. Anybody could just walk up in here, he thought just before he entered the room, where his fear was confirmed.

A tall, middle-aged, balding, black man sat on his bed waiting for him. As Trevor looked closer, he saw that it was Gary McKey.

"What you doing here, man? How'd you even find out where I was?" Trevor asked, without even bothering to greet him. He hoped that Gary hadn't come all the way back to New York with the hope of a father to son reconciliation, like those sappy Hollywood movies. It wasn't going to happen.

"Well I got the information from Tiffany and she said I would find you here. One of your boys opened the room and said you'd be rolling in around about this time," Gary replied.

Trevor shook his head. It would be his adoptive mother to sud-denly have a change of heart towards Gary and he had probably sweet-talked her into giving him another chance to make a connection.

"How'd you even get here?" he asked.

Gary chuckled. "Don't sleep on them Greyhound buses, man. Gave me a lift straight to the city, then I took a cab up to campus," he answered.

Trevor was a bit surprised that his father would go to such lengths to come see him but he wasn't impressed.

"Well, good luck finding your way back. Hope you ain't expecting me to drive you back to the 'burbs," he replied harshly walking over to the door, hoping that his father got the hint that he wanted him out. But Gary didn't move.

"Trevor I know you're mad at me. You have every right to be and I don't blame you. What I did back then in leaving you and your mother was stupid and for that, I'm sorry. But I need your help," Gary said, with a sense of urgency in his voice.

"What could you possibly need my help for and why would I break my neck to help you out? Did you help me out when I needed you?" Trevor asked. After Gary failed to give an answer, he said "I thought so. You could let yourself out, man," he said gesturing to the door.

Gary didn't leave but he stood up from where he previously sat. Taking out his phone, Gary said, "Ok, I'll go, but first I need you to listen to something," and he walked over to Trevor.

Trevor still didn't have a speck of trust in Gary as a father and when he encroached upon his personal space, it was more than uncomfortable. Gary held the phone to his son's ear.

"Just listen to this message," he insisted, accessing his saved voicemails and playing one of the messages back. The voice was deep and barely audible due to the connectivity but it was intelligible.

"Yo G, this is Nate. Just called to let you know that the busta' who did Nina in eighteen years ago is still alive and that nigga working in a car shop now, under some new name. Look, I got a plan so we can get the drop on him. Meet me this Saturday at Rufus King Park at ten o'clock at night. I know you probably gon' tell me to call the police and all that, but I ain't letting him get away again. If you down, meet me at da spot. If not, stay out of my way and you betta' not call the cops," the voice threatened before the message ended.

Trevor stood still, shell-shocked at what he just heard. So his father was right about Nate and his friendship with him. He was also right about

Nate being there when his mother had died because why else would he want revenge against the murderer? However, Trevor didn't see the need for his involvement.

"Why you comin' to me for help in all this? What you think imma do?" Trevor asked.

"Trevor, Nate is my boy and all but he is very dangerous. All that he's been talkin' to me about for all these months since we reconnected was how he was going to find a way to make Nina's murderer pay for what he did. I didn't even think he was alive until I got the message a few days ago," Gary admitted. "Trevor, I need your help to try to reason with him. You're the last part of Nina still left and maybe if you spoke to him, he might let this thing go," he said.

Trevor shook his head. Gary was making this seem so easy when he knew full well that it wasn't. "Why me, man? Couldn't you call the cops on him? He's obviously outta his damn mind. As much as I want a piece of that garbage, I ain't tryin' to get mixed up in this," Trevor replied angrily.

Gary turned to the window, almost reflectively. "I can't dime my boy out like that, Trevor. He's still my friend, but he's in a real dark place right now. I'm gon' try to talk to him again but I can't do it without you. Maybe if he sees that you've moved on, maybe he'll move on and let this thing go," Gary reasoned.

Trevor stepped up to his father's face. "It ain't neva' occurred to you, that I got a lot more to lose than you do? Now you want me to risk it all to save your friend? Why didn't you do that when you had a chance to save my mother?" he asked.

"I'm doing something now," Gary answered. He started to make his way toward the door. "You can't forget that she loved you and she sacrificed her life to keep you alive. If you need me, I'll be at the motel at the corner of Sutphin and Parsons Boulevard," he added walking out of the door. Trevor sat on his bed, watching him leave. This wasn't his fight...or was it?

Arthur Blaylock checked his watch early Thursday morning outside the Queens Police Precinct. Mike was scheduled to meet him outside the building over thirty minutes ago. He never understood why his brother-in-law was never organized about time. He wasn't sure how life worked in the church or the marble industry but he was positive that both places had some type of time discipline. Earlier in the week, he had made arrangements with Mike to meet at the precinct where David Anderson was being held, awaiting his trial. The purpose of the meeting was to be introduced to David and hopefully gain his trust as a lawyer who would defend him against the charges of the state and Loree's family.

Finally he saw Mike's car appear around the corner as he slowed down and prepared to parallel-park behind his own car. Mike had left his job early, leaving the managerial duties to some of the supervisors in the office. When he stepped out of his car he went to meet Arthur at the front steps of the precinct.

"You know how long I've been waiting out here, man?" Arthur asked as he and Mike walked up the steps to enter the precinct.

"Forgive me man. It's been real busy at work this week and even more busy outside of work," Mike answered, shaking his head. It didn't make for a great excuse but Arthur decided to let him slide for it.

"How's Robby and Pint-size?" Arthur asked, referring to his sister and Shania.

Mike needed a second to answer Arthur's question because the scene in Isis's apartment rushed into his head uninvited. Mike still had yet to tell Robyn and the more time passed, the guiltier he felt about it. Robyn didn't seem to notice that Mike was distracted and bothered since she was busy with her own work but Mike had certainly noticed more icy indifference in Robyn than ever before. It made Mike wonder if she already knew about his indiscretion or if she was just working so hard that she couldn't muster the strength to show any emotion. Whichever the case, it made Mike uncomfortable and he knew that before he took to the pulpit on Sunday, he would have to confess to Robyn and hope she would forgive him.

"They're ok and Shania's not pint-sized anymore. She got taller and more athletic. You should go to more of her track meets, man," Mike added.

Arthur laughed. "I know but you know how it be for me, man. Always working never got much time for nothing. But from what I hear, seems like you ain't had much time neither," he replied slyly.

Mike was leery about responding. He was afraid Arthur would figure out that Mike hadn't been spending time with Robyn. His life was already tense enough; Mike didn't need to add Arthur into the equation. He was only too thankful that Robyn had allowed him to speak with Arthur to help David and his grandmother. They walked inside the precinct, checked in, and waited for the officers to escort David to the proper holding room where they could speak. The officers took Arthur and Mike into a small meeting room, which had an officer standing guard, since the room had an alternate exit and police had to be present to prevent convicts from escaping.

After waiting for a few moments, David walked into the room accompanied by two officers. He sat at the table across from Arthur and Mike. If Mike had believed in David's innocence, all those beliefs flew out the window the moment he saw David. Arthur's got his work cut out for him, Mike thought. David's face showed beard stubble from days that he had not shaved and he wore an intense scowl on his face, as if he didn't trust the men in the room and he was ready for a deadly confrontation. The two officers left David in the room with Arthur and the pastor while the one officer continued to stand guard.

"What's this all about, man?" David asked suspiciously.

"How are you doing, David? I'm Michael Hillman and this is my brother-in-law and attorney Arthur Blaylock," Mike greeted.

David still looked at both of them with his suspicions growing before realization set in.

"I think I seen you before; you Shania's father, right? The pastor of that church right up the street?" David asked.

"That's right," Mike confirmed. "I'm sure you've seen my daughter many times at school," he added. David sat back in his chair, obviously a little more relaxed but still leery of his visitors. "Yeah I seen her at school sometimes. Why are you even here? Ain't you with Loree's fam?" David asked.

It was clear David knew Shania and Loree were best friends and he assumed that Mike was intimidating him to get some type of confession.

"Actually David, we are here today because of your nice grandmother," Mike continued. Upon hearing the mention of his grandmother, David buried his face in his hands.

"Damn. My grandmother? I promised her I wouldn't get into any more shit and now I'm in deeper than before," David said.

"She visited my house and confirmed your innocence, so now we're here to help you," Mike said.

David shook his head. "Why would you wanna help me? Why would anybody wanna help me? You heard what her family said about me. I'm as good as finished and it sucks, cuz I'm all my grandmother's got right now," David said.

Mike sat up straight in his chair. "Young man, I want you to look at me now," he said firmly. David obeyed, looking directly at the pastor. "I'm helping you because it's the right thing to do. Your grandmother believes in you, Arthur believes in you, and I believe in you. But there is someone else who believes in you," Mike said.

David still kept his steely gaze on Mike. "Yeah, who?" he asked.

"Jesus Christ," Mike replied. "Son, even if the whole world and your so called homeboys and brothers have written you off, Jesus has not forgotten you. You may not believe in Him, but He believes in you. He believes in the positive change you can make in this community. If you trust Him and if you trust your ability to change and turn over a new leaf, He will make it happen. And it starts with this trial," he added.

David looked up toward the ceiling and Mike thought he had failed to reach him but on closer examination he realized that David had tilted his head upward to keep the tears from falling.

"My grandmother's always telling me about how Jesus loves me and how He's always looking over me, even in my foolish ways. My own parents ain't even want nothing to do with me and it was my grandmother that took me in. Nobody asked her to accept my sorry ass into her life and throughout all the stealin', all the lootin' and gangbangin', she still kept me in her home," David said, unable to control the sobs escaping him.

Mike walked over to the other side of the table and patted David's broad shoulders. "Well, it's because of your praying grandmother that I'm here today with Arthur and we are going to prove your innocence and clear your name. If we succeed, you have to promise your grandmother that you'll stay out of trouble and stop hanging around with guys that'll do nothing but cause you to waste your life. We got a deal?" he asked.

Wiping his tears on his shirt sleeve, David agreed to accept their help, shaking Mike's hand and Arthur's hand. Arthur went on to talk about the plan of action they were going to execute to discredit the charges of the state and the McAfee family.

"David, what you need to understand here is that the prosecution is going to pull out all stops to convict you because of your background. What you need to do is to give them the best presentation in the courtroom. Be mindful of the judge and remember that you are under oath. If, in the likely event you are given a sentence, we can opt to settle for a plea bargain to lessen that sentence. You're looking down at least forty years to life if charged for a first-degree murder," Arthur said.

David nodded his head, confirming that he understood the process and once again showed his gratitude to Mike and Arthur for helping him. Mike left the precinct feeling optimistic about the trial that was scheduled for the following Monday. He had a positive feeling that David would be let off and would not have to serve any jail time, even though the odds were against him. Now, if only he could find the words to apologize to his wife...

CHAPTER
TWENTY-THREE

On Friday afternoon after lunch period, the warning bell rang as students made their way to their classes or their lockers. Some of the students hung out in the halls as usual; talking and joking with their friends. The only person who wasn't in a joking mood at the moment was Jamal. Although the first day back at school went by without any drama, he couldn't verbalize his disinterest and poor morale. School began dragging for him and every hour felt like another day had passed. Jamal never really liked school to begin with, but he hated it more than ever on this particular week. Ms. Peterson had surprised the class with a pop quiz for which Jamal was not prepared. It affected his grade point average since he managed to score only sixty-eight percent on the quiz; the lowest score he had received since enrolling at Richmond Hill High. His mind had wandered, and he found himself distracted most of the time. The unforgettable image of his mother and the pastor having sex on the couch was etched so strongly, he couldn't get rid of it. He was able to drown out the thoughts when he practiced shooting and passing and defensive drills with Nate in the mornings because when he was sweating, his heart was racing, and his adrenaline was pumping, he used the anger brought on by the images as fuel. However, sitting in class for the following seven hours of the day proved detrimental to his psyche.

Another problem for Jamal was his relationship with Patricia. With the drama of Loree's death and David's arrest surrounding them the previous week, the feelings between Jamal and Patricia began to fizzle. Jamal noticed that Patricia's eyes would wander and there were more times when he noticed her talking to other boys. At first he would feel jealous but soon that envy was replaced by indifference. Patricia was a person who acted a certain way and Jamal acted a certain way. He understood that he needed to come to terms with it because he had bigger issues to worry about. That brought Miles Jackson in the picture.

A freshman boy who had a mouth Jamal would love to shut at times; Miles would give Jamal almost five hours of misery every week. Two of those hours were in school, where Miles would make fun of Jamal; from his clothes, to his shoes, to the way he talked. Jamal naturally learned to ignore him, and Omar had always taken Jamal's side when Miles was abusive. The other two painful hours were when Jamal would be at his own bedroom, doing homework or watching TV, relaxing. Unfortunately, Miles lived at the apartment building across from Jamal, and their room windows were on opposite ends. So whenever Jamal left his window open, Miles would start on a new batch of insults. Jamal had always ignored him and shown self- control through Miles' taunts. Miles was slightly taller than Jamal, so he would make fun of his height. Miles had straight short black hair, clean with waves rippling down the back and sides, so he would make fun of Jamal's hair whenever it grew out. Again, Jamal ignored it. It wasn't until Miles began pursuing Patricia and she began showing interest in him instead of Jamal. The lack of attention was a little hard to ignore. There were days when Jamal would catch Miles and Patricia whispering to each other between classes, a smug grin plastered on Miles' face while he eyed Jamal. To make matters worse, Miles' mother was one of Isis's clients. It was his mother who had referred Isis to the Rock of Jacob Baptist Church. So that last painful hour Jamal had to listen to Miles' smart mouth was after church service on Sundays. Jamal clearly wasn't fond of Miles and on Friday afternoon, it all came to a head. Miles noticed Jamal walking toward his locker, while talking to friends.

"You know, I don't know if there's any room on the squad for short niggas," Miles said loudly, as if he was talking to his friends but he knew

Jamal could hear him."Puny, no shot, clumsy, and nappy-headed. That's the reason why his girl with me now," Miles said, laughing.

Jamal looked at Miles, his eyes locked in. He wasn't in the mood. "Shut up, man," he replied.

Miles wouldn't stop. "Look at him. He don't even look like he in high school. Yo, you sure you in the right place man? I. S. 89 is down da street, playa," he said, while the kids with him laughed.

Maybe if I ignore him, he'll get off my case, Jamal thought but it was pretty obvious that Miles wanted to get a reaction from Jamal. Jamal refused to give him that satisfaction. He continued to grab the books he needed for his next class and closed his locker but Miles didn't stop.

"You know? Why would I want Jamal's girl when I can have his mama?" he asked.

Jamal turned around. "What did you say?" he asked. They can talk about me all they want but I swear to God if they bring my mom into this….Jamal looked right at Miles. Sure he was taller, but he was also lanky. Jamal walked right up to Miles, standing with him chest to chest.

"Don't ever say nothing about my mama again, you got that?" Jamal warned Miles just as Omar walked down the stairs to join Jamal.

"Or what? You gonna sic your boyfriend on me?" Miles laughed.

Omar stood next to Jamal. "Yo Miles, chill out man. Jamal ain't in the mood," he said on behalf of his friend. "Come on," he gestured to Jamal, who picked up his bag and started to walk away.

"But his mama was sho' in the mood Sunday night though, ain't that right Jamal?" Jamal stopped in his tracks. Miles, noticing the instantaneous effect, continued his derision.

"I guess I gotta be a pastor to find out how she tastes though, right?" he added, roaring in laughter, not anticipating what happened next.

At the same moment Miles made the reference to Sunday night's events, Jamal rushed straight at him; his force and inertia knocking him to the ground. Within seconds, Jamal was on top of him, landing punches to Miles' groin and midsection. Students started to gather around, trying to get a glimpse of the action. Omar found himself sifting through a myriad of students to reach his friend, who was currently rolling around on the floor with Miles, fists flying. Miles fists grazed the side of Jamal's face but Jamal kept pounding away, as Miles found himself unable to guard his own body and retaliate at the same time. The teachers, who noticed the throng of students forming the small circle in the hallway, fought their way through the crowd and lifted the two boys off of each other. Miles's arm and lip were cut and he had a small bump already appearing just above his left eye. The left side of Jamal's cheek was red.

"I told you not to talk about my mama, man!" Jamal exclaimed angrily as both boys were led to the administrative office.

As Jamal and Miles were led down the hall, Shania and Lisa were heading to class and they saw the students dispersing from the area. It was obvious that a fight had just occurred. Craning her neck to get a closer look at the scene, Shania saw the administrator walking two boys to the office with their clothes disheveled and was surprised when she saw that Jamal was one of the boys.

"Oh my God, that's Jamal. But what happened? He's never been in a fight before," Shania said to Lisa before approaching Jamal from the side. "Jamal, what happened?" she tried to ask him.

Jamal looked at her with the same angry expression that he gave to Miles just moments before. "Why don't you ask yo' dad and leave me alone?" he replied harshly.

The administrator turned to Shania. "Young lady, I'm going to have to ask you to refrain from speaking to either one of these boys right now. Please go to class. Thank you," he said.

Shania had no choice but to watch her young friend and former Sunday school student go the office for disciplinary action and she had no idea what Jamal had meant when he told her to ask her father. What did her father have to do with Jamal fighting in the hallway? She walked back to join Lisa as they walked to class.

"What happened? What did he say?" Lisa asked.

"I don't know. He just told me to ask my dad and to leave him alone. He looked like he was angrier at me than he was with that other boy," Shania answered.

Lisa gave Shania the same quizzical look that was already present on Shania's face. Shania didn't want to take Jamal's statement too seriously because of course, he was a freshman but she still wondered how her father was involved.

Isis was at work and while she was doing a sew-in for a client, her cell phone rang on her table. Apologizing to her customer for the inconvenience, Isis picked up the call.

"Hello?" she answered.

"Hello is this Isis Samuels?" the voice on the other end asked.

"Yeah, speaking," Isis replied.

The administrator proceeded to inform Isis that her son had been involved in a fight at school and her presence was required immediately. Isis, numb with shock, put her phone down and asked one of the other stylists to complete the sew-in. Her manager excused her and Isis drove as fast as she could to get to Richmond Hill. Once she arrived there, she was directed to the administrator office. It was there that she saw her son holding an ice pack on his swollen cheek and Miles, bleeding from his bottom lip as he held a piece of paper to it. Miles' mother, Mrs. Jackson, was already in the office and by the disapproving look she gave Isis, there was no doubt that she believed Jamal started the fight. The administrator told Isis to take a seat.

"Now, Miles please start from the top. What happened?" the administrator asked.

Miles began explaining to the administrator that he was just joking around with Jamal and although the jokes were crude, he said that Jamal completely lost his temper and went after him first. After he finished his story, Mrs. Jackson pointed a finger accusingly at Jamal while speaking to the administrator.

"Sir, it is very obvious that by my son's story, this young man needs a course in anger management and very strong supervision," she said.

Isis couldn't believe what she heard. She felt hurt and betrayed. Mrs. Jackson had been not only a faithful client to Isis over the years but she had also become her friend. Now here she was, accusing Jamal of being unstable.

"Hold up. Where do you get off telling me my son has anger issues? Jamal's never been in a fight one day in his life until today, so if something went down, it's pretty obvious that your son said or did something to piss him off," Isis countered.

"My son?" Mrs. Jackson asked as if her own son was a saint. "You out of all people should know how Miles loves to joke around. If your son is too sensitive to understand or make light of the situation, he needs to learn to walk away," she countered.

This lady needs to walk up out of my face before she gets an ass whooping Isis thought.

The two women were so angry that the administrator had to step between them to avoid another potential fist fight. Immediately he handed out the citations for their punishments. Miles was suspended for three days while Jamal was suspended for four days. Despite Isis's protests, the administrator stated that the punishment was final. Infuriated, she took Jamal out of school for the day and as they walked out the door, Nate was in the hallways, mopping the floors and saw Jamal walking out with his mother. Jamal looked at Nate with an apologetic face. Nate nodded his head as if he understood what Jamal tried to convey.

The car ride back home wasn't much better. As soon as they left the school premises, Isis started on her son.

"Boy, what has gotten into you? Why would you do something so stupid to get yourself in trouble like this?" she asked.

"He knew what happened, ok? Is that what you wanted to hear?" Jamal raged.

"What?" Isis asked.

"He saw you and the pastor Sunday night. He said something about it and I went off. I don't know," Jamal replied and in truth he really couldn't explain his actions, not even when he was in the administrator office. In the scheme of it all, he could've asked his mother the same question. What would have led her to do something so stupid on Sunday night? For a moment, Jamal thought of asking her that very question but thought better of it. He decided to let it go and let reality sink in. He was suspended from school for four days. He had never been suspended before in his life. Immediately a spirit of overwhelming regret came over him. If only he had displayed more self-control in the hallway, maybe this incident could have been avoided. His mother turned to him, her tone softer than earlier.

"Honey, I'm so sorry for what I did. I shouldn't have put myself in that situation. Then maybe you wouldn't have gotten suspended. I can't say I blame you for your reaction. Believe me honey, I still care about your father and I still want things to work out, ok?" she asked.

Jamal nodded his head, indicating he understood but he wanted to be alone in his own thoughts.

Shania arrived at home two hours before her father. Exhausted, Mike returned from work and sat down on the couch to gather his thoughts. Shania was in her room doing homework when her father came home from work but when she heard him she decided to tell him about what happened at school.

"Dad, do you remember Jamal Samuels?" she asked him. Mike jumped slightly at the mention of his name. He wasn't sure if Shania noticed it or not but there was a certain suspicion in Shania's voice that made him uncomfortable.

"Yeah, I remember him, what happened?" he asked.

Shania came around the couch to face her father. "I don't know Dad. He got into a fight today at school with another kid and when they took him to the office, I asked him what happened and all he said was to ask you. So you tell me," she answered, her eyebrows raised.

Mike sighed deeply. It was pretty obvious that Shania was suspicious and if he didn't tell her now, she was smart enough that she would eventually figure it out.

"Ok honey, I'll tell you why he might have said what he did. You may want to sit down for this," he said to his daughter.

Shania obeyed her father and sat down. Mike began to explain what took place on Sunday after church, from Isis's car trouble earlier that day, to the visit in her home, and the ensuing solitary moment of passion that had taken place. Shania didn't react immediately but there was an unmistakable mixture of betrayal, anger, and sadness on her face.

"Honey, I know I've betrayed your trust and your mother's trust. I made a huge mistake and I'm so sorry," he said.

Shania did not want to hear any more from her father, at least not today. "Whatever, Dad," she said, brushing away a tear. "Once a playa, always a playa. Gary was right about you," she said.

"Please hear me out for a second," he pleaded but Shania was already getting on her feet and was headed back to her room.

Looking back at her father, she said "That boy's probably scarred for life now. He looked up to you and you turn around and do this to him. You better tell Mom as soon as she gets home because if you don't, I will," she threatened before shutting the door, closing herself off from the man she called her father.

Mike didn't even bother to call her back. What could he say? His daughter didn't trust him and as soon as he broke the news to his wife, he wasn't sure if she would forgive him or if she would leave and divorce him. For the next two hours that day, Mike sat in the couch in quiet prayer, which was all he could do whenever he was confronted with adversity.

"Dear Lord, my life is such a mess now. I was unfaithful to my wife and reverted back to the person I was before I encountered you. My daughter's best friend passed away and her family's accusing an innocent young man. They won't even allow me to conduct the funeral service tomorrow because they have stopped trusting me. I don't blame them Lord. Sometimes I don't trust in myself and I feel like it's too much of a burden. It's just too much, God. You promised that you will never give your children more than they could bear but I don't know if I can handle this pressure; this burden of being an example of you when things in my life are falling apart," he prayed and he poured his heart out to the Lord as he never did in a long time.

After what felt like an eternity, he heard the lock on the front door turn and he knew his wife was home. The moment of truth had finally arrived. He could no longer duck or dodge or conceal any more secrets from Robyn.

"Hey honey, how are you doing?" she asked as she walked up the stairs.

Mike decided not to waste any time and wanted to get it done. "Actually, I'm not really doing well. We need to talk," he started as Robyn took off her shoes while sitting on the kitchen table.

Oddly, she was more cheerful than she had been in days. Mike walked to the kitchen table and sat across from his wife, unsure of where to start. Before he said a word, Robyn stopped him, her expression suddenly serious.

"You can save your breath, Michael. I know you were at Mrs. Samuels' home last Sunday night and I know you two did more than just talk," Robyn said.

Mike's mouth dropped open in such a way that if one saw it as a humorous moment, they would have laughed out loud but he quickly gained some composure. "How did you know?" he asked.

Robyn stood up and started pacing the kitchen. Mike had known her long enough to recognize that whenever Robyn paced the kitchen, she did it to either calm her emotions or to gather the right words. At any rate, Mike checked his heart. He was still alive and breathing. Robyn had not killed him yet, so he was at least thankful for that.

"Well, believe it or not, the news traveled much faster than you did Sunday night. I didn't have to be told, Michael. I knew it would happen. I saw the way she looked at you on Sundays. I saw how you looked at her and it was the same way you used to look at me," Robyn said and Mike could see her trying to suppress the grief that was becoming more and more evident upon her face.

"Something just told me that you were at her place but it wasn't confirmed to me until Monday morning when I went to work and one of my co-workers reported seeing you get in your car and drive off from her street. When she told me that, even though I knew deep down inside that you was with her that night, nothing could have prepared me for her words," Robyn explained and her tears began to fall. "At first I asked myself, what did I do? What did she have that I didn't have? I was so upset and everyone, from my co-workers to my boss asked if I was ok. I told them that I needed some time to myself. So I went to church and knelt down at the altar that day. My heart and my mind wanted to leave you and never come back home to the deception, the lies, and the distrust. But I don't know what it was, nor could I explain it, but this wave of peace flooded over me, dousing my anger, my bereavement and my despair. It was as if the Lord told me to give you another chance," Robyn said. "That was the last thing I wanted to do, but I listened to Him and I came home, expecting you to confess but you never did. It's been a battle of patience and anger for me these past four days," she said.

Upon hearing what Robyn had to go through after being unfaithful to her, Mike couldn't have felt any worse. Any other woman would have left him and not looked back. The marriage would have broken apart and he would have lost her trust forever and yet she had forgiven him.

"I'm so sorry for what I did," he apologized, tears flowing down his cheeks as well. He knew she was too good for him and it was only by God's grace that she didn't walk out on him like he deserved.

"I forgive you," Robyn said and they held each other in a tight embrace, as they heard a knock on their door. Mike and Robyn looked at each other in curiosity.

"Were you expecting any company tonight?" she asked him.

"No, not tonight," Mike answered as he went downstairs to answer the door. When he opened the door, he was taken aback. Trevor stood on the other side of the door. "Yes, what can I can I do for Mr. Trevor McClain? Or should I say Trevor McKey?" he asked raising his eyebrows.

"I'm sorry to visit at this time of night but I was wondering if you could help the son of Nina Martin," he replied, referring to himself.

Mike looked him straight in the eye to see if Trevor was joking but his face showed signs of urgency. "Come on in," Mike said warmly, inviting Trevor inside his home.

Loree McAfee was finally laid to rest the next morning at the J. Foster Phillips Funeral Home on Linden Boulevard. Amos, Alisha, and Andrea were all standing in the front row as Reverend Morgan Whitefield, a friend of the family, gave the eulogy for the funeral. Ever since the disastrous meeting in his office the past Sunday, the McAfee family had made it clear that they no longer wanted Mike to be involved in the funeral. Nonetheless, Mike, Robyn, and Shania still attended the funeral ceremony. They stood in the back among the various friends, family, and loved ones who attended the funeral. For Shania, it was the scene at the hospital all over again. It was so strange that only a little more than a week ago, she had still been talking and laughing with her best friend. Now Loree was in a cold, hard, empty casket on the verge of being lowered into the earth. It was a mixture of grief and guilt that hit Shania all at once. If Shania had only spoken with Amos or Alisha about what Loree was going through in her relationship, could she have prevented this tragedy?

If only I was in the casket instead of you. It should be me lying in there, not you, Shania thought. She knew those thoughts were dangerous and in most cases unstable but she couldn't have felt any worse. The city was already gripped in a new wave of fear and distrust. Shania couldn't allow herself to be vulnerable and become a statistic. She just wouldn't permit it. Robyn was also in tears, reminiscing about the times when

Loree had visited the house; the sleepovers, the lunches after Shania's track meets; and her undying love for her little sister. Although Mike was also grief stricken and had a grim look upon his face. It had to stop. It all had to stop. The senseless murders, the unlawful taking of human life without guilt or conscience, the endless road of senseless violence must all come to an end. Although Mike surely didn't possess the ability to end all of the violence himself but he would go to any lengths necessary to stop the vengeance pool before it began to spread. He was thinking not only of himself or his family but of all friends who were lost. It was not too late to start a change for future generations. He knew what direction he had to go and the first step in that direction would take place tonight in an undisclosed area where he had to stop another friend from making a crucial mistake that could cost him his life.

At nine forty-eight Saturday night, Antoine Sparks drove Nate's purchased car to Rufus King Park. When he had received the call from Nate earlier, he didn't understand why Nate wanted to meet him at the park. Why couldn't they have met at his house or something? Some people will always confuse themselves and others, Antoine thought as he turned at the intersection and saw the white gate that surrounded the park. The park was just about empty and Antoine's senses became alert at once. Coming back to this area brought back memories; unpleasant, distant memories he wished he had never lived.

Antoine viewed himself as two different people. The first person was the lowlife drug pin who lived off his dealers and mistreated women and men alike. He had caused so much pain to so many people in the past, some he remembered but others were just fragmented pieces. The ones he couldn't remember were probably due to his past overindulgence in drugs and drinking.

As soon as he approached the park entrance, he subcon-sciously rubbed his chest just above his heart with his right hand. It had been twelve years ago when life nearly ended. One of the friends from his past life as a drug dealer had shot him in the chest left him for dead. If a nearby couple had not noticed him, he surely would have bled to death. Once he arrived at the hospital, the bullet was extracted and he made a successful recovery. From the day he opened his eyes in that hospital, Earl Canter had died and Antoine Sparks was born. He changed his name, lost significant weight, and went back to school to re-educate himself. Taking the job at the car dealership had been the best decision he had ever made. He loved the people he worked with and he was thankful that they had provided him a fresh start, given his past. But here he was, at the same place that held the negative memories of his old life. He saw the big white gazebo up ahead but he did not see Mr. Plummer. Holding the keys, the car note, and the paperwork, he decided to sit inside the gazebo and wait. After fifteen minutes of waiting, he decided to try calling Nate again.

I can't be out here waiting. Doesn't he know I'm a busy man? He dialed the number and the phone rang five times, before going to voicemail.

"Where are you?" he said to himself, oblivious to the fact that he was being watched and the figure watching him was quickly nearing him with a closed left fist. The hand to face impact could be heard in the night skies. Antoine's right cheekbone was shattered instantly by the impact. Holding his face in agony, Antoine looked up to see his assailant. He barely got a look before a kick to his mid-section knocked the wind out of him. Antoine grunted in pain as he looked up and saw his potential customer standing over him, holding a gun.

"Are you crazy!!??" he yelled. "What the hell's wrong with you?" he coughed as Nate approached him, his eyes wide open with the brilliant light of revenge shining within his pupils.

"The mouse always comes back to da trap when it falls for the bait. Karma's a bitch, ain't it?," Nate asked in dim tones.

Antoine, still struggling to breathe because of the heavy blow to his chest, tried to rise to his feet. Nate stood over him, watching him struggle to get up.

"Damn Earl, don't tell me you got soft on me, man. Remember when you was kicking my ass back the day with ease?" Nate asked as he leveled

Antoine again with an overhand right followed by a knee that hit him directly in his diaphragm.

"What the fuck are you talking about? I don't even know you!" Antoine yelled with the pain reflected in his words.

Nate stood before him. "Then maybe you'll remember this!" he yelled, hurling what appeared to be dark, thick splinters of wood that were stained dark red. He pulled out his gun.

Antoine looked at the wood splinters. What was wrong with this guy and why was he beating him up? His motive couldn't be robbery so it could only be one other reason: revenge.

"Wait, man hold up please!" Antoine begged, his eyes darting to and from the gun pointed at him.

"Hold up? You want me to hold up? You should've held up before you killed Nina, you piece of shit," Nate replied.

"Nina who?" Antoine asked.

He knew a lot of people in the past and he had hurt so many of them that he couldn't even remember most of their names. Then, out of nowhere, as if it hit him as quickly as Nate's punches, Antoine remembered.

"You mean little Ni-Ni, don't you? Please man, hear me out. I was so high that day, I didn't even know where I was. I remembered fighting her off along with some other dude she was with but I don't remember what happened," he said.

"I was that other dude!" Nate replied angrily. "You murdered her and you left her to die, remember that?" he added insanely.

It was as if the dawn of realization struck Earl. "Look man, I understand why you doing this...." he started but Nate cut him off.

"You don't understand shit!" he countered. "You don't know what it's like living every day for eighteen years without your best friend and nightmares wakin' you up at night. What you know about that?" Nate thundered.

Antoine tried to look for a way to flee but Nate blocked the park entrance from within the gazebo area.

"You once said that my blood was here. Your blood is here too and this time, I'm gonna make sho' it stays here," Nate said as he raised the gun to Earl's left temple. Earl shut his eyes, waiting for the bullet to enter through his head but it never did.

"Nate, please stop!" a voice exclaimed.

Nate turned around, obviously startled by the voice. He didn't think anyone else was in the park other than himself and Big Earl. Three figures came out of the shadow of the night and approached Nate in the gazebo. Nate looked closer and recognized two of the figures at once; Mike Hillman and Gary McKey, followed by a young boy he had never seen before. The voice hailing him to stop, came from Mike. Nate turned to Gary, shaking his head.

"I should've known betta' than to tell you shit. I knew you was gonna dime me out. You should've stayed out of it," Nate said.

"I couldn't do it man. I got too much love for you, I couldn't let you go on with this," Gary said.

"Nate, it's over. Please let it go. It's not worth this. Bloodshed can never be repaid by more bloodshed," Mike explained.

"Says who? You?" Nate asked, pointing the gun at Mike. Mike put his hand up as he found himself held at gunpoint by his one-time friend.

"So you and Gary scheming behind my back now, is that it?" Nate asked, before his eyes fell on Trevor, who started to walk toward him. "What you got to do wit' this, boy?" he asked as Trevor stepped forward.

"If anyone should want payback for Nina's death, it should be me. I'm her son," he replied.

Nate's eyes widened and Trevor saw the shock of this revelation register on his face. Big Earl, who was still sprawled on the ground, also looked at Trevor. Nate pointed the gun back at Big Earl.

"Son, this piece of trash is the reason that you ain't got yo' momma here wit' you and he doesn't deserve to walk another day while Nina was robbed of that same chance," Nate said.

Trevor looked at Big Earl who was reduced to a shell of his intimidating old self. The eyes of the man who murdered his mother stared right back at him. Trevor had two conflicting emotions. The first emotion was the same emotion as Nate; revenge and payback. But there was another emotion that he felt; bred in his heart from the conversation he had with Mike earlier that night. He saw his mother smile in the home video with him as a baby again. He stepped closer to Big Earl.

"You killed my mama in cold blood and you walked around free for eighteen years acting like everything's all good. You don't deserve to live, because of that," Trevor said. "But I forgive you," he added, while Nate gave Trevor a look of horror mixed with confusion. Big Earl broke down and wept in front of Trevor.

"I'm sorry for all the pain I put you through. I hurt a lot of people in the past and until tonight it never occurred to me how serious I hurt people. All I want is another chance. I'm sorry," Big Earl said.

But it wasn't good enough for Nate. "It's too late for apologies," Nate said as he raised the gun over Big Earl's head again.

At the same time, six members of the NYPD surrounded the gazebo. Nate hadn't notice them. The darkness and his rage had concealed them.

"Drop it. Drop the gun and put your hands up now!" one of the cops yelled. Nate did as he was instructed, and the police moved forward and cuffed him and Big Earl. Trevor broke down and cried as he held three bloody fence spikes.

CHAPTER TWENTY-FOUR

It took Mike and Gary over twenty minutes to console Trevor after the police had apprehended Nate and Big Earl at the deserted park gazebo. Mike had to commend Trevor. It couldn't have been easy looking into the face of the person who had murdered a loved one and not react the same way as Nate had. Trevor appeared to have grown up in Mike's eyes and although Mike hadn't taken the time to really know Trevor, he felt a new sense of respect for the young man.

After Gary and Trevor went their separate ways, Mike returned to the comfort of his home. He thanked the Lord that he had made it back safe and unharmed as he still saw Nate's gun aimed squarely at him in a brief moment of insanity. As he walked into his bedroom, he saw Robyn already fast asleep.

After Trevor had visited Mike and explained how Gary had gotten into his dorm room and played Nate's voicemail, Mike knew that of the three men involved – Nate, Gary, and himself – he was the peacemaker and the negotiator. At first Robyn was against her husband's involvement. Unlike the David Anderson case, this had been a personal matter of life and death. If Nate was as crazy as Trevor had made him out to be, then Mike's life would be in serious danger. Mike understood how concerned his wife was but he felt that Nate might listen to reason if he was present.

Mike certainly didn't want to take any absolute chances, so he had called the police department and told them where Nate said he would meet Earl. At first, he feared he would arrive too late; that Nate would have already dispatched Big Earl, would bury the body somewhere, and flee. He was grateful that he had arrived early enough to stop Nate before the police arrived. It was a gamble that had worked in his favor but could have been miscalculated severely.

Mike set his alarm to six o'clock in the morning. He had to visit someone whom he had not seen in some time. As Sunday morning arrived, he got up, got dressed, and drove down Liberty Avenue for fifteen minutes before reaching his destination. He had to look closely at first because he was not sure he was at the right location. He parked outside a small, single-person side home and walked through the thin open fence. Knocking the door with three hard knocks, a familiar face opened the door.

"Pastor Michael Hillman, how you doing this morning my brother?" Trayback Collins asked as Mike hugged him warmly.

"I'm doing good, reverend. I hope I didn't wake you up this morning. I intended to visit after the morning service but I felt it couldn't wait," Mike said as he accepted Reverend Collins' invitation to step inside his home.

Trayback's wife had passed away a few years ago and his sons had moved to Pennsylvania and started families of their own. After Reverend Collins offered him some coffee, he invited Mike to sit down on the couch.

"So I see you've been too busy to visit me nowadays, huh?" Reverend Collins asked, laughing.

"Busy is an understatement, reverend," Mike replied. Sighing, he continued. "Reverend, I had so many hopes and prayers over what God could do for the development of my church and the community. Man, we've dealt with some trials over the past month. My old friends from high school came back and one had his own mission to personally take someone else's life for a murder that occurred years ago. My daughter's been dealing with the same situation with the death of her best friend. I want to do the best I can to be a dependable leader and father but sometimes my past comes back to haunt me. It's all happening at once, reverend, and I don't know if I'm the one God chose to lead the people in my community," he said.

Reverend Collins didn't move, staring deeply into Mike's eyes, as if he wanted to be certain that Mike knew what he was saying. "So are you telling me that you want out of the ministry?" he asked.

Mike shook his head. The way Reverend Collins had posed the question, it sounded like he was painting Mike to be either a loser or a quitter. "I don't know what I want right now, Reverend. God tells us that he won't tempt His people any more than they can bear, but how much more can I bear?" he asked. "I've been unfaithful to my wife and although she forgives me, our marriage is far from perfect. Now I'm defending the boy who has been arrested for the murder of Shania's friend and her parents no longer trust me because I see that the boy's innocent," Mike continued. "Court date is set for Tuesday and if the judge rules him guilty, it's another misunderstood young man locked up behind bars. I know that he may have a past but that doesn't make him guilty of this crime, does it? Am I wrong for believing the potential of our young men today?" he asked.

Trayback Collins sat back in his chair for a moment. Breathing deeply, he replied, "In the Old Testament, when God was looking for another ruler to replace King Saul, He sent Samuel the Seer to seek out David the shepherd. Now David did not look like a king yet, but God saw his potential. Although Samuel did not see it yet, the Lord saw it and He reminded Samuel, saying that man looks at the outward appearance, but He looks at the heart," Reverend Collins walked up to Mike and patted him on the shoulder. "He may be trapped and a prisoner in the system, but the Lord knows his heart and He knows the plan that He has for that young man. He knows your heart as well, Michael," he said. "He knows how hard you've tried to keep peace and harmony within the community, and he sees your efforts. The biggest mistake that we make as pastors is forgetting that we are not the head of the church. Christ is the head of the church, and we are merely appointed representatives used as vessels to lead others to Him. Stay in prayer, brother, and soon the Lord's divine plan and future for your community will be revealed to you. Spend more time communicating with him through fasting and daily devotions and don't worry about the outcome of the trial come Tuesday. I have a great confidence that he will be set free. I remember another high school quarterback who was burdened and imprisoned by similar troubles and doubts about his potential and look at what He was able to do with that young man," Reverend Collins added with a smile.

Mike smiled at the reference Reverend Collins made to him. Looking at the clock, he realized it was seven-thirty. His family would be awake and would be wondering where he was at such an early hour. Mike stood up and prepared to leave. He shook Reverend Collins' hand.

"Thank you, reverend, for the words of encouragement and prayers. I will see you soon," he said as he walked out to his car.

"Have a good one son. Tell the missus and the young one that I send greetings and treat her well now," Reverend Collins said as Mike drove back to his home to prepare for Sunday service.

The church congregation was seated as Pastor Mike resumed his sermon. Taking his cue and his inspiration from Reverend Collins, he preached on the Lord examining the heart of every living person. The message was very well received as it normally was, although there were a few people who were skeptical of the pastor and his words. That few included Mrs. Jackson, the mother of Miles Jackson, who had fought Jamal at school a couple of days earlier. Then there was the McAfee family, who weren't even present at Rock of Jacob Baptist Church. As far as they were concerned, the pastor had lost all credibility in the community and new rumors about him having an affair and cheating on his wife only strengthened their doubts about him. Mike understood their attitudes and hoped that one day he could regain their trust. Only God knew what was in store. Then there was Nate, who was currently sitting in a jail cell, charged with assault and battery and unlawful possession of a firearm.

Although Nate had been arrested, Mike didn't believe for a moment that Nate's anger had subsided. He knew that if Nate was ever released from jail, he would continue to pursue Earl. Nate's stubbornness was his downfall and Mike knew that he had to keep his friend in serious prayer. Mike concluded his sermon.

"I know that there are many of you who feel that I shouldn't be up here preaching a message this morning or even ever again. I will admit that I have made many mistakes recently and I've hurt not only myself but my family in the process," he said. Turning to the front row where Robyn sat, he spoke directly to her. "My beautiful wife and my gorgeous daughter have stood by me each and every day and although I have sinned against God and against them, they have not forsaken me. For this I am very thankful. I want to apologize for my shortcomings and times when I allowed my pride and my vanity to overcome my better judgment. Thank you for forgiving me and for giving me a second chance. Because you were the better woman, it has made me a better man," he said.

Robyn buried her face in her hands, tears streaming down her face with emotion. Pastor Mike stepped down from the podium and hugged his wife in the first row. Ronald Plank, without warning or planning, stepped up to the podium.

"Brothers and sisters, let us form a ring around this family. Let us lift our voices up to the Lord and pray for the health, the longevity and blessings to be bestowed on our beloved pastor and his family," he said.

This was done and a large circle was formed as the members of the church, old and new, gathered around the pastor and his family. The congregants began praying for them. All Mike could do was look up towards heaven and thank God for the overwhelming support he was receiving from his extended family. It was a moment to behold. After church ended and all the members had left the building, Mike looked back at the front of the church where the podium was and the mode cross behind it. He knew it would be a tough battle Tuesday in the courthouse and the future of a young black man was hanging in the balance, but he no longer felt overwhelmed or burdened. It was a battle for which he would be ready. As he grabbed the last of his belongings from the office, he heard the office door open behind him. Turning back, he noticed that it was Robyn.

"Hey honey. That was quite a service, huh?" he asked his wife. Robyn smiled at him.

"It was wonderful. I wouldn't have traded that moment for any other moment that we've had since we came here," she said. "But I have something I need to tell you," she added.

"Sure, what is it?" Mike asked. Robin paused before speaking.

"At the conclusion of the service today, while you were greeting all of our members, I saw Isis," she said.

Mike stopped packing his briefcase. He had hoped that the two women wouldn't run into each other, knowing how jealous and confrontational Robyn could be.

"What happened?" he asked. Robyn sat down.

"Well, we had a talk about what happened last Sunday night. She apologized for what happened and she apologized for hurting me. At first, I didn't want to talk to her or even be seen with her but after talking with her for a while, I realized what she was going through," Robyn said. "Her husband left her and Jamal and she felt isolated. After explaining that to me, I became less and less upset and I started to feel sorry for her. Then she told me that she was planning on moving out of the city to another area," Robyn explained.

Mike was taken aback by the news. "She's moving?" he asked in disbelief. He had halfway hoped to meet with Isis to apologize for what had happened and to apologize to Jamal. He had just fixed their countertop and now they were moving away. It didn't make any sense but it didn't have to make sense to him as long as God knew the whole picture. "When will they be moving?" he asked.

"They are already packing, and they will be on their way out this Tuesday," Robyn answered.

That's the same day as the court case for David Anderson, Mike thought as he closed the light to his office and walked out.

He thought about going over to Isis's house to at least saying goodbye but after reconciling with Robyn, it just didn't seem appropriate to go back to the site of his transgression. Instead he walked over to Robyn and held her hand.

"I'm so sorry," he said.

Robyn rolled her eyes. "I know, I know you've said it about a thousand times already," she said.

Mike stepped closer, confidently and kissed his wife. "I'll say this a thousand times more. I love you," he said as they held each other in a close embrace.

Nate sat in a closed cell with a few other inmates. The last eighteen hours had been nothing short of agonizing. He had been so close to exacting revenge before his plan had been thwarted by Gary and Mike.

These two owe me one, Nate thought angrily as he sat fuming about his second missed opportunity. Big Earl had once again slipped through his fingers and the worst part was that he didn't think the justice system would make Earl pay for what he had done. He might serve thirty to forty years if he was convicted but Nate knew Earl would find a way to get away with it, again.

It's ok, I've waited this long to get a crack at him, I don't mind waiting a few more years to get another chance. I don't care how old he gets, he thought.

Nate knew the police wouldn't release him anytime soon due to the visible wounds on Big Earl and the fact that he had been caught brandishing a gun over Earl's head. Nate's fate was sealed. He hadn't done serious time the first time he had been arrested when he had witnessed Nina's murder but he had a terrible feeling that this time he could be indicted in for a longer sentence.

The chief of police walked over to the holding cell. Looking at the prisoners, he yelled, "Plummer!"

Nate looked up as the officer took the keys out of his pocket and began to unlock the jail doors. He couldn't have heard right? Did they call his name? Were they really letting him out instead of transferring him upstate without the chance of parole? Nate got up and walked to the jail doors. The officer looked at him sternly.

"Your bail's been posted. You're free to go," he said as he allowed Nate to walk out of the jail doors.

"Bail? But who posted it?" Nate asked.

His family had all moved far away, not wanting anything to do with him and he didn't think he had any real friends who would spend a dime on him. So who else could have done it? The police pointed to the front of the precinct, near the entrance. Nate followed his gaze and saw a familiar face looking back at him, the same face he had seen the previous night while pointing the gun at him. Pastor Mike Hillman smiled at Nate as she waited for him to sign release papers and they both exited the precinct. As they walked down the steps of the precinct, after a few moments of silence, Nate finally spoke.

"Why'd you bail me out? I thought you hated me for going after Earl," he said

"I don't hate you man, I just couldn't stand by and watch you throw your life away for a grudge that's held you prisoner for eighteen years," Mike replied.

Nate looked at Mike for a split second, then looked out into the distance of the starry Sunday night. "I was gonna do it, you know, until you got in the way and stepped between us. I could've killed you last night too but you still spent money to post bail. Why?" he asked.

Mike laughed, while Nate stared at him. "Let's just say, I was repaying a debt for myself," he replied. Then his face grew serious. "Nate, I paid for your release on one condition; please stop hunting for Big Earl. Over the years, you've allowed this spirit of revenge to run its course in your life and control your actions. I loved Nina as much as you did but killing Earl will not bring her back. Revenge isn't always sweet," he said.

Nate nodded his head in agreement and the more he thought about it, the more he saw that Mike had a point in what he said. Whether he had killed Earl or not, it wouldn't change the fact that Nina was still dead and he would still be emotionally empty. He had been carrying the grudge for eighteen years.

"C'mon Nate, it's time to forgive and let go," Mike said.

"I can't forget or forgive what he did, man," Nate said firmly.

"Then you'll only be angry for the rest of your life and it will end up destroying you. Please let it go," Mike pleaded.

Nate thought about it long and hard. Mike had been nothing short of supportive and friendly to Nate, while Nate has treated Mike like scum. There had to be a reason that Mike had posted his bail.

"Did God want you to post my bail?" he asked.

Mike smiled at his old friend. "Absolutely. And He wants you to stop living life in anger and start treasuring it. Need a lift back to your place?" Mike asked.

"Yeah, man. Appreciate it," Nate said, shaking Mike's hand and walking to Mike's car.

It felt like the old days whenever Nate had needed help, Mike would always be there for him; no questions asked. He had forgiven Nate for pointing the gun to his face and for the harsh words at the supermarket a few days back. No questions asked. Perhaps, for once in his life, it was time to listen to Mike. He should finally clean all the skeletons from his closet and open his heart and his mind towards others. No questions asked.

Tuesday finally arrived and the citizens of 101 Avenue entered the small court room before eight in the morning. It was a clear morning, one of those mornings when birds were happily and the trees swayed from the gentle breeze. Despite the cheerful day, the mood inside in the courtroom was certainly not sunny. The prosecutor, Dale Rosemond, took his seat at his table with Amos and Alisha McAfee directly behind him. Although Mr. Rosemond's face was serious, he felt more than confident that he would win this trial and achieve justice for their daughter's death by indicting this dangerous person. Rosemond wholly believed that all gang members and even former gang members were a menace to society. He thought they all deserved to be locked up for the good of the citizens involved.

The door opened at the opposite end of the courtroom and Arthur Blaylock walked in, dressed in a solid black suit and carrying his signature briefcase. Following him was David Anderson, dressed in a dark blue suit and tie. He followed Arthur to their table in the court room. David adhered to Arthur's instructions not to look any member of Loree's family directly in the eye. The back door opened and Pastor Mike walked into the courtroom. Robyn had gone to work but she had told Mike that she wanted to know the results of the trial. She assured Mike that she was also praying for David's acquittal. The bailiff suddenly spoke.

"All rise for Judge Henderson," he said in deep tones. The whole courtroom stood up as Judge Cheryl Henderson made her way to the judge's bench. As she did, Shania snuck into the courtroom and sat next to her father.

"Aren't you supposed to be in school?" Mike asked sternly. Shania looked at her father with indignation. "Are you serious? Loree was my friend and besides, Uncle Arthur called me to testify," she replied as she sat down.

The judge made the announcement that the trial was underway and she gave instructions to Arthur Blaylock and Dale Rosemond before they began their cross examinations. As the day wore on, it seemed that the higher the temperature rose outside, the more tense it became in the courtroom. A myriad of people were called to the stand, including the waitress at the restaurant where Loree had spent her last few hours. Cindy Crofton, a few of her classmates, and Amos McAfee all testified. The trend of testimonies given seemed to echo the same tone; that Loree was a girl who bore a strong personality and had few to no enemies. But they all testified that Loree had been increasingly unhappy in the last few months, ever since she had started dating David. The most damning testimony was that they were convinced that David had killed Loree in a fit of rage after Loree broke off the relationship with him.

Amos appeared to be more damaging than any of the other witnesses who testified, stating that from the very moment David had started dating his daughter, he had doubts about him and he had never trusted trust him. After Amos testified, the trial recessed for lunch. When court reconvened Shania was called to the witness stand by Arthur Blaylock. Shania's testimony; helped the prosecution more than the defense but it wasn't as damning to Arthur's defense as he imagined. Shania had testified that she did have her doubts about David but she had greater concerns about the people with whom David associated. She also managed to convey his efforts to stay on the football team, despite some of his teammates' claims that he had explosive anger. Shania was the first witness to divulge the name of Tadarius Hill as a suspicious character and how he was seen with Loree in the days leading up to her death. After a number of witnesses had testified, David Anderson was called to the stand by Mr. Rosemond. Arthur held his breath in nervously. He had warned David that Mr. Rosemond would call him to the stand to get his testimony and would attempt to rattle him and he was right. Mr. Rosemond asked David a lot of questions, most of which concerned his past involvement with Tadarius and M.O.B.

At one point, Rosemond asked David to pull up his sleeve to display the gang tattoo, which was an intricate design that combined dollar bills, blood drops, and guns. As he was under oath, David had no choice but to take off the suit jacket and pull up his sleeve to show the tattoo. There were gasps and murmurs throughout the courtroom when they saw the large tattoo on his right arm and shoulder. Rosemond also broached the subject of David's use of PED's during the season and scolded the athletic committee at Richmond Hill for failing to drug-test their athletes on a consistent basis. Mr. Rosemond was also able to get on the record during his interrogation of David that he had been seen only a few hours after the murder in a secluded area a few blocks from where Loree had been found. When David left the stand, Mr. Rosemond walked confidently back to his table, positive that David's own testimony had been the nail in the coffin for the defense.

Despite Rosemond's boastful swagger, Arthur wasn't done yet. He made a request to the judge to present one more key witness to the stand. The request was granted, much to the dismay of Mr. Rosemond and the McAfee family. Arthur called his last witness to the stand. It was six-thirty and the sun had just begun to dip in the sky when high school freshman Antonio Franks was called to the stand. Standing at six-foot-three inches tall and dressed in a black t-shirt and black pants, Antonio strode to the stand and took oath. As Arthur cross examined him, the courtroom and the jurors suddenly became split. Antonio gave a chilling, detailed first person account of how Loree had been hanging out with some of the other girls who had been seen in Tadarius' company and talked about the animosity Tadarius felt for Loree. Loree had been brash, outspoken, and very opinionated about the gang leader and she had once threatened to call the police on Tadarius and his crew. According to Antonio, Loree had actually attempted to help the other girls who were part of M.O.B to get out. Antonio testified that Tadarius's only option was to eliminate her, thus destroying the only threat to Tadarius's drug and alcohol business.

When Arthur asked if David had any part in the shooting, Antonio vehemently denied that he had any involvement; then he revealed the bombshell that tore the courtroom in two. Antonio confessed that Tadarius had given him and Terrell Washington the job of shooting Loree. After rolling up his sleeve and displaying the tattoo identical to David's, Antonio went on to confess that based solely upon Tadarius's instruction, they were told to take Loree out to eat. They did encounter David on the way out of the restaurant but he and Loree had barely exchanged words. Terrell, who was a junior at Richmond Hill, had recently dropped out of school to join ranks of M.O.B. Antonio further testified that it had been Terrell who had convinced him to join Tadarius and M.O.B.

When he and Terrell had driven Loree to Guy R Brewer Road, Antonio claimed that he and Terrell got in a heated argument. In a fit of rage, Antonio left the car and walked back home, while Terrell drove on with Loree to the secluded area. Antonio rushed home and considered calling the police but his fear for the safety of his family and four younger brothers overtook him. If any member of M.O.B. snitched, Tadarius had threatened to kill their families. Therefore, with pain and regret, Antonio had remained silent. Antonio recalled the day Tadarius and a couple other gang members had cornered him as he was returning from school and they beat him severely, leaving him with several cuts and bruises. Tadarius had called a stop to the beating just long enough to deliver an ultimatum to Antonio. Either roll with M.O.B. or he would be extremely sorry he had crossed him. Antonio, out of sheer terror, agreed and Tadarius had told him what he wanted done. With the courtroom hanging on to every word of his testimony, Antonio explained how Tadarius gave Antonio instructions to place the cloth-wrapped gun in David's backpack to frame him. The police had started their investigation as Tadarius had anticipated and he warned his crew to spread the word that David was guilty of the murder. Antonio continued to explain how he had waited for the opportunity to place the murder weapon in David's backpack.

The entire courtroom fell silent as they absorbed Antonio's explanation of the events surrounding the murder of Loree McAfee. Shania looked across the courtroom at the McAfee family and saw the expression of shock and denial cross their faces. Hearing that their daughter had been involved with the city's most dangerous gang behind their backs was too much for them to grasp. Even Shania was shaken when she heard this revelation about her best friend. It never crossed her mind that Antonio could be lying, but knowing Loree as well as she had, it wasn't like her to be as secretive as she had been during the last weeks of her life.

After Antonio's testimony and the summations, the judge ordered the jurors to jury room to deliberate. The deliberation was painfully long, lasting two and a half hours. Mike closed his eyes in silent prayer. After their deliberation, the jurors came back into the courtroom and the judge instructed everyone to rise while the verdict was read.

"We the jury, hereby find the defendant…." David held his breath and Arthur found himself nervous as well. "….not guilty of the murder of Loree McAfee," the juror finished.

The portion of the courtroom who were supportive of David clapped their hands and rejoiced, hugging David who was still stunned at the reading of the verdict. Breaking down into tears, he looked upward and began thanking the Lord aloud. He didn't care who heard him or who was around him. A broken family and a shady past didn't matter anymore. His football career was probably over because of the testimony that he had taken performance enhancing drugs but he was free. He would not be going to prison. Although many people sought him out to hug him and show their support, he refused to see anyone until he saw Pastor Mike.

"Pastor, pastor!" he called out. Mike approached him. "Thank you for believing in me when almost nobody else did," he said. Mike hugged him.

"No problem, brother. The Lord sees your heart, and may He use this experience as an amazing testimony of your life," he replied as he hugged him.

Shaking Arthur's hand, he said "Thanks man. I couldn't have done this without you," he said.

"No, we couldn't have done this without God," Arthur replied.

Mike looked at him with an expression of surprise. Could this be a sign that his brother-in-law finally realized that the Lord still worked miracles? It remained to be seen but as he turned around to look for Antonio, he didn't see him. He figured that he must have been led to another part of the building to file an official report and get his family under the witness protection program. Mike knew it would be a long road for that young man. Mike walked over to the McAfee family, who were shocked at the outcome of the verdict.

"Amos, I know this isn't the verdict you wanted to hear, but rest assured, they will find the people responsible for this," Mike reassured.

"This ain't over yet," Amos replied, his eyes wet with tears. "I will fight this decision with everything I have, even if I have to go to the state court," he said. Mike bowed his head, knowing that in the emotion of the moment, Mr. McAfee would not be willing to accept the verdict and that their relationship would remain icy and indifferent.

As Amos and Alisha walked away, Mike said. "I understand what you must do. But please, whatever you do, remember this: Not all black boys are thugs," he said as he walked back to Shania, as they made their way out of the courtroom.

The news of David's exoneration had reached the airwaves and coverage was shown on the six o'clock news and the eleven o'clock news. Reporters flocked to the courthouse and tried to interview David's grandmother but the family refused to answer any questions. Willamena Anderson had been staying at a neighbor's home and while she was overjoyed that David had been acquitted, she wasn't thrilled about the publicity. Once the verdict was released, David and his grandmother were put under the same witness protection program as was Antonio's family. Even the police knew the streets always talked. The news of David's acquittal would have reached the ears of Tadarius and his crew. He had to know that he was wanted by the NYPD in connection with Loree's murder and that spoke volumes to Tadarius. It clearly said that either David had confessed or he had a traitor in his ranks. Whichever was correct, Tadarius was more dangerous than ever before.

Everyone had their own agenda in the eyes of Tadarius and he would never be able to breathe easily again. He would once again migrate from city to city, zone to zone, and abandon his old haunts. Tadarius felt like he had moved around forever, until he had finally settled at an old apartment building off of Merrick Boulevard. Tadarius knew the area well, having been born and raised there. Knowing the police were up at Lefferts and 101 Avenue, which was a good thirty minutes to an hour away, it seemed like an ideal location to continue the game.

On a cool Friday afternoon, Tadarius returned from an excursion to 164th Street and Jamaica Avenue. Accompanied by Malik, Terrell, Terrance, and his girl for the night, they returned to count their earnings for the night. Every day for the past three weeks had been tense; from dodging the police who might recognize Terrell's face as well as his own, to plotting a definite yet subtle demise for David and his grandmother.

Tadarius had returned from a night of partying, so his mind was blank. He wasn't worried at all. As the crew entered the dark apartment building lobby, they saw the shadow of somebody standing at the apartment doorway and after getting a closer look, Tadarius realized it was David. With his senses still distorted from the excessive amounts of alcohol and weed in his system, he still recognized David.

"Look who finally got out the pen," he said in low tones that denoted he wasn't at all concerned by with the fact that he had nearly thrown his brother's life away. David looked around him and knew he was outnumbered by Tadarius's gang and that they could beat him to a pulp or kill him whenever they wished but if he was going to go down, he was prepared to bring Tadarius down with him.

David wasn't going down easily. "You framed me, man. It's over. Gettin' me locked up for no reason doesn't make you my brother, homey. It makes you a sick, dirty, low-down piece of crap," he said. "I'm done wit' you man. We ain't brothers anymore so don't refer to me as one because I can't think of anything more sickening than being related to a thug-ass nigga like you," he added.

The gang around Tadarius started laughing hysterically but Tadarius wasn't laughing. He didn't find the humor in it at all. He started to put his hand in his pocket. David braced himself.

"I had to teach yo' ass a lesson, son. If you weren't down wit' us, that makes you an enemy. My enemy," Tadarius said, now deadly serious. Looking back at his crew, he said, "I knew he was nothing but a lil' punk-ass nigga. His grandmother probably got a bigga' dick than he does. Too bad, she ain't gon see her grandson again," he said, and the rest of the crew laughed. Then he turned to David. "You got balls coming down hea' I'll give you that. But you didn't possibly expect me to let you go, now did you?" Tadarius said with a nasty edge to his voice. His companions were no longer laughing either. They each put their hands in their side pockets reaching for their own firearms. Tadarius was already holding his gun, pointing it at David. "You made this way too easy, nigga. Got any last words?" he asked.

It was that extra moment that David needed. Knowing how unstable Tadarius was and his history of acting without any conscience, he took the risk that Tadarius would aim his gun at him and unbeknownst to his 'brother' David was wired by police surveillance so they could hear the entire conversation. Tadarius was unaware that ten police officers had begun to surround the apartment building. One of them got through the door silently and had held his position while the other officers closed in. David saw the shadowed silhouette of Detective Sands in the back of the crew and he smiled.

"Yeah I got some last words. Forget you and M.O.B," David said defiantly. As Tedarius prepared to pull the trigger to send a bullet through David, he heard a click behind him.

"Freeze!" Detective Sands yelled as the police entered the building lobby.

David used the gang's distraction to escape through the building's back door and he was only too grateful to get out of there because within a minute, he heard the gunshots. There were at least ten rounds fired and Detective Sands bent down to take cover under the lobby door as bullets from Tadarius's and Malik's guns shattered the door window, showering Detective Sands with glass. He only had time to yell the one word when Tadarius and his gang started firing.

Detective Sands, using his reflexes, dove out of the way and the moment Tadarius fired, the officers began to fire back. Bullets were flying everywhere and the few tenants who were in the building screamed and ran for cover with their children. Then there was silence. Detective Sands looked up to assess the damage. The whole lobby looked like a scene from a western movie shootout; bullet holes in the walls and his stomach clenched at the scene before him. Terrance and Malik lay motionless on the ground, their bodies riddled with bullets. Although he was a veteran officer who had served overseas in the Gulf War, nothing could have prepared him for this scene.

These boys were young and had their whole lives ahead of them. It never should have come to this amount of bloodshed. He heard sounds of anguish coming from the lobby stairwell. The police had apprehended Tadarius and Terrell, who were both shot; Terrell in the knee and Tadarius in his lower leg. Sophie, the young woman who accompanied Tadarius and was also in the middle of the fray, was apprehended, although unharmed. With both boys in handcuffs, the police led them over to the squad cars as they drove to the precinct to book them. Tadarius was later charged with the attempted murder of a police officer and conspiracy to commit murder in the death of Loree McAfee. He was given life without parole. Terrell was charged with the murder of Loree McAfee and attempted murder of a police officer. He was also given life in prison without parole.

Later that night in Pastor Mike's house, Willamena cried tears of joy when she learned that David had escaped the sting operation unharmed. When David had come to her to explain that he had agreed to help Detective Sands track down Tadarius and his gang, she had rejected the idea due to the danger. After Detective Sands expressed how vital David was to the arrest of Tadarius because he knew the gang's whereabouts and their tendencies, she reluctantly agreed. Pastor Mike walked up to David.

"I'm proud of you, David. My family and I kept you in prayer all night and we're glad He brought you back ok," he said.

"Thanks, pastor," David replied, hugging the pastor.

He also saw Trevor with Gary, Tiffany, and Jack McClain. Both Gary and the McClain couple decided to work out their differences and support Trevor the best way they could. Trevor walked up to David.

"It's too bad you won't be eligible to play football again though," Trevor said apologetically.

Since learning about the PED's that he had been using, the Richmond Hill's football program suspended David for the year and the scholarships that he had garnered withdrawn. Four weeks ago that would have been a problem to David. Now he only saw opportunity.

"Yeah I know but I ain't trippin' on it though. It gives me another chance to find myself and see how I can continue to help my grandmother," he said.

Trevor nodded his head in agreement. "I feel you, man. Just keep doing your thing and stay in them books," he said.

"I hear you, man. Good lookin' out," David said as he dapped Trevor. "Besides, going undercover wit' five-oh to get the drop on Tadarius was kinda dope, though. Got me thinkin' about going into law enforcement," he added.

Robyn came out of the kitchen to announce that she had prepared food and beverages for everyone. On his way to the kitchen, David felt a tap on his shoulder. Turning around, he saw it was Shania. She put her hands up in mock surrender.

"Are you gonna shoot me too?" she asked laughing. David laughed also, remembering their encounter back at the school hallway. "I wanted to apologize for not believing you at first. It's just that I was so upset that my best friend was gone and I thought that you had something to do with it. Can you forgive me?" she asked.

David smiled at her. "No doubt, if it wasn't for your family and especially your dad, I wouldn't be here today. I owe you guys my life. Thank you," he said, hugging Shania.

"No problem," Shania said. Heading toward the kitchen, she added, "I'm starting to see why she loved you so much."

Looking at a new picture of Loree and Shania that hung above the kitchen doorway, David smiled.

"She always used to talk about you when we were together. She would talk about how cool you were, how hard you worked in school and in track, and how committed you were to the church. She was one of a kind, Shania. I never met anyone my age that was real to me, you know what I'm sayin'?" he asked.

"Yeah, I do," Shania replied and they both joined Shania's parents, Trevor, his parents, and Gary and David's grandmother at the dinner table. Before they ate, Pastor Mike bowed his head in prayer to bless the food.

"Dear Heavenly Father, I thank you for gathering us all here tonight to feast in your name. In the last two months, we have dealt with tragedy, lust, unfaithfulness, distrust, vengeance, trials, and tribulation. Although we dealt with them, you did not let us deal with them alone. You've watched us, you've comforted us, and you've kept us safe through all the flaming arrows that the world threw at us. As we prepare to eat our dinner tonight, I pray that you continue to transform the web of lies, deceit, and hate into an endless circle of forgiveness, truth, and love. Please forgive our sins and help us live better in you and through you. I pray this not because we are worthy, but in the name of your son Jesus Christ, Amen," he prayed.

As the extended family started to eat, Mike looked at his table and just reflected on how beautiful it was to see everyone gathered together as brothers and sisters. It was a moment he would never forget.

CHAPTER TWENTY-FIVE

The small Ford turned right at the green light and made its way down the two-lane street. Trevor McClain was accompanied by his longtime girlfriend, Shania Hillman who had graduated Richmond Hill High school and was attending Queens College on a track and field scholarship. Her hair was tied in a long ponytail, and she was wearing a headband that sported the school's red and blue colors. Despite his earlier reservations, Pastor Mike gave permission for Shania and Trevor to start dating and it was a decision that Pastor Mike would never regret. Trevor had shown remarkable maturity and growth over the years. Not only was he exceeding his expectations scholastically, but he becomes an All-American at St. John's in basketball. He was also showing improvement in his spiritual life. Since Trevor had first visited the Rock of Jacob Baptist Church four years ago, he had fallen in love with the overwhelming support and fellowship of the members at the church, continuing to go to services on days when he didn't have games. Whenever he did have practices or games, he got into the habit of reading the books of Psalms and Proverbs and he found them to be very encouraging from which he could meditate on prior to the games. Trevor remembered how unsure he was of himself when he had first arrived in college but reading the Bible and praying daily as pastor Mike had instructed him, gave him a great deal of peace before his games.

He ended up reestablishing his relationship with Jack and Tiffany McClain, who had adopted him, but he never looked at it that way again. As far as he was concerned, they were his parents. They had taken care of him, and they loved him. As he grew through the college years, he began understanding why they had never told him about his biological parents. He understood that they were trying to protect him and to prevent him from looking for revenge like Nate Plummer had attempted. Nevertheless, Trevor still kept in contact with Gary McKey who had moved back to Carlstadt, New Jersey and later remarried.

Shania had completed high school with high honors and was nearly the top of her class in academic achievement. Taking a page from her mother's book, she decided to focus on social work and continue to compete at track and field. She was thankful to have Trevor in her life because although their schedules prevented them from spending as much time together as they would have liked, spend together, he never wavered in his respect for her. They would always make time for each other and were usually together on their free weekends. Loree McAfee's death was still very difficult for Shania at times and especially harder for Andrea, who was now fifteen years old and a sophomore at Richmond Hill.

They were on the way to Long Island City, New York to visit someone. As they approached Newcomers High School, they searched for an empty space to park but did not step out of the car.

"What time is it?" Trevor asked Shania. The clock on his car dashboard was always incorrect. He'd always tried adjusting it, but it never worked. Shania checked her cell phone for the time.

"It's twenty minutes after three. According to their schedule, school's supposed to be over in a couple minutes but are you sure this is the right place?" Shania asked.

"Oh yeah, it's the right place. One of my boys said he started coming here now," Trevor replied.

They were waiting for someone they knew and when the bell rang, all the students began flying out of the building. Kids of all different sizes exited the school and Trevor started to laugh a little bit.

"What's so funny?" Shania asked curiously.

"I forgot how short these high school kids are now. Man, they look like kindergarteners compared to our days," he replied.

Shania shook her head. Trevor could be so clueless at times. "You special, you know that?" she asked, raising an eyebrow. "Do you see him coming out, yet?" she asked, looking at the throng of kids exiting the school.

"Not yet," Trevor answered as they waited a few more minutes. After two more minutes, Trevor smiled. "There's my boy," he said, smiling.

Shania looked in Trevor's direction. A high school senior, standing at six-foot-five inches tall and weighing one-eighty-five walked in their direction. He wore a parka with the Newcomers Lion logo on it with sweatpants and sneakers. He had carved out a reputation at Newcomers in his basketball journey, averaging sixteen points a game and eight rebounds. He led the Lions to a state berth. He also led the city in three-point shot percentage at forty-one percent. He had as much swagger as his game and for good reason. A couple of girls who were hanging out by the school doors hugged him as he walked to his car, which was parked only a few cars away from Trevor. Shania looked at the boy, stunned.

"Oh my God, look how big he got! That can't be him, right?" she asked. Trevor looked at Shania, smiling.

"It's him," he replied and before Shania could say anything or stop him, Trevor got out of his car to greet the basketball player.

It was true. Jamal Samuels hit his growth spurt and grew over 6 inches in three years. Jamal walked over to his car and was about to open it when he saw a face that he hadn't seen in over three years.

"Trevor, is that you?" he asked.

"The one and only, bro," Trevor replied, greeting Jamal. They were nearly the same height now. "I see you got some stilts now," he added, referring to Jamal's height.

"Yeah, just been eating and drinkin' a lot of milk, you know how it is. Just tryin' to maintain," Jamal replied in his deep voice. Trevor smiled. The pre-pubescent voice was long gone and Jamal sounded like a grown man.

"I feel you," Trevor replied. "So I heard you been ballin' out hea' this year," he said. Jamal smiled and nodded his head. Trevor had stumbled across one of the few attributes to which Jamal admitted he felt pride.

"Yeah, man tryin' to be like you. I saw a couple of your games on TV this year," Jamal said.

`"Oh word?" Trevor asked.

"Yeah man. Haven't watched a whole lot but I saw a couple of 'em. Seton Hall and Boston College, especially," Jamal replied.

"That's what's up," Trevor said. "Look, you got any plans later? I'm bout to go get something to eat, you wanna roll with me right quick?" Trevor asked.

Jamal checked the clock on his cell phone. He didn't have practice so he was free. "Yeah man, I'll roll wit' you. You want me to follow you?" he asked, gesturing to his car. Trevor shook his head.

"Nah man, we going to this spot a few blocks away. I'll give you a ride there and back, no sweat," he said.

"Ok that's cool," Jamal agreed as they walked to Trevor's car. As soon as they got there, Jamal saw Shania in the car and the little appetite he had for food was suddenly gone. His mind grudgingly flashed back to the scene of her father lying half-naked on top of his mother. Trevor had never found out about that tryst.

"Jamal, I believe you already know my beautiful girlfriend, Shania," Trevor said.

Jamal didn't let his anger or emotion show right away but he certainly wasn't planning on any long conversations with Shania. Secretly he hoped that the lunch would be quick so he could be on his way. "We're acquainted," Jamal replied icily. He didn't want to sound indifferent but Jamal continued to have a shaky relationship with his mother since that day. He wasn't able to trust her like he did before and it was all because of Shania's father.

"Hey Jamal how you've been?" Shania asked. Jamal shrugged.

"I'm good," he replied.

Shania stopped smiling and turned around in her passenger seat. She knew Jamal would be less than thrilled to see her again after what her father had put him through. The short ride to the fast food restaurant was very tense between them. During the ride, Trevor explained to Jamal how Omar had given him the directions to Newcomers High School so that he could visit Jamal. Jamal and Omar still spoke online, over the phone, and through social media sites. Omar was a senior and still at Richmond Hill High School. He had kept Jamal aware of all the events that had occurred since his departure. Nate Plummer, who in Jamal's recent memory was arrested for assault, had gone back to the school and became the new men's basketball coach. He was coaching Omar, who was playing for Richmond Hill's varsity squad and Omar still talked smack about how Richmond Hill was better than Newcomers but nobody would ever know because their teams would never meet. He also filled Jamal in about Patricia, who Jamal had broken up with before he moved three years ago. She had been in and out of high school relationships until she ended up with a boy who got her pregnant before her senior year. According to Omar, she was only a few weeks away from giving birth. Jamal wished her the best but was starting to see why it didn't work out between them. Finally they arrived at the restaurant and Trevor stepped out of his car and walked inside the restaurant, followed by Shania and Jamal.

Jamal quickly noticed was that it was extremely busy and there were no open booths as far as he could see. "Ain't nowhere to sit, man," Jamal informed Trevor but Trevor seemed to be more of an optimist.

"Nah man, we'll find some place, like right there," he replied, pointing to a booth in the corner wall of the restaurant.

The only problem was there was already a patron there. Jamal couldn't see his face because it was concealed by the restaurant's overlarge menu. "But someone's sitting there though," Jamal began to say, before he realized that Shania and Trevor were no longer behind him.

"Don't worry about your friends. They'll be back," said the man who had been reading the menu.

Jamal didn't know why but the voice sounded very familiar and he saw why after the man put the menu down. Pastor Mike Hillman smiled up at Jamal, who certainly didn't return that smile.

"How are you doing, Jamal?" Mike asked. It took every ounce of will power Jamal had in him to not turn his back on the pastor and walk away. He had nothing to say to him. Jamal suddenly realized that the whole chance meeting was a setup. Trevor and Shania and Pastor Mike must have worked together to drive all the way out here to get Jamal to reconcile with the pastor.

They got another thing comin' if they think I'm stayin' with this guy, Jamal thought but Pastor Mike appeared to read his thoughts. "Please Jamal, just have a seat and hear me out for a moment," he said.

Jamal thought about it for a moment, then sat down. He had to admit, it was clever on the pastor's part to stage this moment and time it just right so they'd catch him after school.

"What, man? What do you want with me? You comin' to ask about my mama or something?" he asked harshly. It might have been a low blow but he deserved it, as far as Jamal was concerned.

"No, I just wanted to talk to you and clear the air between us. I already spoke with your mother and she informed me that I would be able to talk to you today," Mike said.

Jamal shrugged. All this small talk was wasting his time. "Well I'm here. What you got to say?" he asked.

Mike stayed silent for a moment, before continuing. "Jamal, I wanted to apologize for what happened that night. I was struggling both emotionally and spiritually at the time and your mother was too. I wish I had a better reason to explain why it happened but to be quite honest, I don't. But I want you to know that I deeply regret hurting you or losing the trust you had in me as a pastor," he said.

Jamal looked straight at the pastor to see if there was any sign of fear or doubt in his words but there were none. "I looked up to you back then. You were like a hero to me. When my dad left my mama, I knew she was struggling with living life alone and raising me on her own. But I really wanted my dad to make it work with her," Jamal said.

"I know, and that's what she told me as well," Pastor Mike replied. "But all we could do is pray about it and let God handle the rest, Jamal. We can't force what we don't control. I just wanted you to understand that and hope that one day, you would visit us again," he said.

Jamal lowered his head in deep thought. He decided then and there that he was going to let it go. Mike wouldn't have gone through the trouble of coming all the way out here if he wasn't sincere and it took too much energy for Jamal to hold a grudge that long. A waitress came by and picked up the menu from Pastor Mike. She turned to Jamal.

"What can I get you?" she asked.

Jamal ordered the chicken parmesan with a side of mashed potatoes and sweet corn. Pastor Mike smiled.

"Quite a lot of food there but basketball players gotta eat too," he said.

Jamal smiled for the first time that day at the pastor. "Yeah I be wolfin' my food down, man. My appetite grew since I was fourteen, pastor," he said.

"I see that. Hormones have been real good to you," Pastor Mike replied.

While waiting for the food, Jamal asked about everyone else in the neighborhood. "What happened to the dude Nate was going after? The one that got arrested with him?" Jamal asked.

"Well, Earl was held for questioning and initially, they couldn't get a straight response because he couldn't really remember what happened that night. Nate testified and a couple witnesses came forward, claiming they saw Earl flee the scene of the crime and the composite sketches from those days matched his features, give or take a few years," Mike revealed.

"So he's still locked up now?" Jamal asked.

"Yeah, he was locked up but it was later found out that he had a rare form of leukemia and sadly about six months ago he passed away," Mike answered.

Jamal didn't say a word. He remembered the night he had watched the news and saw that Nate had been arrested. At first he couldn't believe it. Nate had been quiet, it didn't seem possible. It was unfortunate that his mother had already considered leaving the school because of Loree's death, then the fight with Miles had happened. It was finally Nate's fiasco that put the final nail in his Richmond Hill coffin. Nate was a man Jamal had credited with teaching him the rudiments of the game of basketball and he owed many of his improvements to him.

"I'll never forget that man, though. If it wasn't for him, I wouldn't have one single college looking at me," Jamal said.

It was true. Jamal's basketball prowess had drawn interest from several schools, three of which were NCAA Division I schools. He continued to catch up with the pastor as Shania and Trevor watched from another part of the restaurant. While Jamal and Mike were mending their relationship, Shania had filled Trevor in on what caused their rift.

"See, I told you they would work it out," Trevor said.

Shania nodded her head and made a noise with her mouth that resembled sucking teeth. "Please, you was just as worried as I was. You didn't think it was gonna work," she argued back. laughing.

"Whateva. Anyway you gonna finish that?" Trevor asked, looking at Shania's unfinished food plate.

"Yeah I'm gonna finish this, what you think?" Shania replied defensively, but was laughing at the same time, pleased that her father had finally made peace with Jamal.

When Jamal returned home at his mother's new duplex, he took his book bag off and walked inside his bedroom. He was still full from the meal he had ordered and he started to feel good and lazy. His mother wasn't home yet, since she was still working at the new hair salon in Elmont. While lying down, his eyes fell upon a memento he hadn't seen in a long time. It was his journal; the frayed and chipped corners peeking out from his dresser drawer. When his mother had first moved into the house he must have carelessly tossed it aside without a second look. He took a look inside the book. The last entry was September 5th 2003. Reading all of his old entries suddenly gave him an inspiration. He took a pen from his book bag, he sat at his desk, and began to write. He didn't know what he was writing, only that the words came out swiftly.

Forever, I've been holding it all in and learning to keep my anger in check
But I was a wreck, the waters of my past rising up to my neck,
Wishing the Lord could take it all away, the grief and the tears,
The taunts and the jeers that I hear are the agents of all my fears
I'm waiting for the skies to clear, but rainclouds get in the way
Desperately I search to see all the good in the bad in a better day
Everyone was tellin' me to pray for a release, but the cycle doesn't cease
My brothers falling victims to the streets, gunshots disturbin' the peace
Mama told me to turn the other cheek but she's no better than the rest
Falling victim to her lust and flesh, but she's still lookin' for the best
Just when I reached my last legs, I can't run; a voice breaks through,
And says, "Forgive my people brother, they know not what they do"
"Don't let the darkness remain in your heart,
your mind, your body, or your soul."
"Take back what the devil stole, make it your goal in a world so cold"
"Be a light of forgiveness that the world can feel and feed off of"
"Don't be a beacon of anger and hate,
but live a second chance and love..."

Jamal looked at the words written before him. It felt refreshing and it felt nourishing. But most importantly, it felt inspiring. A voice had spoken to him, and it wasn't the voice of jealousy, hate, murder, strife, anger, or death. It was a voice of forgiveness, and it was the voice of life.

"Marc A. Beausejour"

Marc A. Beausejour was born on July 28, 1987 in Queens, New York to Haitian parents Jean and Lineda Beausejour. He discovered his passion for writing at the tender age of twelve, with poetry becoming his initial artistic expression. Beausejour showcased his poetic talents in various school talent shows and poetry reading events during his time at North Cobb High School and later at Kennesaw State University after moving to Kennesaw, Georgia in 2001.

Throughout the years, Beausejour continued to hone his craft, writing poems for diverse occasions such as weddings, funerals, and church events. In 2011, he took a significant step by self-publishing his first book, "Words on High," a compilation of spiritually inspired poems from his formative years. Building on this success, Beausejour released his second poetry book, "Rising Higher Than Ever," in 2015.

In the same year, he ventured into a different literary landscape by writing and publishing his first urban novel, "The Preacher's Web." This gritty morality tale marked a departure from his earlier poetic works, showcasing Beausejour's versatility as an author. Expanding his literary horizons, he created the *BlackCyrano* series, demonstrating a wide-ranging creative skill.

While continuing to share his literary work on blogs and social networks, Beausejour remains committed to his education and promotions, earning his associate degree in marketing management from Chattahoochee Technical College in 2018. As a multifaceted writer, Marc A. Beausejour continues to captivate audiences with his words across various genres and platforms.

ALSO BY, AUTHOR

"Marc A. Beausejour"

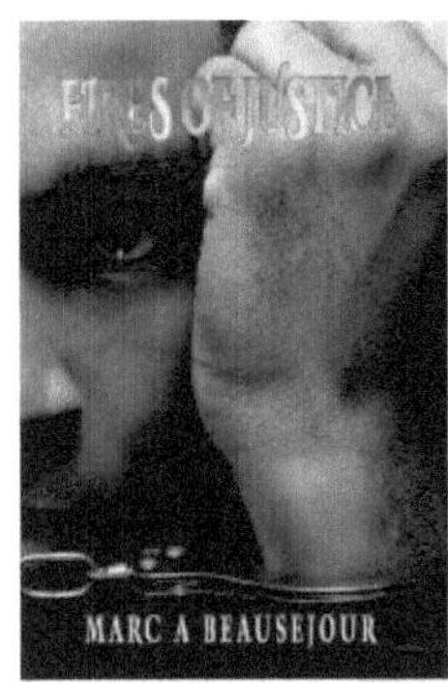

Title: Fires of Justice | Author: Marc A. Beausejour | Publisher: SHE PUBLISHING LLC | ISBN: 978-1-953163-93-6 (paperback) | Publication Date: February 2024 (*second edition*)

English professor Levell Thomas is ecstatic when he receives the opportunity to teach in a metro Atlanta high school. A native of Queens, New York, Levell moves to Georgia with his family and as they settle in their new home, Levell meets his neighbor, a mysterious girl named Raven Roberts. Despite being underaged, she doesn't hide her desires for Levell and pursues him relentlessly. Levell refuses her advances but would soon pay dearly for his decision. The spurned teenager accuses Levell of assault after a physical confrontation and Levell is found guilty in the court of law. Detective Isaac Sands leads the investigation to expose a plot of false accusation and imprisonment in a race against time. Will Sands help prove Levell's innocence by finding the conspirators, or would he put himself in harm's way?

"The controversies confronted, stirred, and then addressed in this story have no choice but to awaken you to new perspectives that might not have ever crossed your mind. Readers, all I can say is be prepared to feel the fire that Beausejour has ignited in this suspenseful masterpiece!"

—D.A. Goodwin, author of The Offender I Once Defended

Title: Adia's Ballad | Author: Marc A. Beausejour | Publisher: SHE PUBLISHING LLC | ISBN: 978-1-953163-92-9 (paperback) | Publication Date: February 2024 (*second edition*)

From the author of "The Preacher's Web", this coming-of-age story explores the life of young Andrea McAfee who struggles to cope with the tragic murder of her older sister. Then a chance opportunity lands Andrea into the music business where she shares a bond with other artists in the hip hop industry and learns she has more in common with them than she realizes. As Andrea immerses herself deeper into the life of recording, touring, and partying as Adia, the new R&B princess, she begins drifting away from her family and her loved ones as her star rises too fast for her to absorb. With fame corrupting her relationships with those she loves, will Andrea find the inner peace and closure she seeks, or will she succumb to the draw of money and celebrity?

Title: Split Decision | Author: Marc A. Beausejour | Publisher: SHE PUBLSIHING LLC | ISBN: 978-1-953163-94-3 (paperback) | Publication Date: February 2024 (*second edition*)

Prepare to enter the ring as cultures clash in this adrenaline-filled drama! Under the tutelage of experienced trainer Jim Shaw, young boxer Sylvio Dominique has taken the middleweight class division by storm, winning bout after bout. Nicknamed "Wolf" for his boxing style and aggression in the ring, Sylvio works hard in the ring and plays even harder out of the ring and there is no shortage of women. Reuniting with childhood friend Valentina Cruz, the two become involved in an intense romance. But as Sylvio falls deep in love with Valentina, he realizes that she is more than what she seems. With a fight against the undefeated Dominican champion Felipe Maximo looming, secrets are revealed, and friends turn to foes as Sylvio later discovers that he may not be fighting only for the middleweight crown, but he may also be fighting for his life.

Title: Split Decision II - The Comeback |
Author: Marc A. Beausejour | Publisher: SHE
PUBLISHING LLC | ISBN: 978-1-953163-95-0
(paperback)| Publication Date: February 2024
(*second edition*)

After Sylvio Dominique's sudden retirement from middleweight boxing following a close brush with death, the former champion hangs up his gloves to continue running the Shaw-Dominique Community Center in Queens, New York. When Sylvio's hometown rival and current middleweight champion Barry Taylor; asks him to help train for his title defense against new contender and former MMA fighter Jun Zhang, Sylvio agrees to the proposition. But Taylor is defeated handily, and when Sylvio suffers a tragic death in the family and the center struggles financially, he makes the decision to return to the ring. Meanwhile, his girlfriend, Valentina Cruz find success as an actress and her relationship with Sylvio begins coming apart at the seams. Sylvio's trainer, Jim Shaw is reluctant to help Sylvio, as he finds himself struggling with his own personal demons. Jun Zhang then challenges Sylvio to fight him for the crown. As he prepares for his toughest ring battle yet, can Sylvio and Jim find the fortitude to emerge victorious while putting all their struggles behind them?

Title: Street Retribution | Author: Marc A. Beausejour | Publisher: SHE PUBLISHING LLC | ISBN: 978-1-953163-96-7 (*paperback*) | Publication Date: February 2024 (*second edition*)

New York City attorney Edward Reed harbors a secret. He was once known as Antonio Franks, a member of M.O.B., the most dangerous gang in Queens, New York. He was also the key witness in the trial that exonerated another ex-gang member, David Anderson, when he was falsely accused of murdering his girlfriend, Loree McAfee. But years later, both men's lives are in danger, as other former gang members are slain under mysterious circumstances by a femme fatale, prompting rumors that M.O.B.'s ruthless gang leader, Tadarius Hill is seeking revenge on those that turned on him and his organization. Will Edward and David survive the bounty, or will they fall victim to the code of the streets?

Title: Divine Vengeance | Author: Marc A. Beausejour | Publisher: SHE PUBLISHING LLC | Publication Date: COMING SOON!

After the murder of David Anderson, LaToya Richardson awaits her day in court while attorney Edward Reed receives a warning from Tadarius Hill, the gang leader of M.O.B. and sexy femme fatale Tina, who gives him an ultimatum. Realizing that he cannot use conventional methods to combat the tactics of his former gang, Edward pulls out all the stops to prevent Tadarius from wreaking havoc in the city. LaToya's son, Chris adjusts to his new home and new school while staying with David's family. Andrea McAfee's relationship with her boyfriend Quentin comes apart at the seams as lust and infidelity threatens to tear the couple apart. Can Edward, Chris, and Andrea summon the strength amidst the chaos in their environment to secure their futures?